THE LOVERS THREE

Book 3 of the Nightcraft Quartet

Shannon Page

THE LOVERS THREE
BOOK THREE OF THE NIGHTCRAFT QUARTET
Copyright © 2022 Shannon Page. All rights reserved.

Published by Outland Entertainment LLC
3119 Gillham Road
Kansas City, MO 64109

Founder/Creative Director: Jeremy D. Mohler
Editor-in-Chief: Alana Joli Abbott
Senior Editor: Scott Colby

ISBN (paper): 978-1-954255-43-2
ISBN (ebook): 978-1-954255-44-9
Worldwide Rights
Created in the United States of America

Editor: Alana Joli Abbott
Copy Editor: Bessie Mazur
Cover Illustration: Matthew Warlick
Cover Design: Jeremy D. Mohler
Interior Layout: Mikael Brodu

Printed and bound in the United States of America.

Visit **outlandentertainment.com** to see more, or follow us on our Facebook Page **facebook.com/outlandentertainment/** .

ALSO BY SHANNON PAGE

NOVELS

Eel River
Our Lady of the Islands (with Jay Lake)

The Nightcraft Quartet:
The Queen and The Tower
A Sword in The Sun
The Loners Three
The Empress and The Moon (forthcoming)

The Chameleon Chronicles (with Karen G. Berry,
writing as Laura Gayle)
Orcas Intrigue
Orcas Intruder
Orcas Investigation
Orcas Illusion

COLLECTIONS

Eastlick and Other Stories
I Was a Trophy Wife and Other Essays

EDITED BOOKS

Witches, Bitches & Stitches (anthology)
The Usual Path to Publication (collection)

PRAISE FOR SHANNON PAGE'S
THE NIGHTCRAFT QUARTET

"Page's enchanting worldbuilding and charming heroine will draw readers in, and an exciting cliffhanger ending sets things up nicely for the next in the series. This fascinating blend of science and fantasy is a treat."

-*Publishers Weekly*

"Page fashions an intriguing and hugely gifted heroine who, nevertheless, struggles with problems that have bearing on our own. The first book in the planned quartet kept me up all night until I had finished the last page."

-Antoinette L. Botsford, *Amazon* review

"The magic system is powerful but subtly intwined. The characters use it so nonchalantly, I sometimes forget I'm not also a magical person walking around San Francisco."

-C. G. Volars, author of *Static over Space: Gravity and Lies*

"The history, the folklore and the world-building in this novel are written together beautifully. The characters are well developed and the information that is given about the world is intertwined with the story in a way that does not feel like an info dump. Some characters I fell for instantly, others I am wondering if they are who they say they are. In a world where warlocks and witches can live for centuries, who knows what hiding in their back closets; but I am looking forward to finding out."

-Richelle Reed, *She Reeds by the Sea*

For Mark
Always and ever

— CHAPTER ONE —

Naturally, witchkind does not observe Christmas, but let no one say we don't have important mid-winter festivities.

When the days grow short, and darkness covers the land—even in bright, urban San Francisco—our kind gather to banish this darkness with warmth and cheer and good company.

Yule was still over a week away, but already my parents had decorated their lovely Pacific Heights home. When I was a child there, I'd wondered why we couldn't just have a brightly ornamented tree in our front window like all our neighbors—with, of course, big shiny presents *for me* underneath it. Once I grew a little older, I began to appreciate the house-wide festooning of real, living fir boughs woven everywhere, braided with red velvet ribbons accented with golden chains, coins, and beads. Our house always smelled so fresh; the humans' trees, being dead, would slowly fade, turning brittle and dusty through the long weeks of their seasons, culminating in a bunch of brown, spidery tree carcasses littering the sidewalks in the first week of January, stray bits of tinsel blowing in the wind.

No, the witchkind way was the best. When the Yule celebrations were finished, Mother would coax the fir boughs back outside, where they would resettle as a few tidy trees in our backyard.

This year would be my first in a house of my own—though I was in my mid-forties, I had lived communally in a coven house since attaining my majority at the age of twenty. There were no fir trees in my small back garden, so I used the excuse to visit Mom and ask her for ideas on how I could decorate my home for the season.

Of course, Rosemary and I visited her a lot these days. Mom always enjoyed spending time with her brand-new granddaughter.

Now we sat in my mother's cozy breakfast room over cups of hot chocolate. A cutting of fir bough was tucked into my purse, which I would coax to life when I got back home. That would be a good start, though I'd need a lot more decoration than that. A fire burned in the room's small, tiled fireplace; Rosemary sat on Mom's lap, trying to reach her hair so she could pull it. Mom's hair, worn loose today, gently pulled itself out of my baby's hands, moving to curl and twine around Mom's face. My mother looked like a pre-Raphaelite portrait—no way old enough to be a grandmother, though she politely kept her apparent age a bit older than I did mine.

I smiled at the picture they made and sipped my cocoa. "So, should I just encourage the ivy vines to come in? That's the greenest thing I've got."

Mom shook her head vigorously. "No, no—never ivy. Trust me: ivy is the last thing you want to invite into your home." She frowned, thinking. "Surely you must have some other evergreen back there?"

She can't remember because she hardly ever visits me, I thought. Well, her strength wasn't what it used to be; she'd had a brush with illness last year and had never quite fully come back from it. It was just easier for her to stay home. As a witch with a botanical focus, she gained strength from her house and garden. "There's that tall one that makes the crazy flowers in the springtime—it's still green, even in December," I said.

I could see her eyes go vague, but I couldn't tell if she was searching her memory or casting her vision over to my house, a half-mile away. Then she brightened. "Oh! Of course, the red flowering gum tree. That's perfect; you might even be able to encourage a few blossoms, if you play your cards right." Her smile grew. "Speaking of cards—did you bring them?"

I had thought about it, but decided not to. "I'm working with them every day at home," I told her, "but today, I just wanted to talk to you about Yule decorations and drink hot chocolate." Rosemary reached for her hair again; it evaded her tiny grip again. "And give you some grandbaby time."

Mom gave Rose a little squeeze and rocked her gently on her lap. "And such a sweet precious cutie she is!" She gazed down at the baby, her eyes filled with love. Rose blinked back up at her, looking for all the world like she was communicating with her.

I smiled to watch them, even as my heart gave a little hitch. I knew Mom loved our visits, and adored Rosemary...and yet, I also knew that Mom had mixed feelings about being a grandmother. I hadn't realized, until the day I gave birth, that Mom had wanted another daughter of her own. She and Dad had seemed perfectly happy just as a couple; I'd asked about a sister many times when I was younger, and had been told *Maybe, someday.*

In theory, *someday* could still come to pass. Witches and warlocks lived far longer than mundane humans; Mom should remain fertile until well into her second century, many years from now. Yet we were also, as a species, far less fecund than humans. The fact that I'd gotten pregnant without consciously trying was still a bit mysterious to everyone.

And that's where my thoughts always went fuzzy. It seemed to me that there was something even more mysterious about my beautiful daughter...yet my new-mom brain kept sort of sliding away from whatever it was. Hormones, let me tell you. And nobody else had even known what I was talking about when I'd asked.

So, I'd stopped wondering, mostly. But it was strange.

Sad, came into my mind. Not my own thought: a message from Rosemary. She'd started using a few more words in her mind-speak to me, though nothing like full sentences. I understood her well enough. She wasn't sad; she was realizing that her grandma was sad.

Which was plain enough. I reached out for the baby. "Shall I take her now?"

Mom gave me a relieved, tired smile. "She's probably getting hungry."

"Or she's curious about what cocoa is going to taste like," I joked, getting the baby settled in my own lap before opening my blouse.

"Would you like some more?" Mom lifted her hands above both our mugs, sitting on the small table between us.

"Sure." I glanced through the tall windows behind her, looking out at the cold winter sunshine, wishing it would ever snow in San Francisco. Wouldn't that be cozy!

Mom moved her fingers, bringing my attention back into the room. Both our cups filled anew. I watched her carefully, while trying to disguise the fact that I was doing so; she didn't seem taxed by the small magic, but once she was done, she did lean back and cradle her mug, as if absorbing its warmth.

I picked up mine with my free hand and took a sip. "Delicious."

She smiled back at me. Was there a bead of sweat on her unlined forehead? "My pleasure. I'm happy you could spare the time."

"Of course."

We sipped in silence for a minute as Rosemary suckled: three generations, drinking a warm beverage together. Soon my daughter began to nurse less energetically. She'd fall asleep in another minute or two.

All right, I supposed this was cozy enough.

Mom set her empty mug down on the table and cocked her head slightly. "Any more thoughts on your wedding ceremony?"

"It's not a wedding," I said, automatically, but she just waved her hand in dismissal.

"You're signing a romantic, domestic, and financial contract with the father of your child, in front of witnesses and guests in fancy clothes, at a ceremony involving cake and Champagne," she said. "I could say all that every time, or I could just be efficient and call it a wedding."

I gave her a helpless grin and a shrug. Point taken. Even so, we were *not* getting married. Witchkind does not do that. "We're still working on the final details of the terms," I told her.

She frowned, just for a moment. "I thought you were in agreement several weeks ago?"

"I thought so too." Rosemary had completely stopped nursing by now, but I didn't want to ease her off the nipple and wake her back up. I leaned back a bit so my arm didn't have to hold all her weight. Amazing how much a tiny body weighs, especially at rest. "But every time we send a new draft back to Gregorio's people, they find one more thing they want to tweak."

"Ah." Her frown ghosted back again, but then she shrugged. "Warlocks and their *procedures*."

I laughed softly. "Yeah. Anyway, once we get a final agreement worked out, we'll set a date. It would be nice to do it in the springtime, have the party outside, maybe."

"That would be nice. But you know you're welcome to have it here. I'd be delighted to—"

"Yes, yes, I know." We smiled at each other. "We'll talk, once Jeremy and I really have an agreement."

At my feet, I felt a nudge. Elnor, my familiar, had been sleeping under the easy chair I sat in; now she was awake and wondering if I'd forgotten her mealtime.

Mom noticed the movement. "I have tuna here, you know."

"I know—but I really should get on home, before she needs changing." I started to unlatch Rosemary and button myself back up. "Plus, I have a lot to do today."

This was a fib. I hadn't done any meaningful work since the baby was born a month and a half ago. Unless you counted, oh, *raising a newborn* as meaningful work. Which of course I did; I just hadn't done any of my biological research since Rosemary had come along.

Mostly this was because taking care of a tiny, nearly helpless creature was pretty all-consuming. But also, I had to admit, I was finding it blessedly hard to remember exactly where I'd been in my research. I'd never been super diligent about my lab notes, but my level of scattered distraction for the last few months was truly above and beyond. The one time I'd been up to my third-floor lab after I got back from my Old Country retreat, I hadn't been able to make heads or tails out of the scattering of petri dishes and vials across my lab bench, or the scribbles in my current notebook.

But that was fine. Gregorio Andromedus—Jeremy's father, Rosemary's paternal grandfather, and my mentor—was fully on board with my taking a good, long maternity leave. Not that he was my employer or anything; my research was my own, meant to benefit all of witchkind. And nobody paid me for it; my coven resources and my parents' long-ago gift of the house I lived in saw to my support. I could go back to work whenever I wanted to, whenever it made sense.

Whenever I felt drawn to do so. I still expected the urge would come back...someday.

I got to my feet, tucking the newly awakened Rosemary back into her little sling-carrier. In just over a month, she'd already grown so much, she was nearly too big for it already. I'd have to get the next size up; for now, I just loosened the side straps. Mom got up too and helped me fasten it in back, where I couldn't see. By now, Elnor was twining around my ankles. "Yes, kitty," I told her. "We'll be home in five minutes."

Mom saw us to the door, then closed it gently behind us. I walked down the front path, glancing automatically up and down the sidewalk to see if any humans were about before slipping onto the ley line that opened up a couple of doors down from my folks' house. Nobody saw us; there were people going by in cars, but to them, it would merely have looked like I stepped behind a tree. They would not notice that I failed to emerge from the other side.

I would see to that.

Once back in front of my house, I stopped on the porch and reached out with my magical senses to touch the wards. They were set, but not from outside. I released them and walked in. "I'm home!" I called out.

Petrana, my golem, walked up the hallway from the kitchen. "Greetings, Mistress Callie," she said. "Would you like a hand with the baby?"

"Thanks," I said, handing Rosemary over. Petrana took her expertly; Rose cooed and giggled at her. They'd really bonded on our trip. I trusted the golem completely.

Yes, it was weird to have a golem in the first place, and it was particularly weird to use her for childcare. But a lot of how I lived my life was considered strange by the rest of witchkind. Hey, it worked for me.

And nasty diapers didn't bother golems one bit.

I heard footsteps on the stairs coming down from the second floor. "Hello, darling," green-eyed Jeremy said, following me into the second parlor.

"Hi," I said, stopping to give him a kiss. Then I sensed the other presence in the house. "Is your father here?"

"Yes. He came to help me with a few things, and I think he was hoping to see the baby. He's upstairs in the study now."

"Ah. I wish I'd known; I wouldn't have left."

"Quite all right." He smiled. "Did you have a nice visit with your mother?"

"I did," I said as I sank onto the plush sofa. Elnor immediately jumped up next to me, clearly more concerned than ever about mealtime. I patted her absently; she nudged my hand, impatient. "I got some ideas for our Yule decorations."

"Oh, excellent," he said, politely.

I knew he didn't really care about this sort of thing. Warlocks loved to focus on business, leaving the domestic realm to witches. So old-fashioned, so many of them. "Mom still seems tired to me, but she did do some household magic, several times."

"It takes a lot of time to recover from a serious illness," he said. "Particularly at her age."

I gave him a quizzical glance. "She's not even a hundred." *She's barely older than you are*, I didn't add.

Jeremy smiled, looking apologetic. "No, of course not—but she's no longer in the first blush of youth either. My father's research has long indicated that as we advance into early middle age, many of us fail to notice a physical decline, particularly as our magical strength grows." He then seemed to catch himself. I'd had to remind him more than once about warlocksplaining. "Of course, I'm not telling you anything you don't already know from your own research."

"Of course," I said, gently. Elnor batted at my knee. "Petrana?" I called out.

"Yes, mistress?" she answered from the top of the stairs on the second floor.

"My cat is starving to death, perishing right at this very moment in fact. When you're done with the baby, would you be so kind as to set a bowl of tuna down for Elnor? Assuming she has the strength to get to the kitchen, that is."

"Of course."

In a minute, Petrana appeared at the doorway, clearly aiming to hand me the baby, but Jeremy intercepted her. "I'll take the little munchkin," he said.

Rosemary happily settled in her father's arms. Jeremy cooed at her and made all the goofy little noises people do at babies. She blew spit bubbles in his general direction—a clear sign of affection.

I leaned back on the couch to enjoy watching them together. Jeremy was such a natural father. I wondered why I had been so reluctant to sign a contract before she'd been born...I did remember that we'd, well, not argued exactly, but debated the issue several times. Maybe I had just needed time to get used to the idea. As I mentioned, the whole thing had been something of a surprise, even though that's not supposed to be possible for witches. I had just recently moved out of my coven house and had been imagining living alone for a few years. I'd had big plans; I was going to get some serious, solo work done.

Just more ways in which I was weird.

Jeremy sat down in the easy chair across from the sofa, bouncing the baby gently on his knee while she reached for his ponytail. He let her grab hold of it. "We're making progress upstairs," he said to me. His sentence was punctuated by a faint bump from above us.

"Oh good." He still had a rental house in the Marina, but he'd been spending more and more time here, in preparation for us combining our households. I'd given him the front second floor sitting room to use as a study. He'd assured me that was enough space, though I felt stingy, giving him only one room in a three-story house, and feeling like even that was a sacrifice. I'd originally envisioned that as a room I would lounge and read in, a more private space than the formal first-floor rooms; but the truth was, I'd probably sat in there three times in the nearly-a-year I'd lived here.

Still. This was *my* house; any contract we signed was going to make that clear.

Which he was perfectly okay with! Yet another sign that this was a good move for me, this not-a-marriage. And the more I watched him with the baby, the better I felt about it all.

I really was lucky.

"I'm not ready to show you yet," he said, after cooing at Rosemary for a minute. "But soon."

"No rush." I smiled at them both. "I mean, I'm excited to see what you do with the space, but it's entirely yours." If I needed a reading nook, I had the whole third floor. It wasn't like I was using the lab, after all.

Elnor sauntered back into the room, pausing just inside the door to sit and wash her whiskers. "That was a close one, eh?" I teased her. "Thanks be to the Blessed Mother that we managed to save your life, yet again."

She pretended not to hear me.

Jeremy grinned at me. "And this is why warlocks don't keep familiars. I'd be hard pressed to say who owns whom here."

"Nobody owns anybody; it's a partnership," I said, smiling back at him. This was another conversation we'd had more than once; it wasn't getting old, either. Was this what having a life partner felt like? I'd had relationships before...but none of them had reached anything near a moving-in-together level of seriousness. Much less a baby. There had been one...my mind struggled to recall the details. A nice fellow, but...there was something not quite right about him. I didn't even remember what.

It was a long time ago.

"Well," Jeremy said, getting to his feet, lifting Rosemary high into the air as he did so. She squealed with delight as he pretended to toss her, while never loosening his grip on her. She still had hold of his hair, pulling it up over his head. It looked painful, but Jeremy didn't flinch. He just brought the baby back down and gave her a little squeeze before turning to me. "I should see what my father is doing up there, unless you need me...?"

"Of course I need you, but not at the moment," I said lightly, reaching out to take Rosemary.

He handed her over, kissing the top of her head, then the top of mine. "You know where to find me."

"That I do."

Once he'd gone back upstairs, I just sat there for a few minutes, holding my daughter and feeling at a bit of a loss. Yes, I had told my mom a fib; I really had nothing to do today, besides work on some Yule decorations, but I hadn't wanted to tire her out further. I reached into my bag and pulled out the sprig of fir, turning it over in my hand as I thought about it. Probably I should get it into some water, let it refresh itself before I pushed magic into it. I set it on the table beside my chair.

Mom kept seeming so determined to prove she was well, insisting on doing magic and continuing to teach me tarot and all the things that…well, tired her out.

Maybe it was time to talk to Dad again. I'd brought this up with him before, but he'd insisted he was monitoring her carefully, and that she was on the mend.

I supposed I'd have to be happy with that.

With a small sigh, I got up, hefting Rosemary onto my hip. "Such a big girl!" I said to her. "Good thing you have such a strong mommy!"

She made little nonsense sounds back at me. It melted my heart; she was so adorable.

I carried her down the hallway to the kitchen, at the back of the house. Petrana was standing over the stove stirring a pot of beans. I hadn't asked her to cook beans; it seemed like she was taking more initiative every day.

"That smells good," I told her.

"Thank you, Mistress Callie," she said. "I'm going to use half of them for bean and cheese enchiladas for dinner tonight and keep the rest for later use."

Bean and cheese enchiladas? "Is that something Jeremy wanted?" I asked.

"Not specifically, but I know he enjoys Mexican food a great deal. He has mentioned more than once that there is nothing like this in the Old Country." She turned to look at me, and I could swear she gave a small smile, though she was still nearly as expressionless as my cat. "It seems he didn't explore Balzst nearly as thoroughly as we did, mistress."

I smiled back at her. "That's the difference between being a tourist and being a native. He probably ate most of his dinners at home. The Blessed Mother only knows what sort of traditional old-world fare his cook or housekeeper or whoever prepared for him."

Jeremy was the son of a San Francisco warlock, but he had been raised by foster parents since a very young age, after his mother had died of a strange illness. He hadn't told me a lot about her—he didn't remember a lot about her—but he'd had a happy childhood, nonetheless. He adored his foster parents and visited them whenever he traveled back to the Old Country. They were both in the diplomatic corps and had raised him to do similar work. I looked forward to meeting them; they would certainly be invited to our contract-signing ceremony, and given enough advance warning so they could make the journey easily.

Now I was sorry I hadn't sought them out when I'd been there, just last month. Well, I'd been on retreat, recovering from childbirth, and had still been thinking over the whole contract question. It would have been deeply awkward to establish a connection with them only to come home and decide not to move forward with the relationship.

So it was all for the best, I supposed.

"Was there anything you needed, Mistress Callie?"

Yeah. Something to do. "No, thank you, Petrana," I said. "I was just going to head upstairs and…" I didn't finish the sentence. I didn't know what I was going to do. Check on Jeremy and his dad? No, I should let the warlock at least have control of his own space. "Oh, wait, yes there is—I left a bough of fir in the second parlor. Can you find a vase for it and get it in water?"

"Of course."

I climbed the stairs to the second floor, glancing up the hall to the closed door at the front of the house. Jeremy and his father were working some magic in there; I could feel it. Were they stretching the space a bit? I again felt a twinge of guilt for my miserliness. Heck, this floor also contained a largely unused guest room as well as Rosemary's nursery, where she'd yet to spend a whole night—we were still co-sleeping, even when Jeremy was in the bed with me. Us. He hadn't made a murmur about it, but the truth was, having a baby in bed did tend to curtail certain...other activities.

It probably shouldn't, but clearly we both felt weird about it. Jeremy and me, I mean; Rose was obviously far too young to be aware of such things, even if she did seem unusually alert and attentive, even for a witchlet.

She still communicated with me only in single words mind-to-mind, and even then not all that often.

She had also still never cried.

I'd been at first relieved and then, pretty quickly, worried by this. Babies cry: that's the one thing everyone on the planet knows about them. They cry when they're startled, when they're hungry, when they're tired, when they're wet. They cry for no reason, just to exercise their lungs.

But Rosemary Leonora did not cry.

The healers at the clinic had checked her over very thoroughly, both magically and physically, and said that she was in perfect health, completely well-developed. Her magical channels were smooth and open, developing exactly as they should. My friend Sebastian, a research biologist who was studying to be a healer, had gone over her systems quite intensively as well, and said he'd never seen any witchlet so robust and strong. I'd probed her magic too, and her biology, as much as I could without endangering her. My birth mother and father had both examined her; my coven mother and nearly all of my coven sisters had looked her over thoroughly. Even my familiar appeared to take her measure on a regular basis and seemed entirely content with her health and well-being.

The only person who hadn't examined her was her grandfather, Gregorio Andromedus. He greatly enjoyed seeing her, but proclaimed himself, at eight hundred, too ancient to be trusted to hold an infant. "Delicate creature that she is, I'd be afraid my old rogue magic would confuse her systems." That made some sense to me, but it also confused me a bit, because…well, I wasn't a hundred percent sure why. I seemed to remember something weird about an interaction between them on the day she was born, but I'd not been myself then—exhausted, filled with pain drugs and spells, worn down from the lengthy labor and the difficult birth. Maybe it was just a strange dream artifact.

Busy as he was, Gregorio still made time to visit us regularly. Rose seemed to appreciate his presence—she followed him with her eyes whenever he was in the room. Probably she sensed something about his great age and power.

Nobody was sure exactly how much a newborn witchlet or baby warlock understood of the world around them. Fortunately, they matured quickly, developing silent, mind-to-mind communication even before their little mouths could handle spoken language.

Anyway, I told myself to just be thankful for her placid, happy silence.

But it was still weird.

I turned away from Jeremy's closed door and thought about heading to the bedroom. Maybe a nap? But no, I wasn't tired; I was…restless. And the baby clearly wasn't sleepy.

My feet carried me up the next, narrower flight of stairs, almost without my conscious decision to do so. Maybe it was because I'd been thinking about it at Mom's...not that I wanted to do any lab work. But I did feel drawn to go inhabit the space, at least for a minute.

Maybe I was trying to talk myself into giving Jeremy (and his father) more space. Not that he'd asked for any. I wondered how long it would take him to do so.

Not till you sign a contract, my mind snickered at me.

I gave a quiet snort back, as I unlocked the door at the top of the staircase. It was pretty obvious that Jeremy was in "best behavior" mode. I mean, he had always been a very marvelous boyfriend, the sexiest warlock in San Francisco and beyond, and a perfect gentleman; but there was an additional sort of—was it wariness? No, not that dramatic, but—carefulness in his behavior. He was thoughtful and attentive, unceasingly apologetic every time his father's people returned the contract for another round of negotiations, and always bringing me little treats—flowers, chocolate, baubles for Rosemary.

And, when he didn't think I was watching, he oh-so-carefully watched *me*.

That was the part I wished I could ask him about. Had I done something to make him think he was on eggshells with me? Had I been unreasonable, or overly demanding, or bitchy? I didn't think so; I didn't remember anything, at least.

But as I stepped into my lab room, I again had that fleeting sense that I was missing something.

Strong, Rosemary said, sending the word to my mind.

"That's right, sweetie," I said, jiggling her a little on my hip. "Your mommy is so strong, she carried you all the way up to the third floor without any help! Now let's see where she can put you down." I looked around the musty-smelling room, its bare hardwood floor with the magically carved pentacle in its exact center, the long lab bench lined up against one wall, the windows at the back letting in the afternoon sunlight. No comfy chairs, no mattresses, no playpens or anything.

Floor, said Rose.

I chuckled. "I'm not putting you down on a nasty filthy floor. I'll see if I can clear some space…"

Floor! Her "voice" was louder this time, more insistent.

It startled me. This placid, uncomplaining baby was suddenly ordering me around? Surprised, I knelt, still holding her, and ran my hand over the floorboards. Okay, it was a bit dusty, but really not so bad.

Middle! she said.

Middle? "You want me to put you in the pentacle, sweetie?"

I felt a strong sense of satisfaction beaming from her as she turned her little head and smiled up at me.

I shrugged and carried her to the pentacle, where I again knelt and felt the floor. "All right," I said, and sat in the middle of the pentacle myself, letting Rose down between my legs.

She immediately started trying to roll away from me. She was far too young to be crawling yet, or even trying to, but that didn't stop her from being a squirmy worm—particularly at diaper time. And bath time. And right now.

"Hey!" I said, grabbing the back of her onesie. "Where do you think you're going?"

She stopped trying to escape and grinned at me again, blowing spit bubbles. Her new favorite trick.

"Fine," I said. "Happy now?"

Still looking up at me, she reached out for my hair, which was in a long braid down my back. It twitched away from her.

A movement at the doorway caught my eye. Elnor pawed the door open slightly wider and sidled in, nose busy sniffing around this room where we'd spent so little time recently. She checked all the corners, as she always did in new spaces, then came to join us in the middle of the pentacle. I could almost see her wondering if we were here to do some spellwork.

"Not without my familiar, kitten," I assured her, petting her on the back, enjoying the feel of her soft fur. Rosemary reached out for her tail, which she flicked away from the baby's grasp.

"You're a force of chaos today, witchlet," I murmured to my daughter. "I wonder what goes on in that fresh little mind."

But the next voice in my head was not that of my daughter. My friend Sebastian said, *Hey, Callie?*

Hey! I answered, happy to hear from him. *What's going on?*

Nothing much, I was just—well, I hadn't seen you or the baby in a while, and I wondered if I could stop by and see how you're both doing?

I thought a moment. Jeremy had never objected to my friendship with the young warlock—for one thing, Sebastian only dated men—but he never seemed all that comfortable around him either. Plus, Gregorio was here. Sebastian obviously wasn't looking for a work meeting. *What about meeting somewhere outside?* I sent. *The baby is restless as all get-out. I was thinking about taking her to a park.*

Sounds good to me. Buena Vista?

Sure. Be there in ten—I have to grab a blanket. I pondered again. *And a snack—make it twenty.*

No, ten—I'll bring the snack.

I smiled. *Deal.*

I closed the connection and started to pick up Rosemary, in preparation for getting to my feet. She squirmed again, nearly making me drop her. I had to add a bit of magic to my strength and balance to save us both. "I promise you will not like it if you land on your head on a hardwood floor," I said to her, once I was safely standing and holding her firmly.

"Ba-ba-ba-ba-ba-ba," she babbled, again reaching for my hair.

Yipes, this child *had* to burn off some of this energy.

— CHAPTER TWO —

Fifteen minutes later, I shook out a blanket on the flat grassy knoll at the top of Buena Vista Park, a lovely small open space near the Haight. It wasn't a secret park, exactly, but it didn't get nearly the crowds and traffic of San Francisco's larger public facilities—like Golden Gate Park, just down the hill. Only a few other people were present, none of them Sebastian—wait, there he was, walking up the hill from the park's east entrance, carrying a large brown paper bag.

I sat down on the blanket and let Rosemary loose. She immediately started rolling, and moving her arms and legs like she was trying to crawl.

Sebastian shook his head, grinning, as he approached. "She's more of a handful every day, huh?"

"Oh, you don't know the half of it. Tell me again why I thought having a baby was a good idea?"

He laughed and sat down on the blanket as the baby squirmed her way closer to him.

"Careful, she's on a hair kick," I warned him.

"Too bad she doesn't eat solid food yet." He opened the bag and pulled out a container of fancy olives, which he opened and set beside me, on the other side from the baby. I popped one in my mouth and chewed, enjoying the oily meaty saltiness.

"Mmm."

He followed the olives with crackers, cheese, and a bunch of grapes. "I thought about wine, but..."

"This is great," I said around another olive. "And I don't want to eat too much—Petrana's making enchiladas for dinner."

"I've totally got to build myself a golem," he said.

We munched contentedly for a while, as the baby rolled around on the blanket between us, reaching for any number of things that she could choke on, or stab herself in the eye with, or otherwise use to do herself grievous harm.

"Maybe we should let her go for it," I finally said. "Maybe then she'll learn to cry."

"I can't believe you want a baby that cries."

I shook my head. "I don't, not really. Just..."

"Yeah." He looked at me sort of quizzically, as if he was studying me, trying to figure something out. Or trying to decide whether to say something.

"What?" I finally asked.

He let out a short breath. "Nothing—I mean, I don't know. You're sure you're...I mean, everything's fine, really and truly? You're feeling...yourself?"

Now it was my turn to look quizzically at him. "I'm fine. I'm totally feeling myself. What do you mean?"

His eyes grew guarded; I could almost feel him retreat behind... something, as he buried his hands in his pockets. A nervous gesture. "Nothing!" he blurted, and then his easy grin came back. "I just want to be sure. You know I know so little about pregnancy and childbirth and young witchlets—so many of us know so little about them. I just feel like I can't ever learn enough about the whole process."

I narrowed my eyes, searching for the bullshit in his words. He wasn't wrong, though; Rosemary was the first child to have been born in our community for several years. Witchkind fertility is a touchy, fragile thing, the result of the long-ago self-breeding project that made us witches and warlocks in the first place. Our forebears selected for longevity and magical power. No one knows for certain whether they also intentionally lowered our reproductive capacity, to keep our numbers in check, or whether it was an unanticipated side effect.

So, children were rare, though not unknown. My own coven was a teaching coven; we had nearly a dozen witchlets, ranging in age from six to fifteen, who took instruction there.

Six to fourteen, I corrected myself; our oldest witchlet, Gracie, had...graduated? She wasn't at the coven house anymore, I knew that much. I really liked Gracie; sometimes she reminded me of my younger self. (Which could be both bad and good, I supposed.)

Had she graduated? At fifteen? No, that couldn't be right. We didn't come of age and choose a coven of our own until we turned twenty. Maybe she had taken some time away from her studies, gone back to stay with her parents for a while. I did remember that coven life had been challenging for her. She yearned for freedom, hated living under stifling ancient rules.

Much as I had myself. In fact, that was a large part of why I'd moved into my own house, last year.

I drew myself back from my woolgathering. Sebastian still watched me, as if waiting for a response. Wondering if I was angry with him? "Me too," I said, belatedly. "I'm learning as we go. Clearly, she's an unusual witchlet, though; you can study her all you like, but I'm not sure that will help you in the future."

He shrugged, looking relieved. "Seems like it can't hurt."

"No, probably not."

Between the two of us, we managed to tickle and tease and play with Rosemary, gently rolling her back and forth on the blanket, keeping her sticky little hands out of harmful (or painful) trouble, and finally wearing her out enough that she might settle down. *Hungry*, she sent to me, after about twenty minutes.

"Huh," I said, reaching for her and opening my blouse. "That's new."

"What is?" Sebastian asked.

I freed up a nipple and she latched onto it. "She always just reaches for my shirt when she wants to feed, or smacks her lips; but this time she sent me the word *hungry*."

"That's cool!" He looked intrigued, attentive. "She's learning new language, then."

"All the time."

As she nursed, Sebastian made up a cracker with a slice of cheese on it and handed it to me.

"Thanks," I said. "Harder to do without free hands."

"My pleasure. As one of your health consultants, I consider it my sworn duty to see that you are well nourished."

"I don't seem to be in any danger of starving," I assured him.

We continued to banter, the momentary awkwardness between us forgotten—or at least, set aside. Yet I realized that this hadn't been the first time since I'd gotten home from my retreat that there had been this kind of weird mis-stepping between us. Sebastian was a good friend, even though I'd only met him last year. He was a fellow trainee of Gregorio Andromedus, but since we worked on different projects, we hadn't encountered one another until our mentor brought him to a dinner party I gave when I first moved into my house.

The same night that my dearest friend since childhood, Logan, had come down with a rare, terrible illness and died.

It still hit me, that she was gone; and then the fact that I thought about her less often all the time brought on a second wave of sadness, and not a little bit of guilt.

Surely I wouldn't ever forget her altogether? But life was long, and she was no longer a part of my daily existence. She would always hold a place in my heart, but…

Then breastfeeding-brain (the successor to pregnancy-brain) took over and the thought faded. There was something more there, I knew there was, but like waking from a dream, I couldn't hold it.

And did it matter? No, probably not. What I had was here and now, alive and in my arms, nursing happily. The future.

Sebastian looked over at me. Again, I got the briefest sense that he wanted to say something important. But what he said was, "Do you want the last grape?"

"Absolutely."

The following day was Tuesday, and Tuesdays meant the weekly Circle at the coven house.

My coven mother, Leonora, called to me in the middle of the afternoon. *Calendula Isadora, please come to the house at four o'clock; I have some business I wish to discuss with you before dinner.*

Yes, Mother, I answered. She'd said "please" very politely, but I knew a command when I heard one.

Besides, my coven sisters always welcomed the chance to play with the baby. The first time I'd let them babysit for an afternoon, I thought I wasn't going to get her back!

Jeremy was still messing about in his study when it was time to leave. I knocked on the door softly and sent him an ætheric thought: *I will see you tomorrow after breakfast.*

Have a nice evening, he sent back. *Give my regards to Leonora and all your sisters.*

I stood outside the door a moment longer, thinking he might come out to kiss me (or Rosemary) goodbye, but he did not.

Shrugging, I gathered up Rose and all her supplies and equipment, and headed over to the coven house, Elnor on my heels.

I left Petrana behind. Not being a witch, she had no place in coven rituals.

When I arrived, Leonora was in her small office off the kitchen—a converted sunporch, with windows overlooking a lovely sweep of downtown in the distance, and the bay beyond. Our own coven house backyard, with its many magical and mundane-but-still-useful herbs and flowers, stepped down the hill in the nearer distance. It was an impressive view; I paused a moment to admire it.

I loved my own house, but the only things I saw out my windows were other houses.

Leonora gave me a warm smile, then bestowed an even bigger one on Rosemary. "How is the precious little sweetums?" she asked, in something as close to a silly voice as my august, dignified coven mother was ever going to produce.

I held off answering a moment, just in case Rose decided to send Leonora a word-thought. Then I said, "She's as marvelous as ever, and growing by leaps and bounds already. I'm going to have to see if I can squeeze a bigger bed in my room here. I'm not sure we're going to fit in that single bed much longer."

Leonora leaned her bulk back in her large, comfortable office chair and brought her grey gaze to mine. Today she was dressed almost informally, for her: an Edwardian gown in a pale green, with a minimum of ruffles about the bodice and sleeves, and no train—at least not that I could see. "That is what I would like to speak with you about, Calendula," she said. "You have not yet signed a contract with Jeremiah Andromedus, but the negotiations are moving forward."

"Yes," I said, a little confused. Leonora was a party to the negotiations: surely, she knew more about their details than even I did. Since I was blood-sworn to this coven from the age of twenty, accommodations would have to be made for me to remain a member while I created a new magical bond with a warlock. It was one of the many conditions I had insisted upon, at Leonora's behest: the more usual path would be for the witch to take a leave of absence from her coven for the duration of the contract, to devote her full attention to the business (and even, perhaps, the romance) of the union.

"Yes," she echoed. "We appear to have arrived at a sticking point with the Andromedus family representatives about your coven status."

"You have?"

She nodded, looking dour. In my lap, Rosemary started making cheerful little chirping noises. Leonora smiled at her absently before going on. "The family is desirous that you and Jeremiah should try for a second child as soon as is comfortably possible. Dr. Andromedus particularly has expressed his concern that your continued coven responsibilities, along with whatever time and attention you devote to your research activities, will unduly tax your energies, leaving you less capable of conceiving."

"What?" I gaped at her. "Jeremy never mentioned anything about any of this."

Leonora shook her head. "I expect he is being told this evening, much as you are."

"But that's crazy!" I said. "I mean, Rosemary is practically a newborn—I'm still nursing her—what's the rush, anyway? We're not even—" I interrupted myself, closing my mouth. Leonora didn't need to know what Jeremy and I were and weren't doing in bed.

"I am certain I do not know what precisely the rush is, though you know as well as I do that fertility is ever a chancy gift."

"I was at least as busy and distracted when I got pregnant as I am now—no, more so," I said, casting my mind back to last year.

It was not long after Logan had died…witches were getting sick… everything had gotten so crazy. That was when Jeremy and I had taken comfort in one another's arms. And then fallen in love.

Logan had had a crush on him first, after all. We both missed her…we bonded over our memories of her…

But then I suddenly was pregnant, and, well, here we were.

"Be that as it may," Leonora said. "You may be sure that I did not rush to agree with the Andromedus family. I wished to speak to you about the situation, and I also intend to bring it before our ancestress this evening."

"Of course." Nementhe might not have anything cogent to say on the matter—at least half the time, her messages were cryptic at best—but often even simply the process of discussing things in Circle with our departed sister in the Beyond helped clarify things later. Something about just asking the question. Like when you wonder about something, and take a shower or go for a long walk, and then the answer becomes clear.

"As you may recall, when we first spoke of this situation, I contacted the Artemis Guild," my coven mother went on. "There were a few candidates available then, but I do not know if they are still seeking positions."

A coven needs thirteen active members to access its full power, to perform important rituals and to keep the levels of magic required to shield and supply a house at normal strength. Of course, each witch had her own power—some more than others— but I couldn't just step away from the coven for ten or twenty years without someone being blood-sworn to serve in my place during my absence. Artemis witches enjoyed the variety of working in a bunch of different covens in different communities, without the vulnerability (and low social stature) of being unaffiliated.

"But—I thought we agreed that I would stay in the coven," I protested. "I thought that's what you wanted. And everyone wants to help raise the baby, and—"

"They do—*we* do," she said, her tone softening and her face relaxing into something resembling a smile. "That is unchanged."

"So why are they suddenly sticking on this? Why do they want a second child so fast?" I hadn't even gotten used to this one, adorable and marvelous though she might be. Then another level of what Leonora was saying hit me: "Wait—another *child*, not another witchlet? They don't want me to have a warlock, do they?"

All softness in her features vanished. "They have not said so, nor even hinted at such a thing, but we cannot rule it out."

Leonora and I gazed across her desk at each other. Warlocks... I mean, yes, I loved one—I loved more than one. I had a marvelous father, and a smart and powerful mentor, and a fun and funny friend who fed me the last grape, in addition to a sexy green-eyed lover. Warlocks were great! In fact, the witchkind world needed more warlocks; we needed them badly. Witches outnumbered them probably ten to one, because when you got to choose the sex of your child, why would you *not* choose to have a witch?

But *somebody* had to produce warlocks.

It was really too bad that we couldn't interbreed with humans. Male and female humans showed up in just about equal numbers at first—in fact, more boys than girls were born, if I remembered my human biology correctly. Of course, boys and men died off faster, so human women made up slightly more than half of their population—

But none of that mattered. It was witchkind we were talking about here, and the crazy notion that Gregorio Andromedus might want me to pop out a baby warlock.

I shook my head, hard enough to send my braid around into Rose's reach. She grabbed hold of it at once and gave it a surprisingly strong yank. It wrapped around her wrist, trying to pry her fingers off; I reached up with my hand and helped. "That's...you're not considering agreeing to any of this, are you?" I asked my coven mother.

"I am not," she said, though not quite as firmly as I might have wanted to hear. "I am well aware of your preferences, and of the interests of this coven. Even if we could manage to secure a qualified Artemis candidate, she would in no way be as strong or capable as you. Our interests would suffer, and I cannot in good conscience agree with that, not without compelling reason."

She paused, still gazing back at me. I could almost hear the unspoken *But...*

"What aren't you saying?" I finally asked.

Leonora pursed her lips. "I will want to speak with Nementhe about this all before we discuss the matter further. But I wanted you to be aware of the issue so that you are not surprised when we are in Circle."

I definitely heard what she didn't say here: she didn't want me knocking our ancestress off her stride with irrelevant questions, confusing her or sending her scattering. Communication between here and the Beyond was tenuous at the best of times, and my older sisters whispered that Nementhe hadn't been a hundred percent sane when she'd moved on. We were lucky we got as much halfway decent advice out of her as it was.

"All right," I said, trying not to feel miffed at the implied accusation. Sure, I was the youngest member of the coven, but I wasn't just some sort of flighty, impetuous witchlet. I was forty-five blessed years old—and with a child, to boot.

Maybe someday everyone would see me as an adult.

"Thank you for your understanding, and for coming by early."

"Uh, sure." Why was she thanking me? Of course I was going to do what Leonora asked—at least, little things. I stifled a smile as I got to my feet, hefting the baby onto my hip.

Leonora smiled at Rosemary, and then at me. "I do believe an assortment of sisters are gathering in the parlor hoping to get some 'auntie time' with the youngling."

I nodded. "Of course." So *that* was why I had to arrive two hours early for dinner in order to have a ten-minute conversation. I turned, but then stopped as I remembered something. "Oh, I have a question."

"Yes?"

"Remember Gracie, who used to be a student here?"

Leonora gave me a puzzled look. "Yes, of course."

"What happened to her? She's not studying here now. Where is she?"

My coven mother started to answer, but paused. Then she shook her head gently and blinked back at me. "She is boarding in a different house at the moment. She is fine; she just needed to learn some skills that we are not able to provide at the level she would benefit from."

"Oh, okay." Now that she said that, I thought it rang a bell. I gave her an embarrassed smile. "I'd forgotten. Pregnancy brain, sorry."

"Quite all right."

I headed out of Leonora's office, nearly tripping over Elnor waiting just outside the door. She followed me to the parlor, as did Grieka, Leonora's familiar.

Then I relinquished my child to half a dozen doting aunties and let myself relax until dinner.

———◖●◗———

At midnight, we gathered for our traditional Circle, seated as always by age. This put me next to Leonora on one side, and Maela on the other. Our cats gathered in the corners of the room, supporting our magic without being overtly involved.

Technically, with Rosemary on my lap, we were fourteen witches in the Circle, but the magic didn't mind. We had all sung her into a deep sleep; she would not remember being here, or the brush of distant, other-worldly magic that Nementhe would bring with her. I knew this because we'd done it before, several times. Of course,

I'd missed the coven Circles that had taken place during my time in the Old Country, but I'd been home for a few weeks now.

After Leonora closed the salt line and we sang the chant, I felt the familiar, comfortable weight of the trance fall over me, the sense that all was right in this world as well as the one—well, beyond. Nementhe glided into our presence. As usual, Leonora communed silently with her for a while, and then each sister shared something.

It was only when Nementhe settled her attention on me that I remembered the sadness and confusion she had brought to our exchanges over the last few weeks.

What is it? I thought to her. *What is wrong?*

Beside me, I felt Leonora's hand tighten on mine, ever so slightly.

"It is not the time," Nementhe said, aloud.

Around the Circle, I could feel, even half-see, several sisters startling. Nementhe very rarely brought an audible voice to our meetings.

"If it pleases you, Ancestress, could you elaborate?" Leonora said. "Not the time for what?"

Leonora hadn't yet mentioned the question of my taking a leave of absence to sign the contract; new business came later in the ritual, after the general weekly reports.

"It is not the time," Nementhe said again, and then, "I know not what more to tell you, Mother."

"Are you perhaps confused, Ancestress?" Leonora asked, after a brief pause.

"I know not."

And then she started to fade away, just draining her energy out of the Circle, slipping back to the Beyond.

"We thank you, as ever, for your wisdom and guidance," Leonora rushed to say before Nementhe was gone entirely. Then the soft lassitude of our trances fell away from us, and we were entirely back in mundane space, sitting cross-legged on the floor of the big front parlor, a bunch of confused cats at our backs, and a bunch of confused witches in the middle.

Leonora, shaking her head, reached out and broke the line of salt on the floor. "Well," she said, but didn't go on.

Well, I thought.

In my lap, Rosemary blinked up at me, wide awake and silent. "How long have you been awake, little one?" I asked. I'd been certain she was out—she had always slept deeply through the ritual before.

Reaching, she sent me.

"Reaching? What do you mean, sweetpea?"

But she just blinked again and started making her "feed me" smacking noises.

Later, in the kitchen, a few of us were having a final cup of tea before bed. Leonora was not among us; she had collected Grieka and headed for her chambers upstairs, promising to meditate on Nementhe's confusing message and hasty departure, and to see if she could contact our ancestress privately. Not many of us could do that; it depended on the willingness of the sister in the Beyond, as well as plenty of strength from this end. But if anyone could do it, four-hundred-and-fifty-year-old Leonora could.

"Circle is always strange," Maela said, sipping her tea. "But, I have to say, that was a bit weirder than usual."

"True that," I said.

Pearl shook her head. "No, Nementhe was always doing that sort of thing even before she moved on."

I turned to look at her. Pearl was one of the younger members of the coven, and—though of course we were all sworn sisters and had lived for decades in this house together, working magic communally, dining together, thoroughly dedicated to one another's well-being—she and I were not particularly close.

"She was?" I asked. I'd heard the whispers, of course, but Nementhe had been retired from active teaching duties even when I was a student here, as a young witchlet.

Pearl nodded. "I always wondered if it was true madness or deliberate mischief."

Maela's eyes widened, as did Sirianna's. "No way," said Siri. "She was definitely mad. I knew her longer than you did."

"Maybe," Pearl said, but there was doubt in her voice. "I mean, I'm sure you're not wrong, but—once she realized how useful the reputation for madness was, what would stop her from, you know, leaning on it when it was convenient?"

"Just for mischief?" Maela asked. "But why?"

"Leonora isn't the easiest coven mother out there," Pearl said. "Maybe Nementhe got tired of being obedient after a few hundred years."

From the shadows on the far side of the huge kitchen, Honor's aged voice piped up, startling us all. "Young witches. May the Blessed Mother preserve us from the collective wisdom of young witches." Then she shuffled out of the room, closing the door firmly behind her.

"I didn't even know she was there," Pearl said, looking at us, abashed now.

None of us had.

We all finished our tea and headed up to bed, chastened. Agewise, Honor was the next in line for potentially moving on to the Beyond. Four hundred was the traditional age (but just try telling that to Leonora, fifty years past that and going strong); Honor was three hundred and ninety-five, almost three hundred and ninety-six, with a birthday in early January. We often combined our Yuletime celebrations with a birthday party for her. Well, Mother Holle celebrations; Leonora didn't think much of fir boughs and gold beads, preferring to recognize a more witch-focused midwinter festival.

I thought about the evening as I got Rosemary and myself ready for bed. Of course the baby needed a diaper change, so I waited till the rest of my sisters had finished in the small shared bathroom. (No, not all thirteen of us shared one bathroom; there were several others, so this one only belonged to four of us. Never, ever wonder why I decided to move out of this house and into a three-story house of my very own.)

Once I finally had us both tidied, hair brushed (mine) and one final swallow of midnight snack (Rosemary), I tried to get comfortable in the tiny single bed. Elnor settled down by my feet, but that still didn't leave much room for me and the baby.

It was hard to believe I used to keep Petrana in this room too — when she was even bigger than she was now, at that.

At least she didn't need any bed space.

My dreams had been very strange since my trip to the Old Country. Well, dreams are always a bit weird, but mine had taken an even odder turn recently. I'd asked the healers about it, but they shrugged it off.

"Sometimes a lot of ley line travel will do that to a body," Manka had said. "The energetic disruption takes a while to settle back out. It should be nothing to worry about — unless they are particularly disturbing. Then you might want to consult a seer or a prophetess and see if someone is trying to use the disruption to get a message through."

"No, they're not very disturbing," I had told her.

Tonight's, however, was.

It started mildly enough. I was walking through a dark forest, but without any sense of danger or fear, just woods after nightfall, with no moon. I followed a path I could barely see, letting my feet find their way as my magical senses reached out, looking for— something. I wasn't sure what.

Suddenly, before me loomed a giant building. It wasn't as though I hadn't seen it in the dark, but more that it hadn't been there before—and then suddenly it was. Yet it had been there all along, in the way of dream logic.

I stopped, trying to catch my breath, but the air around me felt heavy and full, like it did not want to fill my lungs. It made everything seem even dimmer, even the huge building. I put a hand out and touched cold, rough stone, but I could barely see. I gasped for breath, looking for release—for anything. I suddenly understood that I needed to find a way inside this building, that only there would I find relief. There I would find what I was looking for. Yet I could not see any doors or windows—the light was too dim, and my hands found only stone. I began to run alongside the building, trailing my hands along the stone as I ran, cutting and bruising them on the jagged, rough exterior. Even though I nearly couldn't breathe, I began to shout, and to hit my hands on the walls as I ran. "Let me in!"

I startled awake, still gasping for breath, but now I was back in my coven house bed, and Elnor was sitting on my chest.

"Cat!" I exclaimed, sitting up and sending her tumbling off. She nearly landed on the baby, who was snuggled up beside me, deep in sleep—so deep that I gasped again, suddenly frightened that she wasn't breathing.

But she was; she was fine, sleeping contentedly. Her energy was strong and pure, and I even thought I caught a glimpse of her dream, one of comfort and safety.

Elnor sneezed, and then gave me that look that cats give you when they're miffed.

"Sorry," I said. "You were trying to pull me out of the nightmare, weren't you?"

My cat began to wash her whiskers.

"Well, thank you," I said, still catching my breath. "That was very unpleasant. I'm glad I didn't wake the baby." I spoke in a low whisper, and then what I said made me realize how ridiculous that all was: talking aloud to my cat, who wouldn't answer, but quietly, hoping not to disturb a sleeping infant.

I shook my head, trying to let the dream dissipate. But it clung to me: the fear and panic, the helplessness, even the pain in my hands. I looked at them carefully in the dim light of the night, but of course they were not injured.

I finally lay back down, willing myself to settle, to go back to sleep. It felt very out of reach.

Perhaps I would lie here, wakeful, till morning. Which wouldn't be the end of the world or anything; witches don't need nearly the amount of sleep that humans do, though I had been slumbering quite a bit more since Rosemary's birth—and in her last few months in my womb as well. I'd kind of gotten used to it. No doubt this would shift back as I recovered from pregnancy and childbirth. (Not to mention my lengthy overseas trip.)

It would be nice to get a few more hours back in the day, I thought.

To do what? But I had no real answer for that.

After a while, I began to hear the small noises of the coven house at night: several sisters were up and about, doing the quiet things that witches do alone in the darkness. Meditation, private spellwork, even writing by candlelight. It felt both peaceful and a little stifling, my awareness of so many others around me. I let my witch-sight wander the house, seeing who was where, doing what.

Maela, two rooms down the hall on this floor, was sitting up in bed. She held a small orb in her lap: not a crystal ball or anything like that, just a focus she used in her vision work.

Maela was a seer. I remembered what Manka had said about dreams: perhaps Maela could help me with mine. But should I disturb her? She was clearly busy working on something.

I watched her for another few minutes, not shielding my mental presence from her. She noted me but did not pull up from her work. When I was certain she did not want to be interrupted further, I withdrew and let my attention roam more generally through the house.

There was rather a lot of feline energy down on the first floor. I cast my mind's eye down there, seeking our familiars. Elnor, of course, was still up here with me, but there were at least eight cats in the living room, dining room, and kitchen, prowling about, checking corners and perimeters—and their food bowls, of course.

Cats are even more nocturnal than witches, but it was odd for so many to be roaming the house without their mistresses. Maela's cat should be with her, if she was working magic, but the beastie (a white-haired Persian mix named Lotte) was in the kitchen, sniffing by the door to Leonora's office.

A little sound from my daughter drew my attention back to our own room. She babbled and cooed in her sleep, shifting about and punching me with tiny fists. "What is it, sweetie?" I whispered, rocking her gently.

She didn't fully awaken, but she did sort of snuggle into me as I rocked her; she even reached out and put a hand on my breast. I got ready for a middle-of-the-night feeding, but then she drifted back to sleep.

I watched her in the dark, her red curls, her tiny perfect eyelashes, her smooth skin, so astonishingly soft. I drank in the scent of her: clean, baby-pure. A great lassitude came over me, and gratitude: I had never known I wanted a daughter, not until she was forming inside me—and how could I have been so unknowing, so blind? How could anyone not want such a thing?

It's just biology, I told myself. Just pheromones. I should know, after all. A helpless child needed a mother's unquestioning love, her blind adoration. It was how she would survive.

It didn't mean Rosemary wasn't the most adorable child that had ever existed, on this plane or any other.

— CHAPTER THREE —

I did not sleep any more that night, but I arose rested and refreshed anyway once the sounds of the house began to increase and the inviting smells of tea and toast drifted up from the kitchen. Carrying Rosemary downstairs, I settled on the window bench, accepted a cup of tea from Peony, and began feeding my daughter.

Maela strolled in a few minutes later and joined me on the window seat. "I felt your regard in the night; did you wish to speak to me?"

"I did," I told her. "I had a dream of suffocating, and of being locked outside a building I could not see—a building with no doors or windows, but I had to get inside. Its sharp stone cladding cut my hands. I woke up in a panic. I thought about asking you about it then, but I saw that you were awake, but busy."

She nodded. Peony brought her a cup of tea as well. "Thanks," she told our older sister, and then turned back to me. "Yes, I was trying to make some sense out of the Circle last night—as I'm sure many of us were."

I nodded. It was always unsettling when communications with the Beyond didn't go as expected. And yet...I shrugged an ungracious thought away before it had even fully formed.

Of course it was unsettling. I wasn't sure what else I had been on the trail of, in my mind.

"Did you find anything?"

She took a sip of her tea. "I'm not sure," she said slowly.

Lotte walked in from the front of the house—perhaps the living room—and jumped up on the bench with us. Maela began stroking her; Lotte purred and rubbed against her mistress.

"There is a lot that is dark and closed," Maela went on. "So, your dream is interesting. Tell me more."

I told her everything I could remember from it, including the start in the forest, and the sense that the building had appeared from nowhere. And that the answer—what I needed—was inside.

"Yes," Maela said, still sounding pensive. "That does go with what I'm seeing: darkness, a closed-off wall, a need to get inside coupled with the inability to get inside." She frowned. "But this is all too vague to be very useful. Has Leonora come down yet this morning?"

"Not yet," Peony said from the stove. "She was up most of the night in her own meditations."

"Does anyone know if she got hold of Nementhe?" I asked.

Nobody did, including Organza, who came in just then to help get the main breakfast started. "I do know she was up most of the night," she said, which we all already knew.

It went on like that until breakfast was ready, reminding me once again that a tiny bed and a shared bath weren't the only reasons I liked living in my own house. Even with Jeremy and Petrana there, I didn't have to have thirteen conversations about the same thing every day.

When Leonora did finally join us, with breakfast nearly half-over, she reported no further information. She did reach

Nmenthe, after several hours of trying, but our ancestress only repeated the nothings she'd shared with us in Circle.

"It is not the time," said Leonora with a frustrated snort. "Impudent…" She trailed off, clearly unwilling to speak unkindly of our ancestress. Well, more unkindly than she already had.

We all focused on our egg-and-sausage casserole, not interested in attracting our coven mother's notice when she was in a mood like this. And as soon as it was politely feasible, I gathered up my daughter, cat, and overnight bag, and went home.

Jeremy was out; only Petrana was there when we walked in. "Greetings, Mistress Callie," she said politely. "Have you breakfasted?"

"Fully and thoroughly," I told her. "You know what the coven house breakfasts are like."

"In theory," she said.

I was almost getting used to her having a personality, a sense of humor even, by now. "Right, of course. Golems don't eat food."

"Golems do observe witches eating food, and enjoying it," she said. "Golems even understand how to cook food. But no, eating is beyond my capacity."

I stifled the automatic reflex to ask her how she felt about that. Golems also do not have *feelings*, something it took me the longest time to internalize—and apparently, I still hadn't, not fully. Nor would I, if she kept advancing like this.

A sudden terrible thought struck me. Petrana was not some kind of machine artificial intelligence; she was made of magic and mud. But…were the situations comparable? As she spent more time "alive" and learned more, would her mud-mind create more connections and eventually develop independent intelligence? True consciousness?

Or did she have consciousness already, but just in a golem-sense?

I wished I knew anyone on the whole planet who knew anything about golems. When I had created her, I'd done so after studying old books (and new websites with information from even older books). I'd poured my own magic into her, using at first the soil from the coven house's backyard, and then later my own house's dirt, after I'd damaged her doing…something.

Doing what? I couldn't quite remember. Seemed like I was always trying to do crazy things, before I had a daughter.

But that's how you learn, a little voice inside me pointed out. I had always been curious: it was why I'd become a biological researcher to begin with. I had always wanted to push myself to learn more, to grow—not just to grow my own power, but to understand more about how the world worked.

I was not content to sit in a dusty old coven house and tat doilies for four hundred years.

Petrana was still standing before me, waiting politely, patiently. Of course she had infinite patience: she was, entirely, my creature, brought into existence by me for the sole purpose of serving my needs. If I never again asked her to do anything except stand in the corner and wait, she would do that, and without complaint or distress or—well, any feeling at all.

For some reason, the thought made me unspeakably sad. (New-mother hormones, no doubt.) Speaking of which: "Would you take her for a while?" I asked, handing the baby to the golem.

"Of course, Mistress Callie. With pleasure."

I tried not to think about what she could possibly mean by *pleasure* as I headed upstairs to take as long a shower as I wanted.

Jeremy returned to the house in the late afternoon, and again he had his father with him. "Hello, Gregorio Andromedus," I greeted him, leaning in to let him kiss me on the cheek.

"Greetings, Calendula Isadora, Rosemary Leonora."

Old warlocks really do love their formalities.

I had been reading in the second parlor downstairs, trying to work up the impetus to do something more productive; Rose had been sleeping in a little rocker-crib by the sofa, but she awoke when her father and grandfather walked in. Now she was doing the closest thing to fussing she ever really did: little *moops* and *meeps* of unfocused not-quite-distress sounds, which usually came before the lip-smacking sounds of Feed Me Time.

I reached into the crib and pulled her out, jiggling her a little as I smiled at Gregorio. "You sure you don't want to hold her?" I asked.

He shook his head even as I felt my daughter stiffen in my arms. "Oh, no thank you; it is plain to see what she is really interested in." And indeed, she was already reaching for the front of my blouse. "Do go ahead; do not mind us." He smiled at both of us.

"Thanks." Even so, I turned slightly so as not to flash boob at my future father-in-law.

"We need to dart upstairs just for a moment," Jeremy told me. "I've asked Father to help me with one final tweak, and then my study will be ready to show you." He looked proud, even a little excited.

I smiled back at him, happy that he was getting it worked out the way he wanted it. "Take your time. This will keep us occupied for a while."

The warlocks gave me nearly identical little half-bows—polite and formal—before heading upstairs. This time, I couldn't hear anything of what they were doing up there, or feel any residual effect from their magic.

I was maybe even on the point of dozing off with Rosemary on my nipple when I heard them coming back down. Ah, so my night of short sleep was apparently going to catch up to me after all. I blinked and stretched a little, trying to get oxygen back into my body, get my blood circulating again.

"No need to get up," Gregorio said from the doorway. "I must go downtown and finish looking over the preparations. I will see you both this evening." He nodded and stepped away; I heard the front door close softly a moment later.

"This evening?" I said to Jeremy, who came in and sat beside me.

He kissed me on the cheek, then laid a small kiss on Rosemary's crown. "Don't tell me you've forgotten the banquet."

Banquet? Oh, Blessed Mother, I had—the Elders' annual winter fest event. Very formal, very stuffy, very dull. I remembered them from my childhood, as my father was also an Elder. It had been so nice to be able to stop going to them once I joined the coven. "Um, sort of?" I admitted, feeling chagrined. Just what *was* it with my memory lately? I really needed to do something about this. My mind was becoming a total sieve. "Uh, right. I need to figure out what to wear—and what to dress the baby in."

Jeremy gave us both a pained look. "I...do you think we could leave her with Petrana for the evening? Or perhaps get one of your sisters to come over and babysit? It's only a few hours, and banquets don't usually include infants."

I just looked back at him. "What if she needs to nurse?"

Now he looked even more uncomfortable. "Don't you...isn't there...I know the humans have devices for extracting and storing the milk..."

I shook my head. Of course I had one, and that totally wasn't the point. "Seriously, the granddaughter of the Elders' *leader* cannot even come to the banquet?"

"It's not that she's not allowed, it's just that I don't imagine that it will be comfortable for either of you if we brought her. Callie, please understand: this is just a meal and a lot of ceremonial matters. Not a place for a baby."

Every place is a place for a baby, I wanted to say, but it sounded grumpy and unreasonable even inside my own head. Was I over-reacting? It was hard to tell how I was actually feeling—I had so much sudden chagrin over my own memory problems. I was confused, scrambled. "I'm sorry," I said, after a moment. "I—I'm sorry I forgot the event. I could have made arrangements to leave her at the coven house for a few hours, but I just…" I stared into Jeremy's eyes. "What's wrong with me? I can't hold anything in my head these days. Am I losing my mind?"

His entire visage softened with love and concern, and he leaned in to take me in his arms, cradling Rosemary between us. "Callie, I know this is all hard, and new for you. But there is truly nothing to worry about. My father says this is entirely typical of new mothers—human and witchkind alike. The body goes through so many dramatic hormonal changes when bringing new life into the world. Surely you must have studied this during your training?"

"Not a whole lot," I said, letting him hold me. Taking comfort from his strong but gentle touch. "I mean, sure, some; but since so few of us actually have babies, it wasn't a major focus." Then the rest of what he'd said struck me. "You've talked to your dad about this? What did you tell him?"

"Nothing, really," he said, quickly. He pulled back a little so his gaze could find mine again. "Nothing you haven't already expressed openly already, and not just to me. Your concerns about forgetting little things, that's all. And he assured me it's absolutely normal, and that you should start feeling sharper soon. More like your old self."

"Not soon enough to suit me," I grumbled, but nodded at him, feeling a little better at the news.

Still, it was striking, how addle-brained I'd obviously become. And as a biologist, I had to question it: how was this an adaptive or even functional occurrence? If new mothers always became forgetful nincompoops, wasn't that putting their offspring in greater danger? It didn't seem like a very good plan for the ongoing survival of the species. Wouldn't witchkind at least have figured out ways to select this "feature" away?

Jeremy was watching me carefully, clearly realizing I was thinking something through and not wanting to interrupt the process.

Which was another thing. It was great that he was so sensitive and caring. But how long was I going to enjoy being handled with kid gloves?

I shook the thought away and gave him a tired smile. "Sorry again—I'm just not used to being so...fragile, I guess."

His smile was genuine and heartfelt; he pulled me into a quick hug again. "Calendula, my love. You are not fragile. You have just been through a positively miraculous feat, all while showing barely any signs of strain or fatigue. Then, rather than taking a few months to rest and recover at home, as is customary, you undertook a lengthy and difficult journey! I know you've said many times that your retreat to the Old Country was refreshing and restorative, and I'm quite certain that it was, but you cannot seriously believe that it wasn't also very draining—magically as well as physically." I started to reply, but he went on. "You are one of the most powerful witches I have ever met, as well as one of the smartest and most capable. But even you have limits. I believe you are bumping up against one of those limits right now, and it is showing itself in your mental state. Perhaps your brain is letting go of little things because it is trying too hard to hold you together."

Again, I wanted to protest, but I wasn't at all sure that he was wrong. It made sense, it did; but—I didn't feel *tired*, precisely. I just felt, well, stupid. Was that brain fatigue, and I just wasn't recognizing it?

"You might be right," I finally admitted. "I wonder—should I just stay home this evening? If I need to rest?" It might have sounded sulky, but I didn't mean it that way; I was genuinely curious. Maybe I should consider the idea.

He didn't appear to take my words amiss either. "You should do whatever you feel is right. I would absolutely enjoy your company this evening—I have been looking forward to the night out with you, despite its official purpose and, er, lack of entertainment value—but your health and well-being are my most important considerations." He flashed a quick smile. "Yours and that of our daughter as well, of course."

"Right." I smiled back at him, grateful again for his thoughtfulness. How much he loved me; how hard he was working to take care of me, to accommodate me. "No, I would actually like to go with you this evening. I'm sorry I hadn't thought about babysitting—or, well, anything really. I can ask Sirianna if she wants to come over."

He looked *so* pleased; I knew that had been the right call.

—⟨●⟩—

Sirianna was of course thrilled to babysit and asked if she could bring Maela with her. I told her the more the merrier, and that they should feel free to come over as soon as they wanted to. *You can help me figure out what to wear.*

Most of your formal gowns are here; do you want me to bring them?

Oh, that was right: I'd not imagined I'd be going to a lot of old-fashioned dress-up events when I'd moved out; I pretty much had only jeans and T-shirts here. I cast my mind's eye over to my coven house closet, shuddering a little at the elaborate costumes and frippery I saw. *What about just the slate blue?* I sent Siri. *That should fit me even now.*

You're not any differently shaped than you were before your pregnancy, she told me. *But that's a lovely one—very simple.*

I felt different; softer, more fluid. Or maybe that was just my breasts, haha. *Thanks!*

My pleasure. See you soon.

While my attention had been elsewhere, Jeremy had taken Rose and was playing the catch-the-hair game. She squealed with laughter when she grabbed hold of his sleek ponytail, then laughed even harder when it slithered out of her grasp.

"Too cute," I said, laughing along with our daughter. "So," I added, getting to my feet, "want to show me your office while we wait for Siri to get here with my dress?"

"I would be delighted!" Jeremy got up too, shifting Rose to his hip. His hair continued to tease her as we all climbed up to the second floor and walked down the hallway to the closed door, where he stopped and turned to me. "I'll need two hands for this," he said, handing me the baby.

I took her and waited while he spelled open the door, working a complicated incantation that involved both finger movements and muttered words.

That's going to be a lot of trouble to do every time you want to come in here, I thought, but didn't say aloud. His room, his magic.

The door slowly, dramatically, swung open. Jeremy stood aside to let me see.

I inhaled softly, stunned and impressed by the depth and thoroughness of what he and his father had done in here. I was gazing upon a sweeping vista, from the apparent vantage point of the edge of a cliff. Far below was a colorful valley, with a river running through it, leading to the ocean in the distance. Overhead was a vast sky purpling into sunset. Tiny puffy white clouds hovered at the horizon, just enough to be picturesque. I could feel a gentle breeze and smell the freshness of vegetation.

I took a step back, blinking, and looked at Jeremy. "Wow. That's amazing."

"Do you like it?" He totally wasn't hopping up and down waiting for my answer—he was far too dignified for such a thing—but I could still feel it.

"I love it," I told him, honestly. "But...how are you going to get any work done in here?"

"Oh." He laughed and waved his hand. The image faded, though it didn't vanish completely. Slowly, the room's walls and furniture came back into view; the illusion was now more like an elaborate and well-executed trompe l'oeil. "That's just for when I meditate, when I need reality to fade away altogether. Come on in, you'll see."

I followed him in. Indeed, now I could see a large desk against the front wall, between the windows, with a comfortable chair; two matching guest chairs sat by the right-hand wall, with a low table between them. Jeremy sat down in one of them and indicated the other. "Have a seat."

I did, shifting the baby to my lap. "Finally, she finds something more interesting than hair!" I said, because Rosemary was still gazing around the room, rapt.

"Do you think she even understands what she's seeing?" he asked. "I mean, when does a witchlet begin to parse representation—illusion—versus solid objects?"

"I don't know," I said. "She's not reaching for anything, just looking. But that's not really telling us anything."

We both watched her watch the room for a minute. Then Jeremy said, "I wish she'd talk to me like she talks to you."

I looked at him. "She doesn't talk to me all that much, you know."

"I know." He shrugged. "Even a word every now and then would be nice, though."

"She will," I assured him, stifling a little pang of guilt that I had taken her away from her father for so long during her first weeks of life, giving them no chance to grow closer.

But if I hadn't done that, I wouldn't have been able to achieve the clarity I had now—at least about what I wanted from our relationship. We wouldn't be living together like this if I hadn't gone on my retreat. She would grow closer to him in time; she already was. The mother-daughter bond was the first and strongest bond, but others would surely follow.

Jeremy started to say something, but we were both interrupted by a ping from Sirianna. She and Maela were at the door. "I'll get it," I said, getting up.

"*We'll* get it. They're here to take care of our child." My green-eyed warlock leapt to his feet and offered me his arm.

I grinned at him as we headed downstairs to let my coven sisters in.

The banquet was nice, I suppose; it was your basic warlock-run fancy dinner party that still managed to feel like a business meeting, even though nobody was overtly talking business. Maybe it was the setting that was the problem. This room in the Elders' headquarters (a highly warded and disguised penthouse in one of the city's tallest buildings) was just never going to look like anything other than what it was: a conference room. The long table down the middle of the expansive space was laden with food and drink and holiday cheer, along with out-of-season floral arrangements and small decorative bits of magically pulsing colored lights, but it was undeniably a table where warlocks met and imagined they ran the world. Even the floor-to-ceiling windows offering a view of downtown and the dark bay beyond failed to make this feel more like a party.

I felt pretty in my formal gown, though; I'd enjoyed dressing up some in the Old Country, and even brought some fun new things home with me, whereupon I had promptly reverted to Nursing Mother Casual. (Jeans with blouses that buttoned. Which, hey, was a step up from jeans and T-shirts, I suppose.)

I had put a gentle spell on my breasts so that they would slow their milk production for a few hours—not enough to leave me dry when we got back home, just sufficient to keep me comfortable during the meal. If Rosemary got hungry while we were gone, there was breast milk in the freezer that Sirianna and Maela could heat to the exact correct temperature. "Trust me," Siri had said before we left. "I'm a cook; you know I know what to do."

"I do," I'd said, and I did trust her, and it was *still* unspeakably weird to go out for an entire evening and leave my baby behind, so I only went through the precise instructions with Siri one more time to be sure. And now I kept catching myself glancing around for Rose, wondering who I had handed her to.

I sat at the long table, Jeremy at my right hand, my father at my left. At the moment, they were both talking to the witches on their other sides, leaving me without a conversation partner—which was entirely fine with me. I was out of practice with this kind of socializing: scripted, artificial. Dull. It was a relief to just be able to sit and enjoy my meal.

And study the table. Across from me, though too far to chat with without shouting (and pretty much blocked by an over-the-top bunch of fancy flowers), were more of the older crowd of Elders, and their consorts or companions for the evening. Nobody in the room was a stranger, but these folk were several generations older than me, and I had very little in common with them. It was amusing to watch them follow the polite dinner-party conventions they'd been acting out for hundreds of years. Amusing and sad, honestly; even without being able to hear their words, I could likely reproduce the conversations verbatim.

Before the warlock directly across from me could notice my gaze on him through the foliage, I looked away, concentrating on my soup. It was a creamy vegetable-based something-or-other, heavy and fragrant and quite delicious. Comforting for a cold winter's night.

(Or at least the general approximation of a cold winter's night, such as we ever got in San Francisco.)

After scraping my bowl clean, I glanced over at my father. He was still talking to Sapphire, by his side; my mother had not been feeling up to the banquet, he had told me, and the other witch had agreed to take her place as his companion. Sapphire was a coven mother; her coven bred cats, running the cattery that supplied pretty much all local witchkind with our familiars. It was interesting that Mom had chosen her to invite to take her place tonight, I thought. Mom had never replaced her last familiar, Pixel, when the cat had moved on a decade or more ago. Maybe she was finally considering doing so?

Nobody could point to a direct connection between a witch's health and strength and her choosing to have a familiar, but I couldn't help but wonder if there was something to the idea. Elnor was a furry little tuna-eating pest at times, but she amplified and supplemented my magic, and she was deeply invested in my well-being. If Mom adopted another familiar, at least the cat would be a nice companion for her and might even be helpful beyond that. With the long hours that Dad spent working, I knew she was alone a lot of the time.

"The soup was delightful, don't you think?" Jeremy said into my ear.

I turned and smiled at him. "I loved it. I'll have to figure out how it's made and teach Petrana."

The witch Jeremy had been talking to, Isadora, was also a coven mother—actually the head of the coven that Mom had belonged to, before taking what was clearly going to be a permanent leave to set up housekeeping with Dad. She was here as the companion to Henrik, an Elder. Fancy crowd we had here tonight; Jeremy and I were some of the few who were not Elders or coven mothers, now that I looked more closely around the table.

Of course, Jeremy, as the son of Gregorio Andromedus, would no doubt be elected to the Elders as soon as a position opened up.

"I can ask Father to get the recipe from the cook," Jeremy said.

"It shouldn't be too hard," I mused, casting part of my mind back over the cascade of flavors even as the rest of my attention was still observing the guests at this elegant dinner party. One well-placed spell would take out the entire leadership of greater Bay Area witchkind.

Though that would never happen, I assured myself. Here in the Elders' very headquarters, high over the city, heavily warded and magically obscured, we were probably as safe as our kind ever were, anywhere.

Besides, the kind of strife you heard about happening in the Old Country was...

The thought had hardly started before I lost it as Jeremy added, "In fact, I'll ask him now." He turned his gaze toward the head of the table, where Gregorio was for the moment not in conversation. He glanced up at his son with a warm smile; I could see them communicating ætherically, probably about more than just the soup.

Left once more without a conversation partner, I tried to jog my own memory. Something about the Old Country, and...

Suddenly, with a shock, my dream from the night before flashed into my head. Except it wasn't the dream: it was a memory.

I knew that building.

I had been there. It was a real place, and it was in the Old Country. Yet it was out in some deep dark woods, which made no sense. Because I had spent all my time in the capital city, Balzst.

Hadn't I?

I had eaten incredible food and shopped at fun stores, and walked the city streets, and met a zillion terrific witches, and basically just had the time of my life.

I had not gone into the countryside, and I had certainly not tried to get into some creepy scary stone building...

Had I?

Then Sebastian's voice was in my head, very briefly. *Callie. Remember.*

I shook my head, and Jeremy returned his attention to me. "My dear? Are you all right?"

"I...I'm fine," I said, giving him what probably looked like a nervous smile. "I just—my energy is all over the place." I patted my chest, above my breasts. "Maybe my milk is pushing back against the lactation pause spell; I don't know. I haven't used it much."

A look of gentle concern came into his eyes. "We can go home whenever you like, if you're not feeling well."

I shook my head. "No—I don't need to leave. We haven't even had the main course yet, or heard the speeches."

I could see him trying not to smile at this. "I know how much you must be looking forward to the speeches, beloved."

I did smile back at him. My partner in crime. "Eagerly. Raptly. Anxiously. On-the-edge-of-my-seat-ish-ly."

He reached over and patted my hand. "I share your enthusiasm to its exact degree."

I squeezed his hand, and then Isadora said something to him and he turned to her, still holding my hand.

Remember what? I sent to Sebastian. Who, being a very junior warlock, was of course not in attendance this evening.

But he did not reply.

———— ❬●❭ ————

The speeches were exactly as riveting as Jeremy and I had anticipated. But the main course, roasted rack of lamb with tiny new potatoes and a red wine reduction, was delicious. I'm not saying it was worth the speeches; it was the chocolate pot de crème with fresh whipped cream that tipped the balance to the "stay" side of the equation.

Another thing to have Petrana learn how to make.

When the evening was finally over, Jeremy insisted we take a car home, rather than navigating the ley lines. "Indulge me, my love," he said. "I am quite sure you are more than up for the challenge, but let me take care of you. After all, what is a consort for, if not to see to the health and comfort of his lady love?"

"You're too much," I told him, giving him a gentle elbow-nudge in the side. He draped an arm around my shoulders, and I leaned into his strength, his warmth. "I don't know how you can be so crazy-romantic and still sound so, I don't know, serious about it."

"Because I love you," he said, simply.

We stood outside the darkened building waiting for the car to arrive. Most of the rest of the witches and warlocks had gone home via ley line, of course; the few who took human transportation had arranged for cars and drivers in advance and had also long since departed.

"I love you too," I said.

A breeze came up, blowing a bit of trash down the deserted sidewalk. "I do hope we can finish the negotiations soon," Jeremy said quietly, after a minute. "I so look forward to moving to the next phase of our relationship. The more private phase."

I nodded. "Me too. It's frustrating that it has to be this way. You and I have been in agreement practically from the start—we could have just drawn up a contract, signed it, and moved on. Instead…"

He sighed. "I sometimes wonder if we shouldn't just go ahead and do that."

"What?" I looked up at him. "We can do that?"

"We can do whatever we want." But his tone was a little sad, even a little bitter. "There is no law that says my father must be in charge of my domestic arrangements."

He had more to say, I could tell. I waited, giving him time, but he just pursed his lips.

"But you want his…involvement?"

At last, he gave a gentle sigh. "I do, Callie; that's what's so maddening about all this. I came to this city in the first place, as you remember, because my father is here. I love and admire him, but he has been nearly a stranger to me all my life. When he invited me to join him, to learn about his business, his community, his world, I leapt at the chance. When he showed an interest in my own life, that gave me a feeling that...well, I never imagined I would have that. I love my foster parents—they are magnificent people and could not have done a better job raising me—but, my own father..." He trailed off, still staring down the street. I waited. "I never knew my mother, and I barely knew my father. I want to become closer to him, not push him away."

"I understand," I said quietly. And I did.

"I just keep thinking that each new tweak is going to be the last one. By themselves, they are minor; even in aggregate, they are not too onerous. But..."

I did not bring up the *Callie should get pregnant again, this time with a baby warlock* tweak. This did not seem the moment.

Jeremy sighed again, more forcefully this time. "I am trying not to see this as a deliberate stalling tactic, or worse, a capricious and meaningless display of power and authority over me—over us. I am trying very hard. But I am not entirely succeeding."

Down at the end of the block, a car turned the corner, heading this way. Our ride, probably. "Can you...talk to him about this?" I asked.

"I...don't know. I should be able to. But you know Father."

The sedan pulled up in front of us as my cell phone buzzed in my coat pocket, informing me of its arrival. "I do," I said, as Jeremy opened the back door and ushered me in.

We were silent through most of the ride, neither of us wanting to discuss private witchkind matters in front of our human driver. But we were both thinking about it—at least, I know I was, and by the look on his face, Jeremy almost certainly was too.

Sure, contracts could be complicated, and ours was no exception. Balancing the desire of my coven for my continued participation (unless Leonora decided to go the Artemis Guild route after all), and my own desire to continue my research program (despite the fact that I'd spent zero time on it in months), with the fact that our daughter already existed out here in the world and wasn't an abstract to (hopefully) arrive in some imagined future—this was plenty enough to grapple with, without even considering Jeremy's wishes and needs.

Then adding in the requests of Gregorio Andromedus… "Wait, we don't have to take your father's money, if that would make it simpler," I blurted out.

Jeremy looked over at me, clearly startled, then glanced up at the back of our driver's head. *It is customary for both families to provide for the union,* he sent me silently. *As an indication of their support.*

Well, I know that, I said, *but this is getting ridiculous. I have plenty of money—from my family, not just my coven; I've owned that house for decades, and collected rent on it until last year, which I almost never spent. I can support us all without any trouble whatsoever, for twice the length of the contract.*

He gave me a gentle smile. *And I have resources of my own, my love; I would not let you support our family alone. In fact, I have enough so that we would never need to touch yours. But money is not the issue here.*

I know. I sighed. *There's no way we could push your father out of the negotiations—or Leonora, for that matter—without it looking like a rejection.*

Precisely. And that is just the thing I am trying to avoid. So, I fear we must be patient. He squeezed my hand. *The course of true love, et cetera et cetera, eh?*

I smiled at him in the darkened car. *At least we still get to be together while this all gets worked out. In the olden days, the poor witch maiden would be locked away in her ivory coven house tower, never seeing her beloved swain until the powers-that-be had negotiated every detail of her life for her.*

He chuckled softly. *Yes, there is something to be said for our modern times.*

The car turned off Divisadero and headed down our street. "Just here is fine," I said, a few doors down from the house. It had become a reflexive taxicab habit for me, one which made even less sense when using an app where the driver had my address before he'd even accepted the gig.

He duly pulled over and we got out. My phone buzzed in my pocket again a moment later; I pulled it out and added a generous tip before approving the charge.

Jeremy watched me do this as we walked to the house. "I suppose I ought to get one of those devices for myself," he said after a moment. "Though I am not entirely sure what I would use it for."

"Then don't," I said. "I only got this one because...well, it seemed like a good idea at the time."

Why had I gotten it, anyway? Probably just trying to see what living more like a human would be like. Though I did find it useful for, oh, ordering up cars to get around town in. Witchkind insisted that manipulating humans to get what we wanted out of them was harmless to them, but I wasn't a hundred percent convinced of that. How could it be healthy for them to have their minds messed with? Even if we weren't overtly stealing from them (which even I had been known to do from time to time...small things, of course), we were taking their free will and their knowledge.

Something pinged inside me at the thought. A sadness, or a fear; a sense of uneasiness washed through me, then was gone again a moment later as we climbed the porch steps and I began to ease the wards on the door.

Sirianna met us at the doorway, smiling gently to let us know that everything was okay. She held a sleeping Rosemary in her arms and was rocking back and forth on her feet, obviously trying to keep the baby from waking. Despite her efforts, I could see my daughter stirring.

I reached out and took her as she awoke, already reaching for my chest. "Thank you," I said to Siri, and then to Rose, "Sweetie, this gown doesn't undo like that. You need to give me a minute to get out of it."

"We can go if it's privacy you need," Siri said with a grin as Maela stepped up behind her. "Jeremy can help you out of it right here."

He chuckled and laid a hand on my back, at the top of the gown's zipper. "Happy to. Just say the word."

"You people," I said, also laughing as I bounced the baby gently in my arms. "Did she eat anything while we were gone?"

"She did—about half the bottle you left."

That reminded me. "I have to undo the lactation pause spell as well. Can you take her?" I handed Rosemary to Jeremy, who took her with an eager smile.

"And that's our cue," Maela said, slipping her arm into Sirianna's. "Thanks for letting us babysit!"

"Thank *you* for being willing!" I called over my shoulder, already heading for the powder room down the hall.

"Anytime!" And my sisters slipped out into the night; I felt them grab a ley line and vanish.

In the bathroom, I drank a glass of water, reached back to unzip the dress, and let it fall to the floor as I began the incantation to restore the flow of my breast milk. A few minutes later, Jeremy appeared at the bathroom door holding my fuzzy bathrobe and our baby.

"Thanks!" *Best boyfriend ever*, I thought, slipping into the robe. "Want to join us for her midnight snack?"

He guffawed.

"Not like that!" I said, swatting him on the arm. "I just meant…"

"I know, I know. But I liked the image."

Well, I didn't entirely hate it either.

— CHAPTER FOUR —

I awoke deep in the night, not sure what had disturbed me. Rosemary slept tucked into my loose grasp; Jeremy's side of the bed was empty. Had he gotten up, or not come to bed yet? I straightened my legs, trying to move softly so as not to disturb the baby. There was no warmth in the sheets on his side. As the cobwebs in my mind cleared, I remembered he'd told me he was going to stay up a little longer, to do a few more things in his study before joining us. How long had I been asleep?

I was about to "glance" down the hall with my witch-sight when I felt a presence in the room with me. It was familiar...it was benevolent... "Nementhe?" I whispered, astonished. Had my ancestress traveled from the Beyond to appear to me, unbidden?

It couldn't be. She didn't do this, that's not how any of this worked...I blinked into the darkness.

"Nementhe?" I asked again.

Calendula Isadora, came her silent voice, laying itself into my mind with the gentle-yet-uncanny touch of the Beyond. *Take action.*

"Take action?" I echoed, still in a whisper. "What do you mean, what kind of action?"

Your purpose. Your reason. Your work.

"My—what?" My purpose was right here in bed with me, cradled in my arms. What could be a mother's purpose that was greater than her daughter? Or my reason, or my work, for that matter?

Your work, Nementhe said again, more softly this time. She began to fade, just as she did in Circle when her time on this side of the veil was coming to an end.

I wanted to call out to her, to tell her to wait, to stay, to explain to me what she meant—but something held me back. She had come, she'd told me what she wanted to say; the rest was up to me.

Anyway, trying to control Nementhe never worked, even when there were thirteen of us in Circle. Despite the magic and our schedule and the depth of the tradition, she came and went according to rules of her own. And those of the Beyond, which we only imperfectly understood.

I lay in bed for a long time, thinking about the encounter. Wondering what she meant by that, by the words she'd said and the words she hadn't. My work—did she mean my biological research? Why would she care about that? I did feel sort of vaguely uneasy that I was forgetting something—that my scatterbrained state since the birth (or, well, since the last few months of pregnancy) had let something important slip.

I didn't think I'd fallen asleep, but then suddenly it was morning, and the sun was streaming through the window.

Rosemary was awake too, and grabbing at my chest.

I let her latch on and shifted into a more comfortable position while she nursed. We were still alone. I didn't know if Jeremy had ever even come to bed. Now I did hunt down the hall for him with my witch vision; he wasn't in his office either. I cast my mind wider. We were alone in the house.

Well, except for Petrana, in the kitchen, and Elnor, who was just now waking up on the far side of the bed. My cat stretched and yawned.

"I can smell your tuna breath from here," I told her.

She blinked up at me, clearly focusing on the one word in that sentence that interested her.

"You can get the golem to feed you, or you can wait for me, but I'm not budging till the baby's finished."

My cat considered it a moment, then hopped down from the bed and trotted out of the room. I heard the tiny pattering of her feet on the stairs.

Once Rosemary was full, I got us both up and dressed for the day. This was starting to take longer than before; my infant had decided that wearing clothes was an annoyance. It was kind of impressive how much resistance a tiny body could put up, all while pretending not to.

I'd read about this phase, but I could have sworn it came later. Well, nobody had ever said my baby was normal.

Healthy, sure—thank the Blessed Mother. Just...weird.

When we finally joined Petrana and Elnor in the kitchen, my golem had brewed my tea and scrambled up some eggs, which she now set on the table before me, alongside a platter of toasted, buttered banana bread. "Master Jeremy asked me to let you know that he has been called in to help his father at the clinic this morning. He does not know when he will be back, but he hopes it will be some time this afternoon."

"Huh." I wondered why he hadn't told me himself—it was perfectly simple to leave an ætheric message waiting, especially for someone living in the same house with you.

Petrana didn't read my mind—even the strongest of us witchkind couldn't do that—so she must have just seen the question on my face. "He didn't want to disturb you. He said you and the baby were both sleeping so nicely."

"Well, that's sweet," I said, taking a sip of my tea. I hadn't even known he'd been in the room.

Guess I'd needed my rest.

As I ate breakfast, I thought over my nighttime encounter with Nementhe. Assuming it hadn't just been a dream...but I didn't think it had been. It did not have the real-but-not-real sense that even the most realistic dreams do; and I had so clearly woken up before she arrived.

Your work.

And now Jeremy was off with Gregorio, suddenly and mysteriously. Helping at the clinic? With what? Jeremy was no doctor, or researcher, or anything like that.

I finished my eggs and toast and handed my plate to Petrana. "I'll be up in the lab for a little while," I told her.

"Do you want me to watch the baby while you work?"

"No, thank you," I said. "I'm not really going to do much...if anything. I'm just..."

I didn't know what I was "just" going to do, so I left it there.

Petrana did not ask for any details.

Once upstairs, I did the same sort of puttering I'd done when I was up here the other day, still trying to figure out where I had left off, and how to start up again—once I had the motivation and time, of course. "I can't even make any sense of what I must have been doing here," I told Rosemary, who of course could not help me, or even understand what I was talking about, beyond the vaguest of senses. She gurgled and cooed up at me from the floor, where I'd laid her on a blanket, after making sure I'd closed and locked the attic door behind us. Yes, she wasn't crawling yet; no, I did not want to even have to wonder if my baby could somehow roll herself across the huge room and over to the top of the steps, to fall to her certain doom.

Anyway, Elnor was keeping an eye on her too.

I sat on my lab stool at the dusty bench, paging through not just the last notebook but the few before it. I'd been studying witch blood, for some reason; comparing batches and batches of the stuff, collected not only from witches I knew but also from a whole bunch of strangers. My notes were in some strange code. It hardly even looked like my own handwriting. "Was I trying to keep this *secret* or something?" I muttered.

Across the room, Rosemary gave a little burbling laugh, and I felt Elnor's sudden regard—but on me. I looked up at both of them. The baby was waving her hands around, and the cat was staring at me.

"It's almost like you two weirdos are trying to tell me something," I said to them.

Elnor stared back at me.

"*Are* you?"

Let me give you a word of advice: never try to master a cat in a staring contest.

When I finally turned back to the notebook in my hand, it almost seemed as though the notes had shifted a bit. I still couldn't make heads or tails of them, but...a pattern sort of took shape, among the symbols on the page. Was a spell unfolding in my mind?

A sharp cry from Rose snapped my attention back to her.

She was still waving her fat little fists in the air, but she was no longer smiling; her face screwed up into something very nearly like woe.

I was on my feet and by her side before I'd even realized I'd decided to move. I whisked her up from the floor and brought her to my breast. "Rosemary, Rose! What's the matter, what happened?"

She pushed at my chest with her tiny hands.

One of them was bleeding.

I gasped and turned angrily to my cat. "Did you scratch her?!"

Elnor was on her feet, back arched, but looking at me with as much fear and shock as I was feeling. How did I know this? I just did. I'd had this cat for many years now and worked deep magic with her; I knew what I was seeing.

Rose was burbling now, no longer making the angry/surprised sound that had grabbed my attention. I took her hand in mine, examining the cut.

It was a tiny thing, not bleeding much; a puncture wound, maybe? "Is the floor not smooth here?" I asked, kneeling on the blanket, still holding her with one arm as I ran my other hand across where she'd been.

Sure enough, I felt something sharp. I rolled the blanket away, revealing a small nail that had somehow worked its way up out of the hardwood floor. Barely a quarter of an inch; but that had been enough to come through the blanket and poke a hole in tender baby skin.

"Oh, my poor sweetling," I crooned, rocking Rose in my arms, kissing the tiny puncture. I tasted the smidgen of blood on my lips. The baby herself was entirely calm, happy now, all trauma forgotten. "I am so sorry!" I told her, feeling mortified anyway. "We will bring your little crib up here, or your playpen—we'll build you a bed—the softest, safest place! Oh, your mommy is so sorry she let you get hurt!"

Happy, she sent to me. *Happy*.

"Yes, I'm sure you're fine now," I told her. "You have to let your poor neglectful mommy finish freaking out, though."

Happy.

Once I'd calmed down, I went back to the lab bench, taking Rosemary with me this time. No way was I laying her on that horrible dangerous floor again.

She waved her arms around, brushing against my shirt, wiping another tiny spot of blood on it. I thought she was working up to wanting to nurse again, but she had just eaten, and quite a bit, at that.

"Should I get a bandage for you, sweetie?" I asked, examining her hand once more. No, the bleeding had stopped.

Thank the Blessed Mother. Watching one's child bleed has got to rank right up there on anyone's Worst Nightmare list.

I dabbed at the spot anyway, as gently as I could, with a sterile cotton-tipped stick, just to be sure. And there: one more drop emerged. Then, as I watched, the wound closed up, leaving just smooth, unblemished skin.

Witches heal fast, but that was kind of unreal.

I stared at my baby, who was now smiling and looking around the room, her curious little eyes darting here and there.

I stared at the cotton swab in my hand, with its fresh drop of witchlet blood.

Then I pulled an unopened box of slides off the shelf, slid it open, and took out a clean slide.

I brushed the blood onto the fresh slide, covered it with its slip, and set it on the bench. Rosemary was very nearly giggling again and starting to reach for my braid.

"Oh, not this again, little monster," I said to her. Then I called through the æther: *Petrana, can you come up here please?*

Of course, Mistress.

Once I had the baby safely under the golem's capable care, I returned to the slide of her blood.

What was I going to do with it? I didn't know. She'd been examined regularly by all the healers, of course, plus Sebastian, sometimes including samples of her blood. No one had found anything to concern them in it.

However, I myself, as a biological researcher, had never actually looked at her blood.

Telling myself that's all I was doing—just getting familiar with what my own daughter's blood looked like close up—I clamped the slip-covered slide into the rack, turned on the little desk lamp on the bench, and pulled out my Mabel's Glass.

After dusting it off, I put the Glass to my eye and bent over the slide, pausing to adjust the strength of the scrying. It had been a while since I'd used this instrument; it was a bit stale, magically speaking. I pulled back and blew another speck of dust off it, and then sent it a small whiff of my own energy to wake it up.

Then I looked again, focusing my witch-sight and regular sight both as I let the slide tell me what it wanted to tell me.

At first, in fact even for a while, I didn't see it. It looked like normal, if fresh and young, witch blood.

Slowly, the differences began to come to light.

What was distracting, though, was the strong sense of déjà vu I got as I was trying to make sense of what I was seeing. So much of magical biological research has to do with letting your intuition see what your conscious mind cannot recognize. We do this by setting our intentions down, getting almost into a fugue state—a receptive, meditative place. The feeling that I'd seen this all before was getting in the way.

Eventually, I managed to soothe my thinking, striving mind enough for it to sit back and let me see what I was seeing.

Even then, though, I did not truly believe it until I had let a drop of my own blood onto another slide and examined them both, side by side.

But then I finally had to acknowledge the truth: she had tiny, barely detectable markers in her blood that regular witches did not. Markers that could have come from only one place.

Rosemary was only half-witch.

Her father was human.

I know this. I already know this, that little sense inside me kept insisting. I was sitting downstairs in the kitchen, holding my daughter as I sipped a cup of pennyroyal tea, and tried to make sense of it.

My first thought had been, *Is Jeremy human?* But no: he couldn't possibly be. I dismissed that in a minute—a moment. He and I had traveled through ley lines together, we sent one another thoughts easily, we'd built the wards for this house together, he traveled back and forth to the Old Country. He was the Mother-Blessed son of *Gregorio Andromedus*, for crying out loud. He was thoroughly, completely, one hundred percent a warlock.

I didn't have any of his blood in this huge sample supply, unfortunately. But what I did have was proof of his magical essence, in the very wards around me, in all the magic he had done in this house. I built a quick-and-dirty assay using that essence and the profile of Rosemary's blood.

I ran that test four times, refining the assay as I went. Some of the results were weird and wonky, even confusing (I really needed to compare blood to blood), but the answer I already suspected was clear enough: he was not Rosemary's father.

Who, then? *Who?*

Who could have impregnated me with human seed—

But no, that wasn't the first question, or even the sixteenth or fiftieth one. Because it was impossible, literally physically impossible, for witches and humans to make babies together. I knew this—we all knew it. I'd been studying witchkind reproduction all my adult life because of this reality. Not to make us fertile with humans, that wasn't my focus; just to make us more fertile at all.

So how…?

And how had no one else seen this? Rosemary had to be the most-examined member of our community, by a long shot. Why hadn't the healers seen this? Why hadn't Sebastian?

Granted, I'd had to really drill deep to see what I'd seen, but still…

Petrana was in the kitchen with me, as usual, standing near the back windows. She seemed to be regarding me with something more than her usual passive, *I'm available* demeanor.

I turned to her. "Petrana, what is it?"

She gazed at me a long moment, expressionless. Then she said, "With your permission, I would like to call the warlock Dr. Sebastian Fallon to join you."

"What?" I gaped at her. Initiative in meal planning was one thing; this was something else altogether.

"With your permission, I would—"

"Yes, I *heard* you," I interrupted. "It just didn't make any sense to me."

Except maybe it did?

I suddenly had the sense that…maybe this wasn't pregnancy brain I was dealing with. And if it was what it seemed like… "Yes," I blurted. "I would very much like to have Sebastian with me right now."

The young warlock showed up only a few minutes later. Now that I was alert to it—whatever "it" was—I could tell there was something on his mind. Something that had likely been there for… well, since I got home from my retreat, at least.

"No, thank you," he said to my offer of a cup of tea. "Actually, I was wondering if…" He glanced at the kitchen doorway and then back at me. "Where's Jeremy?"

"He's off doing something with his father, probably for a while," I told him.

"Good, good. So he won't mind if I borrow you for a bit?"

I shrugged, watching my friend carefully. "No, of course not. Sebastian, what's going on?"

Now he glanced at Petrana; did I see them exchange a nod? Just how weird was this day going to get?

"Can you come to my house?" Sebastian said.

I was getting past the point of being capable of surprise today. So I just said, "Sure."

"Bring Rosemary and Petrana, too."

Shaking my head in bewilderment, I said, "What about Elnor?"

He gave me a small smile. "She's welcome too, of course."

I gathered everyone, and we all followed Sebastian outside. I set the wards, leaving a short, loving message for Jeremy, and then we walked to the ley line at the end of the block.

Sebastian lived on the upper floor of a small duplex out near the ocean—a converted Marina-style house, with the downstairs apartment built in what had once been the garage. I had only been here a couple of times; the fresh sea air is great, but I could never understand how anyone would want to live so deep in the fog. I teased him about this whenever I got the chance, but we usually met somewhere else—a café, my place, the lab at the health clinic, or even a picnic in the park. "You don't want to hang in my messy bachelor pad," he'd said more than once.

His place was neat today; in fact, it seemed spic-and-span. He undid his wards as we stood on the front porch. It seemed to take him longer than usual, and when we finally got inside and he reset them, they had an odd tang to them.

"Did you make new wards?" I asked him, strolling over to the window that overlooked the Great Highway and the ocean beyond. This was a multi-use space, living room and dining room and a desk for office work; on one side was a small galley kitchen.

"I did," he said quietly.

I turned around and looked at my friend. "Sebastian, what's up?"

Trixie, his cat, wandered into the room. Just a cat, not a familiar: warlocks don't keep familiars. She rubbed up against my ankles, trying to trip me as I made my way to the small sofa, where I took a seat. Then she and Elnor started the customary cat-socializing process: tails lifted, ears forward, backs wary, noses twitching.

Elnor likely wouldn't object to a normal cat, as long as it was friendly. She liked most witches' cats, of course.

Sebastian pulled a wooden chair out from his dining table and gestured for Petrana to sit. She did, even though it made no difference to her whether she stood for months or years on end. It made us living folks feel strange to have a golem looming over them; she understood that.

Rosemary sat quietly in my lap, not reaching for my hair—which made a nice change.

Sebastian grabbed another dining chair for himself, turned it around, and sat stiffly on it. "Callie, I have some uncomfortable things to tell you." Then, bizarrely, he glanced at my golem.

Even weirder, she nodded and said, "As do I."

"Okay, you guys are all creeping me out," I said, trying to stifle a nervous giggle. "The only thing that would be even more strange is if Rosemary started talking to me."

"Ma-ma," said the baby in my lap.

The *half-human* baby.

Somehow, that little random sound out of her (because she was *not* speaking her first out-loud word right at that moment, she was totally not; that was just vocalization) broke the tension. Sebastian and I both laughed, more naturally this time. "Thanks, kiddo," I said, ruffling up Rose's feather-soft red hair.

Red hair. Come to think of it, I had wondered more than once about her hair, hadn't I? Jeremy and I both had brown hair. Sure, his was sleek and shiny and chestnut-hued, while mine was more...well, just plain brown. But my lovely, gorgeous, perfect daughter was absolutely a redhead.

And I was trying to think about anything else right now, rather than raising my gaze to Sebastian so he could tell me whatever earth-shattering thing he'd brought me here, behind new, strong, peculiar-feeling wards, to talk about.

He cleared his throat. "Callie, something happened to your memory when you went to the Old Country."

"Maybe even before that," I said. "The pregnancy—"

Sebastian put his hand up. "I know, and some of that is probably true too, but that's not what I'm talking about. That's not at all what I'm talking about." He turned to my golem. "Petrana?"

She nodded, looking for all the world like an actual independent, intelligent being. Looking like she was gathering her thoughts. "Mistress Callie, what Dr. Fallon says is entirely true."

I stared at her, then at him, my gaze darting between them. "How—just—what's going on here? I'm confused."

"Ma-*maa*!" Rosemary sang.

We all looked down at the baby, who just grinned back at us, her toothless mouth wide open in apparent glee.

"I know," Sebastian said, "and I'm trying to tread carefully here. This…is clearly dangerous. I've researched this matter as much as possible, and I've worked very hard to disable or circumvent the many traps I know are…here…but I can't be a hundred percent sure I've found them all."

I looked back at him, waiting for him to continue. Tightening my hands just a tiny bit on my daughter.

Sebastian cleared his throat, dug into his pocket, and pulled out a gold ring. "Do you recognize this?" I reached out to take it, but he held it back out of my grasp. "No—I don't think you should touch it. Just look at it and tell me if it means anything to you."

Putting my hand back on Rosemary in my lap, I leaned forward slightly, studying it. It was just a plain gold band—no etchings, no design, no stones. The gold was thick, and it looked heavy; it was probably a man's ring, though a strong-handed woman could wear it. "I…" I started, then stopped. I had been going to say no, it did not, but then…I wasn't sure.

"Right. I see." Sebastian closed his hand around the ring and then tucked it into his pocket again. My eyes followed his hand all the way there, as if compelled. Once it was gone, I blinked and looked back up at him.

"I don't know," I said, inadequately. "I *don't* see."

"I know," he said. "I know you don't, and I'm trying to figure out how to do this. I had a plan, but…"

"I think your plan is still good," Petrana said, startling us both. "Just tell her what you know, like we discussed."

Like we discussed? None of this was making any sense.

My golem went on: "I have been watching all the channels, and we still appear to be safe behind your wards. Also, I believe Dr. Andromedus does not know the ring was not destroyed."

"Dr. Andromedus?" I asked, dumbfounded. "What does he have to do with this?"

Sebastian shook his head sadly. "Everything, I am afraid."

— CHAPTER FIVE —

I sat on Sebastian Fallon's couch, holding my daughter, and listened to him tell me the strangest, most incredible story. "Incredible" as in "not believable," and also in the more usual sense, "amazing." He told me a lot more about the mysterious illness that had swept through our community last year, that it was not what it had appeared to be. He told me that he and I had been investigating that illness, covertly, and that I had gone to the Old Country on a mission to uncover tangible evidence: evidence that pointed directly to the involvement of our mentor, Gregorio Andromedus.

"I'm sorry," I said, when he had finished telling me about stolen essence, about a basement full of bodies without souls underneath Dr. Andromedus's laboratory in Berkeley, about the ancient warlock's increasing secrecy and even irrationality. "This just doesn't sound like the Gregorio I know—the Gregorio I've known all my life. He's friends with my *father*. He's the leader of our Elders. He taught me everything I know about biological research. He's..." I'd been about to say, *He's the grandfather of my daughter*, but...

"I'm sorry too," Sebastian said, looking very sad. "I know this is hard to believe, hard to take in. I've struggled with it too." He gave a heavy sigh. "I'm even more sorry that you are having to go through this realization twice."

I bit my lip and leaned back a bit, thinking. It couldn't be, it was all too crazy, too impossible. "Gregorio is at my house all the time. I'm about to sign a contract with his *son*." Which made me shiver. "Ugh, is Jeremy in on all this too?"

"I don't think that Jeremy knows what his father is up to—at least not along these lines," Sebastian said. "He seemed as, well, affably befuddled by everything when you got home as you did. Whatever was done to you to alter your memory, it obviously had to go beyond just you, or the first person you talked to would have immediately started asking questions—questions Dr. Andromedus would not want raised."

"But...why did whatever impacted me and everyone else not touch you?" I asked.

"It did, at least a bit. I was pretty confused at first." He pulled the ring back out of his pocket. "But mostly, it didn't." The ring glinted, picking up light coming from somewhere—not the sun, that much was clear. I shivered. "You wore this ring through the whole second half of your pregnancy," Sebastian went on. "You actually tried to take it off and wounded yourself and Petrana in the process."

I looked at my golem, who nodded. "That was when you rebuilt me," she told me. "It wasn't just so you could make me pretty."

And there was her sense of humor again.

"When it finally released your finger, after you gave birth, you secretly gave me the ring and told me not to use it," Sebastian said, "just to hide it. You told me that it's dangerous, and that we couldn't understand its power. That it was likely still tied to Dr. Andromedus. I believed you, so I did as you asked, despite how tempted I was, until you came home...changed. Then, I knew I had to take the chance."

"What did you do?" I whispered.

"I was very careful. I explored the magic in and around it without exposing myself to it—well, as much as I possibly could. I built new wards so I could work on it here at home, in secret. I know the ring was built to communicate to its maker, to channel thoughts and information and essence and any number of things to him. But it is also a passive conduit; it's not like the magic rings of fairy tales, forever searching for their lost masters."

I snorted softly at this. "Oh good, so I don't have to walk barefoot to Mordor and throw it into the fires of Mount Doom?"

"No, please don't." He gave me a small smile back. "I'm actually hoping you stick a little closer to home for a while—it's not only safer, but I kinda missed my friend and investigative collaborator." Then he grew more serious. "So at least there's that: it was used on you, but I am very nearly certain that Dr. Andromedus is not looking for it now."

"You said it just, what, came off after I had Rosemary?"

He nodded. "I guess. You didn't tell me much about it, just told me to hide it."

"Huh." I glanced at Petrana. "Why do you think Gregorio doesn't know it wasn't destroyed?"

She looked at Sebastian, who answered. "We can't know for sure, but it stands to reason that he would have looked for it—called for it—if he thought it still existed, but it has shown no sign of contact from its maker. I've tested it every way I know how." He shrugged, looking helpless, frustrated. "Maybe you told him it was destroyed? But of course you don't remember, and we certainly can't ask him."

In my lap, Rose started fidgeting. It would only be a matter of time before she started grabbing for my hair again. To distract her, I shifted her around so she was facing the other side of the room, and the cats, who had arrived at some kind of mostly peaceful accord.

"Anyway," Sebastian went on, "like I said, you asked me to hide the ring, and I did. Except then you came back without a whole chunk of memories and acting like, um, not exactly like yourself. So, I started trying to see if I could figure out what happened. And how to restore your memory."

"That's when I contacted him," Petrana said.

I again stared at my golem. "You...you what?"

"You gave the lost memories to me, to hold for you."

I felt my heart rate pick up as what she said sank in. "Oh, wow. Really? That's great!" I turned to Sebastian, suddenly excited. "Oh, Blessed Mother, if Petrana has all my memories—can't she just give them back to me?"

The sober expression on his face brought my hopes crashing right back down. "I hope so. I even imagine so—but it won't be easy. I have no idea how...safe it might be, to feed them back to you. Petrana tells me they were removed with some violence, and in a terrible hurry. She probably doesn't have them all—I mean, we have no real way of knowing if she does or not." He shook his head. "None of this is anything I've ever encountered before, and there is very little in the literature about it, or anything like it. I've run what experiments I can, using proxies and computer programs, but..."

"Proxies?"

Sebastian gave a weak smile. "Don't worry. No sentient beings were harmed in my research. And that's why I'm so hesitant, and want to be so careful: this is your *mind* we're talking about."

I shivered again, shrinking back into the couch. "Right."

"It was not pretty, Mistress Callie," Petrana said. "The removal."

"You were with me? You saw it happen?"

"Not in the same room, no; we were connected by a channel. I was outside the building. But I saw what you saw and felt what you felt. That was bad enough."

"Wow." I wanted to know everything, but also, I was starting to feel a little sick. And scared. Someone had removed my *memories*. Violently. The idea was only just beginning to percolate through my mind. And Petrana—a creature without feelings—*felt* this? "Don't tell me any more about that right now, okay?" I said to her, weakly. "I still need, well, some time to process all of this."

Petrana nodded, and Sebastian said, "Of course. If it's any consolation, you're taking this all really well."

"Um, thanks?" I gave him another small smile. "I guess? I don't feel like I am." *I don't even understand it.*

"No, really, you are. Part of what I was worried about was whether your…attackers…might have left something along the lines of a sleeper spell. Something that would only be tripped by, well, talking to you about it." He reached out behind himself and tapped his knuckles on the wood of his dining table. "I think if there had been something like that in there, we'd have seen it by now." He looked at me a little more intently, I could see that he was looking magically as well as mundanely. "You're still feeling okay?"

"Yes, I think so, more or less," I said, taking a deeper breath as I tried to be sure. "I mean, other than being completely freaked out by the whole thing, of course."

"Good. I think so too." He also took a breath, shrugging his shoulders as if to release tension. "Ready for more?"

I thought about it. "In a minute. Can I get a glass of water?"

Sebastian leapt to his feet. "Of course!"

"Do you want me to hold the baby for you?" Petrana asked.

I almost reflexively told her no—it felt like a great comfort, holding Rosemary, she was anchoring me in place, keeping me from flying off into the æther—but she was still wiggly, and maybe I could use the break. I could always ask for her back if I needed a living, breathing security blanket.

I gulped down the ice-cold water gratefully, then set the empty glass down and steeled myself. "So what's next? What else don't I remember?"

Sebastian laughed gently. "The most important things would be whatever you discovered in the Old Country—" He broke off, watching me closely. "What's wrong?"

I shook my head and put a hand on my stomach. "I...don't know. I felt a little pain, a little weirdness, but it's gone now. Maybe I drank the water too fast."

"Or maybe there's tripwires in your mind after all." He leaned back and folded his arms across his chest, clearly thinking. "Talking more generally didn't do anything?"

"Nothing. I mean, nothing physically; I'm still totally weirded out." I looked at the empty glass. "The water was really cold...?"

He blew out a frustrated breath.

Petrana said, "Mistress Callie still feels healthy and intact to me. And Elnor would be alerted if something was awry with her mistress."

Good point. Sebastian looked relieved, though still wary, as he glanced over at our cats, who were still doing their own thing. He turned back to me, narrowed and focused his gaze, and said after a moment, "Yes, you appear intact to me too."

"All right, well, do you want to try telling me some more things I don't remember? Maybe starting small?"

Sebastian gave me a helpless look. "I don't know if any of it's small. But it might be safer to start with things that are...more remote in time. Less immediate."

"Like what?"

"Do you remember why you moved out of your coven house in the first place?"

"Sure, I...wanted to do more research? I needed more space than I had there? I wanted my own bathroom, I know that. And my renters had recently moved out, and I already owned the house.

Yeah, I think, something like that." But I felt my certainty about that wane with each word I said. "That's not the whole story, is it?"

He shook his head. "No. It's true enough as far as it goes, so they obviously felt they could leave that much of the memory intact, but also, you had been pulling away from coven life in a number of ways, for a while. You even had a human boyfriend."

"It's not weird to date humans," I said, reflexively. "Everyone does it."

"Boyfriend," he repeated. "Not a one-night stand, not a dalliance; Raymond was someone you loved. You were with him for a year, maybe more."

I had no memory of this, none at all. I leaned back again, closing my eyes while I searched my mind, but nothing came up. Just that vague sense of confusion that was getting really, *really* old now. "What was he like? Did you know him?"

"I only met him once—well, hardly even then; he wasn't at his best," Sebastian said with a rueful, uncomfortable smile. There was a story there, clearly. "You stopped seeing him not long after you and I met—you were growing closer to Jeremy at that point."

"Ah."

"But I know you didn't stop having feelings for Raymond altogether. It was something you were still struggling with. In fact, part of your impetus for your trip to the Old Country was what you actually told everyone: that you needed time for reflection, to decide whether you really did want to sign a contract with Jeremy." He shrugged. "Though most of it was...the other stuff."

"Right," I said. The stuff that was clearly too dangerous for me to hear just yet. Maybe. "Was he cute? Raymond, I mean?"

Sebastian shrugged. "Not bad, I think, though I don't suppose I ever got to see his full potential. But you do have good taste in men."

I mock-frowned. "Or at least the same taste as you do."

"Point." He smiled. "He's a construction worker and also a musician."

"Musician? What kind?"

"Bass player in a local rock band."

"Bass! Of course."

The warlock nodded. "Yeah. Kind of burly but muscular, elaborate tattoos, red hair—" He stopped at the look on my face. Or maybe it was my gasp. "What?"

"Red hair?"

"Kind of blond-red, but yeah. I'd definitely call him a redhead." Sebastian's gaze sharpened on me. Then we both turned to look at Rosemary, who had gone very still in Petrana's arms.

"It's not possible," Sebastian breathed, looking between me and the baby.

"It isn't possible," I said. "But it is. I mean, it shouldn't be, but—I did an assay this morning, and I compared her blood to mine, and...that's what led to this whole...conversation." I swallowed, holding Sebastian's gaze. "Jeremy is not her father. She's half human. It has to be Raymond. Oh Blessed Mother, does he even know?"

Sebastian, who had been telling me so many shocking things, now looked gobsmacked. At a loss for words. He just sat in his chair, shaking his head, opening and closing his mouth.

"Did that...was that not part of what you were going to tell me? You didn't know?" I asked him, after a minute.

He shook his head slowly, one final time, then swallowed and stared at me. "I had no idea of that. I wouldn't have even thought to look for it. I mean, who would? Plus, when you got pregnant...you were, everyone understood, no longer seeing Raymond. I know things were chaotic around that time; that's when Logan..." He trailed off, looking very sad.

I felt some sadness too, but it was muted, as if it were being broadcast to me from a very great distance, or as if it had happened many years ago.

But it hadn't. This grief should have been fresher. My *best friend* had died, not even a year ago. So why did I feel *wistful*?

A sudden surge of anger roared up inside me. "Why, they..." I started, unable to even find the words exactly. "Bad enough that they should burn out memories of their crimes and wickedness, but they even dampened my grief! They took all my *feelings* away!"

Sebastian's eyes were filling with tears. "That was when I first knew something truly monstrous had been done to you. You were so strange when you first got home—so light, airy, almost... vapid?—but I chalked it up to exhaustion, and the vicissitudes of extended ley line travel. You even seemed, well, happy, innocently happy. I thought you just didn't want to jump right back into dealing with the hard stuff, that you wanted a day or two to recover before taking up where we'd left off. Before telling me... everything you found out over there.

"But when you acted like Logan's loss was, I don't know, something you'd seen in a movie once," he continued, "I knew this was more than that. And nobody else seemed to notice that anything was amiss. I thought for a moment that maybe *I* was going crazy."

"So that is when I spoke to him," Petrana put in.

"See, that's the part I don't understand," I said, and realized how absurd that sounded. "I mean, that's one of the ninety million parts I don't understand—but it's a big one. Petrana, what in the world—*how* in the world did you even know what Sebastian was thinking? How did you two even think to communicate?"

"When you put your memories into me," my golem explained, "awareness came with them. A lot of what you sent me was what had been going on right before we went to the Old Country, the things you and Dr. Fallon had discovered together."

"Right, but still..." I wasn't even entirely sure of my question. "How did you know it was safe to talk to him, and nobody else?"

"I am not like a filing cabinet filled with manila folders, or a storage unit with stacks of brown cardboard boxes," my golem said. "Mistress Callie, you put your *mind* into me. Or a great deal of it, anyway. You enabled me to begin *thinking* like you do."

"That...should not be possible," I whispered. "You're a golem. I made you out of mud and magic."

"Magic, yes," she said, and there was definitely a ghost of a smile on her face. "Magic is the spark that animates all living, thinking beings. When you put a small portion of your magic into me, when you first built me, I was able to animate, to communicate, to follow commands; but I was not complex enough for independent thought. When you rebuilt me after the ring blew me apart, you redoubled the magic, and used soil from your own house—soil with your own magical imprint all through it. And in the Old Country, when you poured as many of your thoughts and memories into me as you could in the short time you had before the warlocks did their work, I...became something other."

My heart was pounding again—in both fear and excitement, and also disbelief, and a thousand other things. I didn't even have my memories back, but somehow, I felt entirely different now. My mind was open and racing, probing, thinking—the befuddled, lazy unconcern of the last few weeks had been blown away in the fierce wind of all these revelations.

I hardly knew where to begin thinking about it all.

Sebastian, on the other hand, was still processing what he'd just learned. "We're sterile with humans," he said softly. "Everyone knows that."

I laughed, though without a lot of humor. "Oh honey. I was freaked out about that hours ago, I am so over it now. I can show you my assay if you like. Jeremiah Andromedus is not that witchlet's father. I am one hundred percent clear on that."

"No, I believe you," he said. "Just...I don't believe any of it."

"Now you know how I felt when you told me our mentor is not what he seems," I said, with a wry smile. "Yet here it is. So, what does it mean?"

"It means—Callie, it could mean so much. What else of what 'everyone knows' isn't true? What other lies have we been told all our lives?"

"I suspect we're on our way to finding out," I said. And why was I suddenly so calm about everything? It was like my brain had finally gone *tilt*, and all I could be was hyper-rational. "I suspect we already were on our way to finding out...before I went to the Old Country."

Sebastian nodded.

In Petrana's lap, Rosemary had been sitting more or less quietly. As if she were following along with the conversation, impossible though that should have been at her age.

Not that Rosemary had ever been a normal baby.

Now she started making her smacking sounds and reaching her little hands in my direction. I chuckled and began unbuttoning my blouse even as Petrana rose to bring her to me.

While she nursed, Sebastian paced the small room, still incorporating the knowledge and its ramifications. "You must have known this before," he finally said, turning and leaning against the windowsill.

"I don't see how I could not have known it," I agreed.

"But you didn't tell me—or anyone," Sebastian said. "I didn't realize you had...things you weren't telling me."

Then we both looked at Petrana, and I sighed. "I am going to have to get all those memories back into my head," I said.

"As Dr. Fallon mentioned, I do not know if I possess everything they removed from you," Petrana said. "What you sent me were memories of your own choosing. At your instruction, I discontinued the link shortly after they began their work."

I shook my head. "I hope I got all the important ones to you, anyway," I said, then turned to Sebastian. "I have to know what I was thinking, or what was going on; that's the only way I can know *why* I wouldn't have told you such a thing. It's not like you would have been judgey about it."

"No—if anything, I'd have been fascinated," he said. "I'd have wanted to study every facet. I'd have wanted to figure out how it was even possible, and then I'd have wanted to tell the world..."

He trailed off, and we both stared at each other. "I bet I know who knows," I finally said, "and I further bet I know why I didn't tell anyone."

Sebastian nodded, now looking pale and frightened.

"Crap," I added.

"You had a compelling reason for not telling anyone," Petrana put in. "And you're on the right track."

We both looked at her. "I did?" I asked her. "What was it?"

"Dr. Andromedus did order you to keep the information to yourself."

"But why?"

"It is lengthy and complicated. But I could—"

"It's probably best if we can figure out how to restore the memories," Sebastian said. "Then you'll have all the context and nuances."

I sighed, frowning. "Yes. I want my memories back. *All* of them."

———❬●❭———

By the time Rosemary finished up nursing and fell asleep, we were well into discussing logistics. The trouble was, none of us, not even Petrana herself, knew exactly what I'd done to pass the memories to her, and we had even less idea how to safely and effectively return them.

Yes, we'd clearly been mentally linked, and when I'd fallen into the hands of bad guys who decided they needed to rearrange (and delete) a bunch of my memories, I'd sent as many as I could to Petrana. Go, me!

"They could have killed you—they killed the warlock you were working with, and he was one of their own—but they decided not to for some reason," Petrana said. "They did this to you instead."

"I was working with a warlock there?" I felt another stab of grief, and anger. Someone had gotten *killed* helping me?

"Dr. Helios Spinnaker," my golem said. "He was a young researcher who was part of Grand Laurel Merenoc."

I shook my head. "None of those names mean anything to me. This is awful." I turned back to Sebastian. "And they thought nobody would notice that I came back with giant holes in my head?"

"Almost nobody did," he pointed out. "I only knew something was weird because I had the help of the ring's power...which you couldn't have clued them in on, because you didn't know about it."

"Right," I said, thinking it through. "It probably helped that we were so far apart, clear on opposite sides of the world, and that you weren't communicating with me at all."

"And I do believe they were a bit rushed," Petrana added, in what was almost certainly a massive understatement. I still of course didn't remember anything about the episode, but it couldn't have been a long-planned, well-thought-out scheme.

We all nodded and sat there thinking about it for another few minutes. Finally, I took a deep breath and said, "Are we stalling?"

Sebastian gave a surprised laugh. "Probably. But Callie, we have no idea how dangerous this could be. We still don't know what-all they did to your mind."

"Maybe we should just have Petrana tell us everything she knows," I ventured. "Rather than putting the memories back in my head. Then we can know what's missing, and what I thought about it all...it would be better than nothing. And it would probably be a lot safer."

Sebastian looked at me dubiously. "Is that really what you want? Second-hand memories of your own self?"

I thought about my vague, distant sadness over Logan. About whatever role Gregorio Andromedus—my mentor, my lover's father, my daughter's (supposedly) loving grandfather—almost certainly played in it all. And about having zero memories of the father of this beautiful child in my lap. "No," I said with a sigh. "You're right. I want them back for real."

Petrana nodded, as did Sebastian. There was never really any question, was there?

"I thought so," Sebastian said. "But I do think we should start small."

"What's small?" Petrana asked.

Good question. I thought about it. "I know you're not a filing cabinet," I said, "but do you have a sense of how the information is organized? Did I send it to you in a certain way?"

"You sent it to me in a frantic rush. Starting with what was happening to you in the moment, and then with all the secrets you were guarding, things you wanted me to tell your loved ones if you did not make it through the procedure."

"I was afraid of that." I really didn't want to get them all back in the same panicked flood, even if it was safe—which of course we couldn't know. "So, let's try an earlier memory, something from a while ago. Did I send you any happy stuff?" Then the obvious answer struck me. *Of course.* "Send me all the memories about how and when I met Raymond."

"Good idea, Mistress Callie." My golem appeared to think for a moment. In my lap, Rosemary awoke and gazed up at me, probably picking up on my emotions. *I'm going to learn about your father,* I thought to her. Excitement and not a little dread filled my chest.

"Ba-ba," she said, looking pleased and relaxed. I tried to take it as encouragement.

Petrana stood up from her chair. "I am ready to try passing you the memory." She looked at Sebastian.

He nodded. "You two should be in close physical proximity. Touching each other would be best."

"Okay," I said, scooting over a little. My golem sat next to me on the sofa.

Sebastian pulled his chair over and set it in front of us. "I should be right here too." *In case something goes terribly wrong,* he didn't have to say. "Do you want me to hold Rosemary?"

"I don't know." I considered it. "Not for now, but be ready to take her if it seems like you should. If it seems like I'm in danger of dropping her or something."

"Right."

My heart pounded—with nerves, more excitement, fear, curiosity. "I will stop feeding you the memory if I feel that you are distressed," Petrana said.

"Good."

"Or if I tell you to stop," Sebastian added. Petrana nodded.

I took a deep breath. "Okay. I'm ready." *I think.*

"Put your hand here," she said, pointing to her chest.

I did.

— CHAPTER SIX —

I settled my hand against Petrana's skin—or, what passed for skin on a golem—on her upper chest. She was neither particularly cool nor warm to the touch. I felt our shared magic hum softly between us. It eased me as I took another deep breath, feeling myself growing calmer, trusting the process. Trusting Sebastian, and Petrana.

My golem gazed impassively back at me. I closed my eyes after a minute, letting the rest of my senses come more alive, more aware. The sturdy couch beneath me. The clean scent of Sebastian's apartment. The sound of the distant surf, barely there. Elnor's soft fur against my arm (and when had she jumped up onto the sofa?).

I'm ready, I thought, and then I was there.

I left Rose's Bar after a pleasant but unremarkable evening out with friends. Fun enough, and it was good to see some of the younger witchkind set—especially given my staid old coven house, their ancient dull rituals, the endless round of nothing-magic, nothing-conversations, nothing-routines.

Why had I joined this coven, anyway? Oh, right: so that I could teach the next generation of witchlets. So that maybe, just maybe, our lives wouldn't all have to continue to feel so meaningless.

And, yes, Leonora's coven was very wealthy and prestigious, blah blah. I didn't care about that, but I knew that it made my parents happy to see me so comfortably and respectably established.

At my thought of Leonora, I could feel the gentle touch of my coven mother in my mind. Not even communicating, per se; just, noticing that I was thinking of her. Making note of where I was and what I was doing.

A sudden feeling came over me. A feeling of being smothered, stifled...

I had been about to step on the ley line headed toward the coven house, but now I stopped. I was a young, vibrant, powerful witch, bursting with energy and life. It was ten thirty on a Thursday evening, and I had been going home to go to bed.

I turned on my heel and walked the other direction.

Rose's was the only witchkind bar in this part of town, but it wasn't long before I found a human bar. Regular alcohol doesn't do a whole lot for witches—we need the strong stuff, the brews and distillations with that extra magical kick, if we want to really feel anything before our systems shut the buzz down.

But I wasn't looking to get drunk. (Plus, I'd had a few Smoldering Dragonflies already.) I just wanted...well, not to go home and go to bed. Or go home and putter around the heavily warded house with a bunch of witches hundreds of years older than me.

The sound of live music escaped from the bar's door as it opened and a young man holding an unlit cigarette walked out, but even when the door closed behind him, I could hear that the band was pretty good. And loud.

I walked in.

Nobody consciously noticed my arrival, not right at once; but many humans do register when magic-wielders are in their midst. When we were even younger, my friends and I used to amuse ourselves by walking into the big mall downtown and watching the ripple of sub-awareness move through the crowd. Some shoulders hunched, drawing back in instinctive fear; other heads lifted, as if the humans were searching for an alluring scent they couldn't quite catch, or an elusive melody on the wind.

The humans in this bar did the same. I paused just inside the doorway to take the measure of the room, not wanting to sit too close to someone who would be made uncomfortable by me; I just wanted to hear the music.

A group of young women, dressed like they were looking for some fun (short skirts, low-cut tops, high heels, bright lipstick), seated at a table just under the big front window, seemed the most reactive, even to the point of starting to shoot me glares when they thought I wasn't looking. But maybe that was more about how I was dressed, I realized with an internal chuckle: well-fitting jeans, black boots, black T-shirt under a leather motorcycle-style jacket. Ostensibly casual, but I knew I looked good. In an "oh, this old thing?" sort of way.

My witchly glamour, such as it was, didn't hurt either. I'd braided my hair as usual before going out, so that it wouldn't twitch and swish around annoyingly. But, even plainly dressed and French-braided, a witch in a crowd of humans cannot help but stand out.

I gave the group of women a friendly nod and walked away from their table toward the band.

It was only then that the bassist caught my eye. He was yummy, oh yummy indeed. A type of man that was catnip to me, visually: strong and solid but not overly cut or muscle-bound; reddish-blond hair pulled back in a ponytail, from which little damp curls had escaped, framing his ruddy, adorable face. He wore black Levi's and a black tank top that exposed complicated, colorful tattoos all the way down both arms—flames, dragons, swirling designs and symbols. Gorgeous work. He was concentrating deeply on his playing, though I knew that he was aware of me, tracking my movements as I claimed a seat at a communal table near the small stage. I crossed my legs, leaned back, and tried to look at the rest of the band, though my eyes kept being drawn back to the bassist.

The band was really good: energetic, tuneful, and well-coordinated. The lead singer was a tall blond fellow, more conventionally attractive than the bassist; he would be who the young ladies were here for. The drummer was woolly and a little manic, but he kept an excellent beat. There was a guitar player, a thready strung-out looking fellow, who must also play the keyboards set up right next to him, though he wasn't doing so on this song. A second guitar leaned against the wall at the back of the stage, and a second microphone also stood unused. More band members, or more multitasking by these guys?

I found I didn't care. I just wanted to watch the cute redheaded bass player and lose myself in the band's excellent music.

A waitress came over after a few minutes; I ordered a draft beer, intending to sip on it more for the flavor and the hydration than any buzz it would (barely) provide. It was delicious, though, and the crowded room was hot; I ordered a second one after another couple of songs, and then a third before the band's set was finished.

I hadn't even been planning, hadn't been thinking or scheming or anything, really; just enjoying being anonymous and unobserved, taking a small step outside my routine. Enjoying the music. And the scenery, of course.

But when the band crashed to the end of a boisterous, bouncy number that had to be their best of the evening, and the lead singer hollered, "We're gonna take a short break—don't go away!" into the mike, I caught the bassist's eye (which wasn't hard to do) and gave him a look he would not be able to misinterpret.

He grinned, set his bass carefully on its stand, wiped his forehead and the back of his neck with a towel, and hopped down off the stage, his engineer boots making a heavy thud on the wooden floor, to take a seat beside me.

"What can I get you?" I said, before he could open his mouth.

He glanced significantly at my empty beer glass. "That looked good."

I raised a hand and sent just the tiniest bit of magical compulsion in the direction of the waitress. She'd be busy during the break; I didn't want to deprive her of any tips, but more even than that, I wanted a way to keep this man right here beside me.

The waitress caught my eye; I held up two fingers. She nodded and was at our table with the beers almost faster than the bartender could have drawn them.

The redhead looked a little nonplussed as I raised my glass to clink with his. "Cheers," I said anyway.

"Cheers," he said, and took a deep draught. "Ahh. That hits the spot."

I drank deeply of mine too, setting my glass back on the table between us, now only about two-thirds full. He gave me that odd look again. "What is it?" I asked.

Now he blanched, just a little, then seemed to make up his mind. "I watched you drink three of those while I was playing—every sip you took made me want one myself—but, jeez, lady. You can put 'em away."

Oh, that was right, I didn't hang out with many humans; I'd sort of forgotten what this must look like. I laughed. "You don't have to worry about me," I assured him. "I'm a witch, I can drink anyone in here under the table."

"Oh, that's cool," he said. "My sister's a witch too."

I raised an eyebrow at this and did not say, *She most certainly is not.* (Though I did spend a moment wondering about what kind of guy immediately starts talking about his sister when a woman is trying to pick him up in a bar.) Instead, I just kept smiling, nodded at the stage, and said, "You guys are great. My name's Callie, by the way."

He grinned so happily, pleasure bathing his face in light. Okay, he was definitely human, but he shone with an internal fire that could keep a girl warm at night. "Thanks! I'm Raymond."

We shook hands, and I took the opportunity of the physical contact to send a little magical ping through him. Just to be sure. Yep: one hundred percent human, but one of the good ones. One of the open ones. If that makes sense.

He would be the guy in the mall looking around for the elusive melody, not the shoulders-hunched one.

"Raymond," I repeated, after probably just a half-a-beat too long of a pause. I remembered to let go of his hand, as well. "Not Ray?"

"Never Ray," he said, still smiling. "Always Raymond."

"I'll remember that." Enough of witchkind delighted in calling me Calendula Isadora, drawing out ev-er-y syll-a-ble. I would make sure to cry out "Raymond" when he brought me to the heights of passion, later this evening.

Because I was absolutely going to ensure that this guy took me home with him tonight.

———⚬———

The intermission was painfully short. We'd barely managed seven or eight rounds of innuendo-laden banter before the lead singer strolled back over from that table of young women up front and patted Raymond on the shoulder, then stepped up onto the stage.

"Sure, Peter, coming," Raymond said. He turned back to me and gave me a helpless smile.

"The price of fame," I said. "Don't worry, I'm not going anywhere."

I thought I saw him glance at my left hand then—checking for a wedding ring?—but I wasn't sure. In any event, he kept smiling, tossed back the last swallow of his beer, and got up. He put a hand on my shoulder just before turning to climb back onto the stage. A gesture of intimacy, intention, promise?

It sent a happy shiver down my spine.

Their second set was even better than the first. I didn't know any of the songs; I had the sense that they were originals, whereas the first set had featured a number of covers. If the band was writing this much original music and bringing it to fruition so capably, why in the world were they playing to thirty people in a dive bar on a Thursday night?

Well, it was San Francisco, I reminded myself. Talented people flocked here from all over the world. The music industry was fraught and hard to break into.

Still, they were great.

When they finished the second set and started breaking down the stage, almost all the crowd was still there, hooting and whistling and calling out for one more encore, one more!

"Hey, thanks everyone," Peter, the lead singer, finally said into the mike. "But we gotta go, they're kicking us out. Come see us next week—same place, same time!"

The crowd finally relented, and people started settling their tabs and making their way out into the cold night.

I nursed the dregs of my fifth beer. I still wasn't tipsy, of course, but all this liquid was really filling up my belly. And...points south. I stood and caught Raymond's eye as he helped with breakdown. He gave me an alarmed look.

"Bathroom," I mouthed, pointing toward the dark hallway behind the stage.

Now his sweet grin flashed again, and he gave me a thumbs-up.

I don't know why it takes so long to disassemble a simple stage setup, but it was half an hour or more before he was ready to leave.

He looked almost shy as he stepped down off the stage, his bass tucked into a black vinyl case and slung over his shoulder.

I snaked my hand through his free arm. "I believe the traditional line at this point is 'your place or mine,' but my place is complicated, so...your place?" I blinked innocently up at him.

He gave a surprised chuckle, but squeezed my arm closer to his side as he did. "My place isn't much, but it isn't complicated."

"Great. Let's go there."

He nodded, but then said, "Just to be clear. When you say 'complicated,' you're not...I mean, no one's gonna have a problem with this?"

"Not at all," I assured him, even as I sent a quick ætheric message to Leonora telling her that I would not be home before morning and asking if someone could please feed Elnor. "It's, well, kind of a boarding house situation, and I never know who's going to be awake at any hour. Privacy is pretty limited."

"Ah. Cool." We stepped out onto the sidewalk. "Um," he said, looking suddenly at a loss. "I usually hitch a ride with the band..." He glanced toward an alleyway at the corner. I switched to witch-sight and looked through the building, though I almost didn't need to; I saw the expected rally van jammed into the narrow alley. The rest of the band was loading equipment and boxes into it, bickering tiredly at one another all the while.

No thanks.

I brought my sight back to the street and sent out a flicker of magical intention. "Oh look, here's a cab." I raised my arm and hailed it; it pulled immediately to the curb.

"Huh," Raymond said, as we bundled inside.

It was supposed to be a one-night stand. I had every intention of making it a one-night stand. I didn't do such things all that often,

but I had enjoyed human male company occasionally over the years.

Human men were just so much less fraught than warlocks. The fact that it could never turn into anything serious was a huge part of the appeal. Also, warlocks often tended to be gigantic assholes—at least in my experience thus far in life. So full of themselves. So entitled.

Therefore, after a night even more delicious than I had anticipated, when Raymond asked for my phone number, I hesitated. Not because I didn't want to give it to him—I did. I totally did.

My problem was, I didn't have a phone number. Witches don't need phones, not to talk to each other; and when would we ever be calling humans?

"Give me yours," I said. "I will call you."

He looked sad yet unsurprised, though he didn't hesitate, or object, or anything. He just wrote down a phone number on a slip of paper and gave it to me.

On my way home, I stopped at the mall and bought a cell phone. As soon as the service was activated, I called Raymond.

"Hello?" His voice was wary, careful.

"Raymond, it's Callie. Now you have my number."

I blinked and looked at the room around me, deeply disoriented. It had been a memory, but so much more—I had *lived* all that, in what felt like real time. But it couldn't have been; now that I was back, I could tell that only a few minutes had elapsed.

"Oh, wow," I said, taking my hand off Petrana's chest and leaning my head against the back of the sofa. I felt exhausted, and overwhelmed, and a little confused. Also, kind of heartbroken.

"Are you all right?" Sebastian asked. Petrana stared at me as well.

I nodded at both of them. "Yeah. Just—wow."

More emotions filtered in as I processed what I had just experienced. Like rage, and grief, blended together: someone had tried to take that whole reality away from me, had stolen that entire man right out of my awareness! Raymond was a good man, a sweet man, and an astonishingly good lover.

I still did not know why we were no longer together—especially given that we'd made a baby together—but I could probably guess, at least close. "Are all the restored memories going to be that... intense?" I asked. "I feel like I can't take much of that at once." *And that was a "good" one.*

Sebastian shrugged, clearly at a loss. Petrana said, "I don't know if any of us know the answer to that. This is not something that we do every day."

An understatement if ever I heard one. I turned to look at my golem. "Was it like that when I sent them to you?"

"Like what, Mistress Callie?"

"Like..." I trailed off, trying to figure out what I was even asking. "Did you experience all those memories unfolding in real time, like they were actually happening to you? And did they come with such an emotional punch?"

"I do not know how to answer those questions," she said. "I took all the memories in very quickly, but I believe that I do not experience time in the same way as witches. And I do not experience emotions at all, not as you do."

"Huh." I thought about how Petrana could stand idle, for any length of time, until she was needed, and would remain entirely unbothered by this. She had no doubt *not* felt the weight of these memories, the weight of the experience, no matter how quickly or slowly she had received them; I of course didn't remember what it had been like for me when they went out. I had the mental image of ransacking a desk and throwing every possibly relevant piece of paper into a briefcase, while the house was burning down around me. But I didn't know, and I wasn't entirely sure why I was fixated on this. Maybe I was trying to avoid the larger issues. Which were so *very* large. "I guess that makes sense."

"The memory you just gave her," Sebastian said suddenly, to Petrana. "Do you still have it?"

She blinked. "I do."

"Is it the same as it was?"

She cocked her head slightly. "As far as I can perceive. Would I know if it were altered?"

We all looked at each other. Rosemary started to reach for my braid. She'd been pretty patient for a long time, but she was going to need a real nap soon, in her real bed (well, my real bed). Her activity woke up Elnor, who sometime during the memory transfer had also jumped up onto the couch and was snuggling at my side.

"I don't know," I finally said. It felt like I just kept saying that.

"You clearly still had the memories yourself, even after you gave them to me," Petrana pointed out. "Otherwise, the warlocks would have known something was amiss. They had to destroy and alter something, after all."

"That's true," I said. "There is so much here, about all of this, that we do not understand. And me more than most." I exhaled, frustrated. "And yet you can't just dump it all back into me, obviously. I need them all back, but we'll have to take it slow."

Sebastian nodded. "Right." He narrowed his eyes, clearly taking my magical measure. "How are you feeling right now? Want to try another before we stop for the day?"

"I don't know." I took a deep breath. "I'm kind of drained, but other than that, I feel pretty good. Do I, uh, look okay to you?"

"You do—everything seems to be working as it should inside." He smiled. "Which is very encouraging."

"All right, good. Where should we go next?" When they both hesitated, I started answering my own question, thinking aloud. "It's tempting to just move forward, get the memories all in order, but the more recent stuff is probably more urgent right now. Even if it's out of context..."

"I agree," Sebastian said. "I can tell you things, of course, to get you caught up, but that only works for events I actually know about." He turned to Petrana. "We obviously don't want to throw her into the deep end of what happened to her in the Old Country. Can you give her just the start of her research or investigations there? Maybe meeting the young warlock?"

Petrana nodded. "Yes, there is much we did that should be non-traumatic to experience."

"As far as I remember, everything was non-traumatic," I said ruefully. "I just remember a lot of amazing restaurants and fun shops. Those weren't...planted memories, were they?"

"No, that's all true too. You had a marvelous time in Balzst, at first."

"Whew." I gave them both a weak smile. "Okay, let's get this—"

Before I could finish my sentence, Rosemary gave my braid a strong yank. "Hey, kiddo, careful," I said. I pulled her hands away again, then got up and put her on my hip, walking around the room and jiggling her. "Your mama is trying to do something important here, and then she'll take you home and you can have a nice long nap. Okay?"

She blew spit bubbles up at me, but at least she stopped grabbing for my hair. I walked a few circuits before settling back on the couch.

"I can put her down on my bed if you want," Sebastian said.

"No, I liked holding her," I said. "And this only takes a few minutes. She'll be fine." I turned to face Petrana again. "Are you ready?"

"I am, if you are, Mistress Callie."

"I am."

I nestled Rosemary in the crook of my left arm and reached out for my golem's chest once more.

We walked down a bustling nighttime street in Balzst. My belly was comfortably full from yet another amazing meal, this time from a modest sidewalk café; I wore a fabulous new outfit, snakeskin pants with a sexy top and purple illusion-boots. I felt excited and joyful, delighted to have discovered that the Old Country was nothing like I had been led to believe.

I'd spent my first few days there learning the lay of the land—and getting over the exhaustion of ley line travel—but now it was time to get serious about the reason I'd come.

We turned a corner, leaving the crowded central city for a slightly quieter neighborhood. After another block, the main library building came into view. It was a massive building, covered in spells and sigils—

I gasped, a scream lodged in my throat. I couldn't get any air. In my arms, Rosemary twisted; before me, Sebastian shouted a spell.

My vision went blank, and my hand fell away from Petrana—or she fell away from me.

And then I was on the floor, on my back. My entire chest ached, but all I could think about was—"Rosemary! Where's Rosemary!"

"She's fine, she's right here," Sebastian said, leaning over me. He held my baby, who was staring at me. On my other side was Elnor, all her fur raised, tail standing straight up.

"Oh thank the Blessed Mother," I breathed, and closed my eyes again. My heart pounded, but the ache in my chest was slowly ebbing. When I felt capable of it, I opened my eyes and said, "What happened?"

Sebastian leaned back on his heels, still cradling Rosemary. "I'm not sure. Something must have gotten tripped." He shook his head, looking very worried. "You'd barely put your hand on Petrana when suddenly you stopped breathing. And your baby very nearly cried."

"Wow. I'm sorry I missed that," I tried to joke, but it fell flat; nothing about this was funny. I took another breath and began levering myself up to sitting.

Sebastian put a hand on my arm. "No, just rest there another minute."

Elnor's fur was still raised, but her tail was relaxing a bit. I looked behind her, at what appeared to be an empty sofa above me. "Wait—where's Petrana?" I asked.

"I am here," she answered, sitting up. "I do not breathe, but I too experienced a sudden cessation of animating force."

Now I did sit up; my chest was feeling better every moment. "Wow." Rosemary was still staring at me, her eyes large and dark.

Breath, she sent me, mentally. *Air.*

I took another deep breath. It felt wonderful. After another minute, I made my way off the floor, sitting on the sofa.

Sebastian stood before me. "We are definitely done for the day," he said.

I snorted a soft laugh. "I should say so."

In his arms, Rosemary began to twist, clearly trying to reach for me. "Are you—" he started.

"Yep," I said, reaching up to take her. She snuggled into my arms, not even trying to pull my hair or grab at my blouse. "I'm fine now, but that was..."

"Terrifying?" Sebastian asked. "I know it terrified me. I need to figure out what happened and prevent it from ever happening again."

I nodded. "Yes please. Never again." I was still calming down, my heart rate slowly making its way down to normal. "Maybe...we should just go with the 'telling me things' plan instead?"

Sebastian shook his head. "We can. But let me see what I can figure out. I mean, you're never going to be satisfied with half measures; you're going to want to know everything you knew before. Like really *know* it."

"I do want that," I agreed, reluctantly. "I want it all back in my head right now. But..."

"Yeah."

We were silent for a bit, each in our own dark thoughts. "How much would you say I'm missing?" I finally asked.

Sebastian and Petrana looked at each other. "I don't know how to quantify it," the warlock said. "A lot, though. Clearly every single memory involving Raymond. A whole lot of stuff you and I worked on together. Whatever you found out in the Old Country. Probably more than that."

"Definitely more than that," Petrana agreed. "But those are the largest items."

Rosemary had been mellow since the incident, but now she got her little hands around my braid and gave it a strong yank, singing out "Ba!"

"Okay, I have to get this one home," I said to Sebastian.

"Mistress Callie, would you like me to hold her?" Petrana asked. "It does not pain me if she pulls my hair."

"Absolutely." I handed her over, fully expecting her to protest, but she happily settled into the golem's arms, and even stopped vocalizing. She didn't grab for her hair, either.

Babies. Go figure.

"So, you'll work on this, and let me know when you're ready to give it another try?" I asked Sebastian.

"Absolutely." He paused. "One thing, though: you probably don't want to tell Jeremy about, well, any of this. I think he's pretty well in the dark about a lot of things."

"All right." It would feel weird, keeping something so big from the man I planned to bind decades of my life with, but it made sense. "He does seem to think Rose is his baby."

"Yes, I'm quite sure he does. We all did. So…" Sebastian looked frustrated.

I patted his arm. "It's all right. You and I can talk about how I should handle that too, when I have…more of my brain back."

He smiled, weakly. "Okay. Take care of yourself, please."

"I will, I promise."

I was too exhausted to even want to risk travel home on the ley lines, or magically summoning up a cab. Fortunately, that cell phone—which now I knew why I had—was a very useful device for solving little transportation problems.

Jeremy hadn't returned when I got home, to my tremendous relief. "I'm going to nap with her," I told Petrana. "I don't think I can stay awake another minute."

"Good idea," she said. "If you like, I can brew you a mild strength potion while you sleep."

I almost told her not to bother, that I could do it myself. A year now I'd had this golem, and I still couldn't internalize the fact that her whole *purpose* was to help me with things. That being polite and considerate to her, even if it made me feel like a good person, was completely beside the point. She had no *feelings*. She *did not care*.

And yet...that felt less and less true all the time. Was it just that so much of my personality had gotten imbued in her, along with my memories? Was that what it meant, putting part of my mind into her?

Where would it end?

I had no idea.

"Thank you, Petrana, that's a good idea," I told her. "In fact, you can even carry the baby up the stairs for me. It's all I can do to carry my own self."

She did that, and saw the three of us (because Elnor would never miss a nap) tucked into bed. "Rest well," my golem said. "If you're still asleep when Jeremy returns home, I'll let him know not to disturb you."

"Thanks," I said, and then my baby, cat, and I all sacked out.

— CHAPTER SEVEN —

I awoke at sundown, sensing a familiar presence in the house. I sat up, trying to shake the cobwebs from my mind. It wasn't Jeremy; it wasn't anyone who lived here; it wasn't Sebastian…

I sent my senses out, trying to figure out who it was. I heard footsteps in the hall outside my bedroom door, light ones. Someone small, or someone trying to be quiet? "Who's there?" I called out.

Then my door handle turned. I pulled the covers up higher, as though a down comforter would protect me from…whatever had snuck into my house.

Black curls poked through the narrow opening in the doorway, followed by a slender teenage witchlet.

"Gracie!" I cried, delighted.

Now she opened the door all the way and stepped into the room. "Oh, you are awake! Your golem said you were napping and that I shouldn't wake you, that I should come visit another time. But I said that it's hard to get over here, and I didn't know when I'd be able to get back. So she said that I could peek in and see, as long as I was super duper quiet."

"You can always wake me." I patted the bed beside me. "Come, sit down."

She did. I felt absolutely suffused with delight at seeing her, even as I was still confused about where she had gone, and why, and why it was hard for her to get back here.

Even as I thought that, I suddenly understood *why* I was confused. They'd taken those memories too, the bastards. I shook my head, trying to stifle the flood of rage. I needed to just get the dang memories back.

But I didn't need to point any of my anger at Gracie, even inadvertently. "Can I hold her?" she was asking, already reaching for Rosemary.

"Yes." I handed her the baby, making sure she knew to support her head. Feeling like I'd done this before, too. Then I heard another soft step in the hall, followed by a knock.

"Oh!" Gracie gave me a sheepish grin. "I almost forgot. Can I introduce you to someone?"

"Uh, sure." I said, glancing down at myself. "Maybe I should get dressed?"

Gracie giggled. "Okay, good idea." She raised her voice slightly. "Hang on a minute!"

"Okay," said a soft, young female voice. Not Petrana. So, Gracie had brought a friend. How nice.

She handed Rosemary back to me before the baby could start yanking on her black curls. "We can wait downstairs in your living room, if you want?"

"Sure," I said. "I'll be down in a minute."

Gracie hopped off the bed and practically skipped to the bedroom door. Well, it was certainly nice to see her so cheerful, I thought, without really knowing why I felt that. She slipped out into the hallway; I heard whispers and a quiet giggle before the two witchlets (I presumed) headed downstairs.

As I got dressed, I thought about the nature of this memory loss. What the Old Country jerks had done to me. Pretty sloppy, when you thought about it. If they had truly wanted to stop me from knowing things, why had they left me with so much confusion, so many half-memories? How was this ever supposed to work?

Though the scale of the spell, or device, or whatever it was, had to be massive, if it was to control the thoughts and memories of everyone who knew me, everyone who encountered me. Everyone who even know anything about me? Where would it stop? If I had written a book about my life, would the whatever-it-was have altered the pages? Maybe it wasn't just sloppy but impossible.

Maybe what they'd managed was unbelievably impressive.

Well, in any event, I was going to outsmart them. I'd get my memories, my*self*, back. Sebastian just needed to figure out a safe way for us to go about it…

Petrana met Rosemary and me at the bottom of the stairs. "They're in the second parlor, with beverages. What can I bring for you?"

"Just a little elderflower wine, thanks."

I stepped into the parlor to see Gracie and—that was no witchlet. I could tell at once that it was a teenage human girl. She was curvy and cute, with short brown hair and large blue eyes, and she wore a vintage lace dress, red tights, and black and white Converse sneakers. Just the sort of person Gracie would gravitate toward…if she'd been witchkind. "Oh," I said, stopping in the doorway.

Gracie hopped up to her feet, setting her glass of lemonade on the table beside her chair. "Callie! This is Rachel." She beamed at me, and turned to look at the girl with an air of—pride? Affection? "Rachel, this is my friend and teacher Callie, and her baby, Rosemary. Isn't she the cutest?"

Rachel got up as well and came over, already cooing at the baby as she put a hand out for me to shake. I took her hand, surreptitiously checking her essence for any magical elements I might have missed, though it was so clear she was human. "It's…nice to meet you," I said, and gave Gracie a puzzled glance.

"Rachel's the one I mentioned to you," Gracie prompted me. "You know. When I visited last."

"Ah," I said. "About that..."

Petrana appeared at the doorway with my wine. I took the opportunity to get us all settled in chairs before I elaborated.

I took a bracing sip of my wine. "Actually, I'm having a little trouble with my memory." *It's a magical thing,* I added, privately to Gracie. "There are a few gaps...I don't remember your last visit."

Gracie frowned. "You don't? It was just after the baby was born, like, two months ago. I snuck over here in the middle of the night. Minky brought me—we came through the cat portal in your hall closet." She glanced down at her familiar, sitting politely at her feet.

My eyes widened and I looked significantly at Rachel. *Gracie!* I sent silently. *She's human.*

The witchlet just stared back at me before shaking her head and giving me a wobbly smile. "Wow, you really are memory impaired, huh? It's okay, we can talk about magic in front of Rachel. I've told her everything. I told all my human friends everything." Now she got up and walked over to the human, putting a hand on her shoulder. "Shove over, hon."

Rachel grinned up at Gracie and did just that. Gracie sidled down into the easy chair next to her, like...just like...

My confusion was cleared up when Gracie leaned in and gave Rachel a kiss. Then she looked back at me. "You don't remember me telling you I had a girlfriend either?"

"Oh! No, I don't, but...that's wonderful, Gracie! But I thought..." I struggled to grab any stray thoughts that remained in my poor beleaguered head. "Didn't you have a crush on that young warlock who..."

Gracie laughed. "I'm bi! Callie, we totally talked about this. I can't believe you don't remember it."

Rachel poked Gracie in the side, giggling. "You had a crush on a warlock? You never told me that..."

"It was nothing," Gracie said airily. "He was a jerk."

"Most of them are," I agreed, suddenly wondering when Jeremy was going to come home. And what he would think of my entertaining a witchlet and her human girlfriend. Who she was talking about magic right in front of!

Well, whatever he might think, it didn't matter, did it? This was my home, and I could host any visitor I liked. But still. I was glad he wasn't here; glad I didn't have to deal with him right now.

"So, what happened to you, Callie?" Gracie asked with a frown. Minky had gotten up as well—the leggy kitten was half-grown already!—and resettled at her mistress's feet once more. "How did you lose your memories? Was it something to do with having the baby?"

In my lap, Rosemary burbled and muttered happily, enjoying being in a room full of chatting people. It was almost like she thought she was part of the conversation, making noises like the rest of us. I rocked her gently and took another sip of wine. "No, it happened in the Old Country." I looked again at Rachel, who was watching raptly. "I'm sorry," I interrupted myself. "This is just too weird. I can't...Rachel, honey, I'm sure you're a nice girl and all, but we don't generally tell humans about—well, about anything of what we are and what we can do. Except, Gracie has told you?"

Rachel smiled back at me. "I get it. G told me this would be freaky for you—but that you were cool, so you'd be okay with it. Once you got used to the idea." Her smile grew. She really was cute. "Kinda same as how it happened with us, actually."

"I'm sorry I didn't send you any warning," Gracie added. "I only knew we were coming over about a minute before the portal opened."

"The portal..." Okay, I had a bunch of questions about that, but I put them aside for the moment, because I had even bigger questions about…everything else. "Gracie, I'm working on getting my memories back, but for now, I'm totally at a disadvantage. You're going to have to be patient with me, and just tell me things even if you think I should already know them."

She nodded, looking serious, though the effect was somewhat marred by the cozy cuddle she and her girlfriend had going on, snuggled together in the easy chair. Rachel rested her head on Gracie's shoulder, and Gracie squeezed her hand. It was honestly just freakin' adorable. But there was no way I was going to tell them that.

Young love *never* thinks it's cute. Young love is *very* serious.

"Okay," Gracie said.

"Good. So, please remind me, where are you living now, and why did you move out of the coven house? Leonora said you were studying somewhere else?"

Gracie cocked her head, now looking confused. "She said that?"

I tried to remember her exact words. "Pretty much. That you needed to learn things that our house couldn't teach you."

Now Gracie snickered. "True that! But it's weird that she, of all people, would say so." Then she sobered. "Wait, is it just *your* memory that got affected? Maybe she's confused."

I shook my head. "No, not just me; it apparently bleeds off me and touches other people too. So maybe she doesn't remember… whatever she knew about you. That's how it was supposed to work, anyway, I think." I thought about Sebastian and the ring. "There are a few people who seem to be out of the range of it, though."

"Like me, I guess." She shifted in the chair, lifting Rachel's legs and moving them so they draped over her lap; Rachel leaned her head back against the arm of the chair. "I've been living… somewhere else. I didn't tell you where, exactly, so you haven't forgotten that. I haven't told anyone where, in fact. I've only seen you, and only that once—because I wanted to see the baby."

Rosemary gave a little happy burble at that. "And then just now because I wanted you to meet Rachel. But we're going to have to leave soon." Gracie glanced at the doorway, which led into the hall...and the closet, presumably, with its mysterious portal. "But I remember everything—at least, I think I do. How would I know if I'd forgotten something?"

"I don't know for sure," I told her, "but speaking from experience, you'd always have this vague sense you were missing something. And then eventually someone who knew more would explain everything to you. And then...it gets a little more complicated from there, so if you have to leave soon—"

"Right." She sat forward, resting her hands on Rachel's legs, and frowned as if she were thinking hard about something. Then she shrugged and grinned at me. "Well, I think I remember everything, so I'm just gonna keep believing that."

I nodded. "That's probably wise. I expect when I get my own memories back, I can fill you in on whatever you might be missing. Assuming I ever get to see you—"

"I will totally visit you whenever I can!" she chirped. "Assuming you don't tell Leonora or my parents where I've gone."

"Gracie, you know I can't—"

The witchlet put a hand up. "Don't!" she cried. I shut my mouth, surprised. "I know you forgot, but you already promised not to tell on me, except to let everyone know I was safe," she went on. "So, just trust me that you still feel that way." She gave me a winning smile.

"Um, okay," I said. Did that ring true? Maybe?

"Good! I don't want to spend what little time we have going over all the same stuff we did before."

Well, that made a certain amount of sense, though I sure wished I remembered.

Rachel was still watching our whole conversation with rapt attention, not seeming weirded out at all; not even by Petrana, or...

anything. "You really know that we're witches," I said to her, "that we can do actual magic, and you're okay with that?"

"Sure." The human girl shrugged and glanced at Gracie, who gave her an encouraging smile. "I mean, like we said, it was a little weird at first. I didn't know what she meant when she told us."

"Who's 'us'?" I asked.

"Just a group of kids I met at...well, just somewhere," Gracie said. "They all—*we* all, now—live together in a big house in the East Bay. They took me in. They understand me, better than almost anyone else in my life." She blinked at me; were there tears starting in her eyes? "Except you."

"And now I don't even seem to understand you, because I've lost my memories," I said slowly.

"You're going to get them back, aren't you?"

I nodded. "I'm already starting to try. But it might take a while."

"Good. That you're getting them back, I mean, not that—"

"Yeah, I get it." I smiled at them.

Rachel and Gracie both looked relieved. "So, like she said," Gracie said, "it was a little crazy at first, but now everyone rolls with it."

"Some of us more easily than others," Rachel said with a laugh. "Jeffrey was..."

Gracie rolled her eyes. "Jeffrey's a doink."

I didn't ask what *doink* meant; the implication was clear.

"But I already knew there was something different about her," Rachel went on. I could see the love in her eyes as she talked about Gracie. "And maybe I was already predisposed to believe, because of how I was raised. 'Cause when she told me...it really just all kinda made sense, you know?" She shrugged. Gracie patted her arm, encouragingly. "I already felt drawn to her, and already believed in her, *so much*. So when she told me—and then showed me—that she could do real magic things—well, so many things I hadn't understood about the world just fell into place." She gave me a helpless look. "I can't really explain it more than that."

"But you see?" Gracie said, before I could reply. "Almost everyone in the house was like this—even Jeffrey isn't weird or freaked out, he's just…kinda clueless, is all. Everyone is like totally fine with this. It's no different from being gay, or vegetarian, or whatever. The whole world is full of variety—we're not all clones of each other. Humans are totally okay with the fact that some of us can do magic, and some can't. We just don't trust them enough to tell them that, so we hide in our stupid secret houses and mask our abilities, and it's just dumb! It's not necessary at all!"

I was shaking my head, though I didn't have a strong argument against her. It was all too…new, too baffling. "But Gracie, we can't just tell humans we exist, and what we can do. I'm glad you've found some good, warm-hearted people to tell, but you must remember why we hide in the first place. I know you've studied history—"

"That's just it: it's *history*," Gracie said, leaning forward again over Rachel's legs in her lap. "The world isn't like that anymore."

I gave a sad chuckle. "Oh, I think the world is pretty divided, pretty closed-minded. Just glance at a newspaper."

Gracie shrugged off my words. "Not like *that*. I mean the church doesn't run everything, and we're not all living in isolated backwoods medieval villages where nobody knows what's going on anywhere else, and everyone thinks that every spinster with a cat must be having sex with the devil and putting curses on cows and crops and each other!"

I tried not to grin at this colorful synopsis of centuries of oppression against witchkind. "It's true, the world is a good deal different today, but…" I interrupted myself this time. I didn't want to waste our limited time having an argument either, particularly since I didn't even have good points to make. I'd just be repeating what I'd always been taught about the world. And, even without possession of my full memories, I already knew that I had never been a blind acceptor of every bit of traditional wisdom.

I had no idea what I really thought about the matter, all the way down. But I did know that I'd had what had clearly been a real relationship with a human man.

And that some *really pivotal stuff* I'd "always been taught" was a complete lie.

"So tell me more about your friends," I said to Gracie, instead. "The ones you're living with."

"Oh they're so cool! They're all artists, and they took over this abandoned building in—"

"The *East Bay*," Rachel said, forcefully.

"Right," Gracie said, with a smile. "Just a sort of warehouse-type place, but with little rooms as well as big rooms, so we have space for a lot more people, and we want to grow the community. It's a live-work space, and Amelia is the person who started it—she's a painter, she does these huge pieces on found materials, like plywood or broken concrete from a construction site or whatever, so she gets the biggest room on the ground floor, 'cause some of it's *real* heavy, but it's so gorgeous. And then there's Estevan, who does music, but he also cooks. Like, he could be a chef somewhere, if he wanted to be. He feeds us most nights; it's why I'm getting so fat—" She patted her slender belly.

"You are *not* getting fat," Rachel said, in the bored yet indulgent tone of someone who says such a thing so many times a day, she doesn't even hear herself saying it anymore.

"And then Fenny does—"

Gracie cut herself off as her cat suddenly turned and nipped her ankle. She sprang to her feet, nearly tumbling Rachel to the floor. The human girl just laughed and got up as well. "Oh! We have to go right now!" Gracie said, grabbing Rachel's hand in one hand and scooping up Minky with the other. "Sorry! We only have a minute to get this right."

And before I could get to my own feet and see where they went and how they did it, the three of them were out of the room, into the big closet under the stairs, and gone.

Holding Rosemary, I stood at the open closet door. I'd never kept anything in here—there were plenty of other storage places in the house, and I really didn't have all that much stuff. But mostly I left it empty because it was so mysterious and weird, and because Elnor loved to explore the place.

Speaking of my cat, she now nudged the back of my legs as I peered into the depths of the closet, looking for this mysterious portal. I saw nothing. I was about to hunker down to go in and look more closely when Rosemary started fidgeting in my arms. Not just pulling at my blouse or yanking on my hair, though she was doing those things too, but she was squirming like an eel and making her little sounds.

At the same time, Elnor escalated her bumping of my legs with the bony top of her head. And then a moment later, Petrana appeared behind me. "Do you need help with anything, Mistress Callie?"

I sighed and backed out of the closet doorway. "No, I don't, thank you. I'm just going to nurse the baby and…that's it."

Immediately, infant and cat settled back down, but Elnor kept an eye on me until I'd settled into my easy chair and opened my blouse.

So why dangle mysteries in front of my nose if I'm not supposed to be curious about them? I thought, sourly. Oh well. Perhaps when my memories were restored, I'd know more about this closet-portal-whatever situation.

Meanwhile, I fed my baby and thought about the visit with Gracie and Rachel.

Were they right? Was it foolish to keep ourselves secret from humankind? From the memories I still had, at least, I had never considered humans dangerous or scary. In fact, until I had (apparently) decided to date one, I hadn't really given them much thought at all.

At least, that's what I *thought* I'd thought.

Gracie sure had looked happy. From what I did remember about her, she'd always been high-spirited and dramatic, and, though a good student and a smart one, a little impatient with the rules and strictures of traditional coven life.

In fact, she'd always been my favorite student, perhaps for those very reasons.

I was glad she'd come to see me, and further glad that she trusted me enough to tell me even some of what she was up to these days. Including having a human girlfriend! I shook my head and smiled, trying not to think about how I suddenly felt so old.

Jeremy did not come home till extremely late that evening, long past dinnertime. He was full of sincere and loving apologies for having been away, and incommunicado, for so much longer than he had anticipated. I had dined, and had taken another fortifying dose of the strength potion Petrana had brewed, so I assured him that there was no reason for him to apologize, or spend even a moment worrying over me and my health.

Still, it felt so strange to be dishonest with him—and to not ask him what he'd been up to at the clinic. When he asked what I'd done all day, I mentioned nothing about my time with Sebastian (and everything that had happened and that I had learned there) or the visit from Gracie and Rachel. Instead, I told him that I'd puttered around in the lab upstairs, because I was thinking I'd like to start getting back into my research soon.

Sebastian *would* figure out a way for us to work on the memory restoration. I was quite sure of it. And I would need space, time, and privacy to manage it.

"Oh, that's a nice idea," Jeremy said pleasantly. As though I'd told him I was considering learning how to bake scones or trying to decide which kind of tea rose to plant in the garden. "That sounds like a productive use of your time."

I started rankling a bit at this—*Just exactly what about making a baby out of my own body and then taking care of her twenty-four-seven isn't productive?*—and then had to forcefully tell myself to settle down. He wasn't being deliberately judgmental or condescending; he was trying to be supportive. And furthermore, I didn't *want* him looking too closely into how I was spending my time. He was probably also relieved—now he could feel less guilty about staying out late doing mysterious stuff with, or for, his dad. Which, again, would work out well for me.

What *was* he doing with his dad, anyway? Jeremy wasn't a biologist, or any kind of a scientist. He wasn't even really a politician, or a community leader. Was this just another make-work thing of Gregorio's so Jeremy didn't feel so purposeless?

How much did he know?

What even was there to know?

I just smiled at him and sipped a glass of after-dinner elderflower wine. "I may have to order some more supplies," I told him. "Everything up there is fairly stale. And I will likely have to spend extra time at first, just getting everything back running smoothly like it was before I took maternity leave." I gave a soft laugh. "Honestly, I can hardly remember what I was doing, it's been so long."

"And so much has happened," he agreed.

Oh, you have no idea, I thought. *I have no idea.*

Blessed Mother, how was this going to work?

— CHAPTER EIGHT —

I t took over a week, during which time I tried to act as normal as possible. I taught my classes at the coven, I did tarot lessons with my mother, I took care of an infant. I decorated my house for Yule, and Jeremy and I hosted a small holiday party. I tried to be patient.

I tried to pretend that I wasn't aware that I was missing what felt like *half my brain*.

It was at the formal, fancy Yule gathering at my parents' house two days after our party where Sebastian finally pulled me aside. "Great food," he said around a mouthful, and then more quietly, "Can I come see you sometime soon?"

"Are we...good to go?" I asked, feeling the familiar surge of excitement and nerves again.

"I think so. Good to give it another try, at least."

"But I should come to your place, right?" I asked. "Wouldn't that be safer?"

"I actually believe it would be better done at your house. And safer, energetically speaking: working in your own space, behind your own wards. All the magic that is imbued in your home, and which resonates to you—and to Petrana."

Good point. "Hmm, okay."

"I'll need to do some things to the space," he went on, "and we'll need to test what I've figured out in the site where the spellwork will actually happen."

I nodded. "Sure, that's fine with me. Come over anytime."

Sebastian took another bite of whatever melty-cheese-pastry thing he was snarfing down and flicked his gaze briefly over to Jeremy, across the room talking to a couple of coven mothers, including Leonora. "I don't want to interrupt anything," Sebastian said blandly.

"He goes off to work with his dad most days, and stays out for hours on end." As I said the words *his dad*, I felt...something. I glanced up and saw that Gregorio Andromedus had joined Jeremy and the coven mothers in their conversation. He was not looking at Sebastian or me, he was smiling pleasantly at the people he was talking to, and yet...

"Reliably?"

Startled, I looked back at Sebastian. Right. He'd asked me a question. "Mostly," I told him. "I can see if I can pin him down, like, tell him I'm planning a nice dinner or something and ask when he'll be home."

Sebastian nodded, already smiling at my mom as she walked over to us, Rosemary in her arms. "These *belles fromages* are magnificent, Belladonna Isis," he said to her, politely. There was only a tiny flake of crust at the corner of his mouth.

Mom gave him a winning smile. "I do thank you, Dr. Fallon." She turned to me, handing over the baby. "Grandmas can only do so much; she has requested the pleasure of her mother's company now."

"Thanks, Mom." I sent a silent message to Sebastian: *Tomorrow? Just let me know. I'll be there.*

I spent the rest of the party in a state of heightened awareness—always keeping tabs on Gregorio, and with the nagging sense that he was keeping tabs on me, though not a word was said. It was very uncomfortable.

—⟨●⟩—

Sebastian came to my attic laboratory room shortly after noon. In anticipation of our work, I'd gone out in the morning and found a comfortable loveseat and two matching chairs at one of my favorite antique stores. I hadn't had to explain the furniture to Jeremy: he was already out for the day. I'd made him promise to be home by six—and, in the bargain, had pretty much hinted that I did *not* want him around during the cooking progress. That I was going to be trying something new and didn't want to be distracted and screw it up.

At least, I hoped he understood that.

Sebastian sat in one of the chairs, while I took the loveseat and Petrana sat beside me, within my easy reach. The warlock smiled at this. "We're not quite ready to start yet," he told her.

"You have circumvented the threat," she said. "I can feel the difference."

I looked at her, surprised. "You...feel it?"

"Do you not?"

Sebastian broke in. "I've managed to disable the tripwire we ran across before, but I don't know that I caught every trap the Old Country warlocks may have laid. So, I built a second spell to run while we do this, to sort of—well, think of it as running ahead and testing the ground."

"Canary in a coal mine?" I asked.

"Pretty much. It should alert me—and you, and Petrana—if we run into another problem." He frowned briefly.

"What is it?" I asked.

He shrugged. "I have tried to think of everything, to test for every sort of trap that might be within your mind. But it's like proving a negative. If there is something none of us have ever thought of..."

"Right," I said. If we hadn't thought of it, how could we protect against it?

"Anyway." He got up and began to walk slowly around the room as he spoke. I could feel that he was doing magic. Elnor's head perked up from where she'd been sleeping in the corner by the door; she followed his movements with her gaze. "I'm just getting a deeper sense of the space," he explained, "before I put in some supplements to your wards. Assuming that's all right with you?"

"Of course," I said. "Whatever you need to do, to make this as safe as possible. For all of us."

He nodded and made four more circuits of the room before stopping and turning to me. "Now to the wards—do you want to join me in this?"

"Yes." I handed the baby to Petrana and got up. "Which end do you want me to take?"

<hr>

Within fifteen minutes, we'd built a sort of magical Faraday box, wards-inside-of-wards, sealing off my attic workspace far more effectively than the lock on the door ever could. They were gentle but strong, and—most importantly—should be as close to undetectable from the outside as possible.

Sebastian took his chair again, wiping a bead of sweat off his forehead. Though we'd ostensibly worked together on the casting, clearly he'd done a great deal more work than I had.

"So, will the process be the same as what we did back at your place?" I asked, as much to give him time to recover as anything else.

"Mostly; you won't notice anything different," he said. "I'll be monitoring as I did before, but with deeper access to the transfer."

"That's good," I said. "I know it's risky, but..."

Sebastian frowned slightly but nodded. "Well, yes, it is still risky, and we should probably make sure we're both completely clear on all the risks—as many as we can know, that is."

"Oh?"

"The obvious risk is another episode like the one you had before, where a buried spell knocks you out and potentially harms Petrana. Since neither of you experienced any lasting damage from that—so far as we can tell—my guess is that that was more along the order of a warning."

I nodded. "That makes sense. We stopped immediately when we ran into that."

"Indeed. So now that we're going to go back in again..."

I felt a tingle of fear. "You think there's another line of defenses? But how did they even know I'd sent my memories to Petrana?" I turned to my golem. "You said you weren't in the room, and that they didn't know we were doing this, right?"

"That is true, Mistress Callie," she said. "I do not have any sense that they detected my presence outside or that you were handing anything over to me. But they were in your mind. And I do not know what happened after you cut off our connection."

I took a deep breath and leaned back in the loveseat. "Right."

"It would be prudent to assume they at least allowed for the possibility that you'd sent your memories off for safekeeping," Sebastian said. "I mean, if you thought to do it, presumably in the moment, it would stand to reason that warlocks who had developed a mechanism to erase and alter memories would consider such a defense."

"Of course." I began to feel foolish in addition to scared. "Should we not—"

Sebastian shook his head. "No, Callie, I'm not arguing that we shouldn't do this. I just want us to be aware of what we're attempting, and what could go awry. So: there might be further, more painful warnings. There also might be—for want of a better word—booby traps. Something that can harm or destroy the memory as we try to transfer it back."

"So we could lose the memory altogether," I said slowly. "Even Petrana wouldn't have it."

"There is that risk, yes. Now, she has told me many things about your trip, so all the information would not be lost, but it would be..."

"Not like having the real memory back," I finished. "But still, it would be better than nothing."

"I agree."

"It's worth the risk. I'm okay with that," I said, but Sebastian put his hand up.

"There is a third level of risk. I think it's unlikely, but I have to bring it up. Callie, we've discussed how you put a piece of your *mind* into Petrana, by doing this transfer."

"Yes," I said slowly, my fear growing.

"There is a possibility that, if we disable or circumvent the warnings and other barriers, that we could, well, destroy that mind. We could damage Petrana—or you—permanently, beyond repair."

Damaged beyond repair. Petrana had apparently been broken before, and I had rebuilt her—though I didn't remember this directly. But that had been before...all this. Before she had grown so much. Before she'd started developing something of a personality. Before I had put a piece of myself in her.

It was hard not to think of her as a *person* now. And a part of *me*.

As for damaging myself beyond repair...well, when witches left this plane, our souls journeyed to the Beyond, where we enjoyed another lengthy lifetime before eventually choosing to move to the next level.

Except, if what Sebastian had told me last week was true, Gregorio had drained the essences out of a great number of witches, here on our plane, and captured their souls. They were trapped in a limbo, neither alive nor departed. Were they even aware? What a terrible fate.

Even if I could be assured of a safe transit to the Beyond, I was nowhere near ready to go there yet. I had a *lot* more living I wanted to do here first.

Rosemary had gone very still in my arms as we talked. As though she were listening attentively—or even following my thoughts. Now she gave a quiet coo, and sent me *Love. Remember.*

Startled again, I looked down at her. "Sweetie? You think it's safe to go forward—you want me to remember?"

"What did she say to you?" Sebastian asked.

"'Love' and 'Remember.'"

He frowned. "She could be wanting you to remember on your own, without going through this dangerous process."

I gazed into my daughter's dark eyes. She looked back up at me, calm and placid. "I don't think so," I finally said. "I know she doesn't cry, but she fusses when she's not happy about something. And she seems totally cool with this all now. I think we should give it a try."

"All right," Sebastian said. He had caught his breath by now; I could see that his strength and energy were good, just by the color in his cheeks and the brightness in his eyes. "Let's do it."

—◄●►—

We began with the memory that had thrown us out before: the beginnings of our research at the Old Country's main library. This time, the scene unfolded without incident. Again, I had the strange dual sense of the episode happening in real time, but only a minute or two of elapsed time when I "woke up" from it.

"Whoa," I said, blinking as I brought my mind back to the attic. "Did you know that witches *control the weather* in the Old Country?"

"They do?" Sebastian asked. "Seriously? How?"

I shook my head. "It's a collaborative spell, and it's only for the capital city, but—wow. That's serious magic." Too bad we couldn't do that here, in San Francisco. Well, maybe we could if all our inhabitants were witchkind, instead of the tiny fraction that we were.

"I really need to visit the Old Country someday," Sebastian said, his voice wistful.

"You do—everyone does. Even with what little I can remember of my time there, it was amazing."

"So," he said, gazing closely at me, inside and out. "You seem fine, and it looks like that all went well. Should we move on?"

"Let's. But let's try and do them in order, earliest first. Can you do that, Petrana?"

"Of course, Mistress Callie."

And back in we went.

Fortunately, meeting Raymond was pretty early on the list, so I hadn't gone terribly out of order with my first "download" a week ago. Petrana passed back to me a few shorter scenes from earlier in my life, some involving my friend Logan, some others so random I wasn't at all sure why they'd been removed, or why I had shunted them to my golem. Most of the biggest thefts had come after I'd met Raymond and, eventually, moved out of the coven house.

The process was…intense. Anguishing. Even the happy memories—and there were plenty of those—made me furious when I emerged from them, as I understood again and again how much those monsters had taken away from me. They had intended that I would never possess these memories again. They had imagined they were making me a lesser person, a lesser witch, and that this would be a permanent change.

Did they have any remorse, any reluctance, in doing these terrible deeds?

I did not know, because I had not gotten to that part of the story yet.

"It's interesting they didn't remove my memory of making you," I said to Petrana, as I laid my head back against the sofa. We'd gone through a few dozen by now, and were taking a short break, sipping pennyroyal tea that Sebastian had conjured up. "That's a pretty big, and pretty weird, thing that I did."

"Probably they couldn't do that without removing me as well, and for whatever reason, they decided not to do that," she said.

"Thank the Blessed Mother for small favors. What would I have done if they'd taken you from me?"

She very definitely smiled at that. Yes, it was tiny, her lips barely moved, but sitting as close to her as I was, I could see it. "They could not reach me. You have to be able to catch somebody to 'take' them."

"True that."

I finished my tea and set the empty cup down on the couch beside me. In my lap, Rosemary still seemed relaxed. She hadn't napped during any of the transfer process; she also hadn't begun grabbing at my blouse. I wondered how long it would be before she got hungry. Probably we needed to get back to it.

"Well, shall we?" Sebastian asked, picking up on my train of thought, if not all its details.

"Ready when you guys are."

The next memory was another one of Raymond. We'd gone out to dinner at a little brewpub in his neighborhood, then repaired to his apartment for vigorous bed sports, and then watched something forgettable on TV. I'd gone home after he'd fallen asleep, in the wee hours of the morning, slipping back into the coven house like a thief, though of course everyone knew where I'd been and what I'd been up to. I had found Niad in the kitchen, making herself a cup of tea; she had been bitchy and snarky as usual. A perfectly ordinary, mundane memory.

I still could not see why Raymond and I had broken up; we were a blissfully happy couple, though we didn't spend a lot of time together. He was busy with his construction work day job and his rehearsals and performances with the band, and I...well, I was a witch, who had to hide most of the realities of my life from him, and could never bring him to my house or introduce him to any of my friends and family or bitchy coven sisters.

Oh, maybe that was a clue. Still, I wanted to know for sure.

I wanted to see what happened.

We had been going for most of the afternoon when I felt a change in the house's energy. I sent my senses out: yes, Jeremy had returned.

"Crap," I said. "What time is it?"

"Almost five," Sebastian said.

Rosemary had finally fallen asleep—in Petrana's arms. I didn't even remember handing her over.

Now I sent my gaze through the walls and floors. Jeremy stood in the entryway and called down the long hallway toward the kitchen. When he didn't get an answer, he climbed the stairs to the second floor and went into his study.

"Crap," I said again, getting to my feet. "I told him I was making rack of lamb with parmesan soufflé, and crêpes Suzette for dessert, and that it was all so complicated I didn't want him underfoot!" I paced the room, racking my brain. "If I send Petrana out to the grocery store and get the soufflé started right away—"

"Stop," Sebastian said, getting up and leading me back to the loveseat. Not until I sat back down did I realize that I was completely out of breath. "Just tell him it didn't work out—that you're ordering takeout. He'll think that's adorable."

I shook my head. "He'll think I'm a worthless moron, which is nothing new," I said glumly. "But Blessed Mother, this is an exhausting process." I turned to Petrana. "How much more do we have to go, do you think?"

"I would say we are nearly halfway through," she said, after thinking about it for a moment. "It's difficult to quantify it exactly, as some of the memories are very short and some are quite lengthy. I often do not know where we are headed until we embark."

"All right," I said, taking a deep breath and getting to my feet once more, this time hefting the baby onto my hip. "Well, that was pretty good progress. I probably couldn't do much more today anyway."

Sebastian got up too and put a gentle hand on my arm. "Let me just look you over quickly before I go."

I stood still as he checked me out and then nodded. "Okay?" I asked him.

"Yes, you're fine." He gave me a relieved smile. "So, go take care of your dinner, and we'll talk soon."

"Soon? Tomorrow? I want to get this done!"

His smile began to look a little strained. "As soon as possible This isn't easy on me either, you know."

I pulled him into a side hug. "I know, and I'm sorry. I'll be patient."

"No, this does need to be done. Let's just check in tomorrow and see where things are."

I hugged him harder, then let him go. "Thank you, Sebastian. Really."

"You are welcome."

Sebastian slipped out onto a ley line. I unlocked the attic door and carried Rosemary downstairs, Petrana and Elnor following.

After a hurried consult with Petrana, I settled in a comfy chair in the front parlor, the more formal of our downstairs sitting rooms, and then sent an ætheric message to Jeremy. *Join us for a drink?*

I'll be delighted to.

A minute later, I heard the sound of his study door closing, then his footfall on the stairs.

"Before you ask," I said the moment he stepped into the room, "the meat burnt, the soufflé fell, and the crêpes spilled on the floor before they were even fully mixed up. I am never cooking again;

we are moving to Plan B for dinner. And Petrana will be mixing the cocktails as well, so they should be safe too."

He watched me carefully as I made this little speech, clearly trying to figure out whether he should be laughing with me or soothing me. After a moment, I took pity on him.

"Here," I added, handing the baby up to him and giving him a warm smile.

He took her and kissed her, then leaned down to kiss me before sitting in the matching chair, a small table between us.

"I am, er, sorry to hear about your afternoon," he ventured.

"It's all right," I said. "Nothing a little drink won't fix right up." *And the more we both drink, the easier it'll be to make conversation that* doesn't *involve what I've been up to all afternoon,* I told myself. Though Jeremy was likely too polite and sensitive to pry further.

Petrana appeared in the doorway. "Good evening, Mistress Callie, Master Jeremy. What would you like to drink?"

I glanced at Jeremy. "Bulgarian frog brandy, please," he said.

"I'll take a Smoldering Dragonfly," I told her. "A large one."

Petrana nodded. "Coming right up." She turned and walked back to the kitchen, her footsteps light on the hardwood floor.

Jeremy shook his head, smiling. "I know I've said this before, but it never ceases to astonish me how much that golem is developing. How much more lifelike she seems all the time, and her capacity for learning. I don't know if I have ever read about any golem in history who could equal her."

I smiled. "Well, thanks. I guess most golems were never kept animate as long as I've kept her, were they?"

"Traditionally, no—again, as I understand," he said. "Not that I'd ever seen one in person before Petrana. But they were intended to be for a specific purpose, and then unmade when that purpose was done."

"I wonder why."

"I had imagined it was because golems are thought to degrade over time. That's what's so peculiar—and so marvelous—about this one. She only gets stronger and smarter."

The *she* in question appeared in the doorway again, carrying a silver platter with a snifter of greenish-amber liquor and a steaming, bubbling goblet. I could smell the fragrant cocktail from across the room; it made my mouth water. "Here you are," she said, walking over and handing me the glass, then giving the snifter to Jeremy.

I took it and took a sniff. Heavenly. "Thank you, Petrana, this looks perfect."

She nodded. "Will there be anything else? Would either of you like a snack before dinner?"

"No, thank you," I said, and Jeremy shook his head as well.

Petrana withdrew.

"I never wanted servants," I remarked as she left, grateful to have hit upon a reasonably innocuous topic of conversation. "My parents of course had household help—still do—and I always felt it was weird, having people in our home who weren't family. Especially since what they did were things we could easily do for ourselves, with magic or even with our hands. But with Petrana... somehow it's different. It's not that she's an extension of me, because she isn't." *Nope nope she totally isn't, nothing to see here.* "It's more like, since I built her, I still feel, I don't know, proud of her?" I shrugged. "Something like that."

"I think I understand, though that was not my experience. As you know, I grew up with servants as well." Jeremy raised his glass toward me. I lifted mine and we clinked a toast. "I never gave it a thought, until I began my education. And even then, I appreciated having my time freed up. I do not wish to be burdened with mundane household tasks—nor would I wish my mate to be similarly burdened." He held my gaze then, a light shining in his eyes.

I sipped my cocktail (it was as delicious as it had looked and smelled; icy cold, yet bubbling like a pot of boiling water, sweet and crisp and sharp) and set it on the table between us. Mate? Was he trying to tell me something?

His smile grew; he jiggled Rosemary gently in his lap. "I have news to share with you, Calendula. News of the best possible kind."

Now I started smiling back at him, while trying to ignore the small feeling of dread lacing through my stomach. "Oh?" I said, trying for a light tone. "Do tell!"

He produced a cream-colored envelope, a large one, tied closed with a loop of red string. Where had he been hiding it? "This," he said, opening the envelope with a flourish, "is the final version of our contract, approved by all parties and ready to be signed."

"Oh!" I said, trying to look pleased. "Is...everything we asked for included, then?"

"Everything and then some." He pulled out a thick sheaf of papers and fanned them out in his hands. Rosemary immediately began reaching for them.

"Here," I said, laughing. "Give them to me before she has her way with them."

He handed them over. I took another sip of my drink before I even looked at them.

"There's a summary on the first page, and then all the details behind," Jeremy said.

I swallowed, set my drink down, and steeled myself to look.

He watched me carefully, even nervously. I tried to ignore him as I scanned the lines. Yes, the finances were as we'd discussed; there was a provision for me to retain my coven membership (whew), and even a tentative schedule for the time I would spend there; a clause mentioned a table of assets to be found in Appendix D; and then—

"Forty years?" I said, giving Jeremy a sharp look. "We had been discussing twenty."

He held desperately to his smile. "It's like I said—it's what we wanted, and then some."

"Jeremy, you know we can renew a contract—as many times as we want. My parents have. There's no need to lock in such a lengthy period right out the gate. Forty years is nearly how long I've been alive."

He finally gave up on the smile and sighed. Rosemary sat quietly in his lap, again for all the world looking like she was paying rapt attention to the conversation. "Callie, I've told you many times: I love you, and I want to make a life with you. Twenty years is just such a brief moment for our kind. I wanted to...commit to something meaningful with you." I started to answer, but he went on: "Contracts can be dissolved as well, at any time. If it is not making us happy, we can simply undo it."

"I just don't understand the change," I said. "I was happy with twenty years. It will take her to her majority," I said, indicating the infant on his lap, "and we will still both be under a hundred when it's up. I have no reason to expect we won't want to renew. But why lock ourselves up now? As I said, I barely remember forty years back." I cringed internally, thinking about how much else I did not remember. Well, I was working on that. "We cannot know who we will be in twenty years, much less forty."

He was frowning now, and staring down at the baby. Then he looked back up at me. "Yes, she will achieve her majority at twenty. But...did you not want to try for a second child, perhaps? Any further issue we have, even should you be so fortunate as to conceive within the next year, would still be dependent after a twenty-year contract had expired."

And there it was. I was glad Leonora had brought this up, because Jeremy and I had certainly never talked about it before.

I glanced at the summary page again. "I don't see anything here about additional children."

Jeremy was starting to look more and more uncomfortable by the moment. "I...no, it's not specified, but there's a place where we can add in details, on page seventeen...it's one of the things I was hoping we could talk about."

I just looked back at him. Like, *Okay, go ahead, talk.*

"It was my father's idea, actually; he asked me if we might consider additional witchlets...or even a baby warlock."

Again, I was very grateful that this wasn't being sprung on me in this moment. "Is that what *you* want?"

He shrugged, looking helpless. "I hadn't given it a thought—as you know, I hadn't given any of this a thought, before we...found ourselves in this situation." He jiggled Rose on his knee. She gave him that mysterious baby-smile, the one that might be gas. "I had always vaguely imagined that I might settle down and raise a family someday, but it had not been my plan or intention when I moved here, even after I met you. As I know it was not your plan either," he hastened to add.

I felt a sudden mental misstep at this point; here was another memory I did not have. There was something to know here, and it was important, but it was gone.

How in the world did I come to have this baby? How in the world did everyone—including Jeremy and (until recently) me—believe he was her father? We hadn't gotten to any of this yet, in our work upstairs.

I shook away the sensation and gave him a tentative smile back. "No, I don't recall planning such an outcome either, at this juncture in my life." I said it lightly, as though I were joking. *Of course I remember every detail, and so do you, haha, nobody has messed with our minds, certainly not about anything so important as a baby.*

Because I would remember. Soon enough.

Petrana stepped back into the room. "Dinner can be served at any time, or I can keep it ready as long as you like. Do you wish a second cocktail, or would you like to come to the table?"

I looked at my goblet. How had it gotten empty? Jeremy had finished his frog brandy as well. "I'd like another, thanks," I told her.

He nodded too, but then beckoned her over with a finger. She leaned in; he whispered something in her ear.

"Yes, of course, Master Jeremy." She picked up our glasses and left the room.

I eyed Jeremy; he was looking very pleased with himself about whatever secret he was planning with my golem. Suppressing a sigh, I leaned back in my chair and picked up the contract again. The lengthy term stuck in my craw. It was not right; it smacked of manipulation. He said it had been Gregorio's idea...

"You didn't answer my question," I said, turning back to Jeremy. "Do you want a second child, or is that just something your father thought you might want?"

He was making a little circle of his arms around the baby, pretending to fence her in on his lap. She was pulling at his shirtsleeve and blowing bubbles with her spit. He looked over at me. The love written on his face—for me, and for the baby—was genuine.

"As I said, I hadn't thought about it before he brought it up, not in a tangible way, but...yes, I do think so. I had no idea how charming and delightful a little mini-us would be." He grinned down at Rose. "She's so smart, and so adorable, and so much fun. Don't you want more?"

I shrugged. "She's also a handful. I mean, I'm glad you're enjoying her, and you're a great help, really; but remember, the mother carries the vast majority of the burden here. Not to mention carrying the child in her body in the first place."

"I do know that, and so the decision would be entirely yours, but...I'm just saying that if you did decide to try again, I would be all for it. I would help and support in any way I can." He gave a sad smile. "And I do know that we, as a people, are greatly imbalanced. The world could certainly use more warlocks."

"Yes, we do outnumber you guys," I conceded. "But one warlock can impregnate numerous witches, of course. Biologically speaking." I glanced down at the contract again. "I don't see any provision about relations with other partners, casual or otherwise? For either of us?"

Jeremy looked blank. "Is that…something you wanted?"

I wished I knew. "It's a common clause to include, I thought. Given what you just said about more warlocks—if an unaffiliated witch, or even a coven witch, wished to conceive, she could do worse than to choose you as the sire."

"That wouldn't make you uncomfortable? Jealous?"

"I don't know," I said, honestly. "It might. It's hard to say. I certainly wouldn't want to be blindsided by it. I mean, that's why this kind of thing usually gets spelled out in a contract. If it were something we'd talked about in advance and agreed to the terms about it, I could see being fine with it." I tried the thought on, looking inside myself for an internal reaction. But everything was still just too muddy in there. I smiled at him. "Actually, I have a hard time believing you haven't been approached already. Everyone can't stop gushing about how adorable this child is." *And she's powerful evidence of your fertile potency,* I didn't have to add. At least, that would be what everyone thought.

Now he looked suddenly shy. "It is possible that subtle inquiries have been made," he admitted. "I have, naturally, deflected any such overtures; it would be extremely inappropriate to even begin discussions on the topic until you and I had reached a full, legal, and public understanding."

And yet, there was nothing in this contract about it—this contract that had been fussed and haggled over for months now. Why not? I didn't press the matter; I couldn't, not until I understood my own mind more. Instead, I sipped my cocktail. "We should let Petrana know we'd like to eat soon," I said. "Rosemary will want to nurse again, so I should dilute the drink in my bloodstream. Also, I'm hungry."

Jeremy smiled at me. "So...shall we set a date for the signing, then?"

I frowned slightly. "I'd like some time to look this over more carefully—more than just the summary on the front page. And I'd like to think more about the...other issues. Can we talk about that tomorrow, or in a few days, when I've had a chance to read it through?"

"Of course," he said at once, though he didn't entirely hide his disappointment. "It's just that, I know the best places get booked up early..."

"It's early January," I told him. "Any reception and party shouldn't happen before spring at the earliest, and you know June is probably even safer. If I take a week or even two weeks to look this over, we'll still have plenty of time to find the perfect venue."

"Yes, you are right, of course." He jiggled the baby again. She really was being remarkably patient. "Would you like to discuss any of the...other issues...further this evening, or set the topic down for now?"

I got to my feet and reached down for Rosemary. "Let me answer that question after I've gotten some food into me. Those Dragonflies were potent."

"Very well." He rose as well and offered his arm, and together, we strolled into the dining room.

Petrana had worked quickly, laying an elegant table, complete with the fancy china and silver, candelabras on the white linen tablecloth, and crystal goblets at each place. Four or five covered dishes sat on the sideboard.

I smiled, amused, as I saw the setup: Jeremy's place at the head of the table, and mine at the foot. "We're going to have to shout to hear each other," I said.

He nodded, with a gentle smile on his face as well. "It's not that large a table. And it's fitting for a celebration..." He glanced at a silver ice bucket in its stand beside his chair, where a bottle of Champagne rested. "If that is...appropriate?"

"Champagne is always appropriate." I put Rosemary down in the little antique bassinet we had set up in here and stepped over to the sideboard, where I lifted the lid off the largest platter. "Chicken thighs! With barbecue sauce! And crispy skins!"

From the doorway, Petrana nodded. "And mashed potatoes, and the far dish is a green bean casserole. Plus, cornbread muffins."

I turned and beamed at her. "I had no idea this was exactly the meal I wanted until just this moment, but—this is *exactly* the meal I wanted. Thank you!"

"Do I get no credit?" Jeremy asked, still smiling. "I chose the Champagne."

I set the lid back on the platter of chicken and crossed the room to him, where I pulled him into my arms and squeezed him tight. "You are amazing, too." His arms enfolded me, and we stood like that for a minute, in a warm embrace. I could smell the delicious scent of him, combining enticingly with the hot food. The whole effect promised an evening of every sensual delight.

And I didn't have to sign anything in order to drink Champagne and eat crispy-skinned barbecued chicken thighs.

I released him and pulled back to gaze up into his eyes. He leaned down and kissed me, then said, "Shall we eat?"

"Most absolutely."

It felt silly at first to sit at opposite ends of the table—when we didn't just eat at the kitchen table, we usually sat together at a

corner of this one—but it quickly started to seem natural, even fun. Like we were pretending to be grown-ups. Petrana served us flawlessly, and I ate three pieces of chicken, a huge scoop of potatoes, and even had seconds on the casserole. It wasn't just that it was delicious; I had a lot of energy to replenish, after my day.

Besides, eating kept my mouth busy, more or less. Jeremy took charge of the conversation and regaled me with tales of growing up in the Old Country—funny stories of things that happened to him during his schooling, warm accounts of his foster parents.

"I'm so sorry I didn't meet them when I was there," I told him.

He took another sip of Champagne—we were on our second bottle by now. "Quite all right; that was not why you were there. You were relaxing and touristing, not wanting to get to know perfect strangers."

"Yes, but even so. They sound like marvelous people."

"You will meet them at the ceremony and celebration," he said.

I smiled across the table at him. Yes, there would be a ceremony and a celebration, I felt quite confident. We would work out the details, any differences we had...and he was correct, even if I did sign for a longer term, any contract could be voided.

Tonight was about our connection, our love, which was strong and clear.

And it was also about the triple chocolate cake that Petrana carried in, once she'd cleared our dinner plates.

"What is *that*?" I asked, as she spooned something over top of the cake.

"Warm brandy sauce," she announced proudly. "Shall I serve?"

"Oh yes," I breathed.

When all was said and done, I was almost too full to enjoy what happened later, once we retired to our bedroom.

Almost.

— CHAPTER NINE —

In the deep of the night, I lay awake. Jeremy slept deeply beside me, to my left; Rosemary slumbered in the crook of my right arm; Elnor snored softly at my feet.

A cozy little scene. Too bad my mind was overflowing with—well, everything. Raymond was so fresh in my thoughts, courtesy of all the restored memories of him. My heart ached with love and guilt and regret and yearning. I had just...walked away from him. Not knowing how to face the impossible, I'd just avoided it.

And then, there was this be-damned contract with Jeremy. The suddenly doubled term.

Why would they do that?

Who, specifically, had done that? Jeremy, or his father?

Did it matter? Jeremy clearly wanted it.

And more children.

Blessed Mother, I could not sign this contract. I just could not. Maybe I would recover some piece of information once I had the rest of my memories back that would change my mind, but I kind of didn't think so.

I felt railroaded. Controlled. Condescended to. Now I even resented the lovely dinner and the Champagne, even though half of it had been my idea. I lay in the dark next to Jeremy, feeling more and more resentful of him, annoyed with him. Even a little afraid of him, maybe. How much *did* he know? Why was he always being so *careful* with me? Blessed Mother, this was no way to start a life together!

I sighed and wished I could shift in the bed, but I would disturb three peacefully sleeping beings if I did. So I just lay still, which made the urge to fidget almost unbearable.

What's the matter? came a voice in my head. Sebastian's. *Are you all right?*

What in the world? I took a sharp breath in, trying to stay quiet. *What do you mean?*

You're broadcasting discontent so hard, I can feel it from here.

Now I did extract myself from all the sleeping entities and stepped across the room, looking back at the bed. Jeremy stirred but did not wake; Elnor opened one eye, watching me without moving. The baby lay still, settled into the warm spot I'd left on the mattress, breathing softly. I turned and gazed out the window at the dark trees and the house next door. *You shouldn't be able to do that. How are you picking up on my feelings?* I sent him.

I didn't mean to. I was just thinking about you, and I suddenly got walloped with your emotions.

I frowned. *You're not messing with that ring, are you?*

A pause. *I'm being very careful, Callie.*

You need to leave that thing alone! We don't know enough about it, except that it's obviously very dangerous.

I think it increased your power, whatever else it did, Sebastian said, blithely ignoring my concerns. *You wore it for months, while you were pregnant, and gave birth to a healthy witchlet—it can't be that dangerous.*

On the bed, Rosemary moved her little arms in her sleep. She clenched a tiny fist and smacked her lips before stilling again.

I walked back across the room and watched her carefully. I'd just pick her up and go to another room if she woke; but no, she fell back into a deeper sleep.

We think Gregorio was monitoring me through that thing, right? I asked Sebastian. *The added power was—what? A byproduct? Unintentional?* Before he could answer, I added, *You're not wearing it, are you?*

I have never put the ring on my finger.

Somehow, I didn't find that precise, evasive answer all that reassuring. *If you bring Gregorio's attention to yourself before we know even everything I knew before, we won't stand a chance of stopping him. We need to be careful.*

We're running out of time.

Didn't I know it.

But you didn't answer my question, Sebastian went on. *What's wrong? You're practically seething.*

I sighed, looked back at Rosemary one more time, and then grabbed my robe off the bedpost, put it on, and slipped out of the bedroom. *Hang on,* I told Sebastian. Elnor would guard the baby, would keep her safe from rolling onto the floor, even if Jeremy slept too deeply to be aware of the need to watch out for her.

I started to head downstairs, but veered off at the last moment and went up to the third floor instead. On the first floor I would just run into Perana, and she'd want to make me a cup of tea or something, and I just...needed to be entirely by myself. At least physically.

At the attic door, I let myself in and locked it behind me, then ignored the furniture and sat cross-legged on my pentacle in the center of the floor. I felt the reinforced wards settle around me.

It's a long story, I finally sent to Sebastian. *But the short version is, I need the rest of my memories back, and pronto.*

I see. And I agree. Now it was his turn to pause. *I don't suppose we could get together right now, could we?* he said, after a minute.

I thought about it. *I don't think so. That would likely create more awkwardness.*

Then you're just going to have to tell me this way.

I chuckled softly at my friend—letting me *not* be alone, looking out for me. All this time. *Okay,* I said, and proceeded to tell him about the entire evening.

Well, sounds like dinner worked out, he said, after I was done.

Yeah. And I need to know everything there is to know before any of this goes one step further.

Yeah. You do.

We both do. Can we do the rest of the memory transfer tomorrow?

He fell silent, for longer this time. I was about to nudge him when he said, *I'm not sure that's the best idea.*

Why not?

I...well, just trust me, bear with me. I've been doing a little more looking into the magic involved here, and I want to put a few more safety measures in place before we try to access the really telling memories.

All right, I said, slowly. *So...?*

Can I borrow Petrana for a few hours tomorrow?

Petrana? Um, sure, but—

I'll know more after I work with her a bit. Then we can proceed—maybe by the end of the week.

It would have to do, I supposed. *Okay.*

We briefly discussed logistics, then signed off. I was still not sleepy—even less sleepy than before, in fact. My mind was full of questions and the answers weren't available.

Well, they weren't available in the usual, straightforward way, at least.

I got up and went quietly down to the bedroom, retrieving my box of tarot cards from my purse, and brought them back up to my blanket in the attic.

I shuffled the cards and let my mind relax, deliberately sending no intention into the deck, just my queries, my curiosity. After they were well mixed, I began to lay them out. I didn't even let myself consciously decide the spread. Of their own accord, my hands dealt a Draw Six—three above and three below, set out all at once.

Wow, I thought, staring at the cards. Weirdest Draw Six ever. Weirdest spread in general ever. Had I truly not manipulated this in any way?

Across the top, I had the Queen of Wands, the King of Swords, and the Queen of Swords.

The royalty theme continued on the lower three, with the Page of Wands and the Knight of Swords...but the last card was The Devil.

I took a deep breath and just gazed at this crazy story. Wands and Swords: such a collection of pointy things! I liked the Queen of Wands, particularly; maybe it was just the black cat at her feet, but she had long been one of my favorite cards. She is confident and optimistic, yet also passionate and *com*passionate. The sunflowers on her throne and in her hand are a symbol of fertility. A warm and happy card, and as the first one off the pile, it boded well.

The King and Queen of Swords were a fascinating couple. They both signaled truth, clear-headedness, mindfulness, thinking—all the things I was working to get back. That was encouraging too. The Swords suit was a little too rational and logical for my taste, though it melded well with my scientific training. But I liked the order and peacefulness the cards portrayed: both monarchs hold their swords ceremonially, not aggressively, and they sit under calm blue skies in a pleasant landscape.

Then the lower three. Well, the Page of Wands was a fine enough fellow, cheerful and extroverted, ready for adventure. The Knight of Swords next to him, however, was a little wilder, darker: wearing his full armor, dashing in on his white steed, sword at the ready. He symbolizes action but also impulsiveness—rushing into things without exactly thinking them through. (Nope, not taking any of this personally, not me, nope.)

And then. The final card. Always the most pivotal, most meaningful card of a Draw Six—sometimes the most dramatic. Which was certainly the case here. The Devil, despite his upside-down pentagram, horns, and claws, doesn't represent evil. It is rather a card about being stuck, trapped, held captive; it's about loss of control. Being a slave to circumstances, sometimes of your own doing, sometimes not—but in either case, within your power to change. When Mom worked with the cards with me, she always stressed the illusory aspect of all this: "These are *feelings*," she would say, "not situations. If you *feel* trapped, it doesn't mean you *are* trapped." Indeed, as she'd pointed out more than once, the humans at The Devil's feet are only very lightly held; they could slip out of those chains and walk away with very little effort.

I sat back and kept looking at the spread, letting all the messages run through my mind. So much of it seemed to be describing what was happening, what I was doing: working hard to restore my memories, to regain control of my life. To understand the connections between things. To unmask Gregorio Andromedus. The Knight of Swords gave me a little pause: was I rushing into this? Did I need to be more careful, slow this process down a bit till we were sure it was safe? But no, The Devil seemed to argue against that interpretation. I was trapped in my illusions, in the false memories and stories that had been put into my head. I needed the truth, even if it was dangerous.

Even if it would hurt.

Working with the tarot had made me even less sleepy, if such a thing were possible. The thought of going back down to the bedroom and trying to hold still in the bed was unbearable. Sebastian wasn't going to do his whatever-it-was until tomorrow (well, later today). I could just go get a book and cozy up downstairs till sunrise, try and distract myself...but maybe there were things I could get started on here.

I got up from the floor, stretched, and walked over to my lab bench. All the slides and samples were still tidied away, but my lab notebook was out—the one I'd been puzzling over a week ago when Rosemary had pricked her hand and started this whole unraveling.

I opened it to the page that had so mystified me. These memories, at least, had been restored: everything was suddenly clear. I *had* known about human-witch hybrids when I wrote (and coded) these notes. Not only that, but I'd been searching for them.

Unsuccessfully...because I hadn't had the right comparison. Of course I hadn't—Rosemary hadn't been born yet. I'd been looking at the wrong place on the genome.

I knew where to look now.

I opened the cabinet where I'd stored all the preserved blood samples I'd been working with. Strangers and friends, witches old and young and in between. All gathered from Gregorio's clinic. *Goodness, he was busy*, I thought.

I even had blood from nearly half of my coven sisters. I'd been able to collect that more quietly.

There were far too many samples to test them all right now, even with my simplified assay, unless I wanted to stay up the rest of the night. So I went with a faux-random sample, choosing six to follow the thematic logic from my tarot spread: two from witches I did not know (one from San Francisco and one from the South Bay); two from acquaintances (Gentian and Sapphire); and then two coven sisters. I hesitated over that selection, eventually choosing Maela and Niad.

I wiped a bit of dust off my lab bench, released the samples from their preservation spells, and took out the Mabel's Glass. After looking everything over, I flicked my fingers to set the magic in motion.

The assay took only a minute to run, and then I was hovering over the bench holding the Mabel's Glass to my eye.

The first two samples were nulls: one hundred percent witch. Gentian, I was not surprised to see, was also entirely witchly.

Sapphire, the coven mother at the cattery house, had some odd anomalies in her genome, but they weren't human.

I tried not to wonder too hard about that. If I wanted to look into her nature more specifically, I'd have to design a different assay.

Maela was a witch, and—if I was reading the results right—quite a bit stronger than she "read" on a casual scan. Well, she was a seer; that was uncommon magic, poorly understood even though it was also quite ancient.

And then I looked at Niad's results.

And then I ran her assay again.

"No," I said aloud to the empty room, only then half-wondering why Elnor had not felt me using magic and decided to join me. I cast my vision downstairs: she still slept at the foot of the bed. Then I pulled my regard back up here and stared again at this impossible result.

Niad too?

Of all witches, *Niad*? I remembered what Leonora had told me about her unhappy childhood—the warlock father abandoning Niad's mother; the young witchlet always striving to be better, more, over-achieving to make up for some imagined shortfall.

Except it wasn't a deadbeat warlock father...it was a supposedly-impossible human father.

Well, this at least bodes well for Rosemary's strength, I told myself. Niad was one of the strongest witches I knew. If she had overcome mixed parentage, Rose certainly could.

Did Niad know? She must, at some level. How could she not? Her mother would have known, obviously...would she have told her daughter?

Likely not, I thought, after a minute of reflection. That unhappy childhood would have been one full of untold secrets, impossible truths buried, hidden.

I actually felt a rush of sympathy for my bitchy coven sister.

This world got stranger every day I lived in it.

It was after four in the morning by now. And I needed to look at the rest of the blood samples. I needed to know more.

I started with the rest of my coven sisters for whom I had samples here. All witches.

Then I did the rest of the witches I knew, with the same results. It was going faster by now, as I got more comfortable with my process, so I did the strangers and the handful of warlocks in the mix. All null: all witchkind.

I sat back on my stool, looking again at Niad's results. So, so weird.

A small noise caught my attention from downstairs. I cast my vision through the floor down to the bedroom again. Jeremy had stirred, rolling over in bed but not waking. Rosemary was still under too (what a long sleep for her!). Elnor was awake, giving herself a bath as she kept an eye on the sleepers.

As I watched Jeremy's quiet breathing, I realized there wasn't a sample of his blood in my collection. Was that strange, or simply par for the course in Gregorio's universe? Of course, he wouldn't test his own son's blood; he knew exactly what would be there. Anyway, he wouldn't have much access to the boy, not after he'd sent the child away to be fostered in the Old Country.

But now I was curious.

Even using magic, there wasn't a way to get some of his blood without disturbing him. I started to shrug off the notion and then realized that I did, in fact, have a rather fresh sample of an important fluid from his body.

In my very person, in fact.

I will spare you the details of the next minute or so (you're welcome). I was soon tweaking my assay to account for the different nature of the fluid, and then setting the spell to run.

I didn't breathe as I held the Mabel's Glass over the slide, just letting the knowledge sink into me.

I'd found the second case.

Jeremy was half-human.

---c●)---

This fact sent me into a series of new questions and some false trails. Was *Gregorio* part human? No, he was not, could not be; he was demonstrably eight hundred years old, and a bastion of tradition and power. It had to be Jeremy's mother. The one who had very mysteriously died when he was quite small and was thus very conveniently no longer around for anyone to examine, or question, or know anything about.

Since Jeremy was a hybrid, could he be Rose's father after all? No, she had none of his DNA in her blood...not to mention the red hair. Her father was Raymond.

Jeremy was twenty-five, twenty-six years younger than Niad. Gregorio had very likely known about Niad, probably from the start; what had he done about the situation?

He had done *something*, I was sure of that. Even with only half my memories, I knew enough about Dr. Andromedus to know that he wouldn't let something so startling, so anomalous, so *impossible*, just...be. He would have been inquisitive, curious. He would have wanted to understand how it happened. He would have put everything he had into learning from the situation. And then...

Because I did not, for even a moment, believe this was just a coincidence.

He would have turned to biological experimentation—his life's work. He would of course have kept it quiet, biding his time, but he would have absolutely, as soon as he felt he had a handle on it, tried to replicate the case. Tried to breed a hybrid child of his own.

What a scientist.

Had there been failures, before Jeremy? I shivered to think of it. I didn't want to know, yet I knew I had to know, yet there was literally no one to ask, save the warlock I absolutely could not ask...

Did Jeremy know? If he did, he hid the knowledge well. I rather suspected he was as much in the dark as the rest of witchkind were. In fact, I was pretty sure of that.

Should I tell him? Could I tell him?

Blessed Mother, I needed the rest of my memories back.

Soon, I told myself. *Very soon.* Then at least I could talk to Sebastian about it.

Speaking of which: time to start setting our arrangements in motion.

"I have an idea," I said to Jeremy over eggs and toast, after the sleepyheads finally arose from their slumbers.

"Hm?" He looked up and smiled at me, and at the baby in my lap.

"Let's take the day off—go somewhere and do something fun. Remember when we used to go walking, for hours and hours, you and I? We must have covered half the city in our rambles."

Jeremy looked startled. Well, this was kind of out of the blue, and he was undoubtedly uneasy about the contract issue. He glanced at the window before looking back at me. "It's not exactly walking weather."

I waved a hand dismissively. "I just meant that as an example. We can do something indoors—go to a museum, something like that. Or hey, even head down to Monterey and visit the aquarium! I bet you've never seen the aquarium."

"I haven't," he allowed, "but..." He shifted in his chair. "I am supposed to be meeting my father at ten o'clock."

"Oh?" I tried to look very disappointed, but also like I was trying to hide it. "Oh, well, okay, that's fine. I probably do need some time anyway, to think about...things."

Jeremy's visible discomfort grew. "My darling, I—yes, you did say you wanted to—but I could contact my father—I just—"

I let him stammer on a bit before taking pity on him. "No, you're right, it really is fine; it was just a spur of the moment thought. We can make a plan for another day, when you aren't already committed. My mother would like to see Rose and me, anyway; we haven't been by since her Yule party." I smiled down at the baby, who had been watching the conversation in her usual rapt way. "But we really do need to get down to the aquarium someday," I added to Jeremy. "It's amazing."

"I expect it is," he said, nodding, and looking thoughtful.

I took a bite of my toast. My braid flicked itself out of Rosemary's reach.

"Actually," Jeremy said, "hold that thought a moment."

I looked up at him. "Oh?"

His gaze was vague: he was sending an æthoric message to his father, no doubt. Then he refocused on the room and smiled at me as he sipped his coffee. "Just checking on something." Sure enough, a minute later, his smile widened. "My father says that he does not require my help today, and he even offers the use of an automobile and driver if we want to go down to Monterey by car."

"Really? I thought we'd just take the ley lines. It's kind of a long drive..."

"He says it's not more than two hours, and quite scenic, even in the rain. We should make a day of it." Jeremy finished his coffee and set the mug down on the table with a decisive thump. "What an excellent idea, Callie! I'm glad you thought of it."

I grinned and got to my feet. "Well, I should get changed, then, and pack a bag for the baby."

———⟨●⟩———

We were on the road within the hour, heading south on 101. Highway 1 would have been even more scenic, of course, but that was better saved for a sunny day. (We had no interest in getting caught behind—or, worse, under—one of winter's frequent "mud-fall events" at Devil's Slide.) Jeremy seemed relaxed and happy now, obviously taking my request for a family day out how I'd hoped he would: as evidence that I was thinking positively about the contract and its startling new terms. Rosemary seemed to just love the car ride; she had only been on short drives around the city before now. She babbled and laughed in her car seat, frequently turning her head to look out the window.

And in all the confusion and chaos of getting ready for our big day out, it had been the easiest thing in the world for Petrana to slip out to the backyard, where Sebastian awaited. "I'll have her home by six," he promised me.

I had nodded and shut the door behind them, then said, "All right, cat, that's the last time I'm opening that door for you. Seriously."

Jeremy had walked into the kitchen and set a small knapsack down on the table. "Elnor doesn't want to…come along, does she?"

"No, I don't know what she's on about," I had said, rummaging through the cupboards looking for car snacks. "Cats! Who can figure them?"

Now my little family and I rode south in a big fancy car driven by a middle-aged warlock in—honest to god—a chauffeur's uniform, complete with shiny cap. *Wow, Gregorio,* I thought. *Could you be any more pretentious?*

It was a comfortable ride, though, and the warlock was a good driver. We got to the Monterey Bay Aquarium just in time for the rain to let up, and spent a solid four hours making our way through all the exhibits.

Rosemary liked the jellyfish the best.

Jeremy was charmed by the sea otters, which was in turn just about the most charming thing I'd ever seen in my life: a tall, handsome, sophisticated Old Country warlock…nearly giddy with delight at the sight of marine mammals cavorting and playing in the water.

"I've never lived by the ocean, you know," he said to me as we finally walked out to the car. "The Old Country is, of course, landlocked."

"Right. That must be so strange." I'd been born and raised in San Francisco; I always knew the sea was nearby, even if I couldn't see or smell it. I enjoyed its proximity, as any living creature of this earth must.

It's where we all came from originally, after all.

Rosemary slept on our drive back up to the city, and surprisingly, I did too. My missed night of sleep—not to mention everything on my mind—apparently caught up with me. I didn't blink my eyes open until the car slowed on our street.

"Nice nap?" Jeremy asked, grinning at me across the wide back seat.

I yawned and shrugged. "I guess so!" Then I remembered the actual reason for our outing and had to push down a sudden stab of nerves. "Um...what time is it? I'm starving."

Jeremy glanced out the car window at the dark grey sky. "Six thirty anyway, I'd say; I wonder what your amazing golem has prepared for our supper tonight." The car pulled to the curb in front of my house; the warlock driver hopped out and came back to open my door.

"Thank you," I said, hefting Rose out of her car seat and onto my hip. I climbed out and sent a quick ætheric message to Petrana: *We're home. Are you there?*

Of course, Mistress Callie, came her immediate response.

With a quiet sigh of relief, I rounded the back of the car to Jeremy's door. My warlock offered me his arm and led me up the stairs.

Petrana met us at the door as the car whisked silently away on the wet street. "Greetings, Mistress Callie, Master Jeremy, and Mistress Rosemary. Did you have an enjoyable day?"

"We did indeed!" Jeremy practically sang out, shrugging out of his coat and handing it to the golem. She took it and hung it in the hall closet before turning around for mine. "The otters!" he went on. "I've never seen anything like it!"

"Yes, we did have fun," I affirmed. "What smells so good?"

"A hearty lamb stew, with biscuits and roasted cauliflower."

"Oh," I almost moaned. "That sounds perfect."

We were at the dinner table within minutes, and the heavy, rich stew was indeed just the right thing for a dreary drenched day. Despite the nap, once all the food was in my belly, I felt even sleepier.

"Shall we turn in early tonight?" Jeremy suggested, after watching me blink my eyes open for a third time.

I nodded, even as I wanted to grill Petrana about what Sebastian had done with—or to—her today.

I just had to trust him, trust that he knew what he was doing.

And I *did* trust him. But...I was still curious.

Sleepiness won out, though, and my warlock, baby, and I were in bed before the golem had half cleared the table. I just had time to hear Jeremy's snores before I sacked out myself.

— CHAPTER TEN —

I walked through Golden Gate Park, toward the secret communal witches' garden. Mists threaded around my ankles, generated by the powerful spells that kept the garden safe and hidden, turning humans away. It felt even creepier than usual here, somehow; I never liked having to make my infrequent trips to the place, but tonight…well, it was worse.

Perhaps it was because I knew I wasn't really here, that I walked in a dream, a dream I had no control over.

Movement to the right of me caught my eye. I could not stop walking, but I flicked my gaze over. The white tail of a cat flashed briefly in my vision, then the animal disappeared in the darkness.

Another cat miaowed to my left. Again, I could not see the creature for more than a moment before it vanished.

"You have to listen to the cats," I whispered. My voice was uncanny in the dreamscape, and it unsettled me further. I felt the heavy, hearty lamb stew weighing down my stomach.

Had the stew been only stew? Why had we all fallen asleep so readily immediately after dinner?

"It was just a bit of Nyx balm," Sebastian said. He now walked beside me—he had always been walking beside me—but of course he hadn't. It was dream logic once more. "Perfectly harmless to all three of you—yes, even Rosemary."

She had nursed for all of maybe three swallows in bed, I remembered. "Petrana drugged our stew?" I asked. Even in the dream, my voice was logy, confused, slow.

Sebastian chuckled, but there was no humor in it. "Callie, you drug yourself more than that every evening at cocktail hour."

"Yeah, but on purpose." I wanted to reach over and jokingly punch my friend's arm, lighten up the mood, let him know I wasn't mad at him...but I found myself unable to do anything but walk forward, approaching the garden's black gates.

Sebastian reached out his left hand and unmade the spell binding the garden closed. The gates swung open with an eerie creak, though no flakes of rust or dirt fell as they moved.

Beside me, Sebastian kept his left hand lifted, now indicating that I should precede him into the garden. I did; he followed, then closed and bound the gates behind us.

I stopped on the path and turned to him, a little surprised to find I had some control. "Why here? What happened? Tell me everything."

Even in the dream, I could tell he was uncertain. His smile looked strained, worried. "I need to keep you and Petrana in separate places, in case...something goes awry."

"Awry?"

"She should retain the memories even if this doesn't work. We can try again."

"All right."

He took a breath. "First, I have to do this." He reached both hands toward me, as if to cup my face in an embrace.

Frozen, I stood staring at him, surrounded by darkly potent foliage, by warded and spelled metal gates, by the night and all its secrecy and darkness, and by a dozen or more unseen cats. The cats circled the garden, yowling and calling to one another.

Sebastian's hands moved closer to my head. He did not touch me, but I felt the power radiating from him. A familiar power...

You are wearing the ring, *I thought to him, no longer able to even speak with my dream-voice.*

It is the only way.

The power caressed me, insinuating itself into my bloodstream, opening my magical channels. I had lived with this power for months, I knew it; but it was different now. I could not tell if it was better or worse. I told myself to trust my friend, but in truth I had no choice. I could only stand there and let it course through me.

Behind me, a cat cried louder.

"Now," Sebastian whispered.

With a sudden surge, I felt every magical channel inside me swell to nearly bursting. It was painful—it was orgasmic—it was terrifying—it was the best thing that had ever happened to me.

I had a brief, potent memory of Jeremy and me standing together in a field in the East Bay at sundown, burning the magic out of Flavius Winterheart—

—but then that image vanished, too, and I stood before Sebastian—

—in my physical body.

In the magical garden.

In the middle of the night.

I shook my head, letting the dream fall away, and then shivered. "You might have warned me, told me to wear something to bed at least," I grumbled, glancing down at my naked self. The gravel path was cold and sharp under my bare feet, and goose bumps rose on my skin.

Sebastian tried to laugh, but it came out as a gasp. He was breathing hard, exerting himself to the limits of his power. "I'm so sorry," he managed after a minute, as he bent over and rested his palms on his knees. Then he straightened and shrugged out of his light jacket, handing it to me. "Here, this might help."

"Thanks." I put the jacket on, grateful even as I wished it were just a bit longer. I was barely legally covered—not that human cops would ever find their way in here. But still. My shivering grew, and I tried to reach out with my magic to grab a pair of pants and maybe some shoes, but I had nothing in me. My little flare of magic bubbled and subsided, and I was suddenly *starving*.

"I'm really sorry," Sebastian said again, still breathing hard, though he was beginning to pull himself together. "I didn't know exactly what would happen." He peered at me in the dim starlight. "How do you feel? Can you…remember more?"

"I…" I started, then the flood of it all hit me. "Oh Blessed Mother," I moaned, and sank to the cold sharp gravel.

Sebastian was at my side, trying to catch me as I half-sat, half-fell. I skinned a knee on something and landed hard on my butt. "Callie! Are you all right?" The ring glinted in the moonlight. It looked almost oily.

"I…think so. Ow." I wiped a bit of blood off my knee and then closed my eyes, trying to process the rush of…of everything.

Because it all had come back, all of it. Slamming into my brain like a Mack truck. I remembered everything. *Everydamnthing.* I knew how Jeremy and I had gotten together, and I now fully remembered all my hesitations about making a long-term commitment to him. I knew how Raymond had come to be the father of my child—well, I knew everything I'd ever known about it. The actual *how was this even possible* part was still a mystery…though apparently not as much of a mystery as we'd always been led to believe.

I knew every little creepy, manipulative, and downright threatening thing Gregorio Andromedus had done to me, to force me to cover up this knowledge…and everything that it meant. I could almost see all the bodies Gregorio had hidden in the basement underneath his lab in Berkeley, emptied of their souls. I knew exactly why I had gone to the Old Country, and what the warlocks of the Iron Rose had done to me there.

And I remembered every moment of Logan's last evening alive. I gasped as the fresh grief washed through me, finally feeling the loss of her—and then gasped again as the ramifications hit me. "She's not dead: Sebastian, she's not dead!"

"What?"

"Logan! Her spirit isn't in the Beyond, and her body is unspoiled. So she must be trapped, not dead after all. Like all the rest of them!"

Sebastian was shaking his head. "Yes, but nobody knows what to do about that. Unless you found the missing souls on your trip..."

That knowledge poured through me too, and my heart sank. "No. I was about to learn something—that young warlock there who was helping me was going to show me," I glanced at my young warlock friend, sitting here risking everything to help me, "but that's when they caught me, caught us both. That's when they tore my memories away...and killed him."

Still exhausted, and newly despairing, I leaned my head on Sebastian's shoulder and let myself softly weep. He patted my shoulder.

"You have got to take that ring off. You've got to get rid of it," I told him, sniffling back tears. "It's bound to Gregorio somehow. He'll know you've used it. You're in danger."

"I will go into hiding directly from here," Sebastian promised. "I've already made arrangements."

"Take it off now!" I insisted, pulling away from him.

"Callie, it won't matter if I'm wearing it or not." He put his hands on either side of my face, touching me gently this time, urging me to meet his eye. "Think, don't panic. If I pull it off my finger, it's likely to try to bounce away; this way, at least I contain it, until I can get to safety." He held my gaze. "And *you* must go straight to your coven and tell your sisters and your coven mother and everyone you know what has happened—all of it."

"But—"

"No, Callie, listen. It's only through lies and secrets that Dr. Andromedus has been able to get away with everything he's done.

If we shout his secrets from the rooftops, then there's nothing he can do about it."

"He can punish us! He can do to us what he's done to so many other witches!"

"He can't punish everyone. He's increasingly isolated and has had to plunder ever deeper to get what he needs. His crimes won't survive exposure to the light of day. Callie, I *know* this. Trust me."

I looked into his eyes, then finally nodded. I leaned my cheek into his gentle hand and sighed.

"Well, isn't this interesting?" came a snarky voice from behind me. One I knew all too well. "You even fool around with the gay ones? You *are* an energetic witch."

"Niad," I said wearily, without turning around. "What are *you* doing here?"

———⟨●⟩———

Ten minutes later, dressed in clothes Niad had magically fetched from my closet at the coven house, I sat on a bench just inside the gates of the magical garden. Sebastian had slipped out into the night, promising to send word tomorrow letting me know that he was safe, and making me promise in turn not to try to find him. My coven sister paced importantly in front of me, her little herb-gathering basket over her arm, her windrush forgotten in light of this much more compelling drama.

She had demanded to know everything, of course. My first reflexive instinct was to deny, deflect, lie…but that was the old way of things.

It was true, what Sebastian had said. Secrets weren't doing any of us any good.

And I was filled with new empathy for her, and a whole lot of curiosity. *Did* she know she was half-human? Surely not.

Probably.

I cobbled together a semi-coherent explanation, doing the best I could even as the emotions kept pouring through me. Oh, Blessed Mother, this was crazy.

"So, you're saying some wicked warlocks in the Old Country stole memories right out of your head?" she asked, after my story wound down. Her blond hair twitched on her back, reflecting points of starlight. "And then somehow, what, put a spell on you that affected everyone you know here, so that no one noticed, or asked you impossible questions, or...?"

"Something like that," I said. "Since I was the victim, I don't really remember a lot of the actual process."

"It had to have been some form of a deflection spell," Niad mused. "A very subtle but general one. Powerful." She paced further, thinking. "You did seem a little...vague, maybe, when you first got back."

"I felt vague," I told her. "I thought I was just tired, and post-partum."

She nodded. "That would explain a good deal of it. But I still don't like that none of the rest of us even suspected anything."

I took a breath and smoothed the skirt on the silly pink frock Niad had brought me. Of course she would choose this one. Why had I ever even bought this dress? "Like you said: a powerful spell. Holy Blessed Mother of Us All." I leaned back on the bench, overcome by weariness and another wave of emotion.

Niad actually looked...sympathetic? She frowned, at least, and her sharp features softened a fraction. "I felt it," she said quietly. "When the—the whatever it was—when it happened, when your mind came back. It's why I decided to harvest windrush tonight, and not next week like I'd planned to." She looked at me. "How did he break it? How did the warlock release you?"

I shifted on the bench. "I'm, um, not a hundred percent sure I even know." I made a split-second decision to keep quiet about the ring, at least for now. I just hoped Sebastian would keep his promise and get rid of it—if he could. "He had been working on it for days, but didn't want to tell me any particulars, in case it was dangerous."

"Hmm." She continued pacing, her heeled boots tapping on the stones of the path. "If I felt it as strongly as I did, surely others did as well. We should get back to the coven house at once and tell everything to Leonora."

"I have been intending to do exactly that," I said, somewhat tersely. "As soon as I have the strength." And just who elected Niad boss of the situation?

"Good. I can help you, though you seem fine to me now. I'll just get the windrush and we'll go." She glanced around the creepy garden that surrounded us: the potent, poisonous herbs and flowers; the dark, damp stone walls.

"Yes, I think I'm fine, but I need to go home first."

She turned to me and frowned. "Why?"

None of your blessed business, I thought, but I said, "My daughter is there. I'm not leaving her—I didn't even intend to leave her alone tonight, but Sebastian called me out through a dreamscape."

Niad gave me a long look before shrugging and turning back to the garden. She strode to the patch of windrush that now grew along the left-hand wall. Once there, she pulled on a long pair of thin gloves and plucked seventeen strands of the bitter herb, placing them in the basket in alternating rows, heads to toes, roots to flowers. This accomplished, she walked back and looked me over carefully, then nodded. "See you at the house."

After the gates closed themselves behind her, I stretched my arms up over my head, without getting up from the bench. Then I turned right and left, twisting my spine to release tension. "Whew," I said aloud, though softly. This garden always did creep me out.

I got up and stretched again, casting my vision to my house… where Jeremy and Rosemary slept soundly in our bed, still under the influence of the Nyx balm. Shivering, I brought my vision back to the garden. Time to leave.

At least I thought I could probably handle a ley line by now. Unlike when I first woke up.

I put my left hand on the gate handle; it swung open with its eerie creak. As I stepped out into the ordinary night, I already felt a little better, though still pretty overwhelmed. The gates closed behind me, solidly.

I walked through the park, to the shore of Elk Glen Lake, where a ley line would take me back to my neighborhood with a minimum of twists and turns. Even so, I took it gently, emerging on my street a few minutes later.

I stood on the sidewalk in front of my house, catching my breath again and taking the measure of the place.

It was the smallest hours of the morning, past midnight and before any hint of light would grow in the east. The rain clouds had scudded off some time ago; a sliver of moon failed to compete with the lights of the city.

Inside my house, a warlock and a witchlet slept; a cat and a golem did not.

As I thought of Elnor, I heard a clatter and a small thump down the block, as of some animal knocking something over. I turned to look, with both regular and witch-sight, but saw no movement. I stood watching anyway, waiting. After a minute, a flash of orange fur moved between a trash can and a tree.

The park had been full of cats when I'd been there in the dreamscape. None of whom were there when my body and mind finally reunited.

"Cat?" I called out softly. "Here, kitty kitty?"

I saw nothing further, though the edges of my mind still felt like they could perceive a feline presence. Neither dangerous nor exactly benevolent; just, there.

Finally, after another deep calming breath, I walked up the front steps of my house and let myself in. The wards had not been breached.

I closed the door behind me and stepped quietly down the hall into the kitchen. "Petrana."

"Yes, Mistress Callie?"

"I am going to take Rosemary and Elnor and go sleep at the coven house." She nodded, and I went on. "I have all the memories back—everything you had, it's in my head now. Whatever you did with Sebastian, it worked."

"I am glad to hear that."

"Are you—still the same?" I asked her. "Do you still have the memories too?"

She nodded. "I do."

"Wow." I gazed at her, trying to see if she looked any different. Did she still have part of my mind in her, or just memories? I had no idea. "Anyway, I'm completely spent, and somewhat confused, and also, well, upset. I need to tell Leonora everything, and I... kind of don't want to sleep here, right now."

"I agree," she said. "You should see to your own rest and rehabilitation. I will let Jeremy know where you are when he arises."

"No need," I said. "I'm going to leave him a message in the æther."

"Very well."

I tiptoed upstairs and into my bedroom, though they were both sleeping so soundly, I could probably have come in playing a trombone and not roused them. Elnor watched me from the foot of the bed, golden eyes large and curious, but keeping her silence, her stillness—she clearly caught my intention. I stood a moment by the bed, watching Jeremy sleep, struggling with...too many memories. He was kind to me, and he loved me; I knew that was genuine and true.

Yet he had never, so far as I could tell, been entirely honest with me.

This wasn't about privacy, about respecting one another's boundaries or independence or whatever. This was a deception from the start—he had not grown closer to me merely because he was interested in me. He had done so because his father had wanted him to, for reasons which were still not clear to me. Worse, despite whatever mind-altering effects this dark spell had had on him, he had gone forward with formalizing our relationship, pressing for a longer commitment, even rushing to get it signed. Maybe that was all innocent; maybe he was just that much in love, that enthusiastic to "marry" me. But I couldn't be sure of that. In fact, I was filled with doubt.

I was going to have to find out what was really going on before Jeremy and I could ever have a chance at building something true and real between us.

Assuming I even ever wanted that, once I knew everything there was to know.

And once *he* knew all there was to know too. I was going to have to tell him about his hybrid nature.

I gave a soft sigh and composed a brief message, triggered to find him when he awoke. *The baby and I have been called to the coven house. I will let you know when I plan to return.*

I resisted the urge to touch him one last time, to graze a finger across his cheek, to brush his hair back from his face (it lay as lank and inert as the rest of him, spelled into sleep by the balm). Then I picked up my sleeping daughter and nestled her to my breast.

She did not wake, but just shifted against me, aware and comfortable at some deep infant level. Giving a tiny murmuring sigh.

Elnor took this as her hint and hopped down from the bed on silent paws, then stood beside me, waiting for my signal.

"Yes, kitten," I whispered. "Time to head out."

We went downstairs and back into the night.

— CHAPTER ELEVEN —

At the coven house, I again stood a moment outside, sending my senses in first. I didn't feel particularly social just now, to put it mildly. Even Sirianna in the kitchen making potions would be more than I wanted to deal with.

But there was only Leonora, sitting in the front parlor, Grieka on her lap. A small mica-shaded lamp on the table beside her bathed her in a soft amber glow; no other light was on in the room. And every other sister in the house was asleep, including Niad, who couldn't have gotten back from the magical garden all that long ago.

Interesting.

We went into the house, and I remade the door spell behind us. Elnor followed me into the parlor; Leonora nodded a greeting at us.

"Good evening," I said to my coven mother. "I'm glad you're still up. I…I need your help."

She gave me a gentle gaze. "Of course, Calendula Isadora. You may always request my help, even if I am abed."

"Thank you." Speaking of bed…I wanted to just climb upstairs and fall into mine—I could barely stay on my feet—but this had to be done now.

I sighed softly and sank down onto the smaller of the two sofas. Again, Rosemary shifted a bit in my arms and murmured without waking.

Leonora watched all this with a warm half-smile. Our cats also looked at one another. On a normal visit, they'd already be romping together, tumbling around on the floor and chasing each other from room to room, but perhaps they sensed that this was something more. Or at least something other. So Elnor hopped up onto the sofa beside me, turned around three times, and settled at my side, purring softly.

I peered at my coven mother across the dimly lit room. "How much did Niad tell you, when she got back from the garden?"

Leonora frowned. "Very little. Only that a previously undetected spell of some kind had been laid upon you on your travels, and that it was now released. A spell that has been working upon all of us, to lesser and greater degrees."

"Yeah." I sighed more heavily; Elnor purred a little harder. It warmed my heart.

"Of course I felt the spell's release," Leonora added. "I did not know what it was, only that a powerful disruption in our bonds had taken place."

Yes, the whole city probably felt it. I hoped Sebastian had made it to his hideout safely.

"It's a long story," I warned her. "And it might, at times, be hard to believe."

Leonora tilted her head, considering me. "The hour is late. If we are to get to the end, we must begin. Tell me everything."

"Gregorio Andromedus is harming witches, and some warlocks," I started. "And he is doing so for his own personal gain."

She raised a grey eyebrow. "Dr. Andromedus?"

"Yes, and I have proof."

I told her all that I could remember and piece together. I tried to tell it sensibly and in order, but my exhausted and overwhelmed brain jumped around, making confetti of the story, as threads tied back on themselves, and as I made connections that I hadn't earlier.

I had already told her about the Iron Rose warlocks and their horrific memory-stealing device before I started explaining why I had gone to the Old Country in the first place—our discovery of the soulless bodies in the basement of the library building on the Berkeley campus—which threaded back to the night Logan died, or didn't die but was separated from her body, which led forward to my growing involvement with Jeremy, and my wondering how much he knew about any of this...

And then, before I had even fully realized I'd decided to do this, I said, "Because he doesn't know Rosemary isn't his daughter."

Leonora had been listening attentively, but at this, she snapped to even greater focus. "What are you talking about? What other warlock have you been involved with?"

"No other warlock," I told her, my voice quiet. "Raymond is her father."

To her credit, Leonora didn't laugh or dismiss me. She didn't even look terribly shocked, which was interesting in itself. But she did say, "You know that is impossible."

"But it isn't," I said. "That's just what we've been told all these years, so we don't think to question things when we believe we understand how the world works." It might be even more convincing if I could also tell her about Niad and Jeremy's parentage, but it didn't seem right to tell anyone else without letting them know first. "I can show you my assays from a few weeks ago, but I already knew it—my returned memories show Gregorio telling me about it while I was still pregnant with her. And my going home and testing it for myself, confirming what he said."

My coven mother gave me a hard look. "Be that as it may—I will stipulate that you believe it, for the moment. But why did you keep this information to yourself?"

"Dr. Andromedus forced me to. He…said it would be disruptive, to all of witchkind. He said that such conceptions are rare, but they do happen; he said he knew of two other cases, but he would tell me nothing about them. He said for the good of all of us, for the very survival of our species, we must conceal this fact, or everyone will run out and make babies with humans and then our ability to do magic will be diluted. That everything that we are will die out in a few generations."

Leonora snorted softly. "Well, the warlock certainly does have a flair for the dramatic." She shook her head. "I still am not clear on why you did not bring this to me at once, when you learned it."

"I told you, he wouldn't let me tell anyone. He threatened me… and her."

Her expression darkened. "Threatened you how?"

"He wasn't specific, but he implied that…well, that she would only be allowed to live if nobody knew this about her. That he would 'contain' this information in whatever way he needed to. And that, um, that Jeremy and I could try for real, to have an actual baby of our own, later. That Rosemary could have a 'quiet, comfortable life' somewhere, living as a witch with really low powers." My arms had tightened just a little bit around my baby as I said these words, as the memory came back in full force. Did Jeremy know this part? Was that why he was pushing for a longer term to our union, for more children? He couldn't. Could he?

Leonora's face was darkening further with every additional word I uttered. "He has *no right* to threaten you, or your daughter. No matter who her sire is."

I hung my head. "I know, I see that now. I should have brought this to you. But I was just—well, I was frightened. And pregnant. And he's so powerful…"

She shook her head. "A coven exists for the protection of all its members. That is its fundamental purpose. Yes, Gregorio

Andromedus is a powerful warlock, but we are *thirteen* witches. He cannot hope to stand against us."

I nodded. "Thank you." She gave me a soft smile. "But he's wrong, isn't he?" I went on. "Rosemary is not unpowerful—she sends words to me, and her magical channels are open and potent." *And Niad is strong. So strong. And Jeremy is even stronger.* "She's happy. And she...I don't know how the ring Gregorio gave me left my finger, but it was right after she pointed at it."

"On the day she was born? Calendula, you know that nothing about even the most powerful witchlet's bodily movements is under her control in early infancy." She pursed her lips. "No, there is much to untangle here, including the role of that ring and its manner of leaving your body. Where is the device now?"

"I, um, don't know," I said, which was literally true, if dishonest. I didn't know where Sebastian was right now, or where he kept the ring. Was I trying to protect him? I needed to talk to him more about it, force him to stop being so evasive about it.

Leonora frowned. "It is undoubtedly still in existence, even if it is no longer on your finger. I shall have to make some inquiries."

I nodded, feeling more helpless and frightened by the moment. "Do you think Gregorio is still...controlling it? Controlling me?"

"I do not know."

"He's at my house regularly these days," I told her, "acting perfectly...innocent. Benevolent." In my arms, Rosemary shifted and sighed. Her little arms reached for my chest, though she was still asleep. It was just a comfort reflex, I thought. I rocked her gently, soothing her back down into deeper slumber.

Leonora fell silent, clearly pondering all I had told her. After a minute or two, she said, "I shall have to think further on the ramifications of all of this...information. Please say nothing to anyone else until I have had a chance to look into this more myself."

"Not even Niad? She knows some of this, and she will almost certainly have questions. What should I...?"

"Put her off until I speak to you again," Leonora said.

I gave Leonora a small smile. "I'll try."

She was still clearly deep in thought, now speaking largely to herself, it seemed. "We cannot overtly move against the leader of our Elders, even should we want to disrupt the general structure of our community in such a manner. Which I am not prepared to countenance at this point. Yet if this is true...if he has been a party to perpetuating such a powerful falsehood to and about our kind...then I, and the rest of the coven mothers—not to mention the healers!—will be wanting an explanation, and a full accounting of the thinking that has gone into this situation. And the advisability of its continuation." Now she looked more directly at me. "Yes, I must consider this at much greater length, and consult with a few trusted coven mothers and elder crones. You and the child should remain here in the house. Even should Dr Andromedus seek to make good on his promises of harm, to you or to her, he will not dare to broach our walls, or my authority. You are safe here." She drew herself up taller in her seat. Impressive, given her already powerful presence.

In her lap, Grieka responded to her mistress's mood, also sitting up straighter; the fur on her back rose, and her tail twitched. Beside me, Elnor did much the same. I reached a hand down and stroked her back.

"For now, I can see that you are beyond exhausted. Go now and sleep. I shall redouble the house's defenses." She set Grieka on the floor as she prepared to rise, and again her next words seemed directed at herself more than me. "I shall wake Maela and... perhaps Liza, I think; they can assist in the protective spellwork. Yes, that will be a gentle yet effective blend..."

I got up too, though it felt like I was lifting a hundred-pound sack—and that wasn't even counting the sleeping baby in my arms. How was I ever going to make it up the stairs to the second floor?

Somehow, I did. I tumbled into bed and drew my baby close even as I heard Leonora's heavy step in the hallway, heading to wake my sisters. And then I knew nothing, sweet nothing, for a good long time.

I could feel the increased house spells and wards immediately upon awakening. It was the energetic equivalent of wearing thick, heavy winter clothes during an icy storm: comforting and appropriate, yet also stifling and awkward. I sighed softly and rolled over in bed, holding Rosemary close.

Then I blinked and looked at the window as my consciousness slowly returned. I'd missed morning and midday and afternoon altogether—it was dark again outside, after six in the evening. "My goodness," I whispered.

Rosemary blinked up at me, reaching for my chest.

"You must be starving!" I said, helping her to latch on and start feeding. "Blessed Mother—you haven't eaten in a whole day!" Now here was a downside of a baby who never cried.

And yet...I didn't feel overly full of milk, and she didn't seem unhappy, or anxious, or even desperately hungry. She just nursed happily, as if this were all perfectly normal.

"Did you...nurse while I was sleeping?" I asked her, caressing the top of her head as she ate.

Of course, she did not answer me.

Once she'd had her fill on both sides, I sat up, burped her, and then got up and rummaged through my dresser and closet, looking for something halfway normal to wear. Sadly, all my favorite clothes were over at my house, but I did manage to find some old jeans that weren't too terrible. The only button-up blouse I had here was overly dressy, but I put it on anyway. At least it was better than the stupid pink dress.

I missed T-shirts. Oh well, Rosemary wouldn't nurse forever.

Before I left my room to face whatever awaited me out in the house, I sent a message to Sebastian. *Hey, I'm awake finally. Whew. Still trying to absorb it all.*

He did not respond.

I waited a few minutes; maybe his hideout was outside the city? I tried again, putting as much strength into the sending as possible. *Sebastian?*

No response. He had promised to let me know he was safe.

Hey dude? You're kind of freaking me out here. Let me know if you're okay.

Nothing.

The only place I knew to look for him was his apartment. I sent my witch-vision there, but of course he wasn't there.

At my feet, Elnor paced around, clearly growing impatient. "Hey, kitty," I said, leaning down and scritching her head. "I bet you're hungry too—maybe the baby nursed in the night, but I'm pretty sure nobody came in here with tuna for you."

She blinked yellow eyes up at me, in clear and obvious agreement.

And then my stomach growled. "All right," I said. "We all need to eat, but then we have to get a hold of Sebastian."

I tried not to fret too much as I headed downstairs, but it was hard. What was Gregorio Andromedus up to? What more had Leonora found out?

Only then did I realize I'd gotten no response to my message to Jeremy, either.

I stopped at the bottom of the staircase and cast my witch-sight over to my house, but he wasn't there. Only Petrana remained, standing in the kitchen. She wasn't cooking anything, just waiting.

Where is Jeremy? I sent her.

I do not know, she replied. *He departed in the morning and did not tell me when he expected to return.*

Hmm. Well, before I called him, I needed to know what was going on. I walked into the kitchen, but nobody was there. Who was supposed to be cooking dinner? Where was everyone?

I cast my senses through the house. Only about half my sisters were here, all in their rooms.

Curiouser and curiouser.

Boy, was I hungry, though. Dinner or not, I needed food.

"Miaow," Elnor agreed, winding around my legs so insistently now I had to tread carefully not to step on her.

I fed her first, because there would be no peace otherwise. Once she was tucking into a double portion of tuna, I rummaged through the cabinets, stuffing handfuls of almonds and walnuts and dried fruit into my mouth for the quick energy hit while I looked for something more substantial.

Within a few minutes, I stood stirring a pot of pre-seasoned rice as it simmered on the stove, holding Rose on my left hip. (Of course, I didn't have any baby equipment with me here...I hadn't been operating with anything like a fully functional brain last night.)

When it was ready, I sat at the kitchen table—a butcher block structure with built-in benches on each side—and shoveled in the food.

"I thought I smelled something cooking," Niad said as she stepped into the room.

"You can't have any," I said around a mouthful.

She laughed softly. "I don't want any, but thanks." She came and sat down across from me, giving the baby a goofy grin, which looked really foolish on her patrician face.

I scraped my bowl with the spoon and stuffed the last bite into my mouth. "Did I miss dinner?" I asked.

"No. I don't know if there will be a dinner tonight." Niad was trying for her usual casual disdain, but her efforts were falling short; I could see the worry in her eyes and hear the strain in her voice. "Leonora has been out most of the day, and took about half a dozen sisters with her; clearly it's to do with your matter of last night, but no one has had a moment to fill me in." She leaned forward slightly. "I don't suppose there's anything you want to tell me?"

"I've been asleep all day," I said, perfectly honestly, so far as it went. "But actually, there is something you could help me with."

She leveled her gaze on me. I could almost see the suspicion and curiosity battling for ascendancy. "What is it?"

I gave her a sunny grin and got to my feet, lifting Rosemary up and holding her out. "Can you watch the baby for about fifteen minutes? I have something I need to take care of." I even flicked my eyes to the ceiling above me, in the direction of the second floor bathroom. What? I didn't *say* anything about a shower. It was on her if she wanted to interpret it that way.

"Of course." Niad said, after just a half a beat too long. She got up and took Rosemary, giving her a little jiggle. The baby happily went into my coven sister's arms, clearly delighted that Niad's hair was loose today. Rosemary reached for it at once. "Oh no, sweet witchlet," Niad sang, shifting the baby to her other hip as she shot a small containment spell at her hair with her right hand. The hair braided itself neatly and even tied itself off with a golden ribbon.

Show-off.

No matter—now I had my hands free and didn't have to worry about an infant's safety. "Thanks! I'll be back as soon as I can." Then I walked out of the kitchen and headed straight out the front door, pulling a small zone of inattention around me before stepping onto the ley line.

Knowing nowhere else to go, I popped out on Sebastian's street, where I called to him again. *Sebastian? Are you in there?*

Nothing, of course.

I walked up to his house—maybe it could give me some sort of clue. I stood before it, turning around slowly in all directions, seeing if I could pick up his energetic trail. But no—he wouldn't be so careless, especially as he headed off to hide.

I sure wished he would answer me, though.

I could feel his wards bristling about the whole building, even the downstairs unit, where a human family lived. Humans weren't as affected by most of our wards: they aren't that much of a threat to us, so we don't usually bother tailoring them to include human energetic signatures. Ordinary locks generally keep them out just fine.

I stood on the sidewalk, looking up at the house. The wards hadn't let me see much when I'd looked from the coven house. This close, however, I felt as though I could sense a living being inside. His human neighbors, downstairs? No, a quick glance told me they were not home.

What was it? Could I finesse a way to look in? I'd been an invited guest here more than once.

I prodded around the edges of the wards, enduring a few tingles until I found the magical key that would let my sight in. Yes: Sebastian had built in some low-level permissions for me, so the spell would not have to relearn my signature each time. I tinkered with a few threads, and after a minute, I sensed an easing, an opening.

I tentatively began to send my senses in, wanting to see who was inside, ready to pull back at any moment if he'd built in some further repellants past the first line of defenses.

He hadn't; I slipped my witch-sight the rest of the way inside and sent my vision all through his apartment. His small bedroom was on the street side of the building, which was unfortunate, but that was the only way the main living space would have the ocean view.

The bedroom was empty, as was the bathroom, the tiny study, and the hallway.

Only his cat, Trixie, sat in the main room. She reclined on a small plush chair under the huge west-facing windows, half-asleep.

She was the living presence I'd sensed.

I exhaled, letting out a quiet sigh of disappointment. I hadn't really believed he was here, but clearly I'd been secretly hoping I was wrong.

I sent another short message telling him to contact me as soon as he could, and was turning to head back to the coven house when Jeremy's voice came into my head: *Callie?*

Yes?

May I...expect you home this evening? he asked, very carefully.

Not until I knew a whole lot more, I thought. *No,* I told him, *sorry. Leonora still needs all hands on deck.*

All right, he answered. *That's just as well: my father has asked if I am available to assist him with something tonight. I'll go ahead and tell him yes, then.*

Another frisson of fear ran through me at the thought of Gregorio Andromedus. At him asking for Jeremy's help...right now. Help for what? *Okay. Keep me posted, and I'll call you tomorrow.* I strove for a casual "tone" in my silent voice.

Very good, he answered. *Be well.*

You too. I closed the connection, then took the ley line back across town.

I found Niad, the inseparable Flora and Peony, and several of the witchlets in the large front parlor, with Rosemary on a blanket on the floor between them. She was lying on her back and giggling as one witch or witchlet after another competed to see who could make the silliest faces, sounds, or movements and get the baby to laugh the loudest.

"I see I'm back just in the nick of time," I said as I stepped into the room. Elnor jumped down off an easy chair and came to rub against my legs. "You're going to spoil that child if you keep that up; she'll demand I entertain her constantly."

Niad actually looked happy and relaxed as she smiled at me from across the room. She was down on her knees, letting her hair dangle near Rose's grip, then swishing it across the baby's face as she whisked it back away again. "It's too late," Niad said, teasingly. "She has already informed us that she lives here now. You are welcome to visit her anytime, but I'm afraid she's just too cute to let out of our sight ever again."

Everyone laughed, as did I. Because I knew it was a joke, everyone knew it. Yet there must be a primal maternal muscle, deeper than conscious thought, than rationality, than any kind of awareness. A mama-bear reflex. Because that little part of me, way deep inside, was growling and grumbling, and insisting that I fly into the center of the room, snatch up my baby, and take her away from here forever.

Fun, Rosemary sent to me.

I nodded and told my inner bear lady to settle the heck down. Because actually, this was good news. "Oh well, being a mom was fun while it lasted," I said, trying for a breezy tone and mostly succeeding. "Say, has Leonora come back?"

"No, she's still out," Niad said. "She did send word that she is not to be disturbed, and that we will convene a special Circle at midnight."

Midnight...that was still hours from now. "Okay, thanks," I said.

"Place to be determined," Niad added, enunciating carefully, and giving me a glance.

I stared at her, then at the others. "Wait, what? Circle is here. Circle is *always* here." I indicated the room around me, with its carved pentacle under the rug. It was as if Leonora had decreed that day shall be henceforth held at nighttime.

Peony looked at Niad, as if asking permission to speak. Niad shrugged, so Peony said, "We're just as confused as you are."

"Weird." What in the name of the Blessed Mother was going on? "So, um, okay then. Will you all not mind if I run another little errand before I take the baby back?"

"Are you kidding?" Peony asked, seeming relieved that I wasn't pressing further about Circle. "We'll watch her all month, if you just leave us enough milk for when she gets hungry." Beside her, Flora nodded.

"Or you could just come by to feed her," the witchlet Mina said. "And then we can keep her forever."

"Very funny," I told them all, and then sent a private message to my daughter: *You're having fun, sweetie? You don't mind if I leave again for a little while?*

Fun! she told me, again.

"All right," I said to the cozy little gathering. "I'll be back soon—I'm just going to my house for a few things, if you need to reach me."

"Sure thing," Niad said, once again the picture of relaxed cheerfulness.

I stood there a moment longer, then shook my head and turned to go. It was just too strange, seeing Niad act like a normal, nice person.

If I'd have known that a baby could melt the ice queen, I'd have thought about getting pregnant years ago.

Elnor still stood by my legs. "You want to come with me, kitten?" I asked her. She clung nearby as I started for the door, so I took that as a yes.

Once I got back to my house, I let down the wards, then knitted them closed behind us. In the kitchen, I asked Petrana, "Have you heard anything from Sebastian? Since last night, I mean?"

"No, Mistress Callie." Then she added, "Jeremiah Andromedus did let me know that he will be out for the evening."

"Yes, he told me too—and I'm not staying here either. I just came back for a few things."

I headed upstairs and filled an overnight bag, including things for the baby. As I packed, I wondered if I should take Petrana with me, or leave her here? There was hardly room for her at the coven house—and I didn't even know if we'd be staying there, after all. My golem would be fine here, behind my wards.

Then I laughed at myself. I couldn't stop thinking of Petrana as a person now. One who needed protecting.

Back downstairs, I sat down at the kitchen table and waved a finger to conjure myself a cup of pennyroyal tea. As I sat there, sipping it, I thought more about wards.

Jeremy's magic was all through these wards protecting my house. We had built them together, in a time of—well, greater innocence, anyway. A time of lust and attraction and trust. We built them right before we slept together for the first time.

And yet...I had no idea whether I could trust the warlock any longer. If I ever could. He was the son of Gregorio Andromedus, whom I knew very well I could not trust. And Jeremy was with his father right now—at least, presumably.

What were they up to?

How much did Jeremy know? How big a fool had I been, all this time?

Was Petrana safe here? Even though I had my memories back, they still resided in her mind as well. Could someone use that fact against me, or her?

Until I knew whether I could trust Jeremy, I needed to keep him out of my home.

I finished my tea, set the cup down in the saucer with a gentle clink, and turned to Petrana. "We have to rebuild these wards."

— CHAPTER TWELVE —

My golem, of course, didn't even blink at my statement. "As you wish, Mistress Callie."

"Okay then." I shrugged, then got up and shrugged again, harder this time, moving my shoulders in an exaggerated fashion, rolling them, then twisting my back. Trying to loosen up my muscles. Then I focused my attention on the wards.

They surrounded the entire house, wrapping tightly around the outside walls, skimming the roof, and even sinking into the ground underneath the foundation. The house did not have a garage or a basement, so the wards only delved a few feet underground, reaching through hard-packed dirt to make a complete sphere of protection. Well, "sphere" in the most casual of senses; more like a house-shaped bubble. But you get the idea.

I tried to search for the edges of them, to find the handle that would let me take them apart. But of course, they were wards: the whole point of them was that they were not supposed to have unmaking-buttons.

I let them down; they eased away, sitting ready, waiting to be called forth again.

How do you demolish whole-house wards? I thought. I had never done an unmaking of this scope, this magnitude. It was not the same as collapsing a Circle, scratching away a line of salt. These were...infrastructure.

I thought back to the night Jeremy and I had made them. *"If you decide you don't like them, we can take them down at any time,"* he had assured me.

"We." There was the trouble right there. His essence and mine, woven through these. To make them stronger.

It had sure seemed like a good idea at the time.

Was there no way to permanently unmake them without his help?

"What would you like me to do, Mistress Callie?" Petrana asked.

I turned and looked at her. "Honestly? I don't exactly know." I thought about it another minute. "Well, let's see what happens if we try to break the old ones."

"All right."

I reached for her hand, planted my feet in the center of the kitchen floor, and called out a banishing spell in the ancient language of spells: *"Avastå essulian mordente slew chärn!"*

For a giddy moment I thought it might have worked, that maybe it was just that easy. The deep, strong wards shuddered from the impact. Then they tightened again, stronger than before. "Oh, Blessed Mother!" I swore, as the energy rebound gave me a hard thump in the stomach.

I sucked in a deeper breath, shaking my head, and rubbing my belly. Pulling on Petrana's power and weaving it through mine, I scrambled to cast a strong, blunt spell. I called on the forces of iron and chains and stone, summoning all the magic I could grab around me. Including energy from the existing wards. I called out the spell again, growling the final word: *"Chärn!"*

My spell rose—I could feel it whipping around us—but then it crumbled, falling to pieces. "It's fighting me...it must be Jeremy's essence fighting back." Which was what wards were supposed to do, of course. I sighed, sinking to my knees on the floor. That had taken a lot of strength out of me.

I had to work smarter, not harder. I didn't have the strength to just batter away at them blindly. Or the time, really, if I was going to be recovered and back at the coven house (or wherever) for the midnight Circle.

Elnor came up to me as I sat on the kitchen floor; I clutched her close, gathering as much of her essence into me as I could. She purred, but it still wasn't nearly enough.

"You can take more from me, Mistress Callie," Petrana said.

"Really?" I wasn't sure how, but—well, what else was new? I started to reach within myself again, trying to draw deeply of my own power and of Petrana's, but then stopped. *Smarter, fool,* I told myself, and pulled back.

I was doing this whole working intuitively. What is the magic of intuition, of deep truth? What is the opposite of force, and of science, and of *trying harder*?

My purse hung over a kitchen chair, forgotten here since last night. I got up and reached in it for Logan's tarot cards.

I felt a warmth in my belly now, almost a buzz of satisfaction. Power of suggestion? It didn't matter; I was going with my gut feelings, so I might as well go all the way.

I pulled out the deck and took the cards out of their box. It was getting easier to shuffle them; either I was getting used to their awkward size, or they were getting a little less stiff as they aged. As I used them.

After I shuffled a few times, deliberately not counting or looking at the bottom card, I spread them on the table before me, face down. Then I laid my fingers on the cards and chose one, flipping it over. I almost snickered when I saw what it was. The Hierophant: a card of the major arcana, one that stood for tradition, institutional power, spirituality, but in the sense of patriarchal religion specifically—basically everything I was up against.

"Hilarious," I grumbled, and let my fingers choose another one. If the cards were just going to tell me what I already knew...

This time I chose The Star. More spirituality (and more major arcana), but at least this time it was a female figure. She stood for hope and faith, for renewal—perhaps even for rebuilding? With feminine power? I could stretch the meaning to go there, I thought.

What is the difference between feminine power and masculine power? I asked myself.

As witches, we worked our magic very differently than warlocks did. They used strength and brute force, powerful spells and incantations; it was why they chose to live longer, because power grows as you age—to a certain point, anyway. Witches worked in community, much more commonly.

Yes, my career training had been by warlocks, and therefore my career work was more typically warlock-style; but I was a coven witch and worked coven magic for all the important things in life. Like, oh, say, naming babies.

I looked again at the red, draping robe of The Hierophant, and the jugs of flowing water that The Star wielded, and I thought of blood.

It was menstrual blood that we used in our spells that called for blood: blood that flowed according to its own schedule, its own purposes. A menstrual flow was the sign of a healthy witch of child-bearing age (even if she never conceived). Spilled-blood magic was...rather darker, and quite a bit stronger. Trouble was, it was forbidden, because of that strength. Blood carried so much power: it carried our very essence.

Too bad.

I sighed, cast my mind in other directions, and then—

Forbidden by whom, exactly?

Why, the powers that be, of course. Our elders; *the* Elders.

And *why* was I still following their orders? In anything?

I had to protect my home. I was no longer a good obedient little witch, consigning all my strength and power away to my "betters."

I would add my spilled blood to my incantations.

And then there was the spirituality element. Our souls, our spiritual selves, traveled to the Beyond when we were done on this plane. Except for the souls that Gregorio Andromedus had trapped somewhere, separated from their not-alive, not-dead bodies that he was hoarding under his lab in Berkeley.

My thoughts went to Nementhe, and how she had appeared to me here, in this house. Telling me to do my work. I had taken that to mean my laboratory work, and indeed I had discovered...well, re-discovered...the secret of Rosemary's parentage (Through her spilled blood, I reminded myself, however accidentally: the layers kept wrapping around themselves.) But what if Nementhe had meant my spiritual work? My learning the tarot, my working more deeply with witchly magic?

I could not break these combined wards through brute force, through warlock magic.

I would have to do it using the tools intrinsic to me.

Leaving the cards on the table, I got up and went to the drawer for a kitchen knife. But that didn't feel right. I stood, holding the knife, reflecting. Elnor sat on the floor, watching me; Petrana stood by, seemingly as uncurious as ever, yet attentive.

"I'll be right back," I told them.

I climbed the stairs to my bedroom where, in a box on the high closet shelf, I found my jewel-handled athame, unused since my coven initiation over twenty-five years ago. It was an ancient family heirloom, uncharacteristically sharp for a ceremonial knife. It gleamed in the light, alive and eager, as if it had been used yesterday.

Now that I was up here, I realized where we needed to do this: not the kitchen. I hurried over to the top of the stairs and called down for Petrana and Elnor to join me.

We convened on the third floor, standing together over the pentacle carved into the floor, the blanket kicked aside, the loveseat and chairs pushed against the wall. I stood in the center, Elnor at my right, leaning into my leg; Petrana at my left, her hand on my shoulder. I closed my eyes, grounded my energy, and began chanting. I just gathered power at first, continuing the grounding, not reaching for anything or anyone.

After a few minutes, I stopped the chant and held close what I had gathered, examining it. Taking its measure. Petrana and Elnor stood solidly beside me, not moving, not making a sound. They knew what I needed. I rolled the power around in my mind, thinking about The Hierophant and The Star again. Power. Spirituality. The Beyond. Nementhe. The night. Our menstrual blood, the blood that moved through my veins, through the veins of all living creatures. Nurturing, bringing oxygen and nourishment to our bodies.

Slowly, quietly, I began chanting a different incantation, one that had sharp edges to its song. Prickles and thorns. A protective spell, but not a friendly one. At its climax, I swiped the athame against my forearm. It cut clean and deep, and it hurt, but most of my mind was not focused on the pain. I had expected it; it was healthy, it was part of my strong power. I held tight to my focus. Blood spread across the soft skin of my arm.

The wards trembled around us—I could feel them move, sway. For a moment, I felt a gust of nonmagical air leaking through, bringing with it a flash of understanding, of clarity.

I would not, could not shatter these wards.

But I could melt them.

I switched incantations yet again, this time with words that flowed and oozed, like blood itself. Like the water from The Star's pitchers. Like the energy that surrounded us all, the æther we spoke to one another through, the oil in a scrying bowl.

As this chant approached its climax, I readied the athame. When I said the binding word, I took the knife tip and bathed it in my flowing blood, stroking it across my arm. I touched the blooded tip of the athame to my nose, to the center of my forehead, and to my tongue, tasting my own salty essence, then dropped the knife in the center of the pentacle. Digging my fingers into the wound, barely feeling the pain anymore, I dabbed blood on each point of the pentacle.

Then I lowered myself to my knees in the center of the pentacle and took up the athame again, chanting the new incantation a second time, and then a third, growing louder each time. As I spoke the words on the final round, I began to feel movement. A slipperiness, a dissolving, a falling-apart that felt terrifying and exhilarating, and deeply unsettling. My bones ached with it, and a small, frightened part of me wanted to stop—but I would not stop, could not, must not.

When I said the final words, the old wards dissolved around us, melting into nothingness, vanishing into the air.

My home was just a house now, like any human dwelling. Like it had been for the decades I'd owned it, and when I'd moved into it.

But it could not stay this way.

I lay on my back for a moment, staring up at the ceiling, breathing hard. "Are you all right, Mistress Callie?" Petrana asked.

"Yeah. I need to rest, just a bit."

"Would you like me to get you something to eat?"

I thought about it. Yes, I did, but also: "No, not yet," I told her. "We're very exposed here, and I have no idea who noticed what we were doing; we need to finish the job. Then I need to go get the baby. *Then* we will feast."

"Very well." She nodded, and Elnor pushed against my unbloodied arm on my other side, sending her feline strength.

"Okay," I said after a minute. "Let's do this."

I sat up and folded myself into lotus, in the very center of the pentacle. Petrana sat beside me, and Elnor curled into a ball, purring hard. I closed my eyes again and began collecting power once more, but this time making sure to find only feminine power. I reached beyond the boundaries of my house, finding human women who lived on my street, gathering their small but sturdy essences—nothing they would miss, just a hint here or there, a sip or two. They would find themselves gently bound to me, to this house, this street; they would never want to move away from here, would always remember it fondly if they did.

They could live with that.

I rolled and rolled that gathered power within me, coiling Elnor's power with it. Her feline power felt stronger than usual, and that felt good to me, felt right. I was following a rhythm now, almost rocking with the motion of it. I even reached and took some of Petrana's power, though that was really just my own, reflected and stored. That didn't matter; it all counted. I didn't even consciously decide to start chanting, singing, but eventually realized I was making a song—one of my own, nothing I'd ever heard before. A song, a spell, that came from within me, and followed my swaying movements as I rocked in place.

When the spell built, when I could almost see the power swirling around me, around us all, around the house itself, almost a tangible thing I could reach out and poke with my finger, I instead reached inward, lifting the athame and touching its point to my third eye. I just rested it on the skin for a long moment, then pressed harder, drawing a single drop of new blood.

This fresh blood melded with the older blood, and only then did I let loose the power of all the beings in my makeshift domain. Let it flow outward, finding the boundaries it wished to find, the natural limits of *our space*.

With a sizzle, I felt a burst of heat from the tip of the knife. My breath escaped me in a sudden rush, with a moan leading to almost a shout at the end—but it was a cry of joy, not of pain or fear or sorrow. And in that moment, I felt the embrace of the universe.

My new wards shimmered to life, surrounding us, cradling us.

"Oh wow," I sighed, falling back onto the floor in the pentacle once more, dropping the knife on the floor beside me, careful not to poke my cat or my golem. Then I just lay there, catching my breath yet again.

Were we safe?

Elnor nudged against me. I stroked her fur, still breathless and a bit light-headed, trying to pull it all together. Trying to understand what I was feeling.

The previous wards had been cozy and comfortable, a tangible melding of Jeremy and me, of our connection and our combined, and complementary, strengths. The night we'd made them, in fact, they'd felt sexy and delicious: they'd driven us right into bed together. For a long time, they had seemed like everything a witch could ever want. As Jeremy had explained at the time, I'd never had wards made just for me before; I'd always inhabited spaces that were long since protected by others. The wards he and I built had felt so much nicer than the coven's wards, or even my parents'.

Now I understood things at a much deeper level. These wards, these were my own work, resonating strongly to my energy— mine, along with some of that of my loved ones. Well, okay, and some neighbors too. But they were strong as liquid steel, and warm as blood. They would keep me safe: me and everyone I cared about, everyone I wished to shelter here.

They were *mine*.

I stretched my legs out, taking a deeper breath, as my heart rate settled. "Okay I'm ready for that feast now," I said in the general direction of the ceiling.

"Would you like me to prepare something while you get cleaned up?" Petrana asked.

I looked over at her, and then down at my bleeding arm. There was undoubtedly blood on my face too. "Right. Good idea. Let's do that."

"What would you like me to cook?"

"Whatever's fastest."

My golem nodded and headed down to the first floor.

I followed her but stopped on the second floor. In the bathroom, I washed my face and bandaged my arm. I had almost nothing left in my tank, so to speak, but I managed to whisper a small healing incantation before I rinsed the wound on my arm, then dressed it with herbs and a clean cloth. The blood flow, never very strong, soon stopped. The injury didn't hurt much. I hoped it wouldn't as I healed.

By the time I got downstairs, I could already smell something delicious. Whatever fuel I'd gotten from that rice mix earlier at the coven house had long been burned to magical smithereens in the destroying of the old wards and casting of the new ones. "What is it?" I asked Petrana.

"Beef stew with dumplings."

"*Oh* yes." My stomach echoed my sentiments, growling loud enough to make Elnor look up for a moment before she buried her face back in one the largest bowls of tuna I'd ever seen. I chuckled as I sat down; she had clearly reached deep into her own reserves, just as I had done.

Then I remembered that extra bit of feline energy I'd felt during the building of the spell. What had that reminded me of? I tried to think, but my brain felt muzzy with exhaustion and hunger, and it faltered as I tried to concentrate. "We've got to figure out how to make that restorative drink they gave me in the Old Country," I told Petrana. Because now I could remember the thick, delicious beverage I'd been handed moments after I'd arrived at my hotel, and how nourished I'd felt once I'd swallowed it.

"Yes, we should. But for right now, try this." Petrana set a huge bowl of stew in front of me and handed me a large spoon.

I got to work.

A few minutes later, I looked up from the empty bowl. Had I even breathed? Laughing softly at myself, I set the spoon down.

"Would you like another bowl?" Petrana asked, still standing by the stove.

"Maybe, but not just yet. Let's see what this one does." I leaned back in the chair, resting a hand on my stomach, enjoying the feeling of the food settling down into it and spreading energy throughout my veins. "I'd take a glass of water, though."

She brought one over.

I sipped, still trying to decide if I needed more food. I *wanted* more; it was delicious, I thought, though I'd wolfed it down so fast, I'd hardly tasted it.

Elnor looked up at me then, as if to ask, *And what's so strange about that?*

"Right," I said, and finished my water. I got up from the table, standing a moment to make sure I was steady on my feet.

I was, and furthermore, these new wards felt *amazing*. Almost as if I could lean back and they would catch me.

Why didn't more of us build our own wards? I understood why coven houses and other communal-living spaces had more generic wards, suitable for multiple inhabitants, but plenty of warlocks lived alone, and...

Sebastian had built and then rebuilt his own wards. I wondered if they'd felt as good to him as mine did to me. Strong as they were, though, he hadn't trusted them to protect him.

I sighed. *Sebastian?* I sent out again, not really expecting an answer. And I didn't get one.

Elnor licked her empty bowl till it shone, then turned her head to me again. "So, kitty, that was strong work we did," I said to her.

She walked over and butted me on the leg. I reached down to scratch her, but she pulled away and butted me again.

"What is it?" I asked.

She looked up at me, then walked to the kitchen doorway, pausing to look back at me.

"Is there something you want to show me?" I asked.

In response, she practically waddled out of the kitchen. I could almost see the entire bowl of tuna bulging out her midsection. But I refrained from mocking her; I was carrying a bit of a food bulge myself.

I got up and followed her to the front closet, where she sat down at its door and miaowed at me.

"You want me to open this?" I put a hand on the doorknob. She miaowed again, so I opened it. And in she darted.

I started to go in behind her, but she was already on her way back out, pushing past me. When she got behind me, she turned and bit me gently on the ankle.

"Seriously, cat, I wish you could talk," I grumbled, and started closing the door.

She bit me again, a little harder.

"You want me to leave it open?"

No bite this time.

"Fine. But just for now. We don't leave closet doors hanging open all the time around here," I told her sternly. As if she understood me. As if she would have cared, if she did understand.

Then I realized how empty my arms felt, as compared with how full my breasts felt. Seemed like half the food I'd eaten had gone straight into milk.

Niad? I sent through the æther.

Yes, Callie? Did you remember you had a baby?

I grinned at the faux-testiness in her voice. Even ætheric communication couldn't disguise how much fun she was obviously having with Rosemary. *No, I completely forgot about her, but now I need to nurse her, so can you bring her to my house?*

A pause. *Aren't you coming here?*

Is Leonora back? Any word on where Circle is?

Nothing, she sent.

I have a few more things I need to take care of here first, I told her. *Can you please just bring her to me, or send someone else with her if you're busy?*

Another pause, longer this time. *All right. I'll see if I can extract her from all these doting aunties.*

Thanks.

I waited, sitting in the cozy comfort of my new wards. It was a good thing Jeremy planned to be out this evening, but what would happen going forward? I would need to explain this, explain *us*... except I didn't know enough now. Was he villain, or pawn?

I needed more time.

Jeremy? I sent him.

Yes, my love? he answered after about a half-minute.

I took a deep breath. *Could you, perhaps, stay at your own house tonight, when you're done with what you're doing? I need to think about the contract, and all its issues, and it will be easier if I could have the space to do that thinking alone.*

A longer pause this time. Then: *Of course, my love. Whatever you need.*

I'll be in touch—very soon, I promised.

I shall await your call. He broke the connection.

I exhaled, relieved.

And then I decided that maybe another half-bowl of stew wouldn't go amiss.

"What in the Blessed Mother's name are these?" Niad asked as she strode in through the front door, sniffing audibly as she looked around herself. As if wards were visible.

I took Rosemary from her arms. "Come sit down, Niad. And thanks for watching her."

"Any time." She followed me into the front parlor, where I stretched out on the small sofa and got the baby started nursing. Niad took a seat in one of the elegant little chairs I'd found thrifting...with Logan, I suddenly knew.

Maybe someday my returned memories wouldn't ambush me like this. But this was not that day. I covered my emotions by looking down, letting my hair fall over my face as I pretended to adjust the baby and my blouse, and when had my hair unbraided itself? During the spellwork? I hadn't even realized until just now.

Once I had myself under control, I looked back up at Niad.

"You didn't answer my question," she said. "What's with the weird new wards? Your old ones were perfectly fine."

"No, they weren't," I told her evenly. The time for secrets was ending—I knew this, knew it all the way down. "Jeremy and I built those wards together, and I am not at all convinced that he has been looking out for my best interests. He is not welcome in this house—at least not until I know what he's really up to."

Niad's mouth fell open in shock. She stared at me, her strong blue eyes wide. "Why...you..." But whatever spell had emanated from me, covering everyone who came into contact with me and blurring their own memories, had fallen from her as well. Her eyes narrowed. "He's Gregorio Andromedus's son, and Gregorio has been responsible for quite a bit of what's been troubling us all. Hasn't he?"

I nodded, still feeling hesitant about talking to her, and wondering how much she knew from Leonora versus how much she had figured out herself. I could trust Niad with my life—we were blood-sworn coven sisters, after all—but I also knew that she had never liked me. Coven membership invitations are the sole purview of the coven mother, but it is customary for all the house sisters to be consulted, and their preferences to be taken into account. I did not know any of the details which had led to my own invitation twenty-five years ago, but I would bet all the rent I'd ever earned from this house that Niad had argued against my admission.

I could trust her to reach out a hand to save me if I was falling off a cliff, but the jury was out on whether she'd have been the one to push me over it in the first place.

"He has," I told her, "though I do not know the full extent of his actions, or why he's doing these things." At my breast, Rosemary started sucking harder; if there was air in there, she'd be down to that by now. I shifted her to the other side.

"Is your gay boyfriend working on this with you? Is that what you were discussing in your little love-nest in the magical garden?"

"Ha, ha," I said. "Yes, which is why he's gone into hiding. But he was supposed to check in with me, and I haven't heard from him all day, and it's got me worried. For that, and, well, a lot of reasons, I figured new wards were in order."

She nodded slowly. "Makes sense."

"I just wish I knew where he was, and that he was safe."

Niad frowned and looked down at her hands for a moment; I could sense that she was sending an aetheric message. After a minute she looked back up at me. "He is not answering me either; if he were anywhere in range, he should respond."

Oh, how typical of Niad: unable to believe that anyone would ignore her summons.

Just then, Leonora's voice filled my head—and, judging by the look on Niad's face, hers too. *Daughters, I am returned. We must all meet at once.*

She didn't say where, and I had a moment of panic, not wanting to leave my wards. Then inspiration hit.

Yes, of course, I sent to Leonora, letting Niad in on the channel to hear. *It would be my great pleasure to invite the entire coven to my house, for the Circle and any other discussion.* My mind raced. *And dinner—refreshments—whatever anyone wants.*

That is...an unexpected notion, Leonora said.

I think it's a good idea, Niad sent, before Leonora could elaborate. *Bring everyone here. The sooner, the better.*

"Thanks," I said, wondering if my coven sister would keep being so nice when I told her the *rest* of what I had to tell her...after the current crisis was under control, anyway.

"Don't thank me till she actually agrees," Niad said, with a rueful smile.

Five minutes later, we both got word from Leonora: *We accept Calendula Isadora's invitation to gather at her home, and we will indeed require sustenance. We have a number of hungry witches here who should have supped hours ago.*

I gave a relieved smile. *We will have a banquet ready as quickly as possible.*

"Do you want me to just grab food from the nearest restaurant?" Niad asked, already clearly casting her vision around for suitable places.

"No—let's see what Petrana can do." Rosemary had finished her own supper by now, so I handed her to my coven sister, buttoned up, and hurried back to the kitchen.

My golem was already standing over the stove, where the pot of beef stew with dumplings she'd prepared earlier was full and bubbling as ever. The pot itself even seemed larger. "I hear we're having company?" she said to me.

"Yeah, I...didn't I already eat like five bowls of that?" I asked her.

"There will be plenty for everyone," Petrana said, placidly. "Which tableware would you like to use?"

— CHAPTER THIRTEEN —

Thirty minutes later, my entire coven was gathered around my dining room table. It was a little small for thirteen, but we made it work. Leonora had also questioned me about the new wards immediately. She seemed to have accepted my explanation—and then she wouldn't tell me a thing about what she'd been up to all day, what she'd found out. "I can't find Dr. Fallon," I'd told her. "Do you know where he is?"

"We will discuss that all at the meeting," she'd said. "I am not repeating myself twelve times."

"I think I'm going to try to build a golem," Sirianna said now, scraping her bowl clean and giving a little giggle. As if everyone didn't know she was joking. "This is better than anything I've ever cooked."

"It is not," I told her, almost automatically. At my feet, Elnor nudged me before settling back down again. At least we weren't dealing with thirteen restless cats anymore—my sisters' familiars had all had to inspect my house most carefully when they arrived.

Leonora, at the head of the table, cleared her throat and set her spoon down. All small talk ceased at once as we turned our attention to our coven mother.

"Calendula, we thank you for the delicious dinner, and for the invitation to your gracious home." She laid a little extra emphasis on that last bit, and I glanced down at the table. Yes, Leonora had been invited here before—there was that fateful dinner party when I first moved in—as had a few of my other sisters, but this was the first time many of them had even seen the place.

Before I could respond, or even wonder what she would want me to say, Leonora went on. "But now we have important business before us." She looked around the table, making sure we were all attending her carefully. Of course we were. Apparently satisfied, she nodded. "It is unfortunate indeed that the oldest and most esteemed member of our warlock community has taken it upon himself to step outside some of the boundaries of ethical, collaborative behavior, and indeed has reinforced this overreach by attempting to conceal his acts by laying a spell upon us all. We are grateful to Dr. Fallon for his efforts to free us all from this spell."

"Have you heard from him?" I broke in. "Sebastian, I mean?"

Leonora looked unruffled—by either the idea, or by my interruption. "I have not. He told you that he was going somewhere safe, Calendula, did he not?"

I nodded.

"The other coven mothers and I believe this to be the case." She picked up her wine glass and took a sip. "It is our opinion that he will re-emerge when measures have been taken to confront Dr. Andromedus with the inappropriateness of his behavior."

"Wait," I said, feeling uneasy. "You are going to confront Gregorio?" I mean, I knew we had to do this, but the very notion scared me.

"We have sent word out calling for a general meeting of all the Bay Area coven mothers," she said, leaning back in her chair. "We will gather tomorrow at sundown, to discuss whether Dr. Andromedus has perhaps already begun his transition to the Beyond, without being entirely aware of it." She gave a little "tut" sound under her breath, as if she was discussing a silly old man who'd dribbled soup onto his tie. "It happens, sometimes, in the very elderly, particularly elderly warlocks who have been accustomed to enjoying great power. They can ignore the signs that tell them that they should move forward, and they attempt to cling to their place in this realm. Yet the body and the soul know where they belong; they will not be halted forever."

Partway down the table, Honor raised her ancient head and spoke. "Your words are wise and gentle, dear Mother." Then she returned her attention to her stew.

Niad piped up, "Mother, it would be helpful if we could at least speak to Sebastian Fallon. If Dr. Andromedus is indeed starting to lose his mind and drift apart, we could all be in real danger."

"We already *are* in real danger," I said. "Leonora: did you tell the other coven mothers exactly *what* Gregorio has been up to?" I said this as much for the benefit of my coven sisters as myself. A number of them turned and gave her puzzled glances.

"What has he done?" Maela asked her. "Besides spelling us?"

Leonora looked grim—no doubt she had wanted to conduct this meeting in her own way—but she nodded. "Dr. Andromedus has apparently been preying on members of witchkind, separating their souls from their bodies, stealing their essences for his own use."

A few gasps went around the table. Notably, though, some sisters did not look shocked.

"Furthermore," Leonora went on, "he has gone so far as to threaten a witch of our coven—Calendula Isadora."

"Threaten her how?" Liza asked.

Leonora glanced at me then, as if asking whether she should tell them this. I nodded. "Her daughter's sire was a human man. Dr. Andromedus ordered her to conceal this shocking information, under pain of grievous harm to them both."

More gasps, deeper this time. Ruth, next oldest after Honor, shook her head. "Nay, such a thing is not possible."

"And yet." Leonora gazed around the table.

"Dr. Andromedus is our oldest and most greatly esteemed warlock Elder," Ruth protested. "Calendula must be mistaken."

"I am afraid that the evidence suggests otherwise," Leonora told her gently. "And for all these reasons," she went on, addressing the table more generally, "we intend to call Gregorio Andromedus to account. We will require him to provide a full and true explanation for every one of his acts. In the process, we will assess his condition and capacity, and determine whether he should be encouraged to embark upon his journey to take his place in the Beyond."

This all felt a little weak to me. "That's all we can do?" I asked. "*Encourage* him to move to the Beyond?"

"If he's the villain you say he is," Niad said, "there's always the cautery."

The magic-removing procedure Jeremy and I performed on Flavius Winterheart...when we'd thought *he* was the villain. I shivered at the memory.

"That would take the accord of both the coven mothers and the Elders," Leonora said. "And as your elder sister Ruth has pointed out, Dr. Andromedus enjoys the most prominent position among their ranks."

"This is so wrong," I said. Though she had a point, much as it pained me to concede this. Gregorio certainly had all the Elders wrapped around his little finger—either cowed, or (perish the thought) in agreement with him. If we could get some of the Elders on our side... "Why don't I speak with my father?" I asked. "He's an Elder."

Leonora nodded. "Do please send him word, then, Calendula."

I cast my witch-sight over to my parents' house. They were both asleep. Should I wake him? No; nothing would be decided before the coven mothers met tomorrow. No need to disturb his rest. I crafted a message to leave in the æther for him. *Dad, please call me as soon as you wake up. I have something important I need to talk to you about.* "All right," I said, returning my attention to my surroundings.

"Good," Leonora said. "Now, midnight approaches: we must arrange ourselves for Circle."

—⟨●⟩—

It was not nearly as comfortable as the coven house's huge front parlor, but we did all fit reasonably well around my attic pentacle. Fortunately, I had enough salt on hand, though I would need to pick up some more after tonight.

The energy felt a bit different than usual too. Fresher, more vibrant, somehow. We were still in our light trances, and our cats still sat close giving us focus and strength, but it was as though everything was just a bit more charged.

Probably it was to do with the urgency, the pressing need for this Circle. Or maybe the fact that it wasn't a Tuesday night. I hoped Nementhe would be able to give us more helpful advice than usual.

Mostly, though, I relaxed into the ritual, as always. Leonora chanted; our voices echoed; the magic settled around us, binding us to one another, this plane, and the next.

In due time, Nementhe floated into our presence. *Daughters, this is an uncommon occurrence, and an unusual place.*

Hmm, already a bit more on point. That was encouraging.

"Yes, Ancestress," Leonora said. "We have a matter of some urgency to bring before you."

Yet I know what of you speak, and I have been expecting your call.

"That should save some time," I heard Niad mutter.

Before Leonora could say more, a second presence joined Nementhe. Elnor's fur stood on end, and I heard sharp intakes of breath from several of my sisters and growls from their cats.

Greetings, Daughter, and daughters of yours, came a new, and very unfamiliar, voice.

I strained to see the newcomer—but then she suddenly came into clear focus, looking very nearly real. She was a petite, dark-haired witch with sharp features. Her hair was arranged in a very old-fashioned updo, nearly as out of date as her suggestion of clothes.

Leonora gasped. "Mother...Mother *Perrine*? Is that really you?"

The new vision smiled at our coven mother. *Yes, Leonora Scanza, first daughter of my house. It gives me great pleasure to see you once more after so long.*

All around the Circle, my sisters shifted and fidgeted, confusion and curiosity overcoming our yielding to the magic of the trance. Was this...Leonora's coven mother? How many centuries had she been Beyond?

And why was she here now, coming to visit us? This was not the way the Beyond worked, not at all. Only the junior-most ascendant witches had duties to commune with our plane. More advanced Beyonders got to go about their own business, doing...Beyond things. Whatever those things were.

Leonora voiced my question—probably everyone's question. "Why are you here?"

The times are not what they were, Perrine said, *and the planes are not what they were.* She was still smiling, but her voice was grave. *Events are moving far faster than we anticipated, and dear Nementhe here is not yet capable of helping you as you need. So the others have chosen me to intercede.*

"Yes, Mother Perrine," Leonora said. "Please tell us anything you can." She sounded humbler than I'd ever heard her, and perhaps even a little frightened.

And if Leonora was frightened... I shivered again.

The boundaries have grown softer. More permeable. The ancient order is breaking down. Perrine paused, then slowly turned and looked at us all, around the Circle. Her gaze was fierce; it felt like I was being stared at by a raptor.

"What does this mean?" Leonora finally asked. "What has caused this softening?"

You are on the correct trail: you must seek to stop the warlock Gregorio Andromedus, she finally said. *But take care. Though he is diminished, he is still quite powerful. He may harm many more witches before he is stopped.*

"We do of course intend to be careful," Leonora said. "But we—"

My time is short, Perrine interrupted. *Since this is not the usual run of things, the realms are already beginning to relax into their more accustomed forms. So heed me carefully. The warlock Gregorio Andromedus has caused this chaos, though he knows it not. We believe his forbidden disruption of the flow of essence was intended for his own personal, selfish gain; but that matters not. Whether he intended to do harm to all the realms or stumbled into it accidentally, the result is the same: the old ways are no longer holding.*

I heard a quiet intake of breath beside me, but Leonora did not speak.

Perrine continued, *Still he takes ever more, as each swallow proves less efficacious than the one before; his appetite only grows. He may collapse all the boundaries if he is not stopped.*

We have sent you help, but we did not correctly predict the urgency of the timing, so that help is thus far limited. It is also possible that the warlock Gregorio Andromedus somehow learned of our efforts and began countermeasures of his own. No matter. You must act quickly—more quickly than is your wont. Believe the youngsters, even unto the youngest among you. Dispel secrets: it is in the hidden knowledges, the secrets and the shadows, that the likes of the warlock Gregorio Andromedus find their power, and do their harm.

That is all. I must leave you all now. Dear Daughter Leonora, it gives me great pleasure to behold your face once more. I wish you all well and look forward to communing again when you join us here in time.

She began to fade away. As she did, Nementhe, who had stood silently beside her the whole time, came into better focus.

"Mother Perrine, wait!" Leonora called out. "What does all that mean—dispel secrets—which ones, to whom?"

Perrine, however, was gone. Nementhe gazed at Leonora, and after a long moment, she said, *Any and all secrets are no longer serving us. On that we are all agreed.*

Then she too vanished.

Leonora tried again to call our ancestresses back, but they had gone. Even the energy of the Circle felt lessened, deflated somehow. After a minute, she broke the line of salt and sighed.

"I...have much to think on."

The youngest among you, Perrine had said. "Gracie," I blurted out.

"Excuse me?" Leonora looked at me.

"The secrets, how they're not serving us—our student Gracie: she's living with humans and has told them she's a witch." Around the Circle, I heard several gasps. I flushed, feeling a stab of guilt, but I overrode it. I would defend her fiercely if Leonora tried to punish her. "And they're *fine* with it," I went on. "They're not scared, or trying to kill her, or anything. That's the point." I looked around at my gathered sisters. "Gregorio—well, he threatened me, and my daughter, if I didn't preserve a whole bunch of secrets. That's his power over us all: that he's keeping us scared, and divided, and silent."

"I don't know," Niad practically drawled. "I'd say his power over us is the way he harvests our essence and sucks our souls out of our bodies." She gave me a sharp look. "Or our memories."

There was no point in arguing that Gregorio hadn't personally done that to me. It had certainly been done at his behest and for his benefit.

"Again," Leonora said, "I have much to think on, and shall be returning home for the evening. The hour grows late. We shall all talk in the morning." She turned to me. "Calendula Isadora, we thank you most kindly for your hospitality."

"You are all most welcome," I said, to her and to the rest of my sisters. It felt good, I realized, to have hosted a Circle here. To have melded, however briefly, my two homes.

Leonora rose to her feet, followed by the rest of us. A number of my sisters gave me hugs and thanked me for the delicious dinner, and we all started to make our way downstairs.

Your daughter wishes your attention, Petrana sent me.

I chuckled. *I imagine she does.*

In the entryway, I took possession of the hungry infant and glanced into the front parlor. "I'll be up for a while, if anyone wants to stay for a cup of tea—or a digestif," I told my sisters.

Niad said, "I'm not ready for bed yet. I will take you up on that, Callie."

"Me too," Sirianna said.

Pearl hung back too. "Got enough digestif for four?"

I smiled at her. "I have enough for thirteen," I said, to everyone. "But I do understand if you need to get home."

"Thank you, dear," Honor said as she tottered to the doorway. "I do need my rest." I caught the scent of lilacs and dust in her hair, and old-fashioned magic.

In a minute, the nine older witches had left. I turned to ask Petrana to bring us drinks when I felt a needle-sharp pain in my ankle.

Gasping, I looked down. Elnor had bitten me, harder than before. "Cat!" I exclaimed, but then saw where we were, and what was bothering her. "Did someone close this closet door?" I asked her.

"Oh, I did," Niad said, as she headed to the front parlor. "It looked untidy; I figured the golem must have left it ajar while it was cleaning or something."

I opened the door and turned to her. "No, Elnor wants it open. I don't know why, but she does, and that's enough for me."

Niad raised a perfect eyebrow and gave a practiced shrug. "If you say so."

"Do you have slivovitz?" Pearl asked, as she and Sirianna walked down the hall.

"If I don't, I can get some," I told her. "You're ready for the hard stuff, then?"

"After that Circle? Aren't you?" Pearl laughed and tossed her hair. In my arms, Rose reached out for it, but Pearl was past her before the baby could grab it.

"I most certainly am."

We talked and sipped while Rosemary nursed. My sisters wanted to know more about Gracie—where she was, who she was with—but I didn't want to betray her confidence any further than I already had. "I did meet a human friend of hers," I told them. "She seemed to be entirely comfortable with Grace's witchkind nature."

Niad shook her head. "Unreal."

Sirianna was looking pretty relaxed—perhaps it was the three shot glasses of slivovitz. "Of course Grace isn't the very youngest among us," she pointed out. "All of the other students are younger than her. Are we supposed to listen to them?"

Pearl set her own empty glass down and giggled. "Callie's *holding* the youngest among us."

Rosemary's mouth went lax as she fell asleep on my nipple.

I smiled down at her, then up at my sisters. "Well, if my baby gives us any advice, we'll all be sure and follow it."

Although, had she? Not in so many words, of course; but was I meant to more widely reveal her half-human nature? Only a few of us knew that right now—the coven, Sebastian. Gregorio, of course. If we were to stop holding secrets, this was a doozy of one.

I wanted to talk to Leonora about it, though. Surely spreading such news further could wait a few hours, till the morning anyway.

And perhaps a few hours of sleep would be in order. "Well, it's been—" I started, when we all felt something most strange.

"What in the name of the Blessed Mother was *that*?" Niad was on her feet, her gaze darting around the room, though I sensed that the disturbance had been...above us.

It had felt like the energetic equivalent of a truck smashing into the house; the wards were still quivering slightly as they tightened around us, nestling us safely within their bounds.

Then I felt it again, harder, and more pointed.

"Jeremy!" I said, as his voice came into my head: *Callie, what is this? I cannot enter my study—I cannot enter our house!*

Niad said, "Is he here?" All three of my sisters were now standing, staring at me.

"Yes, and I can't actually deal with this right now," I said, my anger rising. "I told him not to do this."

You agreed to stay at your own house tonight, Jeremy, I sent him. *I asked you very clearly to do so, and you promised that you would.*

Callie, this is absurd, he sent. *You asked me to leave* you *alone, and I intend to. But I need something I left in my own study, the one room in this house that you have given over to me. Or so I thought.* I could still feel his presence, just outside, on the sidewalk. He had apparently tried to slip in directly to his study, bypassing the front door entirely. Hoping I wouldn't notice.

Absurd or not, I need you to honor my wishes, I told him. *This is still my house.*

It was at that moment that a large grey tomcat strolled into the front parlor. Rosemary woke up and gave a delighted little shout, waving her plump arms in the air. Elnor, who had been curled up beside me snoring, practically flew off the couch and ran to—

"Willson?" I gasped.

The tom, tail held high and proud, walked up to Elnor. They touched noses, sniffed each other to their mutual satisfaction, and then Elnor licked the top of his head. He lowered his head and butted her gently, and then they scampered off to the kitchen together. They were followed closely by Grayson, Pearl's blue manx.

"Is that...Logan's cat?" Sirianna asked, her voice nearly breathless with wonder.

Callie, please let me in, Jeremy said. *What have you done to our wards?*

Jeremy, we'll talk tomorrow. I shut the channel, for all the good that would do; he could bombard me with messages if he wanted, whether I was receptive to them or not. But he was a polite and well-trained warlock. I felt him withdraw from the vicinity of the house. Good.

Well, not good; but I'd take it.

I got up, handed Rose to Sirianna, and ran back to the kitchen, where all three cats were puzzling over the fact that there were empty bowls on the floor. Bowls that should contain tuna, fresh tuna, a freshly opened can of tuna, or perhaps—in a pinch— canned cat food in the flavor of tuna. Because they were starving, absolutely *starving*, all of them.

"You're not starving," I muttered. Indeed, Willson was sleek and healthy, with bright eyes and clean fur. Looking at him, I felt a confusing tumble of emotions: relief that he was alive and well; grief that I could not say the same about his mistress. And through it all, deep confusion: where had he been, and why had he turned up here, now?

At least now I understood why Elnor wanted that closet door left open.

"Would you like me to feed them?" Petrana asked.

"Sure, just a little," I said. "Let him know he's welcome here, at least."

Once the cats were head-down over their bowls, I gazed at Willson for another long moment, just remembering. Just feeling the emotions the sight of him brought. Then I left the kitchen to go find my sisters in the front parlor.

"Everything sorted out?" Sirianna asked. She held Rosemary in her lap, nestled next to her familiar, Phileen. The baby was getting sleepy again; the cat had long since conked out.

I shrugged. "I guess? I have no idea where he came from, though."

"Strange," Pearl said. "Very strange."

"I just don't know what to make of it," I said.

Niad nodded, frowning. "Well, cats are certainly mysterious creatures." She gazed across the room where her jerk of a familiar, Fletcher, sat washing his whiskers. He treated everyone with equal disdain: us, his own witch, everyone else's cat—it didn't matter.

Sadly, though, I couldn't help but believe that he came by this attitude honestly. I had never seen Niad pet him or give him a treat or say a kind word to him. Even so, I had to agree with her assessment. "Yeah. Mysterious. I'm really glad he's okay."

"Oh, me too," Sirianna said warmly, and Pearl nodded.

After a short silence, Niad asked, "And did you sort it out with Jeremy?"

I sighed. "For now? I guess? I told him we'd talk tomorrow."

"What did he want?"

"He said he'd left something in his study, something he needed." I shrugged. "I mean, that's probably true; but it's also not a very compelling reason to try to sneak in when I've specifically asked him not to."

Niad frowned. "We need to know how much he knows of what his father has been up to."

"Indeed we do," I said.

In Sirianna's lap, Rosemary had now conked out again, and was drooling on Phileen. Siri herself stifled a yawn.

"Time to go?" I asked her.

"Sorry!" she said, smiling. "But, yeah, maybe. Unless you want us to stay?"

She was always just so sweet. "No, we should all try and get some rest," I told her. "I have the feeling we have more *interesting times* in store for us."

Pearl said, "I expect so."

Siri got up and handed me the baby. "Rest well."

"You too. All of you."

I saw them and their cats to the door and let them out through the wards. When I turned around after they were gone, thinking I might just go lie down for a bit, a calico cat poked her nose out of the closet door, looked around, and walked into the hallway.

"Whose familiar is that?" Petrana asked, from the kitchen doorway.

I stared. For a moment I thought it was Phileen, somehow missed in their departure, but this one was much smaller, and she had a lot more orange on her. "I've never seen this cat before in my life."

Elnor and Willson had already approached the newcomer, tails raised, noses busy. All three cats went through their ritual greeting, seeming delighted with one another. As if they were old friends.

"Cat, I have never wished more fervently that you could talk," I said to Elnor, as I reached down and gave the calico a tentative pet on the head. Elnor looked up at me, clearly pleased with herself. I shook my head and turned back to Petrana. "I have no idea what's going on here, but Elnor obviously does."

Rosemary, no longer sleepy, started making her lip-smacking sounds and grabbing for my blouse.

"I can feed the newcomer if you want to see to her," Petrana said.

"All we do around here is serve food," I grumbled, getting settled in the second parlor and letting Rose at my breasts for the seventeenth time today. Whatever day this was. I leaned my head against the back of the sofa and closed my eyes as she nursed. If she could just be the tiniest bit more gentle, I might be able to catch a quick nap...

By the time I'd gotten Rosemary nursed, and managed to doze off several times before being nibbled awake again, two more cats had arrived. Elnor nipped at my heels again as I walked past the closet door on my way to the bathroom, as if I somehow hadn't yet gotten the message that it should be left open. "You-all can travel through ley space and walk through walls, and you expect me to believe that a simple closet door can hold you back?" I said to her, but I left it ajar.

I should install a cat door on it.

The two new cats were also witch's cats; one a wiry marmalade young female, the other a female tuxedo who looked so much like Elnor, I wondered if they were littermates. Elnor greeted them all equally happily, and Petrana just kept opening cans of tuna. "If you have all this under control here, I'm going to bed for a few hours."

"Of course, Mistress Callie."

"Maybe tomorrow I can take them all to the cattery," I said to Rosemary, as we lay in bed. "I don't need a half a dozen cats; maybe Sapphire knows who they belong—"

But of course. They didn't belong to anyone, did they? I really *was* tired, I realized. The first stray cat to arrive had been Willson, whose mistress—or her body, at least—lay under the library building at UC Berkeley...along with dozens of other soulless witches. Suspended, not living, not dead; and therefore, unable to either care for their familiars, or release them from their bonds.

These cats...who had been taking care of them? Who had been feeding them, keeping them sleek and healthy? Because despite what they all insisted, these were *not* starving strays.

Witch cats did have internal resources and intelligence that normal cats did not. But still.

Elnor jumped up on the bed at my feet and sat down, licking her whiskers. The rest of the cats followed, bathing and grooming themselves and each other as they got comfortable for sleep. Barely leaving any room for me, much less a baby.

I sighed and reached down to scritch Elnor. "Sleep well, everyone," I said, as the morning light filled my bedroom.

— CHAPTER FOURTEEN —

I woke up a few hours later. Jeremy had left me a message in the æther, triggered to alert me when I woke.

Calendula, I do not understand why you have broken our wards and barred me from our home. My father informs me that your coven has been meeting there and is preparing to challenge him about his business— about which they can know nothing, as they are not scientists, and certainly not Elders. I am seriously reconsidering our proposed contract. Please contact me immediately so that we can clear this up.

I shook my head, feeling a jumble of emotions—defensiveness, regret, anger, sorrow. "So he's threatening me now?" I said to Rosemary, as she took her mid-morning nourishment.

Rose bit down on my nipple, just a little too hard.

"You too?" I said, easing her off and shifting her to the other breast. "Everyone in this house bites me."

She settled in at the new source of milk and began suckling happily.

What should I tell him?

"No more secrets," I said aloud. Mother Perrine was right. Gregorio's only protection all this time had been in silence, in fear, in controlling information—and ultimately, in messing with my mind, and the minds of many others. What if information ran freely?

What if everyone knew all the secrets?

I am sorry you are angry, I sent Jeremy. *How much do you understand of your father's "business"? Do you know what he has really been up to?*

He took a minute to answer. *Good morning, Calendula. I may not be a scientist myself, but I understand enough to know that my father is working hard to serve and protect witchkind. This is clearly a power struggle between the covens and the Elders, and it pains me to learn that you have been taken in by more senior witches and drawn into their battle. It pains my father, too; he worked closely with you for many years, teaching you everything you know about biological research and the particulars of our magical systems. He thought you were more intelligent than this.*

I thought, *Whoa.* Now that was a loaded message. I bit my lip as I thought about it. He sounded like he believed what he was saying—as I would have, as I *did*, before I learned what I knew now.

Gregorio was almost certainly lying to Jeremy. In a way, that actually made me feel better. It meant I'd been sharing my bed, my life, with someone who was basically honest, if badly misinformed. I didn't want Jeremy to be in on his father's crimes.

I did actually care for the warlock. Maybe even loved him.

I finally settled on, *Jeremy, your father is not being honest with you. I am so sorry to have to tell you this, but it's true. Ask him to show you his research: specifically, ask him to show you what he is doing in the basement of the library in Berkeley. Have him explain to you exactly what that project is for, and how it is benefiting not only its participants but all of witchkind.*

I don't know what you're talking about, he replied.

That's what I'm saying, I told him. *Ask him those things, and then come tell me what his answer is. Then we can talk.*

I just told you I am not a researcher, he nearly snapped. *I will not understand the science. Stop being coy; just explain yourself.*

I sighed. *You will not believe me. You need to see. Just ask him.*

Fine. I will do that. I will speak to my father. Then he cut the connection with the energetic equivalent of a slammed door.

I blinked back a few tears as I sat in my rocking chair nursing my baby. Oh, Blessed Mother. I actually felt sorry for Jeremy, even though he was being an ass right now. But I understood. He was so in awe of his father, wanted so badly to please him.

What would he do when he learned the truth?

—◦●◦—

Petrana served us a delicious lunch—brunch, whatever—at the kitchen table. And by "us" I mean me and what was now eight cats. Or maybe nine? I was starting to lose track.

"Why are you all here?" I asked them. Then I turned to Elnor. "No, seriously, cat: you brought these beasties here for a reason. What do you want me to do?"

She blinked up at me.

"They are still bound to their witches," I went on, musing, "so they're trapped, as much as the witches are." At least the cats could move around in the world.

In fact, several of them did just that, jumping up on the table in an egregious display of bad behavior. Elnor had never in her life—

Elnor jumped on the table and swatted at the tuxedo-cat that was her twin. Tuxedo and the other two cats on the table jumped down, followed by Elnor.

"Thanks, kitten," I said to my familiar. "The manners of some cats!" Did other witches let their cats on the table? I really should call the cattery. They, at least, were set up to house dozens and dozens of the little furry terrorists at once.

Maybe the terrorists would consent to live there until we figured out why they were here and what we were supposed to do about it.

Elnor kept them on the floor long enough for me to finish my meal. She even seemed to be enjoying herself. Was she lonely, being an only cat? She'd been demonstrably delighted when Willson had shown up, and she always enjoyed playing with my sisters' familiars. But no witch I knew kept more than one familiar.

That was one of the benefits of living in covens: our cats got to live in company. Most witch cats were highly social, much more so than normal cats. It was part of what made them good familiars.

I was about to call to Sapphire at the cattery when a well-known, and deeply unsettling, voice filled my head. *Calendula Isadora.*

I swallowed my sudden rush of spit and took a deep breath. *Gregorio Andromedus.*

I know that you have recalled our conversation of some months ago, when I explained a number of situations to you, and made clear the ways in which you were to conduct yourself, he sent.

My heart pounded with fear, but I held to my resolve. No more secrets.

Yes, Gregorio, I do remember that conversation, despite the efforts of your flunkeys in the Old Country to burn it out of my mind.

Then I find myself at something of a loss to understand your current behavior.

I shivered, wishing for the strength of my coven around me. Last night, in Circle, this had all felt...more doable. Clearer. I reached down to pet Elnor, seeking the comfort of her sympathetic magic and the softness of her fur. Understanding, she sat at my feet, and began purring vigorously.

When it was just a question of the parentage of my baby, I sent to Gregorio, *then maybe I could see keeping a secret, if the truth would disturb the safety and balance of witchkind. But what you're doing—it goes far, far beyond my own little personal mystery. Gregorio Andromedus, you are preying on witchkind, stealing essences and harvesting souls, and harming us all. I cannot keep that quiet.*

There was a pause. *I had also been under the impression that you cared for my son, as he cares for you,* Gregorio finally said. *I do not believe he will want to bind himself to you if you continue on this course of action.*

Uh, nope. *I'm sorry I hurt his feelings, and I do care for him. But that is not the issue here. You're lying to him, and you're harming all of witchkind, particularly and generally. I cannot cover that up any longer, and I have told all to Leonora and our coven—and she has spread the word to other covens. You can't control this anymore. You will be called to answer for your crimes.*

He sent a chuckle along the ætheric channel. *Is that so, young Calendula Isadora? Not even a half-century on this plane, and you imagine that you can accuse me of "crimes"? And presume that I will answer you?*

As I've just told you, I am not the only one, by a long shot, who is aware of this, I said. *You won't be answering to me, but to the community of witchkind. The time for secrets is over.*

It pains me greatly, he answered, *that you should speak to me with such disrespect. After all I have taught you, over so many years, and with the great respect and affection I have for your mother and your father.*

I felt a sudden stab of fear, low and sick in my belly; I only now remembered the message I'd sent to Dad last night. He hadn't answered me. *This has nothing to do with my parents,* I sent, trying to project confidence. Trying to hide my unease. *You leave them alone.*

It is so charming that you imagine you may order me about.

Then he closed the channel.

I took a minute or two to let my racing heart settle. Elnor pushed into my leg, as if trying to head-butt comfort directly into me. "Whew," I finally said. "That was..."

No need to finish the thought.

Dad? I sent, into the æther. *Did you get my message last night?*

No response.

Mom? I tried. She didn't answer either. I sent my vision over to their house, but it was empty. Clean, dark, closed. No signs of bad energy or struggles, at least not that I could detect from here.

Should I go over there, check on them?

They did travel, periodically, but they usually let me know beforehand. (*Had* they let me know? Had I just forgotten, in all the drama and excitement? I struggled to remember. I just wasn't sure.)

Mom, please give me a call when you get a chance, I sent. *I need to ask you something. It's kind of urgent.*

I leaned back and pushed my empty plate away, thinking. Around me, a roomful of cats groomed themselves, sniffed corners, went about cat business. "Where are my parents?" I asked them. "For that matter, where's Sebastian?"

Down the hall, I could hear the front door opening. It was Petrana; she walked into the kitchen carrying a shopping bag. I hadn't even noticed her leave; I was too caught up in my conversation with Gregorio.

"Where were you?" I asked her.

She began unloading cans from the bag and arranging them on the counter. "I went to the bodega on the corner. The cats are hungry."

I blinked, looking at her more closely. She appeared almost normal. "Did you...did you pull a glamour by yourself?"

She shrugged. "It is not difficult."

The cats wended around her feet, miaowing insistently. Were there more of them now? It was hard to count them when they never stopped moving.

Petrana opened six or seven cans and portioned food out onto a stack of little plates, setting them on the floor with endless patience, even as the cats were bumping her arm and almost tripping her in their eagerness to get to the food.

It suddenly all felt like too much, and my kitchen was just too full of cats scarfing down smelly canned food to be comfortable anymore. And I needed a shower. "When you're finished there, can you watch the baby for a bit?" I asked Petrana.

"Of course, Mistress Callie." She set down a final plate and came to take Rosemary from me. Now that they were standing still, heads down and tails up, I could see that there were at least a dozen cats in here.

Sapphire? I called.

Hello, Callie, she answered. *What can I do for you?*

I've got a...cat situation here. I explained briefly as much as I understood. *Do you have room for them?*

I do. As they are bound elsewhere, they will be under no obligation to remain here. But they are welcome to rest here if they like.

I'll see what I can do, I told her. After my shower. *Thank you.*

Shaking my head, I headed upstairs, passing the closet door, still ajar. I peered inside, but it was as blank and empty as ever. No detectible portals. Though it did smell a bit like cat.

I took a long shower, feeling like I had to scrub extra carefully to get the oily, creepy Gregorio-threats off my skin. By the time I was clean and dressed, I could sense something different in the house—different energy. It was...quieter, I thought.

Downstairs, I found only Petrana and Rosemary in the kitchen. "Where are all the cats?" I asked.

"They left," my golem said.

"Left?" I echoed, dumbly. "Did they go to the cattery?"

Petrana looked at me. At least she'd dropped the glamour; she looked like herself again. "I don't know. Once they finished their meals, they all sat down and washed their faces, and then they walked back into that closet and were gone."

"Elnor too?" I cast my senses around, looking for my familiar. "She can't just leave me like—"

Elnor strolled into the room, looking up at me as if to say, *What?*

"Where did all your friends go?" I asked her. I called to Sapphire. *Are the cats there?*

No one new has shown up, she told me. *Did they leave your house?*

They did. I shrugged. *Let me know if they turn up.*

I will.

I took Rosemary back from Petrana and sat at the table. On my lap, she was active and cheerful, yet clearly disappointed that my still-damp hair was tightly encased in a single braid down my back, well out of her reach. She wasn't hungry, for once, which was nice.

So I took the opportunity to call Leonora.

I have heard from Dr. Andromedus, I told her.

Oh?

I gave her a rundown of our conversation, including his vague yet disturbing mention of my parents. *And now I can't get hold of them, they're not at home.*

That is unsettling, she said. *Let me see what I can learn. I will call to you soon.*

I closed the channel and sighed, frustrated and worried.

What was Gregorio's game here? Did he mention my parents just to freak me out? To try and keep me in line, or to taunt me?

But no, that wasn't his style. Gregorio Andromedus liked to play the great and benevolent father of us all, teaching and mentoring and correcting gently, leading a student to figure out answers for themselves. All that. I just couldn't see him cackling with glee and rubbing his hands together as he tortured some recalcitrant victim. Even when Jeremy and I had performed the cautery on Flavius Winterheart, Gregorio had taken the stance of *More in sorrow than in anger.*

I snorted to remember it, how easily we'd fallen for it. But we'd never had reason to question the leader of our Elders before. He'd *been* the benevolent father, as far as any of us had known.

Then my mother's voice appeared in my head. *Callie? What's the matter? Leonora said you were worried about us.*

Mom! I sent back. *Where are you?*

At home, of course. What's wrong?

I sent my vision over: indeed, both Mom and Dad were there now, sitting in the parlor. Mom had a cup of tea by her side; Dad, a brandy, though he hadn't touched it.

Sorry, I sent. *I was just being*—then I stopped myself. The urge to not cause trouble sure did run deep—even in me. *I need to talk to you guys. Both of you. Can you come over?*

We cannot right now, I'm sorry, Mom said. *Lucas has a meeting downtown, and I have a commitment here. Perhaps tomorrow?*

Dad's meeting isn't with Gregorio, is it?

Mom sent a gentle laugh. *No, honey, it is not; some of the other Elders are wishing to discuss Dr. Andromedus, and some concerns that have been expressed about his conduct. He's leaving now. He says to tell you he got your message and will speak with you about it soon.*

If they're meeting about Gregorio, that's what I need to talk to Dad about!

He knows that, honey. Don't worry. He has to leave now.

I sighed. *Tell him to be careful, okay?*

I cast my vision over to their house again. Dad was getting up, leaving his brandy untouched. He leaned over and kissed Mom, then left the room.

Of course, dear, my mom sent me. *Now I must go and see to my luncheon. We'll talk later—love you.*

I love you too.

She closed the channel.

Stymied, I sat there a minute. Then I pulled out Logan's tarot cards.

I shuffled the deck in my lap, then held the cards loosely. If Mom were here watching me, she'd chide me for this. *"The traditional spreads are traditional for a reason."* But I liked to just let cards choose me. It felt more...personal this way, somehow.

If this kind of wild magic couldn't handle a little improvising, then what was it even good for?

I held the deck in my left hand, facing away, and walked my right hand over the tops of the cards. When I felt a ping of energy, I plucked the card that seemed to be calling to me.

The Lovers.

I laughed out loud, startling even myself. At the sink, Petrana turned and asked, "What is amusing, Mistress Callie?"

"Nothing," I said, "and everything. I'm getting a rather hilarious message from the universe." I looked at the picture on the card—just as beautiful and happy and sweet as you might expect. Sexy, too; the lovers were naked, Eve and Adam before the fall. Huh, there was even a snake in the apple tree behind her. Yet an angel floated above the scene, and all looked serene and safe.

Lovers. Jeremy and me? Raymond and me?

What in the world was serene and safe—or sexy—about my life right now?

I set the card on the table beside me and lifted the deck again. This time, I walked my hand the other direction, starting with the card farthest away from me and moving closer.

And I pulled the Three of Swords.

"Oh, for crying out loud," I muttered. Three swords, piercing a giant heart as it floats in a downpour. Heartbreak, sorrow, grief, loss… "Now you're just messing with me." I tossed the card on top of The Lovers and set the rest of the deck beside them.

Lovers. Three.

Of course, I only had two lovers—in fact, only one at a time. Well, except for at a certain pivotal moment.

So, *I* was the third? A love triangle?

Except I'd kicked Jeremy out, and I wasn't in contact with Raymond anymore. "Lovers zero," I whispered.

Raymond didn't know…well, anything. He didn't know the truth about me, about the world he lived in. He didn't know he had a daughter.

No more secrets.

Trust the youngest among you.

Gracie had told her human lover. Who seemed delighted by the fact.

What am I supposed to do here? I thought. I considered drawing more cards—either randomly or doing a more traditional spread—but then stopped myself, even as the resolve, the understanding, was growing inside me.

I knew what was next.

Upstairs, I dug around my dresser and closet, finally finding my cell phone in one of my fancier purses. Astonishingly, it still had a charge—seventeen percent. Low but adequate. I punched Raymond's number.

"Callie?" he said, after it had rung so long I was sure it was going to go to voice mail. He sounded very surprised. "What's up?"

"Raymond, um, hi, I'm so, so sorry I haven't been in touch in... well, forever."

"Yeah." He paused briefly. "Christine said you guys got lunch a while back."

"We did, and that was great. I really like her. I can't believe you kept me from her for so long."

He chuckled, a little warily. "I could tell you it was my evil plan all along, but..."

"Yeah." I took a breath. "Say, I need to, uh, tell you some things. Can you come over? Are you busy?"

"Not especially. Supposed to have band practice later, but...you know."

"Yeah."

"What's this about?"

I paused briefly. "I think I'd rather do this in person, if you can."

Now he sounded even more wary. "All right. I gotta do a quick thing first, but I can be there in an hour or so."

"Good. Thank you, Raymond."

"Yeah."

I went back downstairs and waited in the front parlor, restless, impatient. I couldn't really start anything else; he would be here too soon. Plenty of time to begin second-guessing myself, though. What was I thinking? How was I going to explain anything? What was taking him so long? What did "an hour or so" mean exactly?

After basically forever, I sensed Raymond's presence. I loosened the wards and met him at the front door, pulling his confused, sweet-smelling self into a strong hug. Blessed Mother, he felt good. I remembered everything now, and I still didn't love the fact that we weren't together anymore. Or even fully understand it.

No more secrets. Was I serious about this?

What did I have to lose? Truly, what?

Eventually I let him go and brought him inside. "Hey, I like what you've done with the place," he said as he looked around, peering into the front parlor. I had still been finding furniture to fill all these rooms the last time he was here.

"Thanks. It's been a project. Come sit down."

I led him into the second parlor, where he took an overstuffed chair and I sat on the couch. As soon as we were seated, Petrana appeared in the doorway, holding Rosemary. "Shall I bring refreshments?" she asked.

Raymond froze. "Who...is she...what..."

I looked at her, and back at him. She hadn't pulled her glamour on again. Although I was rather proud of the improvements I'd made to her appearance, she really didn't look all that natural. And her voice was a little uncanny-valley too.

I cleared my throat and tried to tell my heart to stop pounding so hard. "Raymond, this is Petrana. She's a golem, and I built her. And this is Rosemary..." My resolve faltered. "My baby." I got up and took Rose from Petrana. "Yes," I told the golem. "Drinks, I think, for now."

"Yes, Mistress Callie." She turned and left without even asking what kind of drinks, clearly understanding that Raymond needed a moment.

Or a bunch of moments.

I turned back to him.

Raymond shook his head, looking stunned and pale. "She's…a what? A Gollum?"

"It's *golem*, not Gollum. She's a creature made of mud, animated by my magic. Because I'm a witch." He looked at me blankly. "Do you remember when we first met, and I told you I'm a witch?"

"Uh, I guess so, maybe, but…"

"Well, it's true. And it's for real—not like your sister's Wiccan faith, but real magic. We're actually a separate, secret *species*. I'm not human. Not like you are."

His brow was furrowed. He was not understanding a word of this, not really. Because in his world, witches weren't real. I might as well have told him the moon was made of green cheese, and that we would later be sailing there in a paper boat.

"Right." He swallowed heavily. "So you're not human."

"No, I'm not."

"And the golem…also not human."

"True," I said, "but different not-human. Petrana isn't truly alive. I am." I gave him a helpless smile. "I mean, if that wasn't obvious already."

Petrana chose that moment to return, with two glasses of elderflower wine. She set them on the side table between us.

"That will be all, thank you," I told her.

She nodded and left the room.

"I…you've always seemed alive to me." He reached for his drink, with the desperation of a drowning man reaching for a life raft.

"Be careful with that, it's a bit strong," I warned him as he took a big sip.

He coughed and snorted, and set the glass down. "Wow. You drink that stuff?"

"Yes. Being a witch, my constitution is different than yours."

"I guess so." He shifted in his chair and glanced around the room. It seemed like he didn't know where to look. His hand tried to reach for the glass again, but then dropped back into his lap. "Callie, I don't...why are you telling me this stuff?"

Through this all, Rosemary sat on my lap, watching us raptly. Did she somehow know this was her father? She knew so much, even if she could tell me so little about it.

I cleared my throat. "I kept secrets from you the whole time we were together," I told Raymond, "and that was wrong. I've realized that I can't do that anymore. You don't have to do anything with this, but I—I can't lie to you anymore."

"But..." He looked at me helplessly. "A *witch*? A *golem*? What does all this even mean?" Was he trying to decide if I was crazy? *Don't be silly*, I told myself, *he's not trying to decide; he's convinced.* The next thing would be him calling the authorities to take my baby away, because I had obviously lost my mind. I needed to make him understand.

I needed to *show* him.

"Don't try and drink that wine," I told him. "Can I get you a beer instead?"

He blinked at the sudden change of subject. "Um, sure?"

I nodded at the table, where the wine glass vanished. In its place appeared an Abita Amber, glistening dewily. "Here, let me open it for you." The cap lifted off and clattered to the table. "Glass?" I brought one from the kitchen without moving a muscle, then watched with him as the bottle appeared to pour itself. "Drink up, but let me know soon if you want another. The bar I snagged that from only has one more." He stared at the glass; the head of foam was settling nicely. "They've got plenty of Anchor Steam, though."

Finally, he looked up at me, eyes filled with fear. "What the *fuck*, Callie?"

"This is what 'I'm a witch' means. I'm not like you. And magic is real."

He stared at me. "You...I..." His face was paler still. "What the *fuck!*"

"I'm sorry, and I didn't mean to scare you. I just didn't know how else to make you believe, to understand. That's what magic looks like." Now I *really* wished I'd asked Gracie—and Rachel—more questions. I reached out for Raymond's hand; he jerked back, then scrambled to his feet and took a few backward steps, still staring at me. I had the brief, slightly hysterical thought that this whole scene was going to be a popular rock song in a few months.

"I—I'm gonna get some air." He turned and dashed out of the house, slamming the door behind him. I heard his heavy boots thumping down the front steps.

"So that went well," I said to Rosemary, biting back tears. She gazed up at me. "No, I can't compel him," I told her, as though she had asked. "I should have known that was a dumb idea. We're not teenagers."

Fifteen minutes later, my doorbell rang.

When I opened the door, he said, "Show me that thing with the beer again."

— CHAPTER FIFTEEN —

The beer I'd filched had gone a little flat, and it wasn't all that cold anymore either. So I brought the second Abita from the bar, then waved my hand over the first beer, magically refreshing it. "I'll join you," I said, lifting the first glass.

He took his chair again. "Thanks." He definitely looked calmer, though he was still watching me warily. And there was something else, something behind his eyes. Resolve? Anger? Whatever it was, he was holding it back carefully. He picked up his beer and made short work of it.

When he set the empty glass down, I said, "Do you want an Anchor Steam? Or I can check another bar if you're set on Abita."

Raymond shook his head. "Why shouldn't I drink the wine?" · My glass of elderflower still sat on the table between us.

"It's witch wine. Much stronger than regular alcohol. Remember how much beer you watched me drink, the night we met? It takes a lot more to get us drunk."

He gave me a humorless smile. "Try me."

"Help yourself—it's not a challenge. I just don't think it's your thing."

He picked up the glass and sipped. This time, at least, he didn't cough and sputter, but it was clear he thought it was disgusting.

"Christine would like it." That hidden thing danced across his face, there and vanished again.

"She would?" She'd been drinking beer the first time I'd met her, and later we'd both had tea when we had lunch together.

"Yeah. I called her when I went out."

I raised an eyebrow. "Oh?"

"Is there a problem with me calling my sister?"

"No, wow, it's fine, really. I'm…trying to dispense with all the secrets, but you see how, er, challenging that is."

"I do." He glanced around. Working up his nerve? "Yeah, I could use another beer. Unless you got something stronger—but not so damn sweet." He motioned at the wine glass.

I sent a silent message to Petrana: *Can you find us a bottle of hard liquor, please? Something sippable?*

Of course, Mistress Callie. Two glasses?

Sure. I said to Raymond, "Petrana will be in here in a moment, brace yourself."

He nodded, still holding himself quite steady. I tried to tell myself that this was a good sign. He'd come back; he was listening. He was trying. He'd freaked out, but he'd done what he needed to do. Now he was doing the best he could.

Petrana walked in carrying a silver tray with a cut crystal bottle of amber liquid and two small glasses.

That's not Bulgarian frog brandy, is it? I asked her silently.

"Macallan eighteen year," she answered aloud. "I didn't want to take the whole bottle, but I can certainly fetch more if you require it. Would you like me to pour?"

I glanced quickly at Raymond. He was watching the golem, still so steady. "No, thank you, I'll take it from here."

Petrana nodded politely, set the tray on the table between us, and left the room.

I started to lean forward to pull out the glass stopper and pour him a dram, but Raymond said, "I got it." He poured himself a healthy splash of the scotch and glanced up at me. "You?"

"Not right now."

"Okay." He sipped and set the glass down. "Don't get the eighteen year that often."

I nodded and settled back on the couch. Rosemary was watching us both avidly. Raymond looked back at her for a long moment. "So," he started, but then stopped.

"So, you talked to Christine?" I prompted.

He took another generous sip before saying, "Yep."

When he didn't elaborate, I said, "What did she have to say?"

Raymond's eyes met mine. "She told me to ask you if I'm that baby's father."

I took in a startled breath. How perceptive Christine was. I'd been working up to telling him, I totally intended to, but I'd wanted to get past the first hurdle first. The *I'm a witch* hurdle. But here we were. "Yes, Raymond, you are."

If I'd thought his face was impassive before, it completely shut down now. He closed his eyes for a long moment. When he opened them again, he looked only at me, not Rosemary. "Okay. Thank you for telling me." He picked up his glass again and drained it. "And thanks for the Macallan."

He stood up in a fluid motion and turned toward the door.

"Wait, Raymond!" I started to get up too, but Rosemary started squirming in my arms. She opened her mouth and made a little squeal, waving her arms around.

Raymond paused in the entryway.

"Wait," I said again, softer this time. "Can we...talk about this?"

He narrowed his eyes at me. "Were you *ever* going to tell me?"

"I can explain—"

He snorted. "Sure. You do that. Explain it to yourself." He turned on his heel and stomped out of the house again.

Don't try to stop him, I told myself. Maybe he'd cool off again—maybe he'd call Christine again, and she'd tell him to at least listen to the whole story…

I brushed away tears once more as I sat back down with my baby.

Several hours later, I finally admitted to myself that he was not coming back.

Which was undoubtedly for the best. It might keep him safer—if Gregorio found out that the actual father of my baby was back in my life, he might try to harm him. Raymond was only human, so Gregorio couldn't steal his essence or his magic.

Humans could be hurt, and killed.

No, Raymond was better off far away from me.

But that didn't mean I had to like it.

I was in the kitchen working on dinner with Petrana when fourteen cats walked in. At least, I thought there were fourteen. It was as hard as ever to count such a mass of wiggly fur.

"Here they are," Petrana said, unnecessarily.

"You guys, seriously," I said to them as they prowled around, nosing at the empty food bowls.

Elnor was delighted to see them, and of course nobody could tell me what they'd been up to or where they'd been. Furthermore, they absolutely refused to be shunted off to the cattery. I could have hauled them there by hand, but I was finding myself more and more reluctant to step outside of my wards.

And if they don't want to be here, Sapphire reiterated, *I cannot make them stay.*

There was really nothing to do but to feed them.

Once they had licked their plates clean and seen to their own whiskers and faces, the cats began drifting out of the kitchen. I followed a small group of them, wondering if they'd go back to the closet and off on another of their mysterious errands. But no:

tonight, apparently, they intended to sleep in my house. They began settling on all the soft horizontal surfaces they could find—well, except for the Elnor-twin, who really, really, really wanted to sleep on the kitchen table.

"I can just wash off the table in the morning," Petrana said.

"Fine. I'll eat my dinner in the dining room." I was halfway tempted to set the golem in charge of keeping the cat off the kitchen table all night—it wasn't like Petrana would get tired, or bored of it, or anything—but then I reminded myself that this cat had lost her mistress, without even being able to communicate with her in the Beyond or choose to go with her. Her witch was almost certainly lying, soulless, in the basement in Berkeley, undead, unalive. So, yeah, tables could be cleaned.

I checked in once more with Leonora. She was aware of the Elders' meeting that my dad was at; in fact, she and her group of coven mothers had spoken with several Elders, which was what had prompted the meeting. Apparently, it was still going on, and was expected to run well into the night.

Will you return to the coven house this evening? she asked me.

Actually, if it's all right with you, I'd rather stay here with Rosemary behind my new wards, I told her.

I understand. Of course you may.

After we signed off, I steeled my resolve and called to Niad. *There is something I need to talk with you about,* I told her.

Oh? What is it?

I'd rather do this in person. Can you come here?

Well now I am intrigued, she sent. *Can it wait a few hours, or must I leave this spell half-cast?*

A few hours is fine.

It was approaching midnight when Niad called to me. *Let me in, please.*

I glanced outside. She stood on my front porch, alone; I released the wards as I walked down the hall to open the door.

Niad stepped inside. "Oh, Blessed Mother," she said, pulling the binding loose from her long blond hair and shaking out the tresses. "Those are powerful wards. How did you even build them?"

I started to brush off the question—what I'd done wasn't exactly approved-of magic, after all—and then yet again reminded myself of my new resolve. Never mind that it had gone so poorly with Raymond...and probably wasn't going to be much more fun with Niad, once we got to it. "I used a bunch of feminine energy, and...a little spilled-blood magic," I told her.

Niad's eyes widened as she stopped in the middle of the hallway and turned to me. "Your own blood?"

"Of course. Who else's?"

She looked at me for another long moment, then shook her head and flicked her fingers at her hair, which wound itself into a tight bun once more, at the back of her head. "I swear I will never understand you," she said softly, then turned and stepped into the second parlor, where she lowered herself elegantly down into a chair. "Do you still have some of that Czech brandy?"

"It was Polish, and yes, I have plenty."

She gave me a feral smile. "Good. I'll have some, thank you."

Petrana must have been standing in the hallway listening, because she stepped into the room at just that moment. It was impressive, how quietly she moved now. "Two glasses, Mistress Callie?"

"Sure."

After she left, Niad asked, "Where's the baby?"

"Dining room, in her bassinet. She fell asleep at dinnertime, and I don't want to disturb her if I don't have to."

"Good plan."

Petrana came back with our cordial glasses and a different crystal decanter. The whole thing felt so much like earlier today, it must have shown on my face.

"I suppose I am wondering why you called me here," Niad said. "Is it something to do with the fact that our most esteemed Elder is basically insane and secretly trying to kill us all?"

I snorted; not exactly laughing, but her dry wit could catch me off guard. "Yes, it is related to that." I lifted my glass of slivovitz in her general direction and then took a small sip. "What isn't, these days?"

She took a drink as well. "Cheers, I suppose. Long life and all that."

We drank in silence for a minute or two. Before she could ask again, I just made myself do it. "In the course of my research, I have...learned a few things about a few members of our community. One of those members being, well, you."

"Indeed." She was doing her best not to look impatient or fascinated, but I knew I had her attention.

"Yes. And, um, there's no gentle way to say this, but, you're half-human. Your father was a human man." The words felt unreal even as they came out of my mouth. I cringed and waited for her reaction.

She looked at me for a long moment. Then she reached out an elegant hand for her drink, took a slightly larger than usual sip, and set the glass back down. "And what makes you think that?" she finally asked.

"I could show you the assays—"

She was already shaking her head. "Please don't. I do not understand even the smallest bit of your biological research. Explain it in terms that have any chance of meaning something to me."

I tried, but every time I got anywhere near even the simplest laboratory terms, like *Petri dish*, she pretended bafflement. Was she just being stubborn?

"Why were you even looking for such a thing?" she finally asked.

"Because of Rosemary, and because of what Gregorio said to me all those months ago—that he knew of two more cases of witch-human hybrids. So I tested everyone I could get samples from."

Her gaze sharpened. "How did you get a *sample* from me?"

I felt my face flame. "The menstrual closet."

"Blessed Mother," she swore, and looked away.

Both our glasses were now empty; I refilled them and took a small sip. "I'm sorry," I finally said. "I didn't mean to violate your privacy, your autonomy. I just...I needed to understand. Our elders have been lying to us for so long—I needed to know the truth. All the truth." I took a breath. "And once I did, I figured that...others would want to know it too."

After a long pause, she gave the smallest nod. "Who else have you told about this?"

"About you? Nobody; I wanted to tell you first. It is your personal business. But as we keep hearing, holding this kind of stuff secret is the problem. If Gregorio can threaten us with this, threaten to reveal our ugly secrets, then he can control us. But it's *not* ugly, and if it's not a secret—then half his power is taken from him."

"Leaving just the half that he uses to suck souls out of bodies and harvest our essence?" she asked, sourly.

I stifled a sigh. "We're working on that part too, as you well know. We're all asking questions now—the coven mothers, even the Elders. His grip is faltering. If we all unite against him..."

I didn't need to finish the thought.

"Who is the other half-human?" she asked.

"I am respecting their privacy as well, for the same reason," I said. "I haven't told them yet. They will be able to decide if, and how, they want to share that information."

"'They'?" she asked. "It's not a witch?"

"I'm not going to say anything more about them."

She looked at me for another long moment. Then she said, very quietly, "Well, I did always wonder."

"You *did*?" I blurted.

"Not about specifics. Nothing absurd, impossible like this." She shook her head. "I know now that my mother...didn't tell me the truth about a lot of things. But even when I was small, I always knew that something was...off. Was other, was wrong. If that makes any sense."

"Yes. It does."

"She always seemed ashamed, but also angry," Niad went on, so very softly. As if she was talking more to herself than to me. "When I was a witchlet, I just thought she was ashamed that a warlock had lied to her and left her, that she'd decided to conceive with him and he hadn't held up his end of the bargain. Hadn't offered her a contract. But she never told me his name, never gave me any clue about who he was, how to find him. And once, just once, she let slip that I was not intentional." She gave a wry look, now watching my face. "Yes, it is clearly not only possible for a witch to accidentally get pregnant, but perhaps even more common than we have ever realized."

"Or maybe it's the human element."

"Humans are far more fertile than we are," she said slowly.

I smiled. "See? You do understand something about biology."

"Very funny." She drained her glass again and set it down. "Why is it that we can't tell a half-witch from a full witch?"

I had wondered this myself. "I don't know for sure, but it might be because we're not actually two different species. How can we tell witchkind from humans?"

She gave a soft snort. "Easy: we can sense their essence. Magical essence means witchkind; non-magical means human."

"So how do you tell how strong a witch is?"

To her credit, she got it immediately. "Ah. Of course. The difference in their essence, naturally." She narrowed her eyes. "So half-witch clearly doesn't mean diluted witch. Because I am far stronger than many of our sisters."

"You are, and I have every reason to believe my daughter is unusually powerful as well. And the third person too: quite strong."

A small crafty smile stole across her face. "Perhaps there's strength in hybridism."

"You're a regular scientist all of a sudden," I teased her. "Because that is certainly true in other species. Anyway, this is all a theory, but it rings true. Humans and witchkind: we're closer than we've always been led to believe."

"Interesting." She leaned back in her chair, thinking. "I believe I need to have a conversation with my mother."

Well, *that* would be interesting. "Do let me know how that—"

The figure of a cat in the doorway caught the corner of my eye. I looked up just as Willson walked into the room.

"Oh, here come the cats again," I said.

Elnor leapt down from the couch to join Willson, but he walked straight to me and miaowed forcefully.

"Don't let him tell you he's hungry, I fed him right before we left my house," came a male voice from the hall.

I gasped; Niad leapt to her feet with an angry shout.

Standing in the front parlor doorway was Flavius Winterheart. The young doctor who Gregorio had framed...and who Jeremy and I had punished. Slicing and burning every trace of his magic out of him, forever.

"Flavius...what are you—how are you..." I stammered, breathless, almost light-headed.

Niad stepped forward and put a firm hand on Flavius's upper arm. She forcefully led him into the room, nearly pushing him down to sit in the other overstuffed chair. Petrana, attracted by the commotion, hurried down the hall from the kitchen. I caught her eye and nodded, and sent, *I think we're okay but don't go far.* I heard

Rosemary stirring in her bassinet in the dining room, making little coos.

"How did you get in here, past the wards?" Niad asked Flavius.

Oh, good question, I thought.

"I guess they only work through mundane or ley space," the ex-warlock said. "Not mysterious portals run by cats." He struggled to keep his casual tone, but I could see the fear and pain in his eyes.

"Well, however it happened, you're here," Niad snapped, still standing over Flavius. "Why? Are you alone?"

"I—was sent, Niadine," he stammered. "And I am not alone—I came with a very insistent cat." He shivered. "Damned uncomfortable journey, I have to say."

"Willson helped you do that? Come through the portal, I mean?" I asked.

"Check and see if it's still open," Niad said. "Who knows what else might come through."

I got up and ran out to the hallway. I could hear Petrana in the dining room, checking on the baby; Rose's cooing was quieting down, and Petrana was murmuring to her. Then I checked the closet. It looked, and felt, exactly as it always did. "It seems fine," I said, walking back into the front parlor. "I mean, from what I can tell."

"Who's Willson?" Flavius asked.

"The cat who brought you here." I sat back on the couch next to the grey tom, who in his turn was now sitting placidly beside Elnor, flicking his fluffy tail. "Logandina Fleur's cat, who's been missing since she...left."

Flavius looked back at me, then at the cat again. "Oh. I wondered...I could tell he was a witch's cat, and I couldn't figure out why he wanted anything to do with me. Why he wasn't with his witch—why any of them weren't. But they wouldn't leave, and I...well, the company was nice."

"Any of them?" I echoed. "How many cats are we talking about?"

He nodded. "Lots. Dozens, maybe. They come and go."

I shook my head. "For how long?"

"Months, anyway. It started slow, with just this big fellow here." He shrugged, looking over at Willson. "I called him Max—he just looked like a Max. He slowly started bringing more strays who were not strays around, and I fed them too. It…grew from there."

"Well, thanks for feeding him—for feeding all of them," I said. "That was kind of you. But you didn't…ask around?"

"Around?"

I felt as uncomfortable as he looked. "I mean, you know, ask any witches."

He gave me a dour look. "I haven't seen any witches since that day. I hadn't seen any warlocks, either, until yesterday. But I don't really know how to talk to humans, so…"

It was terrible, truly terrible, what we'd done to this warlock…to this ex-warlock. Because Gregorio Andromedus had convinced us that we should. To cover up his own crimes.

"Wait, what warlock did you see yesterday?" Niad asked.

Flavius gave a half-laugh, but there was no mirth in it. "Oh, sorry, I'm doing this all backwards. But you keep asking me about the cats. So. Sebastian Fallon asked me to let you know that he's safely in hiding, and to please not worry about him, but he won't be able to answer any of your messages. Also, um," now he looked even more uneasy, "that he hopes you'll have a place where I can be safe for a while."

"You?" I asked, incredulous.

Niad shot me a look.

"Sorry," I added, to Flavius. "I just—I didn't know you were involved in anything of, um, what's been going on lately."

He shivered again, seeming to want to sink into his chair. "The way Sebastian explained it, there is no one who isn't involved. And

I...well, obviously, I am less able to defend myself than any of the rest of you."

I nodded. "Yes, well, of course. I can keep you safe—I mean, as safe as any of us can be."

"Thank you."

"So, Sebastian is okay, truly?" I asked. I just needed to hear it again. I hadn't wanted to admit how worried I'd been about my friend.

Flavius nodded, and even smiled a bit. "He is fine. Restless, and worried about you, but fine. He's sorry that he can't be here, but he...was warned that Dr. Andromedus would likely be targeting him first, for—well, for all his various misdeeds."

"Dr. Winterheart," Niad said sternly, bringing all the authority of her near-century of age to bear in her tone. Impressive, in a witch who kept her apparent age as thirty, and outrageously sexy to boot. "Hints and vagueness are serving none of us right now. The hour is late, and you clearly have something of substance to tell us. I would advise that you do so."

From down the hall, I could hear Rosemary waking up once more. It sounded more definitive this time.

Flavius must have heard her too, but Niad had him pinned with her gaze. He swallowed, looking even more fearful than before. Apparently deciding that Niad was scarier than whatever news he had to tell us, he said, "Well, er, Sebastian has been told that the time for secrets is at an end, but also that revealing them is unbelievably dangerous—that it puts us all at more risk than ever. If we survive this passage, we will find ourselves in a new world of unprecedented freedoms and, um, joyfulness."

Niad narrowed her eyes as I leaned forward to ask, "Who exactly has given him this message?"

Rosemary's call of delight echoed down the hall as Flavius said, "The...the Great Father."

— CHAPTER SIXTEEN —

What?" Niad snapped. "That's impossible."

My mouth hung open. When I regained control of it, I said, "But the Great Father never comes to this plane; he never speaks to you guys." Of course, the Blessed Mother never spoke directly to us witches either, but it was understood that our ancestresses from the Beyond served as conduits between us. Warlocks didn't communicate beyond this plane at all.

"That's what I was always taught too," Flavius said. "He certainly has never spoken to me."

"Should we do something about that child?" Niad asked.

Rosemary had been chattering loudly, clearly wishing to join us in here. "I'll get her," I said.

At the doorway, I met Petrana, obviously coming to find me. "Mistress Callie, I am sorry, but I could not keep her occupied. I think she might be hungry."

Oh, that would be different, I thought with a smile. "Thank you, Petrana, that's fine."

When I returned with the baby, Flavius asked me, "Was that... the golem?"

"Yes," I said, getting Rose and myself situated on the couch. She latched onto my nipple as enthusiastically as usual, keeping her eyes open and darting about, following the conversation.

"Fascinating," Flavius said. "I'd heard about it, but hadn't gotten to see it."

"She's been very useful," I told him. "In fact, she does most of the housekeeping around here. Are you hungry or thirsty?" I should have asked earlier, but, well, I hadn't been expecting him—or anyone—to pop in like this.

"No, thank you, I'm fine." He shook his head vigorously.

Niad leaned forward. "This is all fascinating I'm sure, but I would like to hear more about this supposed 'message' from the Great Father. What danger are we in precisely, and what are we supposed to be doing about it?"

Flavius shrank into his chair once more; Rosemary rolled her eyes toward my sister and stopped nursing. "That was pretty much it—that we have to stop having secrets, but that it's dangerous to tell them."

"Foolish," she muttered. Then, more sharply, she said, "Do you think Dr. Fallon is all right—I mean, in the head? Was this a hallucination, or some sort of madness on his part?"

"What? No, he's himself—"

"But you did not experience any communication from the Great Father yourself," she said. "Did this happen when you were together?"

Flavius shook his head. "No, I was...well, not in the room. But I believe it happened. I do."

"'No more secrets' is the message we have received from the Beyond as well," I said, as much to Niad as to Flavius.

My coven sister nodded and leaned back. "I am just...trying to understand this all," she said softly. "*All* of it," she added, giving me a significant glance.

I noticed she didn't reveal her own secret. No surprise there; she was still processing it, and we were all trying to make sense of this new world we'd found ourselves tumbled into.

"Clearly the danger is from Gregorio," I said, "and whoever might be allied with him—both here and in the Old Country. When I tried to uncover the truths of what he was up to, I had a number of my memories stolen, removed from my brain," I told Flavius.

"Yes, Sebastian told me what happened."

"He's been with you since he went into hiding?" I asked.

"Some of the time," Flavius said vaguely. "And he's not at my home now, so don't go looking for him there."

"I don't even know where you live," I said.

"I don't either," Niad said, "and while I know you're not hungry, Dr. Winterheart, I am. Callie, assuming we're not in immediate danger, can your golem fix us something to nibble on?"

———⊂●⊃———

We settled in the dining room. Petrana had set a lavish table with delicious munchies and a range of drinks. As we ate, Flavius told us the rest of his story.

The last months had been hard for him, which was not the least bit surprising. He had been an intelligent young warlock with a deep and abiding interest in the biological sciences, thrilled to be studying under the eminent Gregorio Andromedus. (Ah, I knew the pain of that one.) He had been even further engaged by the mysterious essence-stealing illness that had swept through our community last year, and had worked closely with Gregorio, and with Sebastian Fallon, to try to find the cause—and a cure. The research had gone very well, and he believed he had found the answer, and quickly. Dr. Andromedus was so proud of him, so full of praise! He had insisted that Dr. Winterheart administer the first vial of treatment personally—and then, without warning, had arrested him for attempting to harm their patients, for causing the illness in the first place. Then came the trial and the swift, brutal punishment, and suddenly, Flavius Winterheart was stripped of his magic and sent out of the only community he had ever known.

"They didn't even bother to provide me with a legal identity, or any money," he said, shaking his head. "I was just essentially dumped downtown and told, 'You're clever, figure something out.'"

"What did you do?" I asked.

He half-snorted, a laugh that contained no humor. "What was I supposed to do? I went for that old standby: amnesia. I presented myself at SF General and said I couldn't remember my name or anything about myself, and I needed help. I knew they would have to take me there—it's the public hospital, after all—so even though they didn't know what to do with me, they tried. I don't know what they found when they looked at my blood, but they submitted my fingerprints to national law enforcement databases." His smile grew even more rueful. "They could find no record of my existence at all. At least they found no evidence that I'd committed any crimes, so they didn't send me off to jail."

"You didn't commit any crimes," I said. "We know that now."

"Yeah, Sebastian told me that too. Better late than never, eh?"

I shook my head. "I'm really so sorry. Which I know doesn't mean anything, but it's still true."

He gave me a brave, sad smile. "Well, it's nice to hear, I suppose." His plate of nibbles sat nearly untouched in front of him, though he'd gone through two cups of greenmire tea and a healthy shot of the scotch that was still here from Raymond's visit. "Oh, one more thing, Callie, I almost forgot: Sebastian said that you should build strong new wards, and you and the baby should not leave the house. Not until it's safe."

"And when will that be, exactly?" I asked, but of course no one could answer. "Well, I have built new wards," I went on. Though

Flavius couldn't feel them, wouldn't know anything about their strength. Another pang of remorse hit me. "And I've already resolved not to leave the house, at least not till I know more."

"Good," he said, then closed his eyes for a moment. "I think that's all for now; my mind is completely exhausted. I haven't slept in..." He sighed. "I don't know. A day or more."

"It is late," I agreed. "We should probably all turn in." A few hours of sleep wouldn't do me any harm.

Niad glided to her feet. "I will take my leave as well. Thank you for the information," she said.

Flavius nodded, but I knew she was talking to me.

"Petrana," I called out to the kitchen as Niad slipped out, "can you take Dr. Winterheart to the guest bedroom?"

"Yes, Mistress Callie," she said.

Once I got in bed, though, I could not sleep. Too much energy, too much uncertainty. Eventually, I got up, leaving Elnor watching the sleeping Rosemary, and headed upstairs to my attic laboratory.

I had told Niad what I knew about her; the next person I needed to talk to was Jeremy. But I wasn't ready to do that yet. Not until I knew how much he knew—about his father, about himself.

Was I just being cowardly? Perhaps.

But I didn't think so.

It was peaceful upstairs, alone in the dark of the night. The blanket I had put down for Rosemary, what felt like so long ago— was it truly only just a few days?—was folded up on the corner of my bench. I shook it out and set it in the middle of the floor, over the pentacle, then sat down in the middle of it, crossed my legs, and closed my eyes.

I thought about hybridization, about Rosemary and her eventual command of magic. I had already hoped, and suspected, that she would not be the underdeveloped magical weakling that Gregorio had said she would be. The memory of his words made me angry anew: how dare he suggest that she would be powerless, worthless? That would have been bad enough if he hadn't had any idea, or if he actually knew that was her future—but he in fact knew just the opposite!

Because he would have known about Niad, he absolutely would have. He had as much as told me so, though he hadn't mentioned any names.

So blending witchly genes with human ones was capable of creating offspring with *more* power, not less. Not "diluting the lines," or any other creepy eugenicist theory. This rang so true for me, I wondered that I had never questioned it before—and this made me feel a little ashamed of myself. Yes, all witchkind had been told a convincing story by our elders our whole lives, and that kind of story was hard to just toss away, without very good reason.

But I was a biological researcher—I *worked* in genetics. I should have been able to see—or at least consider—such things from the earliest days of my training.

Except I had been taught, from day one, never to question them.

By the very man who was tearing us all apart doing precisely that.

I took a deep breath and let the anger flow through me, not fighting it, but just letting it happen as I sat still and alone. Yes: my anger was justified, and entirely legitimate. No: it wasn't helpful right now. It didn't tell me what I had to *do*, to fix this injustice.

I wished I could talk to Sebastian. He'd been my partner in this for longer than anyone else; he understood more than anyone else. I was glad to know he was safe, at least.

I wondered what Gregorio Andromedus was doing, either to retaliate or to protect himself. His secret had already badly escaped its bonds and was spreading at this very moment—the coven mothers were acting, talking to one another, to their coven daughters, spreading the word. My father and other Elders were meeting. Too many people knew too much now. The days of

Gregorio covering up the truth and threatening those few who knew it were over.

Could it be this simple? No, of course not.

I cast my æthereal vision across town, trying to see into Gregorio's house. But he'd cast a shield over his entire home and grounds; all I saw was a pale blur. It almost hurt my magical vision to try, and I withdrew before I'd consciously decided to, taking a deep breath. This warlock was powerful beyond anyone I'd ever encountered before. Of course he'd pull down his shutters, as it were.

I wished I could do that.

I sat on the blanket for a few minutes, letting my energy recover. Had Gregorio sensed my attempt? I wasn't sure; it had felt like a passive shield. But I didn't know; this wasn't typical magic, to say the least.

After a few minutes, I sent a message to Siri, letting her know about Flavius.

Yes, Niad has told us, Siri said. *I've been worried about Sebastian, I'm glad he's safe.*

We've all been worried about him, I told her. *How are things there?*

Unsettled, but all right, I suppose.

Unsettled? I asked.

She sent a sigh through the channel. *I am not certain that I have ever seen Leonora this rattled. Unsure of herself, of the world. She is a very traditional witch, you know.*

I thought about it a moment. *Yeah, but also not. She left the Old Country hundreds of years ago, and lived in several different cities before settling here and starting a coven from scratch, with strays and rejects.*

That was over a hundred years ago, Siri reminded me. *I think she's gotten more and more…conservative, perhaps…over the decades since then.*

You would know, I told her. Sirianna, though one of the younger witches (comparatively speaking), was eighty years older than me.

She was one of the few who had not joined the coven at the age of twenty, but had tried living on her own for a while, much as Logan had done. She had eventually given that up, and joined Leonora's coven when she was closer to the age I was now. She didn't talk about it often. I sometimes wondered if that was why I felt more of a connection to her than many of my other sisters: we had a streak of independence in common.

Not that you'd know it by talking to her now. She was a coven witch through and through, gentle and obedient.

Yeah, she said now. *Anyway, things are uncomfortable in the house.*

You are welcome to come hang out here if you like.

Oh, Callie, thank you, you are so kind. But I think I can be of more help here right now. I'm brewing some moonblossom balm, and baking chocolate chip cookies.

I chuckled. That was Sirianna in a nutshell. *That sounds good. Save me one.*

I shall.

After we disconnected, I again sat for a while. It was the quietest part of the night, often my favorite time. I wondered if Mom was asleep; I cast my vision over to their Pacific Heights home.

It was dark and quiet. Unoccupied.

Father was obviously still with the Elders; but where was Mom? I sent her a message.

I got no reply.

I meditated upstairs until the first rays of sunlight began to touch the room, spreading a golden glow. Then I slowly extracted myself from lotus position and went down to my bedroom, where Rosemary was also just waking up.

Once we were put back together, I went down to the kitchen to begin the process of feeding us—and whatever cats were hanging around.

Flavius Winterheart was already in the kitchen with Petrana. "How did you sleep?" I asked him.

"Very well, thank you." He pushed back from the table and his empty crumb-covered plate. "I don't want to get in your way; I'll go back upstairs."

"No, no, you're fine here," I said, feeling as awkward as he looked. "You're not in my way."

He still looked uncertain, but he stayed in his chair. "I know I'm an uninvited house guest. I don't know how long Sebastian wants me to stay here..."

"As long as you need to. Really."

"What would you like for breakfast?" Petrana asked me.

"Eggs and toast and bacon, and pennyroyal tea, please."

"Of course." She turned to the stove and got busy.

We sat in silence for a minute or two. Then I took a deep breath. "Flavius, I know I said this last night, but I really am truly sorry. If I could turn back time, or if I could restore your magic, I would."

"Thank you." He reached down and scratched Willson's head. Logan's cat seemed quite attached to the ex-warlock. "I know you didn't enjoy doing it."

I shivered. "That's an understatement. Even when I thought it was the right thing to do, it felt...ugly and terrible. Cruel."

"You knew it wasn't right," he said, but without rancor or accusation. "Somehow, something inside you knew that I didn't do...any of those things Dr. Andromedus accused me of doing. I remember feeling that at the time, and I still feel it."

"Maybe. I don't know." We were silent for a long moment while I thought about it. Had I known? Not in any conscious way, surely; but the procedure had felt so wrong. So permanent, so...unfair. Perhaps I knew.

Which was kind of moot, at this point.

I stared at the table, and then at Willson. It was nice that they had bonded. Logan's cat was a sweet fellow; he deserved to be spoiled and pampered and loved. I was glad he wasn't lost anymore.

Flavius glanced up at Petrana, hard at work frying bacon. "She's a good cook," he said, giving me a sheepish smile. "I do appreciate the food and shelter."

"You are welcome."

Then we enjoyed another little spell of awkward silence. I hardly knew him; we hadn't worked together before, and we hadn't run in the same social circles. I didn't even know if he was gay or straight, though I knew Sebastian had been interested in him at one time. "So um…what do you do, now? I mean, these days?" He clearly wasn't a doctor anymore.

He shrugged. "I'm still kind of working it out. Without an official identity or any work history, my options are limited. But I need to earn a living. I mostly do day labor, under the table—construction, yard work, stuff like that. I'm working on trying to get a new ID and figure out a better plan. Maybe I'll even leave San Francisco; I don't know."

"I know you don't want to tell me where you live—for good reason—but how did you even find a place to rent, without identity?"

"Also under the table." He laughed sourly. "It's amazing—there's a whole hidden economy out there. Did you know that? We thought only witchkind was hidden; that it was just us and humans. But humans are so…varied. They have all sorts of ways of getting things done that aren't 'by the books.' There's so much about them we don't know; or, at least, that I didn't know, until I had to become one of them."

"Well, that would make sense," I said. "We're not a monolith either." I thought about the Canadian coven that had helped me on my travels, and the fascinating variety of folk I'd met in the Old

Country itself. It was nice to have *all* those memories back, painful as the latter ones were.

"Humans are far more varied than we are. You have no idea."

I looked at him. He still looked sad, and defensive, and a little angry, and mostly just entirely lost. "I'm sure I do have no idea," I agreed. Thinking about the one human I'd gotten to know to any degree at all...the human I'd kept all the important truths about myself from, until the secrets broke us. "And I think that's a real problem," I went on. "Flavius, is there a way I can help you? Like, pay your rent, or help gin up identity documents for you, or something?"

"You are helping me. You're keeping me safe, here."

I shook my head, "Yes, but as you point out, this is temporary. And as you also point out, you have the rest of your life to figure out. It's unconscionable that we just kicked you out without any resources at all."

"Well, I was a terrible murdering criminal, remember?"

I put a hand on his arm. "We were wrong—*I* was wrong. I can't fix that, but I can do something now. Besides, you're keeping Sebastian safe."

"I'm not—he's not at my place. That's all I can tell you."

"I don't need to know where he is. You're helping me hugely just letting me know that he's alive. You kept Logan's cat alive all this time, and all the other cats. Can I return at least those favors?"

His gaze dropped to the floor. Then he looked back up at me. "Let's see if we make it through the next few days. Then we'll talk."

His comment chilled me. I almost didn't want to ask, but... "Why do you say that?"

"Callie, Sebastian explained plenty to me. We have no idea how Dr. Andromedus is going to react when all of witchkind calls him to account for what he's done." He gave me a wan smile. "And now that I've ruined your breakfast, I think I will go back upstairs. I could actually use some more sleep."

Willson followed him out.

Well, this was going to be fun.

My cell phone rang while Petrana was still cooking. *Raymond!* I thought, glad that I'd left the phone on its charger.

But that's not who it was. It was Raymond's sister.

"Christine, hello," I said.

"Hi Callie." She sounded guarded, and who could blame her? "I suppose you know why I'm calling."

"Yes, I expect I do. How is he?"

"He's quite upset, and he knows I'm reaching out, so you don't have to worry about that. Can you meet me for coffee this morning? I'd like...some answers."

"I am happy to give you answers—and to give them to Raymond too—but can you come here?"

She paused, briefly. "Sure. Text me the address."

Twenty minutes later, I welcomed her in, and invited her to sit in the front parlor. She looked around the room briefly before choosing one of the armchairs. "Nice house."

"Thank you."

"Can I get you anything?"

She shook her head. "Not right now. I just..." She ran a hand through her long red hair and exhaled. "Wow. I thought I was ready, but..."

"It's all right. Take your time."

"No, I'm fine. It's just hard to know where to start, you know?"

"Yeah, I think so."

Now she glanced around again. "Where's Rosemary?"

I'd left the baby with Petrana, who had taken her upstairs. "She's with her nanny right now. After her bath, you can see her. If you want to."

"Yes, I would like to see my niece." She gave the last word just the tiniest extra emphasis.

"Christine, I am so sorry. I never meant for things to get this far, this—out of control."

"Right." She seemed to brace something inside herself. "Okay, so first of all: it's true, then, that that's my brother's kid?"

"Yes."

"And you didn't tell him about this why, exactly?"

I sighed. "The short answer is that I didn't know, for the longest time. The long answer is…quite a bit longer, and involves a whole bunch of things you probably won't believe."

"Like that you're a witch. A witch who can do real magic."

"Like that."

"Right, we'll get to that." She gave me a long look. "How did you not know my brother was her father? I mean, I know the obvious part—you were clearly two-timing him—but it didn't even occur to you that it was a possibility?" She leaned forward. "Even when you got a look at her? Is your other guy a redhead too?"

I felt my face flaming and forced myself not to get defensive. Of course she was right to think this, to feel this way—of course Raymond was too. "That's part of the longer answer. Witches and humans aren't supposed to be fertile together."

"You do fertility research, right?"

I nodded.

"And you didn't know this could happen?"

"I never even thought to question it. It's what we've been told all our lives. It was a terrible shock to me when I figured it out."

"And when was that?"

"A few months before she was born." Before she could ask *So why didn't you tell him then?* I went on: "The first person I talked to about it was my mentor, who had taught me everything I know about our biology and fertility. But instead of being just as amazed as I was, he threatened me—and the baby—and ordered me to keep this quiet. Forever."

"Why?"

"Because he already knew this was possible. It's been one of the big secrets of witchkind, for centuries apparently."

She was shaking her head. "I still don't get why this dude, your *mentor*, gets to tell you what to do, about something so fundamentally personal as the paternity of your *child*. What makes that guy the boss of you?"

"He's the leader of our Elders, who make the rules that govern us. He literally *is* the boss of me, whether I like it or not." Of course that was simplifying matters—just try telling Leonora what I'd just told Christine—but it would do for now.

I could see she wasn't buying it. "You clearly don't like it. So why not just leave the religion, or cult, or whatever you want to call it?"

I sighed again. "We're never going to get anywhere if you don't believe I'm actually telling the truth about being a witch."

"I'm not saying I don't believe you," she said quickly.

"You don't, though. It's obvious. And you're never going to understand anything else if you don't understand this. But I get it! I'm asking you to swallow something that you've been told all your life is completely impossible. Believe me, I know how that feels." I held her gaze. "So. What will it take to convince you?"

She let out another heavy breath. "Raymond said you made a beer appear out of thin air."

"I did. Actually, two of them." I gave her a crooked smile. "Do you want a beer?"

Christine glanced at the late morning sun still lancing through the front windows. "A little early to start drinking. You want to manifest some coffee?"

"What would you like?"

She narrowed her eyes. "A nonfat double-shot mocha, no whip, from Café Curio."

"The one on Haight, or Clement?"

"Haight's closer."

She was right, and it didn't matter. "That sounds good, actually; I'll have one too." I brought two cups—actual crockery cups, with the café's name stenciled on the side, in thick matching saucers. They filled the room with the mouth-watering fragrance of coffee and chocolate.

Christine stared at the cups for a long time. Then she slowly, ever so slowly, picked one of them up. She sniffed it, holding it before her for another long moment. Then she took a sip.

"It's perfect."

She slowly set the cup back down in its saucer on the table. Her hand was barely trembling, but I could see it.

"I'm sorry," I said quietly. "We're not actually supposed to tell humans about what we are, what we can do. This is part of the reason why."

"Wow." She stared at the coffee, then at me. "I mean. Wow."

"Magic is real. And witches and warlocks live among you."

"How...how many of you are there?"

"Not a lot. Just a few hundred in the city; maybe a thousand in the whole Bay Area."

She swallowed heavily. "That actually sounds like kind of a lot."

"There's millions of you guys in the same region."

"So, that's why you're in hiding? Because we outnumber you?"

I chose my words carefully. "That's certainly what I've always been taught. One of the reasons, anyway. But that's been sitting less and less comfortably with me lately—that and all the rest of the lies I've been forced to tell, forced to live. Like about my daughter's paternity."

"Right." She took another sip of her coffee. She was doing a really good job holding her hands steady. "So why is it okay to tell us now?"

"It's not. But I'm doing it anyway, because I recently learned a lot of terrible things about witchkind in general, and my mentor in particular—his name is Gregorio, by the way—and I just couldn't cover it all up anymore. I couldn't keep going along with it. Too many people were getting hurt."

"People, or witches?" I could tell she wasn't trying to be snarky, but it stung a little.

"We're people too. We're just not human, not like you are."

"Wow," she said again. "Sorry. I'm trying to get my brain around this, but—it's not easy."

"I get it. Do you want to take a little break?" I could hear the bath draining upstairs. "I can fetch Rosemary; you can coo at an adorable baby for a few minutes."

Christine stared at me. "Are you going to...bring her magically through the wall?"

I gave a startled laugh. "No, I'm going to walk upstairs and bring her down in my arms." Now was clearly not the time to start talking about ley line travel.

"Okay, good. Yes, I want to see the baby."

I left her in the front parlor with her mocha.

Upstairs, I found Petrana dressing Rosemary in the nursery. "I was just going to bring her down to you, Mistress Callie," she said.

"Thanks, but hang out up here for a while," I told her. "I've got Raymond's sister down there; I'm not sure she's ready to cast her gaze upon your loveliness just yet."

Petrana might have smiled. "I will remain up here until you instruct me otherwise. Or I can put on a glamour."

"Stay here for now. I'll let you know."

Back downstairs, I brought Rosemary over to Christine, who took her with a genuine smile. "Oh, she is still just as adorable as she was the last time I saw her!" she said. "Oof—bigger, too."

Rose seemed delighted to be held by her auntie, and (of course) immediately began grabbing for her hair. Christine let her for a few minutes, smiling and teasing, playing with my crazy child. I just watched, sipping my own mocha.

"All right," Christine said at last. "I guess I'm ready to hear more."

"Want me to take her back?"

"Nah," she said, shifting Rose in her lap, cradling her in her left arm so she could use her right to pick up her coffee cup. "I'm happy holding her as long as she's happy here." She glanced down at the baby, then back up at me with a small frown. "So—is she a witch, or a human?"

"Both," I said, then answered the question I knew she was really asking: "And she will be able to do magic. She already can, a little bit."

Christine got still but did not loosen her grip on Rosemary.

"She won't hurt you," I assured her. "What she mostly does now is send simple thoughts to me, mind-to-mind."

"Wow." She laughed. "I'm saying that a lot."

"You have every right to."

Christine stroked Rose's soft red curls, almost absently. "Okay. So. Start at the beginning."

I snorted. "Which beginning?"

"Tell me why you're now telling humans that magic is real."

"Well, as I said: I found out my mentor was basically a monster." Huh. It got the tiniest bit easier to say this each time. "He was doing terrible things, and not to protect us like he said but for his own selfish benefit. When I challenged him on this, he invoked tradition, history, all the ancient rules—and threatened to harm me and Rosemary to boot. And I just...that was the last straw for me. I'd already been pushing back against what felt like following a bunch of arcane, pointless rules set up hundreds, even thousands of years ago. It was bad enough when it just felt stupid; when I learned it was downright sinister, I just couldn't do it anymore. I couldn't keep living in a world of lies."

"How had you already been pushing back against it?"

"Moving out of my coven house was one of them. Seriously dating your brother was another."

"It's forbidden to date humans?" She looked skeptical.

"Not at all—it's just not the 'done thing' to have a real relationship with them. We don't marry humans. We're allowed, er, casual encounters."

"And no babies."

"Well, that was supposed to be impossible. Witches can actually control conception—we don't release an egg unless we're intending to try for a pregnancy." I nodded at the baby in her lap. "Clearly that was at least a half-truth as well."

"I don't understand how that was even able to be kept a secret," Christine said. "I mean, accidental babies happen all the time. Surely you're not the first witch who ever oopsied?"

"We're not nearly as fertile as you humans," I said. "And like I said: conception is supposed to be conscious, intentional."

She shook her head. "I'm gonna want to know more about that, but I'm stuck on you just purposely having a meaningless fling with my brother, knowing it would never go anywhere. And then getting *pregnant* by him, and still not telling him!"

My heart hurt, even as I wanted to defensively point out that most "flings," especially ones that start with a bar hookup, don't go anywhere. "I never meant to hurt him. It kills me that I have. I want to try to make that better, in whatever way Raymond needs—now, and in the future."

She toyed with her coffee cup, not meeting my eye. "Yeah. I guess he'll have to figure that out for himself."

"In his own time," I added. "And I'll be happy to explain any of this to him directly, or keep entirely away from him—it's up to him."

"Well," Christine said, cradling the baby a little closer to herself, "I can't imagine he won't want to play a part in his daughter's life."

I nodded. "I hope that he will. Whatever that means."

"Whatever that means."

Then we both sipped our coffee for another minute.

"I just can't believe witches are real," she finally murmured. "All this time…"

"We've worked really hard to hide the fact."

"And then we stupid *humans* get together and do rituals and stuff and call ourselves witches!"

"Your Wiccan religion is not stupid," I told her. "Anything but."

"You guys must sit there and laugh at us. Seriously." She fingered the silver pentacle at her throat, seemingly not even realizing she was doing it.

"We do not laugh at you." Well, maybe Niad would, but that wasn't the point. "I know I told you that humankind and witchkind are separate species, but we haven't always been. We're closer than—well, than any of us had been led to believe, I'm just finding out."

"Where did you guys come from? Why are there witches?"

I leaned back on the couch. Rosemary was starting to fidget a little; another mealtime must be coming up. "If you've got time, I'll tell you the long version."

"I don't have a shift till this afternoon."

"All right. Hand that baby over, and get comfortable."

— CHAPTER SEVENTEEN —

I positioned Rose on my lap and opened my blouse. Of course she latched on and gave a couple of token suckles before drooling milk back out all over my breast. It dribbled down, warming and dampening the top of my belly. Great. And now my milk was all coming in, in response to her feeble effort, making my breasts ache. My foolish child grinned up at me, proud of her work, and then fell fast asleep. "Good job, monster baby," I muttered.

Christine stifled a smile.

"Go ahead and laugh," I told her. "She's obviously doing it for effect."

"If I needed convincing that she's a normal baby, that would do it."

We both smiled fondly at the baby, then at each other. It would have been a better moment if I weren't covered in rapidly cooling breast milk and baby spit, but oh well.

"Wow," Christine said. "I have a niece. You and my kid brother made a baby together."

"Yeah. We did."

"So," she said, after another moment. "You were going to tell me the whole history of humans and witches?"

It took an hour or more to tell her even the basics. Yet the whole time I talked, a niggling question hovered in my mind: How much of this was actually even the truth? What other lies had our ancestors and our current leaders told us, that I just hadn't uncovered yet?

How could I ever trust anything or anyone again?

Since I couldn't know the answers, I just told her what I knew, what I still believed.

I covered how, in the earliest times, people with even the smallest abilities and extra powers had first been regarded as village wise women and healer folk, revered and honored; how some bright soul had come up with the idea that these powerful people should marry one another and see if they could produce even more powerful offspring; how this had, over a great deal of time, led to the divergence of our two kinds into actual distinct species, ultimately infertile with one another—or so we'd always been led to believe.

Even so, our two kinds had lived in relative harmony until the rise of certain religions among humankind, religions that could not tolerate the existence of powers outside the scope of their gods. Powers that could not be explained or understood by these early folk and were therefore feared and mistrusted. And so slowly, little by little and occasionally all at once, our kinds separated, creating distinct societies and ruling structures. Humans even went so far as to relegate our kind to myth and legend, denying our very existence.

We had no such luxury; our numbers were far too small, and our reliance on human infrastructure, economics, and culture were too great. So we learned to disguise ourselves and—with the exception of one small Eastern European country—lived in the folds and corners of their world, keeping ourselves secret and safe, "dying" and assuming new identities periodically, or moving, to hide our inhumanly long lives. "Leonora Scanza, my coven mother," I told her, "came to San Francisco just after the great earthquake that devastated this city in 1906. She was already over three hundred years old and had lived in several cities both here and in the Old Country. She bought a great crumbling pile of a house on the boundary between what is now the Castro and Noe Valley—it was called Eureka Valley then—and established our coven, slowly repairing and expanding on the house, improving its magical defenses and assets, and shepherding our investments." Actually, she'd done more than shepherd; she'd grown them into the substantial fortune they were today. But it would be unwise, not to mention obnoxious, to brag about how rich we were.

"Over a hundred years ago?" Christine asked. "How has she managed to hide her age, then?"

"Well, she doesn't get out among humankind much these days." I smiled, thinking of my eccentric coven mother. "But you're right: I think this is the longest she's lived in any one place, as herself. It's probably going to be time for her to 'renew' herself again soon, if she doesn't..." I trailed off, not liking to think of the alternative, although it shouldn't make me sad, if it were something she wanted to do. "It is traditional for witchkind to move on to the Beyond around age four hundred, so she might decide to do that instead, and pass the coven on to a new mother."

"The Beyond?" she asked. "Like...an afterlife?"

So I explained the Beyond, and the realms beyond the Beyond, about which we knew very little, except that, in the general run of things, we progress upward through the realms until we eventually arrive in the domain of the Blessed Mother, and take our place by her side. "The warlocks focus on the Great Father at the end of their line," I added. "But we witches don't pay much attention to him: the Blessed Mother is the source of us all, and our ultimate destination."

Christine nodded, seeming comfortable with this notion, until I got to the next part: the fact that the Beyond was a real, literal place, and that we knew this because our ancestresses who moved there returned regularly to talk to us. "Nementhe visits our coven in its weekly Circle," I told her. "It's really her—in her spirit form, not her body; bodies remain here, and decay, just like everything physical. But her spirit comes here, and gives us advice and guides us."

"Whoah. Like, a séance or something? It's not...creepy?"

I told her no, it wasn't creepy or weird at all; it was something we'd been familiar with all our lives. Going to the Beyond wasn't the same as dying. It was something we did intentionally—usually—and, though we missed our beloved ones who departed, they weren't entirely gone. "It's like they've moved to a really distant country, one with crappy technology," I told her. "The phone lines aren't great, and it's clear that they're really busy there and having a great time, and even sometimes it seems like they're only reaching back to talk to us for our sake—they don't miss us like we miss them. They do sort of remember us fondly, but they'd really rather get on with things there."

"Raymond told me about your friend who died last year. It must be nice, that you still at least get to talk to her."

My heart gave a terrible thump of pain. "Actually, no, I can't; that's part of what's all so awful and crazy right now—part of what my mentor Gregorio Andromedus has done. Logan isn't in the Beyond, but she's not in her body here either." I explained what I'd found out about the soul- and essence-extracting machines, and told her about the warehouse of soulless bodies stashed in Berkeley.

Christine shivered. "That's awful," she said. "No wonder you're disenchanted with the whole system."

"Yeah."

"What's he doing with all the souls?"

"I have no idea," I told her. "He's at least using the stolen essence to amplify his own power, I'm pretty sure; I don't know what he's doing with the souls, or whether we will be able to retrieve them." I told her about my trip to the Old Country, having my memories stolen and then getting them restored. "And once I got my memories back, I knew I had to stop keeping all the secrets. That was just going to get me, and a whole lot of others, killed—or harmed so badly as makes no difference. And if I needed further convincing, a whole different witch showed up in a Circle this week—Leonora's own coven mother, gone for hundreds of years— and *she* told us that the time for secrets was over."

"Is that unusual? A different, um, Beyond witch showing up?"

"Unprecedented."

Christine leaned back in her chair. Our coffee cups were long empty; it was probably time to think about lunch. "Wow. What a story." Then she gave a rueful grin. "To think I just came here to give you shit for lying to my brother."

I snorted. "And you had every right to."

"So. Is this why you wanted to meet here, rather than at a coffee shop?"

She was sharp. "Yes. You can't perceive them, but I've got strong wards around the house. I'm already sheltering someone here, and the warlock I was working with is in hiding."

"Do you think Gregorio might do something to you? Even after you've told so many people about this?"

"I have no idea what he's capable of, or intending to do. I guess I forgot to mention the part about the risk of insanity growing, the longer we stay on this plane…"

I trailed off as an ætheric message arrived from Jeremy. *Callie, I have spoken to my father, as you instructed me to.*

He sounded terse. "Christine, I—have just been pinged by someone. I need to talk to them."

"All right. Do you want me to leave, or—?"

"Stay for now, if you can." I suddenly didn't want her out there in the world, vulnerable. "I'll, er, take the call in the other room." I had started to get up, but I was still covered by a sleeping baby.

"No, you stay. I need a restroom anyway."

"Just down the hall, you'll see it."

She left, and I answered Jeremy. *And? What did you find out?*

I remain at a loss as to why you are behaving this way. Especially given the fact that you have deceived and betrayed me.

I felt a chill, once more. *What did he tell you?*

That our baby is not mine—that you have somehow managed to cheat the very biological realities of our species and conceived a child with your human lover. And then you lied to me, to everyone, about it to cover up your trespasses.

Wow, interesting spin, Gregorio.

Furthermore, Jeremy went on before I could respond, *my father is caring for a great number of ailing witches and warlocks at his laboratories in Berkeley—something you could have learned if you'd simply asked him directly, rather than running all the way to the Old Country to try to lay some sort of trap for him.*

What? This was too much. *Jeremy, he is NOT treating those helpless folks—he made them sick in the first place! He's stealing their essences and ripping their souls out of their bodies! It's plain as day!*

It is not the least bit plain to me, he answered. *I may not have your biological training, but I can identify a patient care ward when I see one. The ill witches and warlocks are receiving around-the-clock care and are being kept in every comfort.*

That snake. Gregorio was probably going to show the coven mothers and the Elders the same thing; he'd obviously been very busy since this all started tumbling out.

So it is your word against his, Jeremy continued. *And who should everyone believe—the highly respected leader of our Elders, or a young witch researcher, barely recovered from a difficult childbirth, who has already lied to cover up an illicit alliance?*

I took a deep breath, trying to stay calm. In my arms, Rosemary woke up and gazed up at me. She lay quietly, as if she were listening to the conversation as well. She could feel my emotions, anyway.

His lies run far deeper than mine, I finally managed. *And mine were at his direct order—did he tell you that? That he himself commanded me to silence about the truth of my pregnancy? That he demanded that I lie to you?*

Of course he told me no such thing, because—

And did he also tell you about your own origins? I interrupted. *Has he told you about your birth mother?*

What about her?

I had wanted to do this gently, and in person. Because I cared about this warlock. Because I knew this would be hard news to take. But this could no longer wait. *She was human. Jeremy, you're half-human. I ran the test myself; I saw the evidence with my own eyes. It's not impossible; it's probably not even that improbable.*

There was a short pause before he said, *Do not be absurd. My mother was a witch—it is impossible for her to have been anything else. My father does not even speak to humans. I can see that you are even more deluded than I realized. I cannot speak to you when you are in this state.*

Jeremy, it's true. If you want me to show you—

Now he interrupted. *Recant your lies immediately, or my father will be forced to take strong measures. You are warned.* And he slammed the channel shut.

Well, I had known he wouldn't take it well. This was no surprise, though it was a deep disappointment. I sat there, mourning the loss of whatever love we had once shared. I had thought he knew me, understood me. Believed me. He had spent so long treating me so tenderly, if carefully. He had seemed like a good man, a good warlock.

I knew he was under the sway of his father—of course he was!—but I had hoped, somewhere deep inside myself, that maybe I could get him to listen...

Had I, though? Or had I always known it would go this way? I did kick him out and build new wards as soon as I remembered the truth, after all.

Jeremy so admired his father, had spent so much of his life yearning to be closer to him.

When would Gregorio turn on him?

I sighed and cuddled my baby. Now she let me know that yes, perhaps she was hungry after all. I got her started and watched her suckle. Her red hair glinted in a ray of sunshine.

Such gorgeous hair. Darker than her father's, but still so beautiful.

And then I spent a few minutes just feeling sorry for myself. I had had two lovers. Now I had none.

But at least I had a marvelous baby.

Christine came back in a few minutes later. "All done with your...call?"

"Yes, sorry, I should have said something," I told her.

She sat down and looked over at me. "What's wrong?"

"Oh—just more of the same," I tried, but that was obviously a lie, and I wasn't doing that anymore. "No, sorry, give me a minute."

"Of course." She glanced around the room. "Actually, I should probably be going before too terribly long..."

"No, stay," I said. "If you can—at least till I see what's going on out there. In fact, I need to pass along what I've just learned." Her eyes widened. "And then I will tell you what it was, but give me another quick moment, all right?"

"Of course." She got up.

"I don't need privacy for this."

Even so, she strolled to the window and looked out at the street. I called to Leonora, but she did not respond, so after a minute I pinged Niad.

Yes?

Jeremy just called to me. Do you know where Leonora is?

She's meeting with six coven mothers to plan their approach for the larger meeting later.

They'll need to know this—can you get word to her?

I can try. They're at Jasmine's house, not here.

I told her everything that had just transpired.

Coward, she said. *That boy needs to show some spine.*

He doesn't know his father is lying to him, I told her, though I wasn't sure why I was trying to defend him. *Anyway, let me know when you reach Leonora, okay?*

I will.

I closed the channel and said to Christine, "That was Jeremy—the first call, I mean."

She turned back from the window and frowned. "The warlock who you were going to marry—Gregorio's son."

I'd explained contracts to her, and how they weren't marriages. But I'd explained a *lot* this morning. "Yeah. He's...taking his father's side, pretty hard, actually. His dad is lying to him, telling him *I'm* the crazy one. I'm not surprised he believes him, but—well, still, it's hard to know that he thinks I'm a liar."

She walked back over and sat down, giving me a sympathetic look. "That must be hard."

"Well, yes, it is." Rosemary was nursing happily; I rocked her gently. "And he ended with a sort of veiled threat, or—okay—maybe not even all that veiled."

"Oh?"

"He said Gregorio will 'take measures' if I don't stop all this—though I don't know how I'm supposed to put the genie back into the bottle. I can't even get hold of my dad; he's been meeting with a bunch of the other Elders for nearly a day now. And Leonora has been talking to a number of other coven mothers. It's not like we're going to contain this secret." *Especially not with the Beyond coming all this way to tell us that the time for secrets is over,* I thought.

Someone was crazy here, and it wasn't me.

"So I'd feel better if you could stick around, inside my house and its wards, a bit longer," I told her. "Maybe even...see if Raymond wants to come over?"

"Oh, I don't know—"

"He doesn't have to talk to me. It's a big house; I can keep myself scarce. But he'd be safe here, in case Gregorio gets any ideas about harming Rosemary's father as a way of getting to me."

"Right." Christine nodded, frowning. "I'll give him a call. And maybe I can order us something for lunch? Or he can bring Chinese?"

Petraia could of course cook us lunch, but though both Raymond and I had told Christine that I'd built a golem, I hadn't introduced them yet.

Given how Raymond had reacted to her, it was probably best to hold off on that.

"Sure. Raymond is great at picking up Chinese food."

We shared a smile as I wondered how much he'd told his sister about our relationship. "Actually," she said, "you don't need to hide in your own house. He's pissed and wounded, and with very good reason; but he's also an adult. I'll explain to him what you've told me and what's going on. And then we'll sit down like civilized human beings and have lunch together." She caught herself then. "I mean, civilized humans and witches."

"Sounds good to me."

I gave her privacy for her lengthy phone call, going into the dining room where I set the table myself, and put Rosemary down in her bassinet.

Then I went upstairs and knocked on the guest bedroom door. "Flavius?" I called softly. "Are you awake?"

"I am. I was thinking about a shower. What's up?"

"I've got a friend here, and another person is coming over with Chinese food for lunch. Would you like to join us?"

I heard his footsteps crossing the room; then he opened the door. His hair was rumpled, but he looked a little better rested than earlier. "That's very nice of you, Callie, but I'm not sure I'm comfortable hanging out with witches right now."

"They're both humans, actually. And one's a guy."

Flavius looked surprised. "Humans?"

"Yeah. One is the man I was seeing last year, and the other is his sister. I want them safe behind my wards till we see what Gregorio does next." He still looked hesitant, so I added, "You're free to do whatever you want, but since they might be here a little while, I wanted to give you the option of not just hiding out. Oh, and they know I'm a witch."

He blinked. "Really." He seemed to digest that a moment, then asked, "What do they know about me?"

"Nothing, honestly. Just that you're someone else I'm keeping safe here. So it's up to you whatever you want to say, or not say."

"All right. I'll get cleaned up and come down."

Petrana was still lurking in my bedroom from when I'd asked her to stay put. I went in and said, "I think Christine is doing all right, but I still want to keep you out of sight for the moment."

"Of course, Mistress Callie."

Back downstairs, I waited anxiously for Raymond. Christine wisely gave me space. Finally, I felt his presence and heard his boots on the stairs.

I eased the wards and opened the front door. There he stood, looking like he had so many times before, except this time there were more bags in his arms. And he wasn't grinning lustfully at me.

"Please come in," I said, standing aside.

"Kitchen or dining room?" he asked, as he entered.

"Dining room."

Flavius came down; I introduced everyone.

Then we proceeded to have the most awkward meal in all of history. Every conversational gambit Christine or I tried faltered out after a few words. We weren't even saved by the presence of an adorable baby; Rosemary slept through the meal.

"Thank you for the food," Flavius said politely, setting his napkin on the table and getting up from his chair. "I'll be upstairs if you need me."

I nodded.

Raymond and Christine exchanged a look. Then she asked me, "How long do you think we should stay inside here? Have you heard anything else from any of your sources?"

"No, and I should probably see if I can raise anyone."

"I'll help clean up," Raymond blurted, practically knocking his chair over in his rush to get up. He made a stack of our plates and took them to the kitchen.

"Sorry," Christine said.

I shook my head. "No, he's fine—as you pointed out, he's got every reason to be upset. He's doing great."

But I was awfully relieved to leave the table myself.

I went upstairs to my bedroom, leaving the sleeping baby under Christine's eye. There, I pinged Leonora once more, but she still did not respond.

What's up? Is everything all right? Niad asked, when I reached her.

Well, no, of course everything wasn't all right, but I knew what she was asking. *Did you get word to Leonora?*

I did.

And...?

She thanked me for the information and told me that they were still discussing matters, and that we would all be informed when they had reached a decision.

I rolled my eyes. *Okay, thanks.*

Nothing new on your end? she asked.

Nothing. Except that I'm now keeping Flavius, Raymond, and his sister Christine safe here till we know what's what.

She snorted. *Regular little coven you're building, aren't you. If you decide to add anyone who can actually still use magic, let me know.*

Very funny.

I lay back on my bed after we disconnected. Niad's snark about Flavius was mean-spirited, but she wasn't wrong either. How sad he seemed, yet how resigned.

What must it be like, to lose your magic? It wasn't just the abilities—the spell casting, the traveling on ley lines, the communication at a distance. The witch-sight. But it was everything that went with it: our longevity, our resistance to illness and disease, our ability to pull a glamour or cast a deflection spell.

Raymond and Christine would live the life spans they'd always expected to—give or take. Flavius had been cheated of centuries on this plane.

And what would happen when he died? He wouldn't get to choose the moment of his moving on, unless he committed suicide.

Would he move on? Would he travel to the Beyond, or would he just...die?

The thought made me even sicker and sadder than I'd been before, when I'd thought about what we'd done to him. The Beyond was real; we had real, tangible knowledge of it. I didn't know much about the humans' heaven, though I understood they were asked to take a good many details about it on faith. Was it truly real? The Beyond, for us, was the next step on our journey, and we all looked greatly forward to going there—even while not being in a hurry to finish up here.

What if Flavius Winterheart was blocked from there?

Who would even know?

Well, Jeremy might. Not that I was going to ask him. But Jeremy was, after all, the one who had brought knowledge of the cautery procedure to us, from the Old Country. It was a tool they had developed there, he told us, to deal with the troubles they were having with the Iron Rose.

(Troubles which weren't at all what we'd been led to believe, I had learned when I was there—actually, before I'd even traveled there. Logan's parents were supposedly killed by the Iron Rose, but their bodies were here in Berkeley. Was *anything* I'd ever been told true?)

The warlocks who developed the cautery procedure might have an idea of what happened to its victims after they died. Or they might have not cared—it was the ultimate shunning, after all. A way of removing its victim from our numbers permanently, yet without killing them.

It might have been less cruel to kill Flavius, I thought.

I sighed, staring at the ceiling, lost in my glum thoughts. Eventually, of course, my baby called to me in my mind. *Mama! Hungry!*

Coming, sweetie, I sent her.

Anyway, I needed to go tell Christine that she should probably call in sick for her afternoon shift.

The day dragged on. Flavius stayed in his room; Raymond and Christine played a desultory game of cards in the second parlor; I kept out of their hair as best I could. Niad got downright testy with me when I asked for one update too many.

I mean, testier than usual.

After an early dinner of noodles and salad made from whatever I could scrounge out of my kitchen, at least it began getting dark. It had been a while since I'd slept; I'd been trying to stay alert and conscious, ready to respond to whatever new threat came my way. But this high level of readiness was exhausting. I could use a few hours of rest and restoration.

"So..." Christine said, drying the last plate and putting it in the cupboard, "how many guest rooms do you have?"

"As many as I need. Just give me a minute to get them arranged."

I walked upstairs, just to make it less weird on the siblings as I stretched walls and rearranged (and imported) furniture, using magic. Halfway through, I gazed at the closed door to Jeremy's study. Should I use that room too? It was mine, in my house. But no, I didn't need to, and I honestly didn't want to.

Later. Maybe.

The house was very quiet after we were all in our separate beds. Elnor slept at my feet; the cats had been scarce today. Not even Willson had hung around.

What were they up to?

And were the coven mothers and the Elders *still* meeting? This was lengthy, even for such deliberative bodies comprised of ancient beings.

Exhausted as I was, I yet again found myself unable to sleep.

After tossing back and forth and annoying my cat for the four-teenth time, I lay on my back and started some mental relaxation exercises. Similar to the chant we did when we formed a Circle: nonsense syllables, repeated enough times to lose even the non-meaning they had, to soothe and distract the mind.

It worked, but I almost immediately wished it hadn't. Because I dropped straight into a dream about Mom.

It started innocuously—we were at her house having tea, much as we often did before a tarot lesson—but then she looked up at me. Her face was painted in misery; she nearly looked her years. "Callie," she said softly. "I am so sorry."

"Why?" I asked. "What is it?"

She shook her head, and reached down to the table before her, lifting up two cards. They were the two I'd drawn a few days ago at my kitchen table, The Lovers and the Three of Swords, only now the happy gentle sky above the lovers was blustery and grey, and the benevolent being above them was a terrifying demon; the pierced heart on the Three of Swords dripped not just rain but bright red blood. The blood, in fact, dripped off the card, into Mom's lap—then it was a flow—then it was a river—Mom was going to drown in blood—

—and then I shocked awake as an ætheric communication crashed through my mind: *Culendula Isadora, I would have a word with you.*

Gregorio. I stifled the flood of rage and fear that poured through me, waking me thoroughly. How dare he! Of course he knew I was asleep; he would time his call deliberately, to keep me as off-balance as possible.

Small mercy to have that dream interrupted, at least.

Dr. Andromedus. I am surprised to hear from you.

Are you? I am reliably informed that you are in frequent communication with the rest of witchkind He paused. *Most of the rest of them, that is.*

What did he mean by that? *Yes, I know that you are able to spy on me. I hope it hasn't been too boring for you.*

An ætheric chuckle. *Not boring at all, Culendula. Not at all. In fact, I am so rarely bored.*

I'm so happy for you. There was a pause. *If that's all you called to say, then thanks and everything, but I really do want to get some sleep.*

Oh no. I was just making polite conversation before getting to the real purpose of my call.

And that is?

He tsk'd. *So unfortunate, youth these days and their impatience. I thought I had trained you better.*

My heart was finally slowing down a bit, but my anger was still simmering. When I thought of how many years I had spent listening to and respecting this snake... *Well I'm sorry to be such a disappointment. Now, you're calling why?*

I have knowledge that I am quite certain you will be interested to have.

Now the fear spiked again. What had he done? I forced myself to sound brave and unconcerned as I sent, *I doubt it.*

Ah, to be so young and so certain. I do hope you have a long life, Calendula Isadora, though you may doubt my words.

And what did he mean by that? *I doubt a great deal about you. So tell me this most interesting thing and let me get some rest.*

Of course, Calendula. And my apologies for disturbing you so late, but your mother was most insistent that I inform you of her whereabouts.

Oh Blessed Mother. I had not even wanted to let myself think this, had told myself that my father—his power, his longtime friendship with Gregorio, his position in the Elders—would have stayed Gregorio's hand. Would have kept Mom safe. I sat upright in bed, struggling to contain my panic. *My mother? What have you done with her, you monster?*

It grieves me to inform you that Belladonna Isis has taken ill once more, gravely this time. At her request, I have brought her to my special clinic for treatment, where she will be given my very focused and particular attention. He sent another chuckle, making my blood run cold. *And now that I have delivered the message as promised, I bid you goodnight. Pleasant dreams.* He closed the channel.

I tried to open another one, but he ignored me.

After I screamed ineffectively into the æther for another minute, I tossed the covers aside and got up, pacing around the room. "What is it?" Petrana asked, from the corner.

"I..." I clenched my hands into fists and tried to force myself to say the words without sobbing. "That bastard. That utter and complete bastard."

"Was it Jeremy? What has happened?"

"No." I took a deep breath and tried to calm my heartbeat. Panicking wasn't going to help. "Gregorio Andromedus has just kidnapped my mom."

My golem stepped forward into the room. Moonlight glinted off her strong features. "What shall we do to rescue her?"

My heart warmed, just a touch. "I don't know. Oh Blessed Mother. I need to get hold of Leonora—"

Downstairs, there was a loud crash. Rosemary woke up and gave a startled yelp. I ran to my bedroom door and yanked it open.

"Callie!" came Christine's voice from down the hall. "Are you all right?"

A second door flew open, and Raymond stepped into the hall, looking sleep-rumpled. "What happened?"

"I don't know!" I cried, and rushed to the stairs, almost tripping over Flavius coming out of the guest bedroom.

"What was that?" he asked.

"Something down here." I ran down the stairs, stopping in the front entryway as I tried to figure out where the crash had come from.

Petrana followed me. "It was everywhere and nowhere," she said. "I cannot trace the source of the disturbance."

Flavius and Raymond were hard on my golem's heels. Christine, in a bathrobe, had paused to pick up Rosemary before following us. Now my baby watched the whole scene, wide-eyed, from her auntie's arms.

Then Rose lifted up her little hand and pointed to the under-stair closet.

We all turned and stared as two white cats walked out of it.

I could feel my stomach plummet in fear and terrible knowledge: I instantly knew them. These were the cats from my dream…the one Sebastian had had to rescue me from.

"Haven't seen these guys in the mix yet," Flavius said, puzzled.

Rosemary and I both stared at the cats, who turned to look up at me, moving their heads almost in unison. Just like they'd done in my dream. Then they turned and walked back into the closet, pausing only to glance over their furry shoulders at me.

Listen to the cats.

And the closet *felt* different. I had never been able to sense the portal before…but now I could. It was open. It was waiting for me.

I had to follow the cats. I had to do it *now*.

As they disappeared into the darkness, I looked at Raymond, Flavius, Christine, Petrana—and Rosemary. I couldn't leave my baby.

I couldn't take her with me.

Elnor bumped into my ankle with her hard little head, trying to nudge me forward.

"Go," said Petrana.

Flavius glanced at the golem in surprise, but Christine nodded. "We got this," Christine said; after a moment, her brother echoed her. Rosemary watched me, looking entirely calm.

Elnor bumped me again, harder this time.

Then Rosemary sent, *Go.*

"Okay," I said, and shivered. I bent down, scooped up my cat, and walked into the dark closet.

IF YOU'RE ENJOYING
THE *NIGHTCRAFT QUARTET*,
YOU MIGHT ALSO ENJOY THIS
FANTASY FROM SHANNON PAGE,
ALSO PUBLISHED BY
OUTLAND ENTERTAINMENT

— PROLOGUE —

A century and a half after the island nation of Alizar had freed itself from continental rule, in the seventeenth year of Viktor Morrentian Alkattha's troubled reign as Factor, a giant corpse washed up onto the eastern shore of Cutter's, at the island cluster's very center. The greatest typhoon in generations had blown spume for three days over the walls of even the mightiest houses on the highest hills, swamping the rotting, coastal boat-towns altogether, drowning legions of the poor, and flushing every darkest alleyway and sewer tunnel with a boil of cold, salty rage.

On the storm's fourth day, dawn was accompanied by a peculiar pearlescence to the east, as if the clouds were loathe to release their clammy grip. Those first few to venture out onto the streets of Cutter's — guards, priests, looters, the desperate — found on the shingles of Pembo's Beach a body so large and long that all agreed it couldn't possibly have been a man. And yet, it had the form of one.

Its pale complexion was, by then at least, the color of a Smagadine, that unhealthy tone indicative of life lived underground, or solely under moonlight, far from any sunlight's benediction. Its wrinkled fingers were the size of longboats. Its gelid, unseeing eyes as large as the wine tuns stored beneath the Factorate House. The cock across its thigh, a toppled watchtower.

The corpse was an instant nine-days' wonder, and a panic. Nearly two hundred years earlier, gods had returned to faraway Copper Downs. Had they at last come to Alizar? The nation's streets were flooded for the second time in days, this time with rumor, prophecy, and hushed prognostication. Had the storm birthed this monster or slain it? Would it rise to lay waste to the city, vanish back into sea like a dream half-remembered, or just putrefy, poisoning Cutter's scenic bay and vast commercial port as it rotted on the beach? Might it be an omen of some even greater calamity in store?

While the Mishrah-Khote, Alizar's ancient priesthood of physicians, maintained a careful silence in regard to their position on the corpse, the nation's Factor did not find the unexpected arrival of a *dead god* convenient in the least. Already struggling to navigate his country's growing pains, he had no need of ominous portents inciting the poor and ignorant to erratic imaginings and potentially volatile assessments of his governance. He just wanted the great body gone! Though not in any manner that might make him look defensive or afraid, of course.

Fortunately for him, Alizar was virtually swimming in very poor and hungry citizens after such a devastating storm. His advisors assured him that the giant carcass was still at least as sound as many others hanging in that tropic nation's butcher shops on any given day. Why not address two problems with a single cure? Thus, the Factor demonstrated his consideration for the city's starving masses by ordering the inconvenient corpse butchered quickly, before it started rotting, and distributed — for free — to all and any wishing to fill their bellies with its meat. Since animals alone — never people, much less *gods* — were ever butchered and consumed, he asserted dubiously, the corpse's fate must somehow prove its nature. Whatever superficial form it might have borne, this creature had been "nothing but a great sea monster of some sort."

Huge crowds rushed to Cutter's bloody shingle to accept their portion of this windfall, by which their desperate families were kept fed for some weeks after. Despite this fact — or perhaps because of it — memory of the giant corpse did not fade as hoped. If anything, the common folks' awe of this *dead god* increased. New tales began to circulate, of teeth and bones extracted, giant finger-nails pared, and god-meat scraped from long, pale flanks not just to feed the desperate, but to bless and heal them as well. From the furtive repetition of these stories, a new cult emerged around the *Butchered God*, if at first just in cautious whispers and anonymous graffiti.

After a while, as no other evidence of returning gods appeared, the wealthy and the comfortable middle class put the event aside. Life went on. New urgencies seized attention — new wonders, scandals, and attendant gossip.

Old storms are eventually forgotten. Old flotsam always drifts back out to sea.

As long as what is buried stays that way, and its memory is left unstirred.

— ONE —

Domina Sian Kattë hummed quietly as she poured two glasses of *kiesh*, worked the cork back into the stout little bottle, then brought the drinks to the sitting room.

Captain Reikos smiled up at her from his seat on the rattan sofa; he moved to rise, but she waved him back down. His pale eyes were as warm as the early-evening air fluttering the curtains at the front windows of her Viel townhouse. Sian could hear the murmurs of street noise from below — the cries of cart runners, the sound of dishes in the tavern's kitchen three doors over, at the head of Meander Way. "I thank you, my lady." Reikos lifted his glass in a formal toast.

Sian laughed and took a seat in the armchair, arranging her golden silks comfortably about her. "None of that, Konstantin; when we come upstairs, we are friends."

"Friends." He tasted the word, then the sweet liquor, before setting his small amber glass on the delicate table between them. "Domina Kattë, I had imagined us more than that. Please forgive my presumption." But now his courtliness was a tease. He went on before she could reach over and give him the gentle swat he so clearly deserved. "Ah, Sian, it is good to see you."

"Yes. It's been too long. What news of the wider world?"

"Well, much of it is still covered in salt water. And little of it is as warm and lovely as these islands are." Reikos leaned back and stretched a bit, without seeming to fill any additional space. He was a trim, agile man able to live comfortably aboard his ship for months on end; entirely at home in a cabin only four or five paces wide in any direction, with its narrow little bunk. He looked quite natural on her small sofa, she thought. "We spent half the voyage here pushing through squalls to make a sailor think seriously about buying a plow. Lost Port's upstart new vineyards have suffered a blight for their impertinence. Some little fly, they are saying, has come by boat from the City Imperishable and developed a liking for grape leaves. The price of wine has soared there now, and every ship that comes to port is treated like a threat."

"That's unfortunate," Sian said. "I've been enjoying the Stone Coast wines."

"Many folk have. I am certain the vintners will do all they can to rescue their investments." He took another sip. "Beyond all that, though, I've seen nothing half so interesting as what I find in Alizar. And not merely because you are here."

She smiled again at this. "I'll bet you say that to all your women."

"Only the best ones." He grew serious. "But tell me: is everything all right here?"

"What do you mean?"

Reikos waved an arm vaguely in the direction of Cutter's, the next major island in the chain, where foreign traders docked. "I almost couldn't find a berth for *Fair Passage*. Ships just aren't leaving — though not because trade is lively; quite the opposite. Yorgen told me he's waited a month or more to fill even half his capacity. The Kenner brothers have lost a good number of their crew to desertion. And I find the streets filled with rabble now, marching around and chanting."

"Oh, the prayer lines." Sian sighed. She thought she could hear one now, in fact, out beyond the end of Meander Way — the leader's call and the crowd's mumbled response. "They follow the so-called Butchered God."

"So-called? You don't believe it was a god, then?"

"I don't believe it was a sea monster, no matter what the Factor would have us think. But a god? Do gods die?"

He shrugged. "I am not a religious man."

"I have little use for priests myself. But if there were gods anywhere near Alizar — and if one should die — I can hardly believe they would allow their bodies just to wash up on a beach somewhere, much less be carved up to feed the poor."

"What a bizarre gesture that was. Your cousin is a... an interesting man."

"You speak as though I know him." Sian shrugged. "Even so, I can't imagine a god's appearance was convenient for him."

Reikos smiled as he finished his drink. "I expect the Temple Mishrah-Khote was pleased."

"Perhaps," Sian said. "Though one must wonder whether the arrival of a god was any more convenient for them. They do not seem to embrace the new cult."

"Such interesting times, as I say." Reikos toyed with his empty glass. "You live amidst these giant ruins. Does no one wonder at the coincidence — or worry that whoever built them might be coming back?"

"From the age of legends?" She took a sip of wine, and sighed. "The Factor may ask himself that question every night. But I don't have to. We've had no Green Woman here, that I'm aware of. And the thing was dead, which is *very* convenient for everyone. Will you have another before dinner?"

"Yes, I will — delicious. I believe I recognize this vintage?"

"Indeed you do. A certain well-traveled sea captain brought me a case on his last visit. I hope he's brought more; my stores could use restocking."

"It's eminently possible that he has."

After checking to see that their bouillabaisse from the tavern was still warm, Sian brought the bottle to the table. "You're right, though: matters here aren't what they should be, and not just on the docks. I can't retain my workers either — I need new weavers, and probably a new dyer, if I can find anyone suitable. I've been to the hiring hall four times this season already." She smiled wryly. "Not that anyone is happy to see me there these days."

"I cannot imagine who would not be pleased to see your lovely face at his doorstep. Show me these ungrateful men!"

Sian laughed. "Ah, flatterer, you warm an old woman's bones."

Reikos gave a half-bow, elegant even from his seated position. "Always happy to be of service. Though you are *not* old."

Sian raised an eyebrow. "Nor am I young."

"You are ageless, a creature of great and abiding beauty."

Sian gave him a long look calculated to wither.

Reikos cleared his throat. "So, what are these marches, then? Some sort of protest?"

"Our work force abandons honest labor now to roam the streets in prayer, begging their Butchered God for a more equitable distribution of wealth. As if coins might just fall on them with the rains!" She shook her head. "I don't know what they hope to achieve. But they seem reasonably peaceful. Enough of this gloomy talk. You must be famished — shall we dine?"

"Eager as I am for fish soup, my lady, I find myself in the grasp of a…different hunger at the moment…" He glanced beyond the small kitchen to the daybed behind its gauze curtain at the back of the townhouse. The fabric around the bed stirred gently in the fragrant evening breeze. "I was a long time at sea, far from the comforts of shore."

Laughing, Sian got to her feet and gave Reikos a hand up. "A man after my own heart. So we shall have dessert first, and dine afterwards."

The bouillabaisse had kept perfectly, making a fine late supper. Sian found a bottle of Stone Coast claret to accompany it, hoping indeed that Lost Port's blight should pass. When the meal was done, Reikos carried his dishes to the sideboard, then took the empty wine bottle downstairs and set it outside the back door for the glass-scavengers.

It was not his custom to stay the night when he visited. A ship's captain had responsibilities early in the morning that required a well-rested body and an alert mind. This equally suited Sian, being well past the age when sleeping like piled pups in the townhouse's small daybed would leave her refreshed at dawn. And though the place was no storefront, clients and associates did happen by with some frequency when she was in town; it was just easier, and more professional, for her to rise alone there.

When he returned from the alley, Reikos nuzzled the back of Sian's neck, planting a few small kisses on the tender skin there. "When shall we dine again?"

"How long are you in port this time?" Sian scraped the soup-bowl into the covered scrap container, lest she encourage the islands' large roaches, and set it aside for return to the tavern. A bright green gecko climbed the wall behind the sideboard, ever alert for mosquitoes.

"A fortnight, perhaps; until I can turn over my cargo. I have you down for one case of *kiesh*, at the very least."

"I thank you." Sian thought a moment. "I need to go to Little Loom Eyot tomorrow, but business will bring me back to Viel within three or four days."

"I look forward to it." He kissed her again, pulling her close. "Such a brief respite this was from the desolation of my days. Will you not come with me this time?"

Sian smiled, turning around in his arms to face him. "My dear, your shipboard bed is even smaller than mine."

"No, not just tonight. Sail with me when I leave. I will show you the world!"

"And what will all your other women think when I show up?"

"There will be no one but you, Sian."

Laughing, she said, "Now that is going a bit far, even for you." She gave him a gentle push. "Go on, get back to *Fair Passage*. I shall see you in a few days."

Reikos let go of her and took up his jacket and satchel. "I hope your husband knows what a lucky man he is."

Sian looked up at him, a little surprised. "Of course he does. As I know how lucky I am. Comfort, and freedom, and interesting work — I have it all."

"Yes, you do." Reikos gazed at her. "He truly does not mind your ...independence?"

"We have long since passed the time of caring about such things. Our arrangement is clear: he runs the manufactory, and I manage the business in town. Our free time is our own." She frowned at her lover. "As I believe I have explained to you."

"Yes, you have." Then he grinned, the mischievous glint returned. "May your dreams be filled with delightful adventures involving dashing sea captains."

"You sleep well too." She walked him down to the front door, then kissed him farewell as he slipped quietly into the night.

She watched his trim form retreat down Meander Way, then bolted the door.

Sian spent a productive morning visiting a new dye-seller on Three Cats, buying several sacks each of ochre and indigo and putting in an order for some rare carmine at a decent price. At least *some* businesses were still thriving. After closing up the townhouse, Sian walked through Viel's crowded streets to the public dock, looking around for Pino, finally spotting him near the end of the wharf, waving madly at her. She and Arouf had hired the young man just a few years back, but he was proving to be a very dedicated worker, cheerfully filling in anywhere the firm of Monde & Kattë required — from hauling supplies to the storehouse, to general repair and maintenance, to fetching whatever Sian acquired in town, as well as ferrying her back and forth between home and Alizar Main.

Resting her feet on the dye-sacks piled in the bottom of the boat, she let herself daydream during the hour-long passage across the smooth waters of Alizar Bay to their private island — perhaps she had had less sleep than she'd realized — only noticing their approach when the boat bumped against the dock at Little Loom Eyot. "Thank you, Pino," Sian said, alighting. Unencumbered, as usual. No matter that she managed fine in town; Pino would never let her carry her own bags when he was there.

"Happy to have you home, my lady," the boy answered, pushing his dark brown hair out of his eyes and grinning at her.

After a perfunctory glance around the lush grounds, she went to her little office upstairs in the loom house to file and sort the documents, orders, and purchase receipts she'd brought from town. Always so much paperwork! Once again, she resolved to hire clerical help.

When the bell chimed for change of shift, she looked up, startled to see the afternoon entirely passed. She straightened her desk, then began the short walk up the hill. She passed alongside the loom house and in front of the dye works, the two largest buildings on the island. Blue-and-red macaws shrieked and hopped about in the chinaberry trees above her head, scolding her for disturbing their evening congress — without offering food. "Peace, you little beggars," she chuckled at them as she turned beside the unmarried women's dormitory, nestled in a riot of blooming lacuina vines next to the refectory for her workers. Beyond that came the cottages of the older, married employees, and the few bachelor couples of whom she did not inquire so much.

Her own house stood on the highest part of the island, an often cloud-capped bluff situated on the rain-shadowed western face of the peak. Like the compound's cottages, it was built raised on poles in the traditional Alizari style, albeit with the modern conveniences of plumbing and a decent indoor kitchen. Its sweeping teak gables were pierced with tall windows and wide, elaborately carved lattice shutters to close against ocean storms or open to the sun's benediction.

The walk might be short — the entire island was little more than a thousand paces north to south — but the rise was of a steepness, and Sian was of an age (no matter what Reikos might say), as to leave her half out of breath by the time she'd passed the stand of bony Dragon's Blood trees outside their gate, and slid aside the soft peg that held the front door closed. No need for guards or even locks when you owned your own bridgeless island.

Inside, a warm glow came from the kitchen, bearing with it the welcoming aroma of food on the stove. "That you, wife?"

"Yes, Arouf, it is I." Sian unwrapped her elaborately patterned silk shawl and hung it on a hook by the door, next to its many mates. Today's had been blue, with the spectacular image of an iridescent morpho butterfly picked out along its length.

In the kitchen, she found her husband standing over a large pot, a long wooden spoon in his hand. Bela was nowhere to be seen; Arouf must have given their cook-housekeeper the evening off. "That smells good," she said, going to kiss him on his damp and bristly beard.

"It's cold enough out for a spicy sweetprawn stew, I should think." He gave her an affectionate pat on the arm, his attention still on the pot.

"Cold?" She lifted an eyebrow, smiling as she went to the cool box to find an open jug of tart white wine. She poured herself a glass, then refilled Arouf's. "Only a man from the farthest reach of Malençon could possibly call this weather cold."

"Or perhaps one who had a particular craving for spicy sweet-prawn stew." Arouf sipped his wine. "It should be ready soon, don't wander far."

"I won't."

Without mentioning any names, she began to tell Arouf about conversations she'd had with 'several trading partners' — news of the Stone Coast grape blight, the increasing labor shortage, the stagnation at the harbor at Cutter's. "And the city feels…less civilized all the time. Jamino Fanti tells me that his runner-cart was ambushed by a mob of angry vagrants last week, demanding money from him."

"Or what?" Arouf asked.

"Or they'd push the cart over and break its wheels, they said. That's what he told me."

"Did he give in to this? Where was his runner while all this happened?"

"There were too many of them for the runner to fend off, apparently."

Arouf shook his head, his dark eyes flashing. "I do not like you going there."

"Oh?" She gave him a wry smile. "Does that mean *you* will go next time?"

He scowled at her. "That is your world, down there, wife. This is mine."

Such a powerful-looking man, Sian mused, *and yet such a child, to be so upset by even a mention of the outside world.* She bit her lip and went to set the table, refraining from telling him that someone in the crowd had flung a fistful of mud at her as she had left the townhouse in Viel to meet Pino that afternoon. They had missed. So what did it matter?

"Did you do any entertaining while you were in town?"

Sian looked up at him. "No. Why do you ask?"

Arouf shrugged, not looking up from the cutting board where he was dicing firefruit. "Why doesn't the Factor *do* something about all this unrest?"

"I don't know." She thought a moment. "He might be too distracted. I hear his son is not recovering quite as quickly as they'd hoped."

"That's unfortunate." He dropped the peppers into the stew and stirred vigorously. Then he lifted the spoon to his lips, frowned, and returned to the board to dice another.

"Indeed." Sian thought about their own daughters, with the mingled love and fear that fills any mother when she hears of a child's illness. Because they would always be her babies, no matter that they were grown and gone. Maleen, at least, still lived in Alizar; Sian had been meaning to visit her and the grandchildren for far too long. Life just seemed to crowd out every space she tried to clear for such things lately. She shook her head and resolved more fiercely to do it — soon.

"Well, supper is ready," Arouf said, ladling stew into a serving bowl. A good measure remained steaming on the stove when he brought the filled bowl to the table.

She dipped her bread in the fragrant broth as the first bite seared pleasantly down her throat. "Your best yet."

Arouf patted his belly and swallowed his own generous spoonful. "A little bland." Tears leaked from the corners of his eyes and his cheeks flushed slightly. "But, it was the best I could do with these poor ingredients."

"Any better and this old body could simply not stand it."

"Well, then. It must be exactly good enough."

"Exactly."

As they ate, Sian asked Arouf about matters in the dye works. He had nothing much to report, beyond complaining of being short-staffed, and soon enough they were passing their supper in silence.

"I'll take the sacks out to the shed, if you'll see to the dishes," Arouf said, pushing back from the table with a contented sigh.

"Of course. Go ahead." Sian rose and gathered the bowls, carrying them to the washbasin. "A one-pot meal shouldn't be much trouble." *Though if you wouldn't keep sending Bela home early, I wouldn't have to do even this,* Sian thought. It had been a long day, and she had more to do before bed.

Her husband pulled his boots on and went out the kitchen door. He hefted the sacks of dye two at a time, which made Sian cringe in sympathetic pain. Small as they appeared, they were dense and weighty. Arouf must not be feeling arthritis in his joints, like she was.

Or maybe it was all the spicy meals he ate. Sian felt her insides burning as she scraped the bowls into the bin for the flamingos and tamarins. Not an unpleasant burn, exactly; but she couldn't make three meals a day of the peppers as Arouf could.

The dishes done, she moved to the sitting room and lit a lantern by her reading chair, batting off a Luna moth that fluttered toward it through the window. After going to pull the shutters closed, she sat down, took a report from the large stack on her side table, and began to read, making occasional notes on a small sheet of paper as she went. The reports were gathered from everywhere Sian could acquire informants, and spoke, in one way or another, of the future of the market for silks and other luxuries. Unfortunately, this general topic was the first and last thing they had in common. It seemed nobody knew what was going to happen: demand would increase; it would most certainly decrease; unrest would interrupt the supply channels, or facilitate them as nervous investors dumped inventory; no two reports could agree.

Some time later, she had filled her sheet with notes and marked up a handful of other documents, putting several aside to keep. She looked up as she started to ask, "I wonder whether we should —" but her husband wasn't in his chair as usual. Come to think of it, she hadn't even heard him come in from the shed. She stretched and rubbed her eyes, glancing down the hallway that led to their sleeping chambers. Arouf's door was closed, and no light burned under it.

Extinguishing the lantern, she went back into the kitchen and checked that the shutters were pulled down there as well against invading night-tamarins, then plodded down the hall to her own room. It was, in theory, the marital suite, though Arouf had not made this bed his home since Rubya, their younger daughter, was born. He did tourist here on occasion, sometimes by entreaty, sometimes in a burst of drunken ardor, and once for a long, sweet passage of nearly six months, during which time Sian had let herself believe that their distance had passed. But, eventually, he had complained of his head, and of her shifting while she slept, and of her cold feet, and returned to his own chamber.

Sian let down her hair and rummaged through her overnight bag for her brush and sleeping shift, wondering just when, and why, their desire for one another had cooled. Their nights had once been as passionate as any she now shared with Reikos. Would she and Reikos drift apart someday as well? She shook her head with a wry smile. No. More likely she would just lose him sooner and more quickly to some younger woman — or some dozen of them. These were not questions to be pondering just before sleep. If ever.

She climbed into the tall, mosquito-netted bed, stretching her legs out across the cool, soft sheets. It did feel good to get into bed of a night.

She thought about reading a while — there were always more reports — but instead extinguished the lamp, and was asleep before she'd had a chance to reconsider.

Arouf lay awake, listening to his wife move around her bedroom, unpacking from her trip. Sian did so love her journeys to town, enjoyed dressing up in her fine silks, being the social and business face of Monde & Katté. Arouf was more than happy to cede her the responsibility. He had no taste for mingling with the traders and merchants; it was an unwelcome change of pace, as far as he was concerned. It was very convenient that she had been willing, even eager, to take this task on. And she was very good at it, better than he'd ever been. The smartest thing he had done was to promote her to the counting house.

No: the smartest thing he had ever done had been marrying Sian Katté in the first place, followed closely by agreeing that she should keep her own name. As Sian Monde, she would have vanished into obscurity; as Monde & Katté, their dye works claimed an undeniable family connection to the ruling Alkattha house, which had hardly hurt the business.

That wasn't why he had married her. Of course he loved her, and their two magnificent daughters perhaps even more. Arouf was still taken by surprise at times by his wife's beauty — her long dark hair, still thick and glossy even as it grew streaked with gray; her smooth copper skin; and those startling eyes, so dark as to seem almost black, until lamplight lit them up, revealing the amber glow within. And when she laughed, she became a girl of twenty again, her cheeks rosy and glowing, her whole face shining.

That she didn't laugh so often these days — that was simply a matter of the inevitable aches and weariness of growing older. Arouf understood growing older; he didn't fight against it as so many men of his generation did with dyes and perfumes, and squeezing into confining clothes to hide the evidence of a healthy appetite. Youth had been lovely. It was over now. Fighting the inevitable was a foolish waste of time. He did the best he could to remain active, for he knew that the longest-lived men in his home village on the eastern shores of Malençon were the ones who chopped wood and dug post-holes to the very end of their days, refusing to let the younger men take these tasks from them.

So all was as it should be.

Even if he had not made the success that he had dreamed of in his youth, Arouf was satisfied enough with the enterprise he and Sian had built. They employed almost three dozen weavers, dyers, and other hands; they had built and furnished this fine, comfortable home; Maleen had made a good marriage match, and Rubya was pursuing her education far away in Dun Cranmoor, on the mainland. And the grandchildren! Arouf smiled in the dark at the thought of them. If only Maleen would bring them to visit more often. Arouf did not like to leave Little Loom Eyot. So much to do here. The older he got, the more daunting travel became. After all the years he'd given to raising his children, why could they not take just few days now and then to come back and see their father? And their mother too — though it was hard these days to catch Sian at home. Or anywhere else, he supposed.

Soon the sounds of Sian in her chamber grew quiet. She would have gone to bed, and quickly to sleep, tired from her work in Alizar Main. Well, he supposed it must be exhausting, though she seemed to thrive on it.

He did sometimes find himself wondering what went on in that townhouse she'd chosen and retrofitted. He'd seen the renovations, shortly after they had bought it for use as an in-town *office* — the addition of sleeping quarters, for when business kept her overnight. The curtained-off upstairs rooms. For additional privacy from the street.

Ever since they'd moved to separate bedrooms, Arouf had wondered if she were…satisfying certain needs elsewhere. They had never spoken of such things openly, not in so many words.

Speaking of it would make it real, somehow. He hadn't even wanted to think of it.

And he despised himself for thinking of it now.

One could not run a successful business entirely from afar. Sian needed to go to town periodically. And the dyes she'd brought home today were certainly fine; Arouf would likely have never heard of the new dye-seller from here.

Arouf shifted in the bed, arranging his pillow more comfortably beneath his head, listening to the kakapos calling one another in the night, and whatever might be rustling through the hisbiscus under his shuttered window. His sleeplessness had grown worse of late, but there was nothing to be done for that. More wine, less wine; a change of diet; being weary or well rested at bedtime; powders from Viel or farther; nothing made any difference. Sleep would find him when it chose to, and not a moment before.

He was almost ready to rise from bed and find something to relieve his wakefulness when he realized that it was in fact morning. He had slept after all, even if his body believed otherwise.

"Ah, me." He sat on the edge of the bed and rubbed the grit from the corners of his eyes. Kava: that's what he needed. He heard Bela's uneven steps in the kitchen as she shuffled around, probably rewashing the dishes Sian had cleaned last night, and putting them where they actually belonged. Yes, his wife's strengths most decidedly lay on the business side of things.

Pulling on his trousers, he tugged his long tangled hair back into a tail, capturing it with a stretchy band. Clever stuff, this tree sap which expanded and contracted. Idly wondering if it could be put to use in textiles, he walked down the hall and poked his nose into Sian's room.

It was vacant: she must already be in her office over the loom house.

Time for kava. He followed the aroma to the kitchen.

ABOUT THE AUTHOR

Shannon Page is a Pacific Northwest author. When she's not writing, she can be found reading, editing, cooking, gardening, doing yoga, drinking wine—or some combination of those pastimes. She has no tattoos. Visit her at www.shannonpage.net.